A
Winter Wish

A Winter Wish

a novel

EMILY STONE

DELL
NEW YORK

A Dell Trade Paperback Original

Published in the United States by Dell, an imprint of Random House, a division of Penguin Random House LLC, New York.

DELL and the D colophon are registered trademarks of Penguin Random House LLC.
RANDOM HOUSE BOOK CLUB and colophon are trademarks of Penguin Random House LLC.

Originally published in the United Kingdom in 2024.
Published by arrangement with Headline Publishing Group Limited.

LIBRARY OF CONGRESS CATALOGING-IN-PUBLICATION DATA
Names: Stone, Emily, author.
Title: A winter wish: a novel / Emily Stone.
Description: New York: Dell, 2024.
Identifiers: LCCN 2024029834 (print) | LCCN 2024029835 (ebook) |
ISBN 9780593872253 (trade paperback) | ISBN 9780593872260 (ebook)
Subjects: LCGFT: Romance fiction. | Novels.
Classification: LCC PR6119.T6743 W56 2024 (print) |
LCC PR6119.T6743 (ebook) | DDC 823/.92—dc23/eng/20240705
LC record available at https://lccn.loc.gov/2024029834
LC ebook record available at https://lccn.loc.gov/2024029835

Printed in the United States of America on acid-free paper

randomhousebooks.com
randomhousebookclub.com

1st Printing

Book design by Diane Hobbing

A
Winter Wish

Chapter One

Lexie stood between the two girls, holding the big gold star above their heads—which was no mean feat, given Bella, at thirteen, was nearly as tall as her.

"I want to put the star on top of the tree!" Bree shouted at Bella.

"Well you can't reach, short-arse, so too bad."

Bree put her hands on her hips, over the green sparkly dress that was, apparently, her designated Christmas outfit. "I'm not short, I'm six."

Bella rolled her eyes and flipped her long blond hair behind her shoulder in a melodramatic fashion. "Your point?"

"OK!" Lexie clapped her hands together, trying to fix a bright smile on her face while wondering what on earth had possessed her to get a job as a nanny, even if it was only for the winter. "Why don't we finish putting the baubles on and then we can decide on the star?"

"I think we're done with the baubles," Bella said, a slight sniff in her voice, like Lexie should automatically have known that the other three full boxes of Christmas decorations on the glass coffee table behind them were completely redundant.

Bree gave Lexie a pleading look. "I really want to do the star," she said, her little lip pouting out.

"Fine," Bella said, throwing herself onto the sofa and crossing her arms. "This is stupid, anyway."

"How about I put the star on?" Lexie said, and reached on her tiptoes to do just that.

Both girls stared at her. Clearly this was a faux pas. Not having grown up with a sibling in the house herself, she wasn't sure of the ins and outs of sisterly arguments. God, perhaps she should have stuck with a job on the ski lift, like the last time she'd done a ski season a few years ago.

"Ah, shall we put up the rest of your snowflakes, Bree?"

Slowly, like she was coming to terms with the terrible thing Lexie had just done, Bree nodded, then gathered up the paper snowflakes they'd made earlier. Bella sighed and got out her phone, slumping on the sofa and pulling one of the fluffy white pillows toward her.

After sticking snowflakes on nearly every spare space of wall—as well as the wooden beams—Bree looked down at the remaining ones in her hands. Then she smiled up at Lexie, grudge over the star forgotten. "Let's decorate your room now," she announced.

"No, I'd rather we . . ."

But Lexie's protests were ignored as Bree marched through the chalet and opened the door to Lexie's room. It was the smallest room—a single bed, with a wardrobe and chest of drawers—but it was still beautifully done, and the big window held one of the best views of the whole place, looking down over snow-tipped fir trees along the wilder side of the mountain.

Bree started sticking snowflakes on Lexie's walls without invitation, while Lexie did a quick scan of the room. Some people might say it was depressingly bare—there were a few second-hand books piled on her bedside table and a couple of photos of her and her mum on top of the chest of drawers, but apart from that it was distinctly lacking in clutter. Lexie, however, was pretty proud of the fact that she could fit her entire life into two suitcases—it made it a lot easier to travel around, and she never liked to stay in one place for too long.

"What's that?" Bree pointed to the glass jar on Lexie's chest of drawers, next to the mirror. It was one of the only things she carted around with her from place to place—and even though she wasn't usually big on decorating whatever room she was in at the time for Christmas, this was the one thing she made sure she always had out in December, no matter what. Bree made to grab it but Lexie stepped up beside her, blocking her access.

Bree frowned up at her. "I want to see," she said, doing that pouty lip thing again.

Lexie looked at Bree for a moment. The fake tears were there, ready to accompany a wail, should Lexie refuse. For a second she weighed it up. Then she sighed, reaching behind her to pick up the jar and holding it up for Bree to inspect. It wasn't anything particularly special to look at—a clear glass jar, tall and slim, decorated with glitter and a snowflake on the front, with gold-and-silver handwriting on it. Lexie had made it when she was a little younger than Bree.

Bree read the words slowly, stumbling over Lexie's terrible handwriting. Handwriting that hadn't ever gotten much better, come to think of it. *Lexie's wish jar.*

There was a snort from the doorway of the room—from where Bella was now leaning—unable to stay away despite herself. "A wish jar? Seriously?"

"What's a wish jar?" Bree asked.

Lexie felt the back of her neck heating. Even with the girls, it was weird to be talking about it. It was a silly tradition, and she didn't want people—like Bella, apparently—scoffing at it. Her mum knew about it, but that was about it. "It's a Christmas thing," she said, her voice dismissive in the hope they would drop it.

"But what *is* it?" Bree pressed—and Lexie just knew she wouldn't leave off.

So Lexie caved. Because apparently, she was pathetic enough that her desire to avoid conflict even extended to avoiding an argument with a six-year-old. "I make a wish, every Christmas, and I write it on a little piece of paper, fold it up, and put it in the jar. See?" She indicated the pieces of paper sitting in the jar.

"And they come true?" Bree asked excitedly.

"Ah . . ."

"Course they don't," Bella scoffed from the doorway. "Things don't come true just because you wish for them."

Well, quite. And Lexie couldn't help thinking about the one big wish she'd made when she was seven, the one she'd put into the jar with such hope. The one that hadn't come true.

She'd started the wish jar when she was four—and it was one of her earliest memories. It had been her mum's idea—a Christmas activity—but Lexie had loved it and had made sure to get her jar out every Christmas, thinking carefully about what she should wish for. The first few had been silly, in hindsight, though they'd felt like a big deal at the time—a new bike, a pet hamster. And those first few had actually come true, and even though as she'd gotten older she'd known that magic couldn't *really* exist, she hadn't been able to stop thinking that maybe her wish jar did hold some Christmas magic, like her mum always told her it did. Until the year that illusion had come shattering down around her and she'd learned the hard way that wishing for something was futile.

It hadn't stopped her from continuing the tradition, though.

There was something cathartic about writing a wish down and putting it in the jar—like she was letting the wish go, setting it free.

"You don't know that," Bree said, sounding hurt. Bella had the grace to look a bit guilty, shifting from foot to foot. Perhaps because she'd nearly let it slip about Santa earlier in the week and had gotten a *look* from her mum.

"I want to do it," Bree announced, already looking around for paper. "I want to put a wish in the wish jar. I think I'll wish for a puppy. Julie has one and he's SO cute."

Bella huffed. "You can't tell us what you'll wish for—then it won't come true."

"So you *do* believe in wishes, then," Bree said slyly.

Bella just rolled her eyes. It's an art form, isn't it? The eye roll. And Bella had it down.

"Where's the paper?" Bree asked.

Lexie felt a little flutter of panic. She knew it was stupid, but she didn't want someone else to put a wish in her jar—even little Bree. So she put it down and clapped her hands. "Hey, I've got an idea!"

Bree looked up at her out of those big blue eyes.

"How about we make *you* a wish jar?"

Bree was all for this, and although Bella refused to make her own, she did help Bree decorate the jam jar they found, and that activity was enough to keep them busy until Nicole and David got home.

Lexie was in her own room after saying good night to the girls when a message came through on her phone.

Lounge?

Mikkel. She smiled a little as she thought of leaving him in bed this morning. Of how easy it would be to go home with him again tonight—no strings for either of them.

She gave it half a thought, then quickly changed, grabbing a top that wasn't covered in glitter but not worrying too much about what she was wearing—a lot of people would have come straight from the slopes, so it wasn't like she had to dress up. She put on a subtle shade of lipstick, dashed on some mascara to try to make her brown eyes look less dull. After a moment's thought she put on a pair of star stud earrings as a nod to the festive season. Then she pulled a hand through her dark curls and considered herself ready. She tapped out a quick response to Mikkel.

Be there in ten.

MIKKEL CAUGHT LEXIE's eye as she stepped into the warmth of the bar, pulling her bobble hat off her head. He grinned and gestured her over to where a group of them were sitting on benches in one of the corners of the bar, up against the wooden walls, which were decorated with forest-green tinsel. Lexie wove her way through the crowd, past the huge Christmas tree that she had absolutely no idea how they'd gotten inside, breathing in the smell of pine laced with beer and sweat. Mikkel moved up to make room for her on the bench and pushed a full pint of beer over to her as she sat.

"Good day?" he asked.

"Oh, you know, the usual. Lots of glitter with a side of sarcasm."

"You must make sure you get onto the slopes tomorrow."

"I will," she said firmly. "The girls are in ski school for the morning, so I have a few hours to myself."

"Good. I have a gap at eleven—we'll do a few runs together." He smiled and placed his hand on her knee under the table.

"What about you, Lexie?" Amelie, one of the regular seasonal workers, looked over and Lexie frowned as she took a sip of her beer, trying to catch up on the conversation. "Christmas next week, what are you doing?"

"Oh, I guess the family will expect me to be with them, won't they?"

"You should ask," Amelie said. "We're all going to do Christmas dinner at Mikkel's—a turkey, the whole lot. If you're free, you should come."

"Yes, you should definitely come," Mikkel said. He had great eyes, Mikkel—gray-blue to go with his light hair and pale complexion, a classic Scandi look. He was also *the* advert for a nomadic lifestyle, in Lexie's opinion. So confident and content, even though he never spent longer than six months in any one place, spending every winter as a ski instructor and every summer teaching surfing in a different location. Despite being in his early thirties, he showed no signs of being tired of all the moving—and Lexie wished she could hold him up with a *Ha!* to her friends at home, who often wondered when she was going to "get a proper job" and "settle down" like the rest of them.

Lexie shrugged out of her coat with some difficulty, sandwiched as she was on the end of the bench, and slipped her phone out of her pocket. One missed call. She bit her lip when she saw who it was from.

"Everything OK?" Mikkel asked.

"Yeah. It's just . . ." She glanced at her phone again. "I'll be right back, OK? I have to make a quick call."

"OK. Hurry back, we're doing shots."

Lexie laughed. "*I'm* not—I have to be up early with the girls."

Mikkel grinned. "One won't hurt."

She made a flapping gesture in his direction as she pulled her coat back on and headed out into the snow. She wouldn't usually worry so much, but she'd missed the last call from her mum a couple of days ago, and knew she was bound to start getting anxious if she didn't hear back from Lexie soon. Lexie moved to the quietest point she could find, the sound of Christmas music—which had been playing on repeat for weeks now—rising over her and into the mountains.

The phone didn't even get to two rings before there was an answer. "Hello, Lexie love." There was something oddly strained about her usually bright voice.

"Hi, Mum—all OK?"

"No, not really."

Lexie's heart lurched. "What is it?" The cold air misted out in front of her in a sharp burst. "What's wrong?"

"It's . . . it's your dad."

Her stomach settled into a leaden weight. "I don't want to know," she said shortly. Which her mum should know, perfectly well.

"Yes, you do," her mum said, her voice gentle in a way that should have been a warning sign. "He's . . . he's dead, Lexie."

Chapter Two

The funeral was awful. It was quiet, barely thirty people standing together outside, so few that Lexie had felt the need to hunch
over and make herself as small as possible. Her dad hadn't been
religious so there was no church, and the ceremony took place
in a woodland burial ground, where you could hear the rustle
of animals brave enough to venture out in the cold. Despite the
shelter of the trees, icy wind bit at her fingertips, making them
numb. The rain held off, but the air was still damp enough to
feel suffocating, like everything was too close. And it had been
stupid to wear heels. They were only small black ones, ones she'd
found hidden in the back of her wardrobe at her mum's house,
but still—they sank into the soft ground underneath her, meaning she had to shift position every few minutes. Then it felt like
something was wrong with her because she was worrying about
her heels in the mud rather than the fact that her dad was dead.

Her dad was dead. He'd died of a cancer that she hadn't even
known he'd had. A cancer he'd been battling for six months. Liver
cancer. She tried repeating it over and over, but still it didn't feel
real. Or if it did feel real, then it was somehow separate to her. She
tried to listen to the celebrant's words as she talked about what
a loss this was, about how Richard had been a force of nature,
how he'd added vibrancy to those around him, how he would be
hugely missed. Lexie couldn't match the person she'd known to

the person who was being described. Who had given the celebrant these words to say?

She wondered if it had been Rachel. Rachel, who was all grown up, a proper adult now. She was still young, really—what was she, twenty-two? But the last time Lexie had seen her, she'd still only been a teenager. She had the same dark curls as Lexie and their dad, and without that, Lexie wasn't 100 percent sure she'd have recognized her half sister—who was now getting up in front of everyone and speaking about what a wonderful father he'd been. She told a story of her twenty-first birthday, and how Richard had surprised her with a dinner party. Rachel broke down halfway through the story and couldn't finish, the piece of paper shaking in her hands, until the celebrant went up and laid a comforting hand on her shoulder.

Where is Rachel's mum? Lexie wondered, as her own mum gripped her hand in silent comfort. She'd expected her stepmother—if you can call a woman Lexie had barely ever in-teracted with by that title—to be by Rachel's side. But instead it was a friend of Rachel's, about her own age—a tall girl with near-black hair—who went over to Rachel, helped her to step back into the crowd. And through all this, Lexie was trying to match what Rachel was saying to the father *she'd* known. Think-ing of her own twenty-first birthday, and how that had been the final straw, the moment she'd decided to give up and cut her dad out of her life completely.

So yes, the funeral was awful. But the wake was worse. It was held in Bath, where her dad had been living—in a dull func-tion room in a middle-of-the-range hotel where everything was white with the exception of the beige carpet. A few Christmas decorations had been put up, with a small tree in the corner and a line of snowflakes—more tasteful than the ones Lexie had done with Bree—hanging along the double doors that led to a court-yard outside. Lexie hated places like this—one of a chain, with a blandness that was impossible to escape. She'd never had much money to stay anywhere fancy, but when she had the choice she tried to stay at places that were part of the local community, and that were independently owned and run. It wasn't always possible, of course, but she always thought you got a better sense of the area that way, and she liked supporting small businesses.

Lexie's mum squeezed her shoulder. "Are you OK, love?"

Lexie nodded. Thank God for her mum. She didn't know what she'd do without her, standing in this room, trying to pay respects to a man she felt she barely knew, whose memory was tainted by disappointment. Her mum hadn't needed to come—they'd been divorced for over twenty years—but Lexie suspected she'd done it for her sake. What must it be like, for her? She must have loved him, once. Loved him enough to marry him. Loved him enough to cry in her room, over and over, when she thought Lexie couldn't hear, after he'd left.

"Are you?" Lexie asked, and her mum smiled her reassurance. She had such a pretty smile, all soft and warm. It felt unfair, that Lexie had gotten more of her dad's looks than her mum's—her dad's dark curls, murky brown eyes. Her mum's frame was somewhat similar to hers, but her features were gentler, her hair a straight honey blond—dyed for years now to stay the same as her natural color, and she had a soft, heart-shaped face that immediately made her look kind—whereas Lexie was all angles, with a too-large forehead.

"I have to go to the bathroom," her mum said. "Will you be OK for a minute?"

"Of course." Because what was she supposed to say—*No, Mum, don't leave me*? So she watched her head away, already feeling hot around the collar of her high-necked black dress—one of the only black dresses she owned, one that she hadn't worn since her stint working in an office in London, which had lasted a little over eight months. She helped herself to a sausage roll—comfort food, she supposed—then headed to the small bar and ordered a glass of red.

Had it been Rachel and Jody, Rachel's mum, who organized this? She risked a quick glance around. Rachel was in the corner, with the black-haired friend she'd brought along, surrounded by people offering her condolences, but Lexie still couldn't see Jody anywhere. She knew that Richard had left Jody too, a few years ago—so perhaps Jody wasn't quite as forgiving as Lexie's own mum, despite the fact that she'd been married to Richard for longer. What had made Richard leave her, in the end? Had he just gotten bored, like with his first family?

She should go over and talk to Rachel, she knew she should. They'd exchanged a brief hello earlier, an awkward hug, but they hadn't really spoken. She should be polite, ask if she was OK, ask what she was doing these days. Was she still in Wales? Lexie had absolutely no idea. And fine, OK, it wasn't Rachel's fault that her dad had decided to go and have another family—Rachel had been caught in the crossfire of that. But it didn't make it easy, and Lexie wasn't sure she was emotionally ready enough to have the kind of conversation that would be expected of her right now. Besides, Rachel had avoided eye contact with her, too. There was a seven-year age gap between them—a gap that had made it obvious that Richard had been cheating on Lexie's mum before he'd actually left—and it had meant they'd never gotten close, the handful of times they'd been shoved together, because as kids that age gap had felt huge. And even though they were both adults now, what did you say to someone who was technically your sister, but who you barely knew at all? What did you say at the funeral of a man who had technically been a father to both of you, but who had arguably only been a *dad* to one of you?

Lexie gripped her wineglass tighter, trying to bite back the rush of hot fury that rose up seemingly out of nowhere. Then there was guilt, squirming in her stomach. Guilt that she wasn't a better person, that she couldn't get through today without feeling angry at her dad, that she couldn't try to be a real sister to Rachel. She felt tears sting the backs of her eyes, tried to blink them away. Really, she'd lost her dad years ago, so there was no reason to be crying now. She shouldn't be here. She should have stayed in Austria, with the girls and her friends.

She felt her phone vibrate in her handbag by her side. A message from Fran, one of the few people from home she had remained good friends with after she left for university at eighteen—and made it her mission to keep on the move ever since.

Hope you're doing ok. Call me after if you want to chat. Xx

Lexie let out a shaky breath. For some reason the message made her want to cry even more. She and Fran had gone to the same secondary school in Frome, near Bath, where Lexie had grown up—where she and her mum had stayed, even after Richard had left for his new family. Fran lived in Bath now and had offered to come today. She'd said she remembered meeting Richard a few times when they were teenagers. But it would have felt weird, bringing a friend along to her dad's funeral. Still, she should make time for a coffee with Fran before she flew back to Austria.

Lexie glanced around for her mum as she sipped her wine—seriously, how long did it take to go to the bathroom? Her eyes skimmed over a woman with deliberately gray hair, cut into a sleek bob. She saw Lexie looking, even as Lexie tried to look away before that moment of eye contact. She was talking to a tall man with dark brown hair, but shoved her empty glass in his hand and made a beeline for Lexie.

Lexie felt panic rise. She'd so far done well to avoid the condolences, to avoid any real acknowledgment that she was a family member. When she'd overheard someone saying, "But didn't he have two daughters?" she'd swiftly walked in the other direction. But now here was this woman, walking very purposefully toward her. And the room was small enough that she couldn't get lost in a crowd, and there was no one here she wanted to jump into a conversation with, so despite a frantic glance around, Lexie was standing stock-still when the woman reached her. She had very distinct pale green eyes, eyes that gave Lexie an appraising look, scanning her from head to toe in a way that made her feel self-conscious, wondering if the tiny ladder in her tights was noticeable, if she should have tried to clean the mud off her heels. The woman was in a black dress—of course—and heeled boots that had somehow avoided the mud from the cemetery. She had on bright red lipstick, and her eyebrows were in a perfect arch that must have taken some time to perfect. Lexie cast around in her memory, trying to place her.

"You won't know me," she said by way of introduction.

"Ah . . ."

"You're Lexie, though." The woman smiled—a smile that managed somehow to be both efficient and warm.

She wasn't sure what she could say to that other than "Yes."

"I worked with your father."

"Oh. OK." She had on sailboat earrings, Lexie noticed. Amid all the black, this woman was wearing bright, big sailboat earrings.

"You're a bit older than the photos he has of you, but I could spot you anywhere." She gave Lexie another look up and down, as if double-checking. The sailboats bounced with the movement. "You age very well."

"Um . . . Thanks." Here it was—the condolences. Though— her dad had photos of her? She somehow doubted that, and with that doubt came an immediate suspicion of this woman.

"It's not a compliment, it's a fact. I was Richard's PA. Have been since he started the company."

Lexie nodded slowly, not sure where this was going. Shouldn't there have been a "sorry for your loss" by now? She hoped she didn't get asked any questions about the company her dad owned—this woman looked like she might be about to quiz her on something. But she knew nothing about it—other than the fact that there *was* a company, which her dad had started around five years ago, when he'd left his second family and moved to Bath. It had something to do with travel, but that was the extent of her knowledge.

"This is an awful time," the woman continued. "I know that. And I know I'm this strange woman accosting you at your dad's funeral, but I don't really see a way around it."

"I'm sorry, I don't really—"

"You need to come to your dad's office the day after tomorrow. There's a meeting and you need to be there."

Lexie stared at the woman, waiting for her to say something more. When she didn't, Lexie spoke. "But why on earth would I need to be there?"

"I can't explain now. It would take too long and it's not the time or the place. But it will affect you and several others, so best to do it all together at once."

Lexie waited for her to elaborate, but she didn't. "I'm sorry," she said, making sure her voice was polite, apologetic, "but I have absolutely no idea what you're talking about."

"No. I imagine not." The woman's face softened, those green eyes filling with such obvious sympathy, it made Lexie's throat close. "I'm the one who's sorry. Really, I am. But it will make a lot more sense when you come to the office. Do you know where it is?"

"Ah . . ."

"No matter, I have the address." She fished in her handbag—a bright red one that, like the earrings, stood out against the black—and handed Lexie a card.

> **Angela Wilson**
> **Personal Assistant**
> **R&L Travel**
> *See the world through celebration.*

So that was the name of her dad's company, then. She frowned. It was a bland name, she decided. And the slogan—it didn't make any sense. Then she looked at the first line. Angela. It was only then that Lexie realized that the woman hadn't actually introduced herself by name.

"You'll be there?" Angela prompted. "The day after tomorrow, eleven A.M."

"I really don't—"

"Everything will become clear in the meeting, I promise you." Angela offered her another warm smile, her eyes creasing at the corners. "See you there. And it was nice to finally meet you, Lexie."

Lexie watched Angela walk away, not really sure how she'd ended up agreeing to something without actually agreeing. She would just have to make an excuse. Feign a contagious illness or something. She finished her wine, put the glass down on the bar, and saw her mum finally heading over to her.

Lexie looked down again at the card in her hand. "Do you know someone called Angela Wilson?" she asked as her mum drew near.

"Ange? I think she's your dad's PA, isn't she? Or was," she added after a beat. She rubbed Lexie's arm in a soothing gesture. "How are you doing, Lex?"

"I'm . . . God, I don't know." Out of the corner of her eye she noticed Rachel moving a little closer. Soon, they'd be right next to each other. But Rachel wasn't looking her way—Lexie suspected she wanted to avoid the awkward conversation, too.

"Mum, I think I'm going to go home. I've got a bit of a headache." It wasn't a lie—she could feel the pressure, a tight band around her head.

"OK, love, I'll drive you."

"No, you—"

Her mum gave her a look. "Lexie, you're staying at my house—how else are you going to get back to Frome? Besides, I think I'm done, too." She glanced around and Lexie wondered again how her mum had the strength to get through this with grace and dignity. "Let me just say goodbye to one or two people and I'll meet you outside, OK?"

Lexie obeyed, feeling relieved to have an instruction to follow. She slipped her coat on, headed out of the function room. As she was walking through the doorway, concentrating on her feet so that she didn't make eye contact with anyone, she felt a solid body slam into hers. She stumbled a little, felt a hand catch her arm to steady her.

She looked up. It was the man she'd seen talking to Angela earlier—dark hair, a strong jawline with the beginnings of stubble, and a faint scar through one eyebrow.

"I'm so sorry." His voice was deep, with a slight rough edge. "I wasn't looking where I . . ."

His eyes met hers. They were a darker brown than her own eyes, with an amber glow in the center that made her think of hot coals glowing orange in a fire.

His hand dropped from her arm and his eyebrows pulled together in a frown. "You're leaving?" he asked, and she swore she heard disapproval in his voice. Maybe he knew who she was— one of Richard's daughters, bailing on the funeral.

"I, er . . ." She cleared her throat, told herself to stop being ridiculous. This stranger had no right to judge her. "Yeah. So if you don't mind . . ." Lexie gestured to the doorway, indicating that he was in her way.

He gave her a curt nod, then stepped aside so she could pass.

She walked away quickly, hugging her coat to her. Before she turned the corner that led to the hotel lobby, she risked a quick glance behind her. The stranger was turning away, but she swore she caught the edge of a scowl he'd been shooting in her direction. Seriously? What was wrong with this guy? She told herself to shake it off as she stepped out of the hotel into the cold, damp air to wait for her mum. Tried to tell herself that she was being silly, that she was imagining the disapproval in his voice. It was just her being self-conscious, that was all. She was sure of it.

Chapter Three

Lexie stood on the street outside R&L Travel. It was uphill from the center of Bath, where there were lines of gorgeous, golden Georgian buildings with big, inviting window displays on ground level and enviable flats above the shops. The sky was a bright blue today, the air crisp and cold, and around Lexie people were rushing to get their Christmas shopping done. She imagined the city would look beautiful after dark, once the Christmas lights lit up.

She'd walked past a few Christmas pop-up stalls, and the smell of sweet roasted nuts hung in the air. It made her think of a Christmas market in Germany she'd been to as a child. She didn't remember much of it, but she had a fuzzy memory of clinging to her dad's hand as he held a cone of nuts, the sound of her mum's warm laugh filling the air. She frowned and shook the memory away. She didn't have a lot of memories of her dad from before he left, having only been seven at the time—and those she did have she didn't think of often. But when they'd been a family of three, they'd gone away every Christmas, without fail. Not always abroad, but always somewhere new—her parents saving all year to make it happen. She'd never asked why they'd done it. Given the company her dad had set up, maybe it had been driven by him. When he left, they'd stopped going away in December, no doubt because her mum couldn't afford it alone. Lexie remembered their first Christmas at home in the cottage, her mum handing her a hot chocolate, red-eyed after trying and failing to call someone on the phone, making excuses for why her dad hadn't come to visit. And the whole day had been tainted, full of hope that got crushed as the day went on and he still didn't show. All she'd gotten from him that year was a Christmas card with a ten-pound note inside—and the tradition of just a card and money was something he'd continued, year after year.

Snap out of it, Lexie.

She squared her shoulders as she stepped into the building. It was customer-facing, stands with brochures around the shop so that people could browse through the holidays on offer. One wall was completely covered in photographs of real people on holiday, presumably people who had taken one of these holidays and didn't mind their snaps up for anyone and everyone to see. On the other three walls there were various styles of artwork with no distinct theme holding them together. Somehow it worked, though—despite the anxiety currently rolling through her body, Lexie could admit that the shop felt intriguing. There was a Christmas tree in one corner with presents underneath—presumably fake—and chocolate coins in a bowl on the reception desk. In the background, "Last Christmas" was playing.

A guy who looked like he was in his early twenties, with floppy blond hair and glasses, looked up. He smiled, showing his teeth in a scarily enthusiastic way, and lurched toward her. He had a Christmas tie on—bright red with white snowflakes. "Hello, come on in—are you just looking or would you like . . . ?"

Lexie was backing away without really meaning to, startled by the overeager reception, but was saved from having to answer by a bark to the left. "No, Harry, she's not here for a holiday. And try to look less like you're going to chase her down the street and hit her over the head with a brochure if she leaves the shop. But well done, that was better."

Lexie couldn't help wondering what the usual greeting was like, if that was better. Still, she looked over at Angela, who was wearing a bright polka-dot dress over black tights, her lips the same color red as at the funeral. This time, she had Christmas-tree earrings on—the biggest earrings Lexie thought she'd ever seen.

"Come on in, Lexie." She smiled. "We're all upstairs, ready for you."

Lexie followed Angela through the shop, feeling Harry's curious gaze on her back. She was wearing a big red roll-neck jumper and jeans, and suddenly wondered if she should be dressed more formally. God, she shouldn't be here. She shouldn't have let her mum talk her into it, shouldn't be such a bloody pushover. Her stomach curdled as she stepped through the door at the back of the shop, then followed Angela up a staircase.

When they reached the top of the stairs, Angela let them through a door with a shiny gold number 2 on it—and straight into the entranceway of a flat.

"Um . . ." Lexie began.

Angela smiled over her shoulder. "Come on, they're just through here." She led Lexie into an open-plan kitchen–living room, stepping behind the island onto the tiled kitchen floor. "We thought we'd have the meeting up here—bit less formal than in the staff room downstairs, and less likely to be interrupted with a question from Harry every five minutes. Now, would you like a cup of tea? Or coffee? Water?"

"Um, just water, thanks."

She glanced around the space, saw two people waiting for them in the adjoining living room. Both were men, one with a balding head and reading glasses, licking his finger before flicking through a bundle of papers, and one with a dark head of hair who was shoving a piece of paper into his jeans pocket. He stared out of the big mullion window to the left, so she couldn't see his face. Neither of them seemed to notice that they'd come in.

Lexie dropped her voice. "What am I doing here, Angela?"

"Call me Ange, everyone does." She handed Lexie her water, gestured to where the two men were sitting around a glass coffee table.

"Is this part of the office?" Lexie asked. At that, the balding man seemed to notice her and looked up from his papers, took off his reading glasses, and gave her a polite smile. Lexie gave him a nod in return, moved farther into the living room—and stopped dead. Because she could see his face now—the man with the dark hair, the man who, although he was resolutely looking out the window rather than at her, she knew would have dark brown eyes with a fiery amber glow at their center. The man from the funeral, who'd looked at her with disapproval as she'd left. The judgment she'd seen on his face still gave her a sour feeling.

"Ugh, what the hell is he doing here?"

She blurted it out without thinking, and now she felt heat rush to her face as he turned to look at her, raising one eyebrow—the one with the faint scar through it.

Who was this guy? Why was he here, in this flat above her dad's office? What the hell was going on?

"Sit down, Lexie love," said Angela—Ange. She had taken the other armchair, opposite the balding man—which meant the only space left was next to the man on the sofa. She hesitated, but saw no choice, so she perched next to him, as far from him as she could get, and crossed one leg over the other, trying to take up less space.

"Now, Lexie," Ange said, seemingly oblivious to Lexie's discomfort, "this is Howard—he was your dad's solicitor."

Howard gave her another polite smile. "Very nice to meet you, Lexie. Though I wish it were under better circumstances."

"A solicitor?" Lexie sat up a bit straighter. "Wait, you're not . . . Is this about my dad's . . . ?"

"It's his will, yes," Howard said gently.

Lexie glanced at Ange. It made sense that she would be here, as her dad's PA. But who was this random glowering man? And why was she even *in* the will? She felt a headache pressing in against her temples.

"Look, I'm sorry if I'm being really dense here—"

She broke off at the tiniest snort from the man next to her, so quiet she wasn't sure if she'd imagined it. When neither Ange nor Howard reacted, she continued.

"But could someone please explain what's going on? My dad left something to me in his will, is that it? Or do you need a signature or something?" She and Rachel would be his next of kin, she supposed—did that mean she had to sign off on something? She glanced at the front door, wondering if Rachel was coming too. Was Rachel the type to be late? She had no idea.

The solicitor put his papers down on the glass coffee table, then bridged his hands on his knees. "I'll jump right in, then. As per the instructions in your father's will, you have been left half of R&L Travel."

She blinked at him, the words landing all wrong in her brain. "I'm sorry. I don't understand."

"R&L Travel—the company your dad founded." He gestured to the travel brochures on the tables. "Half of it is now yours."

The man next to her clenched his jaw, the muscles spasming, and Lexie swallowed, rubbing her hands on her jeans. Why was it so hot in here? And what did that mean—that he'd left his company to her?

Ange picked up the thread. "Lexie, I know this may come as a bit of a shock, especially as your dad hadn't had a chance to convey this to you before he passed, but—"

"I don't want it," she blurted out.

The solicitor and Ange looked at her—and the man next to her did too now, his gaze burning the side of her face. She wanted to scowl back at him. What was he, some kind of solicitor's assistant?

"This isn't . . ." Lexie swallowed. "Look, this must be some kind of mistake. I have no interest in owning this company. I don't even know what it does."

"It's no mistake," Howard said gently. "Half of the company now belongs to you—and half to Theo." He gestured to the man next to her.

She let out a sound of disbelief. "What? To . . ." She turned to look at him. "Who even *are* you?"

"I'm Theo," he said blandly.

"Right, I gathered that thanks, but what—?"

"Theo worked with your dad," Ange interjected, "almost since the company's inception."

The throbbing in her temples grew stronger, and Lexie put her hands to her head. "So what . . . ?" She gestured at Theo. "We're supposed to split the company? Do we sell it and share the profits or something?"

Howard cleared his throat. "Well, there are some stipulations."

"Of course there are."

Lexie could feel Theo giving her another raised-eyebrow

look, but she refused to look at him. She was perfectly capable of being all cool and aloof too, if that's how he wanted to play it.

"If you want to sell the company and split the profits, you and Theo first have to commit to one year of running the company together."

Lexie stared at him. "To *running* it?"

"That's right. And if you make a profit at the end of the year, then you can choose to sell it if you both wish. But if you don't turn a profit, you'll be locked in for another five years—after which time the choice of what to do is up to you."

It felt like the room was spinning around her. Honestly, could they not open one of those impressive windows, or were they just for show? This was starting to feel a lot more like a cage than a gift—she could end up stuck with a job she didn't want for up to *six years*. She didn't even like to stay in one place for six *months*. "And if I don't want to do that? If I just want to sell my half?"

Howard glanced between Theo and Lexie, looking a little pained. "It's important that you make a joint decision on this, but if you were to decide to sell now, you'd walk away with nothing—the profits would go back into the company, to who-ever takes it over."

"Un-fucking-believable," Theo muttered.

"Theo," Ange barked. He scowled at her, but she shook her head. "Don't you go looking at me like that, you know better than to try me."

He looked at her for a second, and Ange raised her eyebrows, almost a dare. His expression evened out as he leaned back against the sofa, folding his arms. Point to Ange, apparently.

"You have to admit this is totally ridiculous," he continued, clearly trying to keep his voice even. Now that he'd managed to string more than two words together, she could hear the trace of an Irish accent. It was faint, but definitely there. "She's never shown any interest in what Richard built, has she? She has no idea what we do here, she said that herself. She's never even been in the shop before. I'm surprised she managed to find it today." He looked at Lexie then. "And no offense, but do you even have any idea how to run a business?"

Lexie felt heat rush down her spine—but not from embarrassment this time. "What, are you some kind of award-winning entrepreneur?" He only offered her a glance, seemingly unbothered by her attempt at an insult. He was annoyed about this all for sure—but he didn't seem surprised. She wondered if he'd already known, at her dad's funeral. Maybe he hadn't been disapproving of her leaving early, after all. Maybe he was just generally disapproving of her.

Lexie turned her attention to the solicitor. "Is there any way for me to get out of this?"

Howard offered her a sympathetic smile. "I'm afraid not, no."

Lexie looked between Howard and Ange, hoping for one of them to say, *Haha—gotcha!* "So I'm just supposed to run my dad's business with someone I've never even heard of?"

That got a retort out of Theo. "Why would you have heard of me? You never bothered to answer your dad's calls or ask him anything about his life—and it's not like you're ever actually around."

Lexie felt the sting of that, even though she knew it was stupid to let some stranger get to her. "You don't even know me," she snapped. "You have *no* idea what I—"

Ange held up her hands to stop them. "OK. Let's just stay calm, shall we? Howard is a busy man, and I'm sure he wants to get this all wrapped up."

Lexie took a breath, did her best to bite back her temper. She was usually pretty good at staying calm—but she'd like to see anyone calmly deal with this being dropped in their laps. "What about Rachel?"

There was a pause, then Howard said, "She's been left the house."

"The *house*?"

"Your dad's house. It's on the outside of Bath—a little cottage, really."

Lexie wondered briefly if he was saying *little* in an attempt to mediate the sting. Well, that about summed it up, didn't it? Rachel, the favorite daughter, had been given a *house,* whereas she'd been left a job to do—one she by no means wanted—and not just that, but she had to manage it with a stranger who seemed to despise the idea of her already. And she had to commit to running the damn thing, whereas presumably Rachel could just sell the cottage and be done with it. Nice one, Richard.

"No. I can't do this," Lexie said, shaking her head for emphasis.

"What a shocker," Theo muttered.

"Theo!" Ange barked.

He held both hands up, a sign of surrender.

"Why don't you let it all sink in, Lexie?" Ange said. "Howard, you'll be around to answer any questions Lexie might have, won't you?"

"Of course. I'll leave my card; you can call anytime."

Howard stood up, gathering his papers. Were they done, just like that?

"Would you like to sit up here for a bit, hmm? I'll make you a cup of tea—award-winning, is my tea."

Lexie looked around at the flat. The walls were pale blue, a little bare. No attempt at Christmas decorations up here. "Is this part of the office, then?"

"No, it's my flat," Theo said bluntly.

Ange leveled a look at him. "You'll want to be controlling that temper, young man, or you and I will be having words again. You know perfectly well none of this is Lexie's fault. Besides, it's not *your* flat." She smiled at Lexie. "It belongs to the company—Theo rents it out at the moment. We also use it for certain meetings, the odd staff drink and whatnot."

"Well, if we're done dividing up Richard's assets like the man himself meant nothing, then I'll just head downstairs and check on the company I helped him run for the last five years."

Theo got up off the sofa and didn't even look at Lexie as he stalked away.

Ange frowned at his back. "You'll have to forgive Theo." She sighed. "Well, you don't *have* to forgive him, not sure I would, the way he's acting right now, but try to believe me when I say he's not always this bad. Let's just say I think he's a little lost, without Richard."

Lexie had no idea what to say to that. At the idea that he *wasn't always this bad,* or at the idea that this Theo had some kind of relationship with her dad that went beyond the nine-to-five. She found it hard to believe. She imagined Theo's antics had more to do with losing a potentially large sum of money, and while she could appreciate that might be annoying, it gave him absolutely no right to be a total dick, whatever Ange said.

"I think I'll go," Lexie said, standing up. Absurd. This whole thing was completely absurd. "I'm meeting a friend for coffee, anyway." *Fran!* Fran, who was a solicitor. Well, she'd see what

Fran had to say about all this, wouldn't she? Surely there was some way around it all.

"OK, love, you do that. Chat it through, hmm? And we'll see you tomorrow."

"Tomorrow?" Lexie repeated dumbly.

"I thought it would be good to show you round, help you understand what it is you've taken on." The way she put it made it sound like it had been an active decision on Lexie's part. "We close for a couple of days over Christmas," Ange continued, "so you'll want to come in before that. So tomorrow, have a little lie-in, maybe just come in for the afternoon?" And again, as Ange showed her back down the stairs, Lexie had the feeling of being steamrolled, with absolutely no choice in the matter.

Chapter Four

Lexie sat on her mum's sofa, blanket pulled up around her knees, sipping the mulled wine that her mum had made them. "Made" being a fancy way of saying "heated up"—it was out of one of those premade mulled wine bottles from Tesco. But it was still good, and they'd stuck some orange slices and a cinnamon stick in there for good measure. The Christmas tree was up in the corner, decorated in red and gold, and a fire crackled in the center of the room.

Everything felt comfortingly familiar. This was the house where Lexie had grown up. She'd thought, once, that they might have to leave after her dad left. She'd thought her mum might have wanted a fresh start, when she'd heard her sobbing in her bedroom, or seen her break down over a stray men's sock that she'd found. But Lexie had hated that idea and had made that clear—crying all night one time at the suggestion. Because this was her home, and she hadn't wanted to leave it. And secretly, she'd been worried that her dad would never come back if they moved. She wasn't sure of the ins and outs of it, but at some point it had been decided that they'd stay. But even though her mum had moved on, had redecorated her bedroom and gotten Lexie to help with the painting, and even though *Lexie* had been the one who'd wanted to stay, over time she'd come to resent the house a little. Because it became the house her dad had left, the one he *hadn't* come back to.

She had so many good memories here. Sleepovers with friends, film nights spent in with her mum. But isn't it funny sometimes how the bad memories can consume the good?

Her mum was in the adjoining kitchen, stirring a homemade pasta sauce. She did pasta very well—any type of pasta you could imagine. But anything else in the kitchen had the tendency to go a bit wrong.

"It doesn't make sense," Lexie huffed as she sipped her mulled wine. "Did you know? Did he tell you?"

She didn't know how much her mum and dad had talked. When Lexie was little, they'd undoubtedly liaised on timings for when Lexie was supposed to see him, and as she'd gotten older, she knew her dad had sometimes tried to go through her mum to get to her, when she wouldn't answer, but presumably the conversations were limited.

There was the briefest hesitation. "No."

"Mum!"

"He didn't, Lex. He just . . . We spoke a few times in the past year. I didn't know it, but he was ill and he wanted to connect with you and I didn't know for sure but I thought there might have been something he wanted to . . . ."

"Forget it. I don't want to know."

Hearing this made her feel all bitter and twisted inside. Partly because her mum seemed to be insinuating that she should have answered her dad's calls, should have magically forgiven him after he'd let her down again and again. And her mum had been there the day she'd turned twenty-one—she knew exactly why Lexie had decided that enough was enough. So, what, was she supposed to feel guilty now? Because in the last year of his life he'd finally decided he wanted to be a dad to her again? Well, it didn't work like that.

"I didn't know, Lexie," her mum said again. "We didn't speak all that much. And he didn't tell me about the cancer, I think because he didn't want you to hear about it from me, but . . ."

"But what?" She snapped the words, then took a breath. She sounded like a teenager—something about being in this house, perhaps. She shouldn't have been taking this out on her mum. "Sorry. I just . . . I don't know how to process this. I don't want to run his stupid business. I don't even live in the UK right now. Am I supposed to just change my entire life for this?" Though it looked like she didn't have much of a choice. Fran, much to Lexie's dismay, hadn't immediately seen a "get-out clause" in that fancy solicitor brain of hers.

"You could move back, if you wanted to."

"I have a job in Austria, Mum. They let me fly home for the funeral, but they want me back on Boxing Day."

Her mum didn't respond to that—Lexie knew her mother didn't take any of Lexie's jobs seriously, probably because they never lasted all that long. But Lexie would be letting the family down if she quit, and even if it was only a seasonal job, that didn't mean she didn't care about it.

"Think of the money at the end of this. If you sell the company for a profit you might have enough to put down a deposit on a house."

"*If* it makes a profit. If it doesn't, I could be stuck for five more years. And besides, Theo is annoyingly right. I know nothing about running a business or how to make a profit."

"Theo is the man you have to work with?"

"Yes, the man who hates me. The complete stranger Richard deemed important enough to give half his company to."

Lexie looked over to the kitchen stove to see her mum raise

her eyebrows at "Richard" rather than "Dad," but she didn't comment. Instead she said, "I'm sure he doesn't *hate* you."

Lexie said nothing—it seemed petulant to argue.

"And I'm sure your dad had a reason for this, Lexie."

"Right, because all his actions in the past have been so reasonable."

Her mum glanced over at her—and she could feel the assessment in that glance. "I think it's worth remembering that things are always a little more complicated than they seem."

Lexie snorted, then groaned. "Sorry. Sorry I'm being cranky. It's just . . . It's been a long day." She didn't know whether to bring up the fact that Rachel had been left a house—or whether that would highlight the divide between Richard's two families. Her mum had always been so great, tried to encourage a relationship with her sister, no matter how much it hurt her. It was part of the reason Lexie had shied away from having a relationship with Rachel, really—she'd seen how much it hurt her mum, the fact that her dad had started over with someone new, and she'd seen her mum try to put that aside, for her. At that thought, she got up, set her mulled wine down on the coffee table, and went into the kitchen.

She wrapped her arms around her mum, breathing in the floral scent from the same perfume she'd worn since Lexie was a kid. "I'm sorry for moaning."

Her mum squeezed her arm. "It's a lot to take in. But one thing at a time, my darling. Go into the office tomorrow, see what's what. Try to understand what's expected of you. Then go from there."

One step at a time. Surely she could do that?

———

AFTER AN HOUR with Theo in the office, she was very much thinking she could *not* do that, and repeating *one step at a time* inside her head was doing nothing to help. He'd shown her around, but grudgingly—and only because Ange had watched them from the corner of the room before disappearing off somewhere. Despite the brevity of Theo's tour, Lexie was pleasantly surprised to find out that the art decorating the walls was all from different countries—all places R&L Travel arranged trips to.

Lexie had, at least, learned more about what the company actually did. She'd done her research last night to be prepared but had let Theo explain it to her—in a ridiculously condescending manner—just in case she'd misunderstood something. The whole idea was based around cultural traditions and allowing people to experience key holidays around the world and get to know a country through the way they celebrate. *See the world through celebration.* There were trips for the more universal holidays like Christmas, but there were also trips specific to certain areas, like the Tomato Festival in Spain or St. Patrick's Day in Ireland. It was a travel company, yes, but based entirely around celebrating different cultures and experiencing new things.

Though she'd prepared herself last night, Lexie had to try very hard not to feel bitter as Theo explained this. Because the more she thought about it, the more it seemed like her dad had taken something she'd thought of as their family tradition when she was growing up—experiencing Christmas in a different place each year—and turned it into a moneymaking scheme. The whole thing left a sour aftertaste, one she was having trouble swallowing away.

There were two desks out front, and Theo and Lexie were currently hovering around one of them, while Harry—with the blond hair and tortoiseshell glasses—alternated between sitting at the other desk, watching Theo and Lexie, and jumping to his feet to attempt to deal with customers. Lexie wasn't entirely sure why Harry had been let loose with said customers, because he didn't seem to know anything, declaring every holiday in the brochure an "awesome" one, and answering any query with "You know what, that's a great question."

After Harry failed to deal with the latest inquiry, Theo shoved the brochure that he was running through into Lexie's hand, marched over to where Harry was smiling and nodding as a couple explained they weren't sure where in Germany they'd like to go, and grabbed his forearm, pulling him to one side. Lexie smiled weakly at the couple as they looked over, the brunette woman arching her eyebrows as she flexed her fingers on the brochure, engagement ring very clearly on show.

"Harry," Theo said in an undertone, "you know you do need to actually learn the *answers* to some questions?"

"I know," Harry said, nodding serenely, playing with his tie—another Christmas one, with little Rudolphs staring out at Lexie. "It's just a lot to remember, my man."

Lexie hid a smile, then cleared her throat. Both of them looked over at her. "Harry, if it helps, the German Christmas Market trip can be done in Munich or Aachen, and it can be from three to eight nights, depending on what they want to cross off." They continued to stare at her, and she shrugged. "It was a question about forty-five minutes ago."

"See, even *she* knows the answer and an hour ago she had no idea what we bloody did here."

Theo let go of Harry's arm and Harry bounded off back to the couple with an undimmed toothy smile.

Lexie crossed her arms, leveling a look at Theo. "I'm going to point out that *she* has a name. Maybe you ought to learn it, given it appears we'll be working together in some capacity for the next year."

He said nothing, but the amber in his eyes flared.

"And I knew what you did here before you explained it to me like I'm a five-year-old."

He flicked one eyebrow up. His unimpressed, scathing look. "Is that so?"

"Yes. And the Lemon Festival in France is the one I'd pick to go on, in case you were wondering." She deliberately named one of the holidays he hadn't run through with her yet, adding a sweet smile for the hell of it.

He gave her a long look—one that made her begin to feel self-conscious enough to ask, "What?"

"Nothing. Your dad liked that one too, that's all."

There was a moment of quiet and Lexie wondered whether she should say something—acknowledge the man who had put them in this situation.

But Theo spoke again, and the moment was lost. "Come on." He gestured toward the back room. "I'll show you how we do the accounts."

"Yippee," Lexie muttered under her breath.

Theo led her to the back room, where she'd stashed her suitcase earlier that morning. There was a mini fridge, an old armchair—and one desk. Clearly, at some point the room had been made to look nice—with bright green walls and a fancy coffee machine—but it had become inundated with clutter. Theo and Lexie both stepped around Lexie's abandoned suit-case, and then Theo sat down and woke up the monitor—though Lexie was pretty sure this must be Ange's desk. There were homemade Christmas cards sitting there, clearly made by young hands—one a weirdly shaped Christmas tree, the other a star with many points. Next to the cards was a photo of Ange with two toddlers—grandkids, maybe?

"The password is Mothball23—Ange's suggestion."

Lexie placed her hand to her heart in mock sincerity. "Wow, you're telling me the password? Have I proved myself worthy?"

Theo didn't bother to answer her, and he moved his chair an extra inch away when she came to stand behind him so she could see what he was doing.

She cleared her throat. "So are you planning on—?"

She was cut off by the sound of the office door opening as Ange came in, holding two steaming mugs. "Here, I brought you some—Argh!" She stumbled, nearly tripping over Lexie's suitcase.

Lexie lurched toward Ange and managed to rescue the mugs before the liquid spilled everywhere.

"Sorry!" Lexie said. "I didn't know where to leave it."

Ange frowned down at the suitcase.

"I'm staying at my friend's tonight," Lexie explained. Fran had invited her round for a proper girls' night in—facials, wine, popcorn, the whole lot.

"Right. And, ah, how long are you planning on staying there?"

"Just one night." Then they were doing something together for Christmas Eve tomorrow. "But I hadn't really unpacked at my mum's so it seemed easier to bring the whole thing . . ."

Which clearly sounded stupid, from the look on Ange's face. But it was something she'd gotten used to doing—packing everything up, taking it all with her. She decided not to mention there was a green canvas bag too, which was sitting in the corner by the coats, out of harm's way, due to the fact that her breakable wish jar was stowed in it, along with some overnight essentials.

"I see. Well. I brought you both tea. I put an extra sugar in yours, Lexie—thought you could probably use it."

Theo leaned back in the swivel chair and crossed his arms but said nothing in response to the dig. And fine: even through the shirt he was wearing you could tell they were impressive arms. Just because you hated someone didn't mean you couldn't appreciate a nice set of arms.

"And what is it you're lecturing her about now, Theo? Or are you just going to keep reciting the brochures, which she can look at herself?"

"He's showing me the accounts," Lexie said, injecting a healthy measure of sugary sweetness into her voice.

"Accounts? For God's sake, Theo."

"We have to make a profit—she needs to know the accounts," Theo said, deadpan.

"The way you 'know the accounts,' you mean?" Ange held up her fingers to demonstrate the air quotes. She huffed out an impatient breath. "We have an accountant, Lexie. And then the rest is down to me. None of the rest of them would have any idea if we were turning a profit or not if I didn't explain it to them in the quarterlies."

"And, er, who are the rest of them?" She was thinking of Harry—she doubted very much that he got an invite to the P&L meetings.

Ange put her hands on her hips and gave Theo a look that made him shift uncomfortably in the chair. "You are boring her with *accounts* rather than telling her who she's going to be working with? I swear to God, T-Rex . . ."

Lexie let out a short laugh. "T-Rex?"

Theo said nothing to that, but Lexie saw a muscle in his jaw spasm.

"He only gets called that when he's behaving like a bigheaded dinosaur. Like now. And get out of my damn chair while you're at it, Theo."

Theo did as he was told, while Lexie wondered if he had been deliberately trying to bore her—maybe he thought she'd quit if it was too dull? But what use would that do anyone? He could whine about it all he liked, but they were stuck in this together. Or maybe he just wanted to punish her. Which boded well for the next twelve months.

Ange sat down, while Lexie took a sip of her tea—sweet, like Ange had promised. "Your dad was the founder and director, of course—and he had the largest stake in the business, which is why he could hand it over to you. Then there's Mike. I was hoping he'd be here to meet you, but he's spending Christmas abroad. Anyway, Mike's a director, so he gets bonuses and the like if the company does well, but he doesn't actually own any of it—that's now you and Theo."

Theo perched on the corner of Ange's desk, slurped his own tea. "Which Mike *loves,* I'm sure."

Ange said nothing, but a look passed between them—so perhaps there was another reason Mike hadn't come along to say hi.

"Then there's me, obviously," Ange went on, pushing her gray hair back. "But I just do a bit behind the scenes, I'm not the one doing the important bits."

"I'd beg to differ there," Theo said quietly, in a tone that surprised Lexie a little.

Ange offered him a small smile before carrying on. "We have a couple of girls who work part-time, and then Harry. Say what you want about the boy, but at least he shows up when you need him." She clapped her hands together. "Now, how about we all show some holiday cheer, hmm? We're supposed to be the ones people come to when they want an epic holiday somewhere they've never been before—and one look at the two of you on the shop floor earlier would suggest that we are, instead, the place to come when you want a holiday filled with disappointing overpriced food and a mediocre hotel room."

Lexie couldn't help the smile that tugged at her lips.

"Why don't you show her the Iceland trip you and Richard were working on, Theo?"

A shot of unpleasant electricity ran down Lexie's spine. "Iceland?"

"It's a trip your dad was thinking about for years, but we've never been able to get it off the ground. Theo, have you got the folder?"

She gave him a little push and he put his tea down, heading to the back of the room, where a filing cabinet was half hidden among the clutter.

"We have folders for each new idea," Ange explained to Lexie, "and the idea is to be creative, stick on things that might work, lots of just throwing everything in before the team sits down and works out what the holiday will actually be." She smiled encouragingly. "It's the fun part. And there's loads to love about Christmas in Iceland—they have thirteen Father Christmases, which we figured would draw in the family crowd. And the geothermal pools, for the honeymooners. Theo! Where is the folder?"

"I'm trying to find it, give me a chance."

But Lexie had put her mug down on Ange's desk and taken a step back. She felt suddenly light-headed and took a breath to steady herself. "No, that's OK. I don't need to see it." She put a hand on the handle of her suitcase. "Actually, do you know what? I think I'm done. I'm so sorry. But it's Christmas and I've got loads to do and I just can't . . . We can make a plan another time, OK?"

Theo frowned at her from the corner of the room, one hand still inside the filing cabinet. "You can't just—"

But Ange cut him off with a look, before turning to give Lexie a searching look. After a moment, she nodded. "OK. Don't worry, we close early ahead of Christmas Eve anyway—I for one want to spend some time with my family over the next few days, and I have an appointment at the panto with my granddaughters this evening. You're right. I'm sure this has all been overwhelming. We'll sit down and make an action plan after Christmas, OK?"

"Yes, thank you," Lexie mumbled, feeling a rush of gratitude toward Ange. Then, without looking back, she grabbed her suitcase and lugged it from the room, taking the escape route she'd been offered.

The door had only just closed when Lexie heard Theo's voice. "What did I tell you? I knew she wouldn't even last a day. Harry owes me ten quid."

Despite herself, Lexie hovered, listening.

"For Christ's sake, Theo! And as if you're placing bets on her. You're behaving like a complete dolt, and you know it."

There was a pause, then, "You're right. I'm sorry. I just . . . Ange, I don't want the company to flop, after years of . . . you know. Building it up. Especially after the last couple of years. He wouldn't have wanted that either and I don't want everything he did here to be lost." *He*. Richard?

Ange's voice was a little gentler when she spoke again. "Well, the one way to ensure it *does* flop is to act like you are."

"She doesn't want it to work. She clearly didn't care about her dad, so why would she care about the company?"

"Why don't you give her a chance instead of deciding for her what she does or doesn't care about? Her dad's just died, she's been thrown into this, and all she can do is her best—but you're making that impossible. You ought to know better than that." The last statement was loaded—like there was a reason he ought to know better.

But Lexie didn't want to know. She started walking again, dragging her suitcase through the shop, past the desks and Harry, who quickly shoved his phone out of sight and pretended to look busy, and onto the street outside. It was just getting dark, and the Christmas lights had lit up around the city, giving the whole place a golden hue.

She blew out a breath. She didn't care, she told herself. She didn't care about Theo betting against her, *wanting* her to fail, and she didn't care about his stake in the company. She didn't give a fucking damn about the company one way or the other. Maybe she should walk away now. If she walked away they both got nothing, right? And maybe that was what she wanted.

Iceland. She knew all about Iceland at Christmas. She knew about the thirteen Yule Lads, and about the geothermal pools. She knew, because that was supposed to have been *her* holiday. It was the holiday they'd been planning—the three of them— for Lexie's eighth Christmas. They'd been talking about it for months, like they did every year, planning what to do. Lexie had been researching Iceland, telling her friends about it. That September, she'd stuck up a chart on which she could cross off the days until Christmas. She'd made her dad tell her all about the types of food they ate there, and she'd begged her mum to buy her a new swimsuit, because of the pools.

Then, at the beginning of October, her dad had left. And Lexie had spent the remaining weeks before Christmas hoping—sure that he couldn't just leave, because the three of them needed to be together, and because they had their holiday to go on, something they did every year. The week before Christmas, she'd placed a wish in her wish jar. Wishing for her dad to come back. Wishing for Iceland. But by that point she hadn't really cared about the holiday—and she'd written a postscript under the wish, explaining that it didn't matter, as long as he came home. But he hadn't—and Iceland had never happened. Instead, years later, he'd remembered that trip, the one they'd never been on, the one it still hurt to think about, and had been planning to monetize it. So do you know what? Screw him and his company. And screw Theo. They could damn well do this without her.

Chapter Five

Lexie took the coffee her mum offered her on the sofa, and re-adjusted the blanket so it covered her bare feet—the fire was on, but the room was still warming up. It was quiet in the living room, and Lexie took a minute to drink that in. There was something different about quiet on Christmas morning, a sense of anticipation. Even as an adult, even moving around every year, it was something she hadn't been able to shake. Outside, the sky was a pearly gray, waking up slowly, and inside her mum's cottage the Christmas lights on the tree flashed in a soothing rhythm.

"Happy Christmas, my love," her mum said, sitting down on the sofa next to her.

Lexie smiled. "Happy Christmas."

She couldn't remember the last time she'd spent Christmas at home. It must have been eight years ago now, while she was still at university. She felt an uncomfortable surge of guilt, even though she knew that her mum always had people to spend Christmas with. In recent years, they'd made sure to video call—and her mum was usually getting ready to go and spend Christmas with a friend. She had an endless number of friends, her mum. Over the years, the two of them had also formed a tradition—instead of buying presents for each other to open (one year a present her mum had sent to her had gotten lost at customs somewhere), they decided on an experience that they'd do together—each paying for the other. Last year it had been a cookery course, the year before it had been the spa. They'd already decided on this year's activity—an experience where you got to go and feed the meerkats at a local wildlife center—before Lexie had got the call about her dad. But Lexie still sometimes wondered if it made her a bad daughter, the fact that she was never around for Christmas Day itself.

"Who were you planning on spending Christmas with this year, Mum?" Lexie asked.

"Hmm? Oh just the usual, you know."

Lexie raised her eyebrows at the very vague answer, but her mum plowed on.

"I was thinking we'd have blinis for breakfast in a bit—that's what Kirsty, you know, Fran's mum, did last year for Christmas, and they are truly excellent with smoked salmon."

"Sounds good." Or it would have—if she had any confidence in her mum's cooking skills.

On the coffee table, Lexie's phone buzzed, and she leaned forward to look at the message. It was a group photo from her friends in Austria, all outside in the snow. It made her smile—made her feel like it was the right decision, to be flying back out there tomorrow. Everything was packed, ready to go. Well, nearly everything. She grimaced as she thought of the green canvas bag, still sitting at R&L Travel.

"Mum, I'm really sorry, but do you mind if I pop out? I'll be two hours, max."

"What on earth do you need to pop out for on Christmas Day?"

"I know, it's stupid. It's just that I forgot something in the office and if I don't get it now I'll be in a rush to make my flight tomorrow."

"You're going through with that, are you? You're definitely going back?"

"Yes," Lexie said firmly. Her decision was made, and nothing her mum could say would change that. Which her mum seemed to gather, because she didn't press the issue.

"All right. But don't be too long or all the sherry will have gone by the time you're back. I plan to crack it open any minute now."

Lexie laughed, then gave her a kiss on the cheek. "I'll be back before you know it."

WHEN SHE GOT to the office, she let herself in with the key code that Ange had made her memorize. The whole city was eerily quiet—only a very few people out in the open—and the office had that same kind of spooky, empty feel. It was dark, but Lexie didn't switch on the lights—she felt the need to keep quiet and hidden.

She tiptoed to the back room and used the light on her phone to find her bag. She felt inside. There, next to her hairbrush, was her wish jar. She took it out of the bag, placing it on the desk next to Ange's photos, just to check it wasn't broken. She hadn't put a wish in this Christmas. It was only now that she realized. She'd left Austria in a hurry, and then things had been so messed up since she'd landed that she hadn't even thought of it. It gave her a slight pang, looking at all the folded-up pieces of paper inside. It was the first year she'd not done it. What would she wish for now? She closed her eyes, took a slow breath. She didn't have a clue.

When she opened her eyes, she saw a folder on the desk. Automatically she reached out and flipped it open, shining her torch to look. She knew immediately what she was looking at. Cutouts from magazines of people in steaming pools, and a photo of bright blue-green light flashing across a darkened sky.

Maybe we'll even see the northern lights, Little Lex, if we're really lucky.

Lexie slammed the folder shut and tried to shove her dad's voice out of her mind. But she couldn't quite block the memory of him telling her where they'd be spending Christmas that year, his face poker-straight as he listed destinations, trying to get her to guess which one it was.

"Iceland!" And she'd leaped into his arms, something she was starting to get too big for, and he'd swung her around the way he'd done when she was really little. She remembered the way he'd grinned at her, the way it had made his eyes, so like hers, crinkle at the corners.

She stared at the folder, a lump forming in her throat. She didn't remember him leaving. Didn't have one definitive memory of him storming out the house, never to come back, like you see in the movies. It had just seemed to her that he was always there, her dad who made jokes and took her on adventures through the woods on the weekends, and then he wasn't. And she'd never really understood it—no one had explained why, other than it just *hadn't been working* and *of course he still loves you, Lexie.*

The sound of the office door opening made Lexie jump. She lifted her phone torch to look toward the doorway and Theo moved out of the bright glare, his face mostly obscured by shadow.

"Any reason you're standing in the dark?" he asked, flicking on the office light. She lowered her phone, pushed back her hair self-consciously.

She frowned as she took him in. His stubble had grown a bit over the last two days, and he was wearing jeans and a casual jumper. "What are you doing here?"

That scarred eyebrow flicked up. He moved into the room, closer to her. "I live here, remember?"

She lifted her chin in the air. "You don't live *here,* in the actual office." But did that mean he was spending Christmas in the flat above, on his own? Though maybe he had someone up there, waiting for him.

"What are *you* doing here? Come to sabotage the place? Burn it all down?"

"What would be the point of that?"

"Well, you've made it perfectly clear you don't want any of this."

She folded her arms. "And why would I? Want this?"

"Interfering with some grand plan, is it? What was it you were doing, off babysitting some posh kids while they're on their skiing break?"

She felt her cheeks flush, even though she had nothing to be embarrassed about—he could think what he liked, it didn't make her choices any less valid. "As opposed to jumping on an old man's company so you can take it all on as your own idea?"

He looked at her for a moment, assessing her. Then he said quietly, "I would never portray it as if it were my idea." She frowned, opening her mouth to speak, but he cut her off. "And your dad wasn't that old."

It was a punch to the gut, even as she tried to ignore it, and she dropped her hands to her sides. There was a flash of memory, coming from nowhere.

Do you have to be such a cliché, Richard? Sleeping with some-

one younger and prettier? You're too old for this shit—you need to grow up.

I'm forty-three, that's hardly old! And she's only a few years younger. It's not like . . .

Then her dad noticed her, hovering in the doorway, having come downstairs in the night for water. *Hey, Little Lex!* The smile he gave her was awkward. *Do you need something to drink? Here, I'll—*

I'll get it, her mum snapped. And her dad looked between them, then sighed, leaving the kitchen, running his hand across Lexie's shoulder as he did so.

Her mum was quiet as she got a glass down, filled it with water. But Lexie could see her lip trembling. So she went over and gave her a hug. *I think you're pretty, Mummy.*

Her mum wrapped her arms around Lexie, squeezing so tight it hurt, but Lexie didn't tell her that. *Thank you, my darling.*

She'd nearly forgotten moments like that—or had tried to, anyway. Moments like that were why she didn't like people arguing around her as an adult—why she tried to avoid conflict when she could. You didn't have to be a genius to work that out. Yet here she was, arguing away. Theo seemed to know just how to get under her skin.

Theo was watching her, a frown playing across his forehead. He opened his mouth to say something, but Lexie cut him off. "Look, let's just—"

But she didn't finish, because her phone started ringing in her hand. Turning her back on Theo, she answered. "Hi, Mum."

"How are you getting on?"

"I'm coming back now."

"OK, just trying to decide whether to start the blinis."

"Oh, I can help you do that when I'm—"

"Nonsense, I'll get cracking." Then she laughed. "Cracking! Like the eggs!"

Despite herself, Lexie let out a little laugh too. "I'll be as quick as I can."

She turned back to Theo to see him standing there, holding her wish jar. "What's this?" he asked, his voice mildly curious.

"It's mine," she snapped. "That's what it is." And OK, she was trying not to argue, but you shouldn't go around just *grabbing* other people's private possessions, even if they are sitting out in the open. She went to take it, but he moved it out of reach. "Give it back."

His lips twisted into a smile. "I'll give it back if you tell me what it is."

"Seriously? What are you, ten?"

His smile grew a little lighter, and she wondered for a moment what his *true* smile looked like, and whether it would make his eyes flare like they did when he was angry.

She pushed her hair back impatiently. "It's a wish jar, OK?"

"A what?"

"It's where you . . . Never mind." It sounded stupid, saying it out loud. And it was none of his damn business, anyway.

He gave it back as promised, putting it on the desk, and she cleared her throat.

"Look. I've been thinking."

He sighed. "Here we go."

"You have no idea what I'm about to say."

"You don't want the company, right? It's all you've said since you first found out about it."

"You mean, since I first found out about it less than a week ago?" She took a breath. *Stay calm, Lexie.* "Anyway, not the point. You're right. I don't want it." Plain and simple language, that was the key.

"If you walk away, you get nothing."

"*We* get nothing."

He cocked his head. "You'd do it to spite me, would you?"

"Well, why not? You've been nothing but nasty to me since the moment we met."

"Or is it about spiting your dad?"

"Fuck you." *OK, so much for calm.* "I'm leaving. I don't want any of this. So go ahead, see how you do without me—maybe you'll find a workaround to the will." Though she knew, from talking to Fran, that that was highly unlikely.

She shoved the jar into her bag, hitched it on her shoulder, and made for the exit.

He stepped in front of her to block her path. "We need to talk about this. Figure out what to do."

"I just told you, I'm out."

"Yeah? Well, that doesn't actually solve anything, so I don't accept that."

"You can accept it or not, doesn't make it not true."

She tried to move past him, but he mirrored her like they were in some kind of stupid sports game.

"Get out of the way, Theo."

"Look, what if you didn't have to do anything?"

"What?"

"You clearly don't want any part of this—and OK, maybe I can't blame you for that."

She scoffed. "Seems an awful lot like you blame me anyway."

He took a slow breath, like he was praying for patience—like *he* was the one who needed patience in this scenario. "Regard-less, what if you didn't have to do anything? Would you stick the year out then? Because I doubt very much there will be a workaround—your dad would have made sure of that—and I really don't want his company to go bust just because you . . ."

She glared at him. "Because I what, exactly?"

They were very close—close enough that she could smell him. Sandalwood and something muskier layered underneath it. He hadn't backed down at her glare, just kept his eyes level on hers. She could see the different colors, the way brown gave way to amber. She should step back. But she didn't want to be the one to back away, didn't want to look like she was uncomfortable around him. She brought a hand up to play with her loose curls—a nervous tic—and he followed the movement with his gaze. He frowned at her hand and she dropped it.

"Never mind," he said.

He eased back an inch, and she let loose a relieved breath.

"Look, I'll do the work. I already know how to do it. You can do whatever—go back to your ski chalet, hit the slopes. Whatever makes you happy. And just be a silent partner. Then at the end of the year, when we've made a profit, we . . ."

"Sell the company?"

He said nothing to that, just slid his thumbs through the belt loops of his jeans and waited. She really wanted to throw the offer back in his face. But she could do with the money. She had no savings, a ton of university debt. Moving from one job to another had lots of perks, but a steady income wasn't one of them.

"Maybe," she said eventually.

His shoulders relaxed, just a bit. "Maybe?"

"I'll think about it, OK? But right now my mum is drinking all the sherry without me and will soon be murdering some blinis."

He gave her a brief, searching look, as if checking for the honesty in her words, then nodded. "OK. Thank you."

Lexie hesitated as he stepped aside, giving her a clear run to the door. *Thank you.* She wasn't really sure what to do with that thanks. "Are you . . . ? I mean, are you doing anything, today?"

She flushed as he gave her a look. She wasn't really sure where she'd been going with that. It had just occurred to her that it seemed like he was spending Christmas alone. But what was she going to say if he was? *Do you want to come round for a glass of sherry and a burnt blini to talk about how great you think my dad was to the woman he left?*

"I'm just hanging out here this morning."

Lexie bit her lip. It was a nonanswer, and she wasn't sure if it meant that he'd be spending Christmas here, in an office, on his own.

He gave her that infuriating one-eyebrow raise, like he knew exactly what she was thinking. "Don't worry about me—I've got plenty to be getting on with, and I've got plans later on. Don't you have to go and rescue some pancakes or something?"

She rolled her eyes. Clearly, he didn't want her sympathy, even if she'd been about to offer it. "OK, fine."

"Don't forget to think about it," he added, as she headed for the exit.

"I won't." She'd do little else now, probably. And OK, yes, maybe that meant point to Theo.

"And Lexie?" She turned back, and he gave her a small smile, which hinted at the fact that he *could* smile, if he really wanted to. "Happy Christmas."

Chapter Six

12/28/23

Dear Theo,

After our recent discussion I'm writing to let you know that I accept your terms. I am happy for you to take the lead with the company, aiming for a sale early 2025, provided a profit is made. Having read through the contract from the solicitor it appears our year started when we both agreed to take on the running of the business, which I'm thinking should count from the first day I came into the office before Christmas. So would you agree we are looking at a January 2025 sale? I will be in Austria until this coming April, but will be contactable via this email address should you need to get hold of me. I would appreciate it if you could keep me abreast of any major developments—I'd like to feel confident should I get asked any questions about the business at any point. It would also be great if you could keep me up to date as to whether we look on track to turn a profit—perhaps we should check in on a monthly basis?

Many thanks,
Lexie

1/15/24

Dear Theo,

Further to my previous email, I just wanted to check that all had been received and understood? I'd appreciate it if you could confirm receipt, and let me know if this is all acceptable to you. As I've said, I'd also like to be kept up to date as to whether the company looks on track to turn a profit, and with any big developments or new ideas you may be bringing in.

> *Many thanks,*
> *Lexie*

2/3/24

Dear Lexie,

Sincere apologies for the delay. Given it was my idea to run the company this way, you can be sure that I accept the terms. However, as the tax year runs April–April, we will not have all the information as to whether the company has turned a profit for "our" year in business until April 2025. I suspect your dad was assuming you would be happy to wait a full tax year. I will ask Ange to send you the P&L sheets after each of our quarterly meetings. The only person who would question you on the running of the business would be, I assume, the solicitor, to make sure that we are fulfilling the terms of the contract. However, he's not suggested that he will be checking up on us in any way, and as you've agreed to be a silent partner, so to speak, I see no reason for you to have a say in any developments I may or may not implement—it would only confuse matters as you wouldn't have the context. Rest assured that I know what I'm doing and will be working hard to ensure the legacy of the business. I certainly don't want to see Richard's dream fall apart now.

If you ever need more information, please do call Ange in the office. I'm sure she'd be only too happy to help.

All best,
Theo

2/3/24
~~Dear Fuckwit,~~
~~If you could take the time to drag your pompous head out of your pompous ass, you'd see that a) what I'm asking for is perfectly reasonable, b) you're really not as clever as you apparently think you are, and c) you're a total dick.~~

2/7/24
~~Dear Theo,~~
~~Given that the solicitor may ask questions, like you said, I really think that keeping me up to date on the basics might be a good idea. I'm not asking for much here—I don't want to know the day in and day out, I just don't want to get caught out and risk losing the money from the sale of the company. Also, you don't have to treat me like I'm a complete imbecile—I'm not. Trust me, I would rather speak to Ange than you—if Richard had left half the company to her we wouldn't be in this mess at all. Maybe that's why you and my dad got on. Because you are also a complete wanker.~~

2/12/24

Dear Theo,

While I appreciate I will be taking a back seat here, I think it is advisable for you—or Ange, if you prefer—to keep me relatively up to date as the year progresses. The P&L sheets would be great, but perhaps you could send me updates at the same time? I don't want to be involved with the running of the company, I know we are both clear on that, but as you say, there is a possibility—albeit slim—that I will be asked questions by the solicitor to make sure I am fulfilling my side of the contract. I wouldn't want to risk all your many hours of hard work by failing to ask a few simple questions—wouldn't you agree?

> *Many thanks,*
> *Lexie*

2/13/24

Dear Lexie,

Noted.

> *Theo*

Lexie gritted her teeth as she read Theo's reply. The fucking nerve of him. She took a calming breath of cold mountain air. The sky was a bright blue today, sunlight glittering off the snow. It was half term, so there were people everywhere, but she could still draw a sense of calm, being up here. She hadn't wanted to be involved, she reminded herself. She didn't really *want* to know the ins and outs of what Theo was doing with her dad's company—she didn't care. She was in it for the money, that was all. And Fran had looked it over with her, and declared Theo's idea sound—there was nothing in her dad's stipulation, from a legal perspective, that said they had to split the running of the company fifty-fifty. Still, Fran had also advised that Lexie ought to be *seen* to be involved: that even though she wasn't going to be hands-on, there should still be a paper trail that showed she had participated to some extent, in case this was called into question when the time came to sell. Theo was just being deliberately obtuse.

Arms covered in a dark blue ski jacket came around her waist, and warm breath tickled her cold ear. "What are you doing looking at your phone when you've got all this?"

Lexie twisted to give Mikkel a wry look over her shoulder. "You mean the mountains? Or you?"

He grinned. "Both."

She smiled and put her phone back into her jacket. She'd invested in a ski suit a few years ago before her first ski season, and she thought it was a cool one—turquoise, white, and purple—but she still didn't quite pull off "skiing chic" the way Mikkel did in his Viking God way. "I'm just checking up on . . . some stuff." She hadn't really explained to him what was going on. He knew her dad had died—all her friends here did, because she'd come back into the bar the night she'd gotten the call, in total shock. But she hadn't been able to dredge up the emotional energy to tell him everything else, given it would mean explaining some of the backstory with her dad, too. And he hadn't asked. They didn't talk much about their pasts or wider lives outside the Alps—kept things casual to the extreme. Lexie preferred it that way.

Mikkel rested his chin on her shoulder. She could smell his cologne—a fresh citrus scent—and though it made her want to stay like this with him, in a little bubble, she sighed. "I have to get the girls from ski school soon."

The family had left in early January, back to London, where the girls went to some fancy private school, which meant Lexie had had the chalet to herself until this week—though it hadn't actually been as freeing as she'd imagined, given she was constantly worrying about spilling something or leaving a mark that hadn't been there before. She'd also had a lot of time with not a lot to do—which she'd thought would be great, but in reality had meant her mind refused to let up, turning the situation with her dad's company over and over. Still, she'd had plenty of time to work on her skiing—and plenty of time for sex with Mikkel.

Mikkel pulled back, so she could see her reflection in his sunglasses. "Race you to the bottom?"

She laughed, but he was already off, pushing away with his poles and executing a perfect parallel turn a little way down the mountain. She snapped into action too, pushing herself off and feeling a familiar lurch of excitement. She never won their races—and she had a suspicion that Mikkel might actually be a bit put out if she did—but it pushed her to try to go faster each time. Halfway down she hit a mogul at the wrong angle and was thrown into the air for a beat, before landing at speed. She nearly fell, her heart giving a painful thud, but she regained her balance and pushed herself into the turn. By the time she got to the bottom she was breathing heavily and full of adrenaline. *This* was what she loved about this place—this was what made living out of a suitcase worth it.

Unbidden, a flash of a memory came to her. This had been happening to her more and more since her dad died—the memories that she'd spent years trying to bury were now resurfacing. Good memories, as well as bad. Like this one—she and her dad, at the top of a ski slope. She'd been six, she was pretty sure, and they'd flown out to the Alps on Christmas Day itself, no doubt because it was cheaper—something she'd only realized years later. Her dad had sat next to her on the plane, and the whole thing had been impossibly exciting, getting up early to go to the airport on Christmas Day.

Keep your eyes peeled, Little Lex. Maybe we'll see Santa and his reindeer flying next to us on their way home to the North Pole.

They'd spent a week in a tiny chalet with just one bedroom—the three of them all camped together. And she'd learned how to ski for the first time. Her mum had hated it, declaring skiing "not her thing," which meant Lexie had spent lots of time with her dad, as he tried to teach her how to do it. Not that he was an expert at skiing, but he'd always been willing to give anything a good go. It had been one of the things she'd missed the most about him, after he'd gone—that sense of adventure, the excitement she'd feel when she saw the glint in his eye and knew he was about to pull her into something fun.

Race you down the mountain, Little Lex. It could only have been a tiny slope, she knew that now—but it had seemed huge at the time. She hadn't wanted to show him she was scared, and anyway, she had felt brave because he was there, and he was always brave. She could hear the faint echo of her mum's voice in the background, her mum oddly faceless in the memory. *Oh, Richard, please be careful.* But they were off, reaching the bottom in no time.

You beat me! Richard's voice, coming up just behind her. *If only we lived near a mountain, you'd be an expert skier in no time.*

It was odd, now, to think about it. Maybe that holiday was what made her want to spend time in the Alps all these years later. She stuck her poles into the snow, looked around for Mikkel. She saw him by the queue to the chairlift, chatting to a woman with long, cascading red hair. Didn't having her hair like that get in the way when she was skiing? Her ski suit was bright turquoise and somehow she managed not to look like the squished marshmallow that Lexie always felt she was when she put on her trousers. When Lexie shuffled closer, she heard the woman laugh brightly at something Mikkel said, then watched as she brushed her hand over his arm before she left for the chairlift.

Lexie rolled her eyes as she unclipped her skies and put them over her shoulder, heading toward the pickup area for ski school. Mikkel hadn't noticed her yet, and she didn't want to embarrass herself by going up to him. She knew he flirted with other women, and it wasn't like they were exclusive. But still, seeing it didn't exactly feel *good*.

She waved to Bree and Bella as they shuffled toward her, fishing her phone out of her pocket when she felt it vibrating. Her heart gave an unpleasant little spasm when she saw who it was.

Rachel. It wasn't the first time she'd called recently. She kept calling every couple of weeks, like it had become a habit. Lexie waited for it to ring out, then slipped her phone away again as the girls trudged up to her.

She should call Rachel back, she knew she should. Or she should answer, next time. She wasn't a total bitch—she'd replied to a few of her text messages. But she didn't know what to say to her. Rachel probably wanted to talk about Richard's house—clear the air, or whatever. The problem was, Lexie didn't want to talk about it. She was trying not to blame Rachel. She knew, logically, that it wasn't her fault that she'd been the favorite daughter, the one her dad had bothered to get to know, the one he'd valued more highly in his will. And she didn't *want* to blame her—but she worried she'd accidentally say the wrong thing, and she really didn't want to end up in an argument. It was pitiful, she knew, that she didn't know Rachel well enough to predict how the conversation might pan out, whether Rachel was likely to get defensive or not.

Next time, she told herself. She'd answer next time, when she could figure out what to say.

Chapter Seven

Lexie was stirring a tin of tomatoes into some browned mince when her phone rang. She made a grab for it, splattering Bolognese sauce on the stove as she did so. She swore under her breath, then glanced over at the living room to check the girls hadn't heard. Neither of them were paying her the slightest bit of attention, Bree watching *Encanto* for the hundredth time and Bella on her iPad. It was nice, though, to have someone to cook for. Despite the worry that she'd do something wrong, she definitely preferred it when the girls were around. But they were only going to be here another five days, and then they were going back to London.

She looked down at her phone, stirring with one hand. It was an unknown number calling, but she recognized the Bath area code. It could be Theo. Her stomach squirmed unpleasantly. She didn't want to answer if it was. So she let it ring out. He could email her if he needed to. But seconds after it stopped ringing, it started up again—the same number. She bit her lip. It might *not* be Theo. And surely it must have been something important for whoever it was to be this insistent.

"Hello, Lexie speaking." She kept her voice formal, business-like.

"Lexie, love, it's Ange. I'm calling from your dad's office. *Your* office, I should say," she added pointedly.

"Ange!" Lexie almost dropped the wooden spoon in the

sauce, picked it up again. "Hello! How are you?" Even as a warm rush of relief washed through her on hearing it wasn't Theo, she felt heat around the base of her neck, knew her voice was too high, too enthusiastic. She should have called Ange before now—at least to say thank you. Ange had been kind to her, defended her—and she'd scarpered without a word.

"I'm fine, though we could do with some brighter weather here. I hear you're in the Alps?"

"Ah, yes."

"Well, good."

"Good?"

"Yes. You're not too far from France, then?"

Lexie frowned. This was really not where she'd thought this conversation would go. Wasn't Ange just ringing to give her an update of some kind? Or even, potentially, to tell her she needed to come back and properly fulfill her side of the bargain? "Well no," Lexie said slowly. "I'm not too far away, I suppose."

"Excellent. The Fête du Citron starts at the end of this week. In Menton. Which is in France."

"Um, that's nice . . ." Lexie stuck a fork into the pasta—bows, because Bree only liked bows—to check if it was done. "That's one of the holidays you organize, right?"

"We organize, you mean."

"Right. Is there something going on with it? Something I should, er, know about?" Not that she had any idea what she should know about it. She had no idea what would constitute a "development" in all honesty—even if she had insisted Theo keep her up to date on those.

"It's the holiday you said you'd pick, isn't it?" Ange continued. "When Theo showed you around the office."

"I . . . Well, yes, I suppose so." Though she'd mainly said that to show she didn't need to read through the brochures. Had Ange overheard—or had Theo told her?

"Good. I've bought you a plane ticket from Zurich to Nice. You can get to Zurich pretty easily, I'm sure?"

"I—"

"And then from Nice it's around just over an hour bus journey. If you keep the receipt for the ticket the company can pay you back."

"Ange." Lexie tried to make her voice firm as she gave the Bolognese another stir. "What do you mean you've bought me a plane ticket? Why?"

"You said you wanted to go, didn't you? And the company can pay for it. So, consider it a nice little holiday."

Lexie let out an incredulous laugh; she could tell Ange was someone who could always get her way. "I can't just go to France next week!" Although actually, she could. She didn't have the girls, and the chalet would be fine left unattended if she wasn't away for too long. But that wasn't really the point.

"It's only for a couple of days. I thought you might like to see what the company does, and who doesn't like a free vacation? And Mike, the other director, will be there—he's said he can show you around so you can get the VIP experience."

"I don't know, Ange. Did Theo tell you . . . I mean, we've sort of agreed I should take a back seat for the year, and he might feel like this is stepping on his toes. I appreciate the offer, really, I do, but—"

"Your dad left the company to both of you, Lexie." Ange was good at the stern voice, you had to give her that. It was enough to make Lexie stop her protests. "Now, I know you have a life, and I know you have commitments in Austria, but the least you could do *as an owner of the company* is see what we're all about.

I've booked you into the hotel and Mike has arranged the itinerary so you can join in."

"I—"

"The contract is very clear, from what I understand. You must both *participate* in the running of the business while you own it."

Lexie said nothing. Was Ange *threatening* her? Suggesting that she'd report Lexie if she didn't go on this trip? But she wouldn't go through with it, even if it was a threat; Lexie was sure of that. Almost sure.

The water covering the pasta started boiling over the pan, and Lexie turned the heat down quickly. "Look, Ange, I'm in the middle of something. I'll call you back, OK?" If in doubt, play for time.

"Wonderful. I've got your email address from Theo. I'll send everything over to you."

"That's not to say I—" But Ange had hung up.

LATER, ONCE THE girls were in bed, Lexie called Fran.

"She just wants me to drop everything and head to France at the drop of a hat—I mean, can you believe that?"

"We-ll," Fran said, drawing out the word, "you said yourself that things were boring when the girls aren't there."

"Yes, but . . ." Lexie let out an impatient breath. "That's not the point, is it?" She leaned against one of the French doors. It was dark outside, but you could still just about make out the mountains in the glow of the nearby bar lights.

"As far as I can tell she's offering a free holiday—why not take it?"

"I doubt it'll really be free. She'll rope me into something, I'm sure of it. I'd admire her for the way she gets things done if she wasn't currently using that ability against me."

"Look, I know you don't want to get involved in the company, but she's right—shouldn't you at least find out more about it, before you sell it? The more informed you are, the more you can make sure you get what you deserve in a sale. And wasn't it partly that guy—?"

"Theo." She said his name like a growl.

"Right, Theo. Wasn't it him making life difficult that put you off in the first place?"

"It wasn't only about him." Richard's name hung in the balance—but Fran had been tactfully avoiding talking about him, no doubt waiting for Lexie to be the one to bring it up. Something that Lexie appreciated.

"Still. He won't be there, will he?"

"No," Lexie said slowly. "Ange said Mike would show me around. He's another director, but I haven't met him yet."

Lexie let the curtains fall over the French doors. Inside, the fire was crackling in the corner and Lexie was warm enough to be walking around on the wooden floors barefoot. And she needed to walk right now. There was a curdling in her stomach making her jittery, and she wasn't totally sure where it was coming from.

"I'm just saying, it's a free trip to France. I'd take it."

Lexie walked to the kitchen, opened the fridge. There was still half a bottle of that fancy white wine Nicole liked to drink sitting there, open. Nicole had offered her a glass last night—would she mind if Lexie poured herself one now?

Fuck it. She got down a glass, unstoppered the wine. She could always replace it, if need be. It would only cost a week's worth of wages.

It was the idea of going on one of her dad's trips, she realized. That's where the jittery feeling was coming from. She'd spent a lot of time stewing over being left with half a company to run and feeling like she was set up to fail, and a lot of time being pissed at Theo, but she had tried not to think too much about her dad, and what he'd built. Tried to push away the fact that it all came from a tradition he'd started with her when she was a kid, only to drop her when he found something better. And she'd done a pretty good job of that, so far—staying focused on the practicalities of it all. So she wasn't sure she wanted to be confronted with it face on like this. She didn't want to condone what he had done by going on this trip.

"Maybe you should make a list of pros and cons," Fran was saying. "For going to France, I mean."

"Sure, I'll get right on that." She poured herself a glass of the wine, took a sip. And yes, it was nice—but she honestly couldn't tell the difference between this and a good supermarket Sauvignon. "Anyway, tell me how *you* are. How's work?"

"Urgh, work is work, let's not talk about it. I don't think I realized how boring being a solicitor would actually be. And I convinced myself it would get better once I moved up the levels a bit, but here I am, up the levels, and it's still just as bad."

"Yes, must be terrible earning all that money."

"The other day this woman came in crying because her marriage was over and she didn't know what to do, and I had to sit down and talk her through the legal options and I just felt evil. Evil, Lexie. I am one of those evil lawyers now—how did that happen?"

"You're not evil. Besides, this is what you've been working for, for literal years." Lexie could remember Fran declaring she'd be a lawyer when they were only sixteen, and she had been absolutely set on it since then, complete conviction all the way—until the last six months or so.

"What? Listening to couples arguing? Feeling powerless in the face of custody battles? Or listening to people cry at my desk as they wonder how things ended up like this and then telling them exactly how much worse it can get before I charge them for preventing that?"

Lexie's stomach squirmed. Fran didn't talk much about specific cases—client confidentiality or whatever—but occasionally she'd say something that made Lexie think of her parents' divorce. And right now, she supposed, she was thinking of her parents more than usual. They must have gotten a lawyer to at least draw up the paperwork, but there had been no big court battles, no arguments over who got what. It was a good thing—Fran had told her that once, over wine, and Lexie knew it was—she wouldn't have wanted her mum to go through what Fran's clients did. But the fact that her dad had walked away without looking back sometimes made Lexie wonder how much he'd ever cared about any of it. How much he'd ever cared about her.

She took another sip of wine. "Why don't you change specialty or whatever—can't you do that?"

"What and go into property law or something equally boring? No thanks. I think when I imagined myself as a lawyer I had images of standing up in court fighting for justice, but I sort of got sidetracked. I blame American TV. That and a ton of university debt I now need to justify."

Lexie laughed. She missed Fran. Yes, she had friends here, but it wasn't the same as friends you knew in and out. "OK, so work's shit."

Fran snorted out a laugh too. "Yes. Work's shit. But . . ."

"But what?"

"I may have met a guy . . ."

"Ooh, do tell." Which was all Fran needed to start gushing about a man she'd met on a dating app. But the thing was, as much as Lexie hated to be skeptical, Fran did this quite a lot. It often baffled Lexie how much hope Fran routinely had about relationships, considering she was a divorce lawyer. She had a tendency to fall head over heels very quickly, then inevitably he would break it off and she was left brokenhearted. The fact that she was able to pick herself up and try again and again was something that both flummoxed and impressed Lexie.

"What about you?" Fran asked. "How's your guy?"

"Mikkel? He's not *my* guy."

"No, of course not."

"What's that supposed to mean?"

"Nothing, nothing."

"Free and single is what I need right now," Lexie said firmly.

"Right, as opposed to all those other times you've been in serious, bogged-down relationships."

Lexie huffed out a breath. "It's better this way round than overly clingy. Remember Ben?"

"I thought Ben was sweet."

"Ben cried when I broke up with him," Lexie said, deadpan. "After we'd only been on about six dates."

"Well, maybe he just really liked you. Anyway, he wasn't as bad as Toby. Remember Toby? He was the one who broke up with me because I wasn't good enough at role-play—after about the sixth date."

"And people ask me why I'm still single, what with all the catches out there." Then she sighed, thinking about her phone bill. "I better go. Are you still going to try to come out here?"

"Yes, if I can ever get time off from all the ruining of marriages I'm doing."

Lexie rolled her eyes. "Bye, Fran." She hung up, then padded to the living room, cocking her head down at Bella.

After checking they were at least *trying* to get to sleep, Lexie checked her emails. Ange had sent a plane ticket, hotel information, and instructions on how to get to Menton from Nice. According to this, Lexie was supposed to leave next Friday.

She drummed her fingers against the granite countertop in the kitchen as she finished her wine. Maybe Fran was right. Maybe she was overthinking it. So what if Ange had some grand plan here? She could still say no to whatever it was.

So she sent Ange a quick email back.

Thanks, Ange. I'll be there.

Chapter Eight

The back of Lexie's neck pricked with sweat as she hitched her rucksack farther up her back, walking the last few feet from the bus stop to the snazzy boutique hotel she'd be staying in. It was warmer than she was used to at this time of year—a balmy fifty-five degrees—and the long-sleeved T-shirt, big jumper, and winter coat were too much for the sunny day, despite the cool breeze whisking the smell of the ocean toward her. She couldn't see the beach from here, but she could hear the cawing of seagulls nearby.

She headed past the bright blue hotel sign, under the domed entrance, and into the lobby area. It was the type of place Lexie loved to stay—proudly independent—and it had a distinctly modern feel, classy and tastefully understated. Sleek wooden flooring, lighting that managed to be neither too bright nor too dim, and stairs to her left that led to a bar area, complete with big white pillars, plush armchairs, and high stools at the backlit bar. It had been a while since she'd stayed in a hotel this fancy, and it made her feel out of place in her travel clothes, like she should be wearing something other than leggings and trainers. Plus, even though it hadn't been a long flight, she still had that travel-tired feeling after taking a bus to the train station, the train to Zurich, waiting around in the airport, then jumping on a plane before finishing the whole thing with two more buses. She wanted a shower and a toothbrush, stat.

She headed for the reception desk, which had an orchid on

one corner of it. The woman sitting there was very chic—the type to be able to pull off a blue blazer and a neckerchief. She had flawless skin, peach lipstick, and neat eyeliner, her hair looped into some fancy knot on the back of her head. It made Lexie feel even more unkempt as she dumped her rucksack at her feet, ran a hand through her curls.

"Bonjour, mademoiselle. Puis-je vous aider?"

"Oui, bonjour. Je . . ." She bit her lip, her limited French completely deserting her. She tried again, telling herself, the way she always did, that she must get better at languages. "Je m'appelle Lexie Peterson. Je, er . . ."

The woman smiled brightly at her. "Ah, oui, you are with the R&L Travel, yes?"

Lexie nodded, pathetically relieved. "Yes."

"I remember you are coming today. The others arrived yesterday." She started tapping at her keyboard with perfectly manicured nails. "You are in room 202, and I think—ah, oui, here he is." The woman gestured behind Lexie's shoulder, and Lexie turned to see an older man with salt-and-pepper hair walking toward her, wearing smart trousers, a shirt, and an expensive-looking jacket—along with a broad grin.

He held out a hand as he approached. Lexie couldn't help but notice his black shoes were very, *very* shiny. "You must be Lexie. You look just like your father, just like him."

Lexie shook the hand he was offering, and he gripped hard before letting go. "I'm Mike. Ange told me to expect you and she was spot-on with the timing as always. Delighted to meet you, truly, delighted. Heard so much about you, of course. You've given Lexie her key, Simone?"

The receptionist—Simone, apparently—fumbled behind the desk, then held out a key card to Lexie. "Voici."

He winked at her. "You're an angel." He checked the time on his gold watch. "Now, Lexie, I'm heading off with our group of clients in a tick. We're going for a look around the basilica— not strictly about the lemons, I know, but the building is a sort of lemony yellow so we're leaning into that—and then we're going to have lunch at a delightful spot. It's reserved just for us: we work with them every year and their *tarte au citron* is to die for—honestly, never tasted anything like it. You'll want to freshen up, I'm sure . . ." He gave her a quick glance up and down and Lexie felt sure he was taking in every inch of her frazzled appearance. "But you'll join us for lunch, yes? Ange said to give you the full tour experience, and I fully intend to make you our guest of honor while you're here."

Lexie couldn't think of much to say to that other than "Oh, right. Thank you." She worked up a smile. "And yes, lunch sounds good. Great, actually." She'd eaten nothing all day apart from a disappointing croissant on the plane. "But how will I know where to find you? Do you have the name of the restaurant, or . . . ?"

"Not to worry, Lexie, not to worry. I'll leave Theo at the hotel. He'll wait for you and can bring you over whenever you're ready."

Lexie realized she was staring at him in a way that might seem rude, and she tried to twist her expression into something more appropriate. "I'm sorry, did you say—?"

"Ah and here's the man himself!" Mike boomed, loud enough to make Lexie jump. She looked around, dread coiling in her stomach, to see Theo coming around the side of reception, where the arrows indicated there was an elevator. Theo jerked to a stop, staring back at her. And it was clear, from the slow frown that crossed his face, that he hadn't known she'd be here.

He managed to school his expression as he tore his gaze away from her.

"They're waiting outside, Mike."

"Marvelous. You know Lexie, of course, don't you?"

"I do. Although I didn't realize she'd be joining us." He gave her a look then, like it might be *her* fault—like she'd somehow deceived him.

"No," she said shortly. "I didn't know you'd be here either."

"Really?" Mike said, his graying eyebrows pulled together as he looked between them. "Not like Ange to forget to bring everyone up to speed. And I thought you knew there was a reason there were two of us out here, Theo." Mike's tone somehow managed to be both mild and condescending at the same time, but he bustled on before Theo could comment. "No matter, you're both here now. Theo, I've told Lexie you'll wait with her and show her to the restaurant. That's not a problem, is it?"

"I don't need—" Lexie began, but Theo interrupted her.

"No, it's not a problem."

And Lexie could hardly force the issue, could she? She wondered why Theo was taking orders from Mike—shouldn't Theo, and she, come to think of it—rank above him?

"Excellent. Well, I best be off. See you at lunch!"

For a brief moment, after Mike left the lobby, Theo and Lexie just stared at each other. Why—*why* did he have to look all . . . put together like that, with his dark, windswept hair, wearing a coat that seemed to highlight his shoulders. She hated that he looked attractive, hated that she *realized* he looked attractive, when he was the last person she wanted to see right now. It tipped the balance in his favor, when her hair was sticking up all over the place and she could feel where the sweat had grown cold on the back of her neck.

"So," Lexie said. "You're here."

He looped his thumbs through the belt loops of his jeans. "Looks like."

She swore under her breath at the sarcastic tone as she bent to pick up her rucksack.

"So nice to see you too," he said, voice all faux-sweet.

She gritted her teeth, but they were at a stalemate. Neither of them could get out of this—they'd both been played. Lexie was going to have to have words with Ange—she didn't appreciate being manipulated. She wouldn't have agreed to come if she'd known Theo would be here—which Ange must have known. It felt like Ange was putting them in the same room and shutting the door with a "Play nice, children." Then again, Ange hadn't actually told her Theo *wouldn't* be here, had she? And Lexie had been dumb enough not to ask.

"What time is lunch?" Lexie asked.

"In about an hour and a half."

"Right. Well, I'll just go up and get sorted, then."

"I'll wait down here, then."

She frowned. "I've got to shower and change."

He gestured toward the elevator. "By all means, take your time."

She hesitated, then walked past him, rucksack over one shoulder, key card clutched in her hand, and jabbed the button on the elevator harder than strictly necessary. Out of the corner of her eye she saw him head into the bar area, his phone now pressed to his ear. "Hi, Ange. I think there's something you might have forgotten to tell me."

———

Her hotel room was gorgeous, the wall behind the huge king-size bed a dark sea blue, pristine white sheets, and polished wood floors to match the lobby. The best part, though, was the view—that and the fact that on the second floor, she had her very own balcony to step out onto, looking out across a long stretch of beach on the French Riviera, where the water glistened in the sunlight and green mountains stretched out behind the line of hotels. She'd have loved to stay out here and just breathe it all in, but it was probably best not to give Theo even *more* reason to be pissed off.

She showered and changed, taking her time to enjoy the fancy water jets. She should have thought better about what clothes to bring—she wished now she had something sleek and sophisticated to wear to lunch. She settled on jeans, pumps, and her go-to red jumper, then assessed herself in the mirror. The lighting in the bathroom was that dim, flattering kind, so by her estimation she looked perfectly fine. Still, she put on some mascara to make herself feel better, scrunched up her damp curls, then took a breath, bracing her hands on the porcelain sink. It was only a couple of days. She was here now: she might as well try to enjoy it—especially as she'd never been to this part of France before, let alone a *lemon* festival, of all things. She wouldn't let Theo ruin her time here.

Her "make the most of it" attitude was put to the test, however, the moment she got to the lobby—and Theo wasn't there. Nor was he in the bar area, moodily sipping whiskey or something. She felt her palms prick as she looked around. Why hadn't she insisted Mike tell her the name of the restaurant? Why hadn't she taken his phone number, for God's sake? She got out her phone to see if there was an email from Theo explaining where he'd gone—but nothing.

"Excusez-moi?" Lexie looked up to see Simone smiling at her. "You are looking for your friend?" Lexie nodded—deciding that now was not the time to point out that he was not her *friend*. "He is in the garden." Simone pointed to the back of the hotel, through the bar area and out the other side.

Lexie followed her directions into not so much a garden as a beautiful courtyard with cobblestones, small wooden tables, and towering green plants that gave it a tropical feeling. Theo was sitting in one corner, his face partly obscured in the shade from the nearest tree. There was an espresso cup in front of him and he was frowning as he tapped something out on his phone.

"You said you'd wait for me in the lobby," she said as she walked over to him.

He didn't even look up at her as he continued to write something. "I trusted in your problem-solving skills to be able to find me."

She pulled her coat on over her jumper and rolled her shoulders. *Do not engage, Lexie.* "Right. Well, shall we go?"

He pressed a final button, shoved his phone into his coat pocket, and stood up, barely sparing her a glance before setting off and leaving her to scramble to keep up.

He walked them through the town, and though she'd only caught a fleeting glimpse of the lemon sculptures they were here to see, everything seemed fitting for a place known for its *citrons*. The buildings were a mixture of orange and yellow, with the occasional sunset pink, which made it feel warmer, somehow. The streets were narrow and there were a lot of tourists around, meaning they had to dodge past the ones stopping to window-shop or take photos.

After five minutes of walking in silence, Lexie was starting to feel awkward. She was usually good at this—small talk. She'd had to get good at it, because she moved around so much—there were always new people to get to know. But right now, she couldn't think of what to say. What she really wanted to ask were questions about the company—about how things were looking, whether he was planning any changes. Whether the Iceland trip was going to be implemented this year, for instance. She opened her mouth a few times, on the verge of broaching the subject, but chickened out each time.

The fourth time she went to open her mouth, Theo gave her a look. "You know, I can *hear* your brain going, even if you don't say anything out loud."

She bit her lip. "I was going to ask about the company. Whether there's anything I should know—any changes or big new trips or . . . anything," she finished lamely. "But you've made it perfectly clear you don't want to talk to me about any of that—so I was trying *not* to ask."

He shot her that annoying raised-eyebrow look.

How had he gotten that scar? she wondered. No. She wasn't wondering—she didn't care one way or another.

"Given *you* made your lack of interest in anything your dad created perfectly clear from the outset and are literally counting down the days until you can be shot of the whole thing, you can see why I'd be reluctant to discuss it."

"It isn't . . ." She shook her head. "That's beside the point. I need to know," she insisted. "I need the money when this company sells."

"Did we actually agree we'd sell the company?" he asked, his voice mild. "I can't remember an explicit conversation about that."

"What?!" she spluttered. "Are you kidding me right now? That is the whole reason I am even—"

"Here we are." He came to a stop outside a rather shabby-looking building, nothing to distinguish it from the two deep yellow terraces on either side. But Theo seemed sure, opening the door and ushering Lexie inside. It was a small place—beyond the bar there seemed to be only one room, which was almost entirely taken up by a long table, covered in a white tablecloth, wineglasses glinting in the sunlight streaming through the high windows. It was nice enough, and the waiter who greeted them was friendly, but it didn't seem like anything special—there was no grand view or stylish interior, as she would have expected from somewhere on a travel company's itinerary.

"What is this place?" Lexie asked, without consciously making the decision to speak out loud.

"Some people would call it a restaurant."

Lexie rolled her eyes at him—he was the type to bring out an eye roll. "Right, I got that, thanks."

Theo headed farther in—and Lexie could see that everyone else was already there, Mike at the middle of the table, currently handing round a bottle of white wine. There were about ten of them in total and they already seemed to know one another, if the way they were chatting away was anything to go by.

"We've been working with the family who runs this place pretty much since the company began," Theo said, and Lexie glanced up at him. "It's a small restaurant, and when Richard found it they weren't doing too well. It's a touristy town, but that still doesn't make it easy, competing with the fancy hotels or places that *look* a certain way. But this place honestly has the best food." He gave a little shrug as she continued to look up at his face. "It's part of the whole ethos of the company—work with small, local places, support the community and people like these guys, who work hard and love what they do. It adds to the feeling of discovering the place behind the tourist traps." He paused, then added, "It's one of the things I love about this company—about what your dad built here. I'm not sure I said that enough to Richard, but . . ." He trailed off, and Lexie looked away, unsure what to make of the hint of emotion in his voice. The hint of someone who might not just be mean for the hell of it—but who genuinely might miss her dad. Maybe miss him more than she was capable of? She didn't know how to answer that.

Instead she glanced around the restaurant again. She loved stumbling on places that weren't the Hilton or the chains aimed at tourists, loved the idea of getting to know the community that way. And she hadn't quite clocked that her dad's company was all about that, too. She'd assumed the smaller hotels advertised on most of their trips were more about marketing than a company ethos, but maybe they weren't. Had this been important to her dad? Or was it just to try to be trendy, stand out from the crowd? She hated that Theo probably knew the answer to this when she didn't.

Lexie grabbed Theo's arm as he made to join the table. And added another thing to the hated list—that she noticed how *solid* his arms were, even beneath his coat. "Look, Theo—" she began, intending to pick up the conversation about selling the company. But she was cut off by Mike's booming voice.

"Lexie! Theo! Come and join us, we're all just getting settled. Lexie, I've saved you a seat opposite me. Come on, come on. Everyone, this is Lexie." He beamed around the table and she got a few smiles and one awkward wave.

Theo looked down pointedly at her hand on his arm, and she let go. She plastered a smile on her face as she went to take her seat opposite Mike, in between a redheaded woman in her thirties—the one who had waved—and a man in his forties, who was talking to another man next to him in a low voice.

"Feeling better, Lexie?" Mike asked, immediately filling her glass with wine. She took a sip—why not?—and was surprised at how good it was. She shouldn't have been, really—this was France, after all. But it was much better than the expensive wine from the chalet—this was cool and crisp and dangerously drinkable. And even she, with her limited wine knowledge, could taste the citrus undertones.

"Much, thanks." She glanced down the table. Theo had taken a place at the end and a woman wearing a pale blue blouse, in her thirties, maybe, with short brunette hair, was leaning in, nodding along at whatever Theo was saying, while the man opposite her—her husband?—looked a bit bored. The woman looked *charmed,* though. And Theo was smiling, telling some kind of story. So, it was only her he was a dick to, then.

"You're just in time for the starters," Mike said, smiling to the two waiters as they came out. "Put them down anywhere, chaps, they're for everyone." Either the waiters spoke perfect English, or they already knew what to do, because soon the table was filled with starters for them to pick at. There was lemon ricotta bruschetta, lemon crab bites, mini salmon cakes with lemon, and a fancy white bean lemon dip.

"Lemon is incorporated into every dish," Mike explained, unnecessarily.

"What if someone doesn't like lemons?" Lexie asked wryly, before she could stop herself.

At the end of the table, she saw Theo look up. He briefly caught her eye and his lips twitched like he might be about to smile, but he didn't give in to it. Mike, however, didn't seem to get the joke.

He took a crab bite, then leaned across to Lexie conspiratorially. Either side of them, people were engaged in conversation. "Now, Lexie, tell me. How are you doing?"

Lexie put her hand over her mouth as she swallowed her first bite of bruschetta. And OK, she could immediately see why Richard had picked this place. The food was amazing. How did they get a simple bruschetta to taste so good? The ricotta melted in her mouth, with just enough burst of lemon, managing to be both sweet and sour. She swallowed sooner than she would have liked to answer Mike's question. "I'm all right, thanks. How was—?"

"I know it must be tough. Your father was very dear to me, of course, very dear. I do know he was a bit of a rascal, though, back in his day."

Lexie was trying hard to like Mike, but him describing her dad as a "rascal," like he was just a kind of playful puppy, made her want to grit her teeth. She took a sip of wine instead.

"I know it must be hard, having been thrown into all this. Have you talked to the solicitor, to see if there's any way out of it for you?"

Lexie spooned some of the bean dip onto her plate. Presumably Theo and Ange had filled him in about her reluctance to take on any responsibility for the company. "I asked—and I got a friend of mine who's a solicitor to check, but they both agreed the terms were pretty clear." And she didn't want to talk about it. "Do you always have one of you on the trips? From R&L I mean?"

"No, not always. We mainly use local guides, so part of the job is recruiting those people, working with them to offer the best experience with customers. Support the local economy, you know." He said it with a wave of the hand, like it didn't really matter to him—but Lexie knew that kind of thing *did* matter. "But it's good for us to be here on the ground when we can. Makes the customers feel loved and appreciated—it's the reason they come back to us. The personal touch, you know. Plus free holidays for us—a perk of the job." He gave a jovial laugh, and Lexie tried to join in. "Now," Mike said, dropping his voice and adopting a serious face once more, "is there anything I can do to make this easier on you? From what I understand you've chosen to take a step back from the running of things. A wise decision, I might add."

"Is it?" For some reason, the way he said it made her bristle. She didn't know why—it had been *her* decision, after all. But it was said like maybe she couldn't handle it. And that, she realized, was what was annoying her so much about the way Theo was being. They were behaving like she *couldn't* do it, as opposed to simply not *wanting* to.

"Absolutely. If you're not planning to take the company on long-term, then I think it makes perfect sense to let it tick along with Theo. And of course I'm here, too. I might not have an active stake like you two, but I do care about the company—like Theo, I've been with your dad on this since the inception. I was here before Theo, even—your dad brought me in very early on. Perhaps he mentioned we were friends before this?"

"Ah, no." Lexie cleared her throat. "My dad and I . . . I didn't really know much about his life anymore, to be honest." There had been a time, when she was little, when she'd wanted to know everything about his life. Wanted to know what he did when he wasn't with her. Wanted to know, if she was being honest with herself, why his *new* life was better than his old one. But over the years she'd stopped asking.

"No, no. Understandable. Anyway, maybe we ought to have a think about this mess you've been left in."

"Nothing to think about." She raised her voice very slightly, in case Theo was listening. "When the company is sold it won't be my mess anymore."

"Ye-ss," Mike said slowly, his eyes flickering around the group of them.

Lexie flushed. She shouldn't have spoken so callously—and so loudly. Luckily, no one else seemed to have heard her. For the first time, it really hit her—people's lives were going to be affected by this. Not the clients—she was sure they'd find someone else to have holidays with. But Mike and Ange—the other people who worked there—they might lose their jobs, depending on who took it on. She could see why they didn't love the idea of her coming in, making money, and leaving. A rush of guilt flooded through her, even as she tried to push it away. It wasn't her fault. Her dad had put her in this position.

"I'm sorry, Mike," Lexie said, meaning it. "I know this can't be ideal, me coming in and, well . . ." She picked her wine up.

"Not at all, not all. Hardly your fault, eh?"

Lexie couldn't help glancing toward the end of the table, to where Theo was sitting. For a second their gazes met, held. Heat flashed through her body, making her tighten her grip on her wineglass. But so what if he'd overheard? She lifted her chin slightly, as if in a silent dare. Then his gaze slid away, back to the woman in the blue blouse, and Lexie let out a slow breath, flexing her fingers on the stem of her glass. Was that a point to her? Regardless, she made sure not to look down his end of the table for the rest of the meal.

Chapter Nine

Lexie walked a few paces behind Mike as he led the group through the Biovès Gardens—the main point of interest in the Lemon Festival, where there were giant sculptures, all made out of lemons and oranges. Among them was a sculpture of a woman throwing a javelin, a man holding a torch, a gorgeous horse. And some of them were *huge*. At least thirty feet tall. Around the gardens people were posing with the sculptures, queueing up to get the best spots. Lexie had a moment of wishing she was more of the arty type—what must it be like to build a sculpture out of *lemons* of all things? Pretty bloody cool was the answer.

The smell was incredible, the sharp and sweet citrus filling the air. The sun was beginning its descent, but it was still light—not like the dark winters of England. Still, it was getting cold, and Lexie was glad of her winter coat as the breeze tugged at her hair. The whole group of them were ambling through the sculptures together, Mike chatting to the two men who had been sitting on Lexie's right at lunch, while Theo had the attention of the woman in the blue blouse with the bored husband.

Theo glanced over at her, noticing her looking his way, and she turned determinedly away, catching sight of the nervous-looking redhead she'd been sitting next to at lunch. She moved a little closer to her.

"Hey. Lucy, right?"

"Oh, yes, right." Lucy had been holding her phone and nearly dropped it, before stashing it in her coat pocket. "Hello. Mike introduced you, but I'm so sorry, I've forgotten your—"

Lexie smiled. "Lexie."

"Lexie, of course. I'm sorry, it's just if we had a conversation and then I still couldn't remember, it would be even more awkward to ask, so I thought I'd better get it out of the way." She let out a laugh that was a little too high-pitched. "Are you here on your own too? Or, no, sorry, you're with your boyfriend, aren't you?"

"My . . . You mean Theo?" Lexie shook her head. "He's not my boyfriend."

"Oh. It's just you came in together—to lunch, I mean. That's all."

"Right. But he works . . . I mean, we both work at the company. We sort of . . . Well, it was my dad's company and now . . ." Lexie huffed out a breath, annoyed at herself for floundering. "Well, anyway, we're with the company."

"Oh that's wonderful. How amazing, that he started up something like this. I always admire anyone who starts up a business; it must be so tough."

And it took determination, didn't it? Determination to start something, to see it through. How had Richard had the perseverance to build a successful business, yet not been able to stick with either of his two families, in the end?

"How about you?" Lexie asked, wanting to change the subject. "What brings you here?"

"Well, I came on my own." She made a face. "Recent breakup." Then she sighed. "Well, not that recent now. But I've never been anywhere on my own before—I know, don't laugh—and I thought, France can't be that hard, can it? And it's nice being in a group. So if you work for the company, does that mean you know all about the festival?" Lucy's eyes brightened, and Lexie felt the urge not to let her down.

She cleared her throat. "Well, ah, the idea behind the festival can be traced back to 1928—to bring back some winter business, one of the hotel owners had the idea to host an exhibition of flowers and citrus fruits in one of the hotel gardens. It was so successful that they did it the year after—and made it bigger."

"That's cool," Lucy said, glancing around at the sculptures.

"Yeah. The official Fête du Citron didn't begin until 1933, though."

This was all stuff you'd find in a brochure or on the internet, but Lucy was nodding along.

"Ah . . . Every year is based around a different theme—last year was rock and opera, this year is the Olympics."

Lucy shot her a look, then nodded toward one of the sculptures. "Hence the massive hoops."

"It would probably explain that, yes." The two of them laughed, slipping into an easy conversation after that.

"What are you doing tomorrow?" Lexie asked.

"Well, we've got that crêpe-making thing, don't we? Presumably we're supposed to have them with lemon and sugar—they'll get the lemons in somehow, I'm sure."

"Oh right, yes." Lexie nodded, trying to pretend she knew all about the schedule.

"You're coming, aren't you?"

"Yes, of course." Was she going? She had no idea.

"Good. Because I was a bit nervous, coming alone. It can be hard, sometimes. So it's been really lovely talking to you."

"Lucy, darling!" The woman in the blue blouse, the one who seemed to find Theo a bit *too* interesting, called over, and both

Lexie and Lucy looked in her direction. She was standing by one of the stalls at the edge of the garden, which were set up Christmas-market style. "These are the candles I was telling you about! You *must* come and see."

The smile Lucy gave back, to accompany her "I'll be there in a minute" wave, seemed to take a bit too much effort. To be fair, Lexie would have felt the same. That woman managed to make the word "darling" sound like an insult. Not that she could comment on that out loud, given the woman was a client.

"I better go," Lucy said. "I promised myself I would give everyone a chance and make the most of everything, so . . ."

"So you're off to look at candles. Got it."

Lucy laughed, and Lexie couldn't help but feel a little proud that she seemed more relaxed than at the start of the conversation.

"You're a natural!" Mike's booming voice made her jump and she spun to face him. "Like father like daughter, hey?" It made the breath stick in her throat a little. Because she didn't know what he'd been like, did she? Had he been the chatty sort? For a moment, she wanted to ask Mike what he meant by that—how, exactly, was she like her father? But she couldn't bring herself to. She wasn't sure what the right answer would be. She didn't want to be like him—didn't want to be the type of person to leave a family like that, to miss birthdays and break promises. But he was gone now. It hit her occasionally, for the briefest of seconds. He was gone, and she'd never see him again. So *did* she want a small part of her to be like him? She honestly didn't know.

Mike saved her from having to think of a response, in any case, by carrying on, talking to those in their group who were nearest. "Now, who wants to have a look at the wish fountain?

A wish made during the Fête du Citron"—he put on a cringe-worthy French accent to pronounce the festival's name—"is twice as likely to come true, so they say."

"You should ask Lexie—she's big on wishes."

Lexie glanced at Theo as he came to stand next to her, hands in his jeans pockets, casual as you like. So—he hadn't forgotten about the wish jar, then.

Instead of ignoring him this time, she cocked her head as she turned to look at him fully. "Sure, I've got a few wishes I'd like to make about you right now, in fact."

He raised one eyebrow. "Spending time wishing about me now, are you?"

"Oh, Theo." She batted her eyelids. "I don't think you could handle knowing the things I wish for."

It got a surprised laugh out of him, one that softened his features, easing out the sometimes harsh lines of his face. Point Lexie?

Mike had walked away toward the wish fountain, taking a few people with him. Lexie headed in the direction of the stalls, taking her time to browse the lemon soaps, before hitting a stall that was all lemon sweets and deciding to buy some for herself.

"Saw you talking to Lucy Caraway."

Lexie jolted a little as she glanced over her shoulder. She hadn't realized Theo had followed her, all stealth-like. "Huh?"

"Lucy. The nervous redhead. Thirty-three, first time traveling alone. Usually goes for an all-inclusive beach holiday."

"You memorize that, did you?"

He just waited.

"Yes, I was talking to her. Are you going to make me feel bad for that now, too?"

"No, I just . . ." He pulled a hand through his dark hair. "I tried to talk to her a bit yesterday, because I knew from her profile that she'd probably be a bit worried, but she was on edge the whole time. But you had her laughing and looking like she was starting to actually enjoy the holiday."

Lexie gave Theo a deliberate look. "Well, you do have your whole evil villain face down to a tee. Maybe you should work on that if you want people to relax around you."

"Oh, I save that face just for you, don't worry."

"Flattered, I'm sure."

Theo huffed out an impatient breath. "I'm trying to give you a compliment here."

Lexie raised both eyebrows. "Are you?"

She wasn't sure if he'd heard—he was looking over her shoulder, at where Mike and the others were clustered around the fountain. "Mike's right, you know. Your dad was good at it too—chatting to people, making them feel welcome right away, like part of the gang. It just came naturally to him, you know?"

Lexie studied the side of his face—his dark eyes had turned unfocused, like he was looking beyond what was in front of him. Or looking back into a memory. It hit her again—the fact that he knew Richard so much better than she did. He'd only known her father for five years, but here he was, making comments about what he was like, when all she had were hazy memories or a sense of anger after more recent encounters. She looked back toward the stalls, not wanting to delve too much deeper into that thought right now.

"Anyway." Theo's voice was more businesslike when he spoke again. "It sounded like you know a bit about the festival already. You been before or something?"

"No. I just did my research. You know, shockingly enough, given you seem to think I have the intelligence of an eight-year-old, I actually *can* look things up online *and* read them." She kept her voice wry and light, enough so that he knew she was joking. Mainly joking.

He let out a fake gasp. "No! Not *both,* surely."

"I know," Lexie said, nodding serenely. "It's impressive, a skill I've tried to keep hidden in case it turns me into a circus freak."

"Very wise," Theo said seriously. "No one will ever look at you the same if they know you have skills like that."

Lexie felt her lips tugging, but refused to give in to the smile. A man selling flowers—yellow, of course—came up at that moment, trying to convince Theo to buy one. Lexie left him to it, returning to browsing the nearest stalls. If only she had a garden, then she could take some lemon plants back with her. Although, did they let you take plants on a plane? She could hear Theo trying to say no to the flowers, and then cave, a bit more easily than she'd expected him to.

She shook her head at him as the flower seller walked away. "You'd have thought you'd be better at avoiding all the tourist traps if you run a travel business."

"Yeah. Well, your dad drilled into me the need to support local businesses as much as possible, to the extent that I'm a pushover, apparently." He frowned down at the flower, then thrust it at her. "Here."

"Oh. Thanks." She took it, looking down at it as she twirled the long stem in her fingers. Tried to ignore the stupid little fizzle of pleasure in her stomach at being given a flower. Then she looked up at him again. "Look, I wanted to talk to you."

He gestured, inviting her to carry on.

"About what you said before lunch."

"Which part, exactly?" His voice was infuriatingly mild.

"The part where you said you didn't want to sell the company."

"Is that what I said? I thought I just referred to the fact that we've not actually had a conversation about it—that we haven't, technically, agreed on anything yet."

She shook her head, disbelieving—and the fizzle of pleasure evaporated. "I want to sell it. You know that."

"OK. Noted."

"Noted? *Noted?*" It reminded her of their little email exchange, and she felt her blood heat. "What is that supposed to mean?" Out of the corner of her eye, she saw Lucy glance over at them from a few stalls down.

Theo glanced that way too, then stepped in toward her. Close. So close that she had to tilt her head up to look at him, so that she could see the way the amber had flared in his otherwise dark eyes. That hint of sandalwood washed over her, mingling with the citrus all around them.

"Can I remind you," he muttered in a rough undertone, "that we are supposed to be helping the guests have a good time? Not arguing in front of them."

"I literally cannot believe you," she hissed back. And to think she'd believed they might be finding their way to a more even footing around each other.

He cocked that stupid eyebrow.

"Fine," she bit out, keeping her voice low. "I'll find you later and we can talk about it then."

"Right. You do that."

She glared at him as she pulled back. Then she shoved the flower he'd given her back into his chest and walked away, leaving him to catch it.

Chapter Ten

In the end, Lexie didn't see Theo properly again until the following evening. She'd gone to bed early the night before, tired after having a drink with Lucy in the bar. Even though he'd also been at the crêpe-making class, she'd been distracted by the actual activity of making said crêpes, getting covered in flour in the process, and although he'd glanced her way a few times, she hadn't actually managed to advance the conversation at all. But maybe that was for the best. She needed to think about how to play it all, what to say. There was no point getting into a stalemate—and surely he couldn't *actually* just refuse to sell the company? It would have to be a joint decision, as per the contract. Which was what she kept repeating to herself as she headed downstairs to the hotel lobby, ready to meet the group for the evening carnival celebration.

Nearly everyone was down in reception, coats already done up as they waited for the last stragglers. Mike and Theo were standing a bit apart, talking in low voices, Theo's mouth pressed into a serious, considering line. Lexie bit her lip, wondering whether to join them or go and make small talk, but Mike saw her, broke off the conversation, and smiled, beckoning her over.

"How were the pancakes?" he asked as she approached.

"A lot of fun," Lexie said, smiling at him and acknowledging Theo with barely a glance.

"You missed the daytime parade," Mike said. "We went to see it the day before you got here. It was fabulous, acrobats and everything. But the nighttime extravaganza is the highlight, wouldn't you say, Theo?"

"Sure."

"Such a high recommendation—don't contain your excitement just for me."

He met her gaze. "Trust me, it's not my excitement I struggle to contain around you." She swore there was a challenge in the way he looked at her right now, and she only tore her gaze away when Mike spoke again.

"I'm so sorry, Lexie," Mike continued, ignoring the tension, "but I can't join you this evening. I would have loved to spend some more time getting to know you, but I really must catch up on some things."

"Oh, OK." She wondered if Ange was somehow behind this.

"But Theo can hold the fort, I'm sure. Ah, there's the last two," Mike said, and Lexie turned to see Cynthia, the woman who'd been flirting with Theo yesterday, along with her husband, coming into the lobby. "I'll leave you to it, then. And don't you two go sniping at each other all evening—we have a professional reputation to uphold." He gave Lexie a wink, as if to make it playful, but she still cringed at the condescending tone and next to her, Theo's jaw clenched. It was the only sign of annoyance he gave, though, before promising to take care of everyone.

Theo led the group out of the hotel and into the town. The light was fading, the sky pink above them, making the whole place glow a dusky orange. Somewhere in the distance, Lexie could hear drums starting up, and though the town generally had a peaceful feel, there was a sense of anticipation in the air, with tourists all heading toward the beach road. Despite herself, Lexie felt excitement hum through her, the drums making her heart pick up speed.

She stayed at the front of the group with Theo. She wanted to peel off, maybe find Lucy, but was too aware of the fact that everyone probably thought she was an insider at R&L, and so would expect her to be taking charge, with Theo. Or maybe an insider would go mingle? She wasn't really sure.

They passed the Biovès Gardens, the citrus sculptures all lit up, adding a whole new feel to the place. "Do you know," Lexie mused, "I was half expecting us to be set to work building a sculpture of our own?"

She said it more to herself, but Theo answered anyway. "What, like a weird team-building exercise?"

"No, like, I don't know, create your own mini lemon sculpture to take home or whatever."

"Where would you get the lemons from?"

She let out an impatient sigh. "I don't know, Theo. From the lemon shop? I mean"—she gestured at the enormous lemon sculptures—"I'm pretty sure lemons could be found."

Theo's brow furrowed. "Would you get someone to teach everyone how to do it, or just hand out the lemons?"

"Jeez, you aren't half making it difficult. It was just a random thought—remind me to censor those when I'm around you."

He glanced at her. "It's not a terrible idea."

"You don't need to sound so surprised—not all my ideas are inherently terrible." Behind them, she could hear the rest of the group chattering away as they got to the street where the parade would take place. Other tourists and locals were already there, waiting for the parade to begin. The drums grew louder.

He raised his eyebrows. "No sniping at each other, remember?"

"I'm not sniping. This is called *talking*. It's where one person says something, then the other person says something back."

"Oh, is that what we're doing? This is your version of talking, is it?"

Lexie cocked her head. "Why, what's your version? Because if you've figured out another way to talk that no one else has cottoned on to by now, I'm pretty sure *you're* the circus freak, not me."

He let out a low laugh, and she felt her own lips tug in response despite herself. Felt an unwelcome prickle along her skin, at the sound of that laugh. *Don't go there, Lexie.*

They'd reached the Promenade du Soleil now, just by the seafront where the parade would take place, and the rest of the group were craning their necks to look past the other tourists, wanting to get the first look at the giant lemon floats that were now being lit up.

"It's not a bad idea," Theo repeated quietly. "The lemon sculpture. I mean, I don't think people would be able to take them back as a souvenir or anything, but maybe it could be an activity, for those who wanted to. Maybe there's a local artist we could work with, who might be able to teach a class or something."

His tone had turned musing, like he was already thinking through the logistics—and Lexie wasn't sure what to say to that. It had been an offhand comment—and he was taking it seriously.

Luckily, Lucy came up at that moment. "Is it weird that I feel excited?" she asked. "Like a child on Christmas morning or something."

Lexie laughed. "I think it's the drums."

"Yeah. Impossible not to get excited when drums are involved."

Lexie felt it too, could hear the laughter in the air around them, children sitting on the shoulders of parents, people chatting and pointing around them. It wasn't a huge space, but instead of feeling overly crowded it felt intimate, like they were all in for a shared experience—locals and tourists alike. *See the world through celebration.* For the first time, Lexie thought she understood the slogan of the company.

Night had fallen now, the pink sky giving way to blue-black—maybe that added to the whole thing, like they were all sharing in some nighttime secret. And then she caught sight of the floats, making their way down the street toward them. A huge horse came first, rearing up as if it were jumping something, a rider made of lemons sitting on top. It was lit up, and the lights shifted as the float made its way toward them, changing color from the natural bright orange and lemon to an eclectic mix across the whole spectrum. From atop the floats, people threw out confetti, and Lexie, laughing as some landed in her hair, couldn't help waving back.

There were more floats—a huge tiger, a rowboat complete with oars, a giant snail. She wasn't quite sure how it was all Olympic-themed, but they were brilliant, each a complete work of art, and the lights added a magical feel to each one. Between the floats were street artists, jugglers who threw lit skittles in the air, women and men in elaborate costumes who performed acrobatics as they walked, their sequins catching the light and glittering as they moved. Even the drums were lit up, the drummers creating a pulse of energy that was impossible not to get lost in. For a while, Lexie was content to watch, to soak up the atmosphere. To marvel at the celebration of a fruit, to think of how cool it was that this tradition had kept going all these years. This was why she loved the way she lived—because she got to experience these things. And apparently, her dad had loved experiencing things like this too—why else would he have started this business?

The parade made its way around the short circuit twice, before the lights were switched off, amid whines and cheers. And then there was bustling as everyone shifted position. "Fireworks now," Theo explained to the group at large. It turned out he'd reserved seats for them all in the grandstand, leading them up to a higher viewing point. Everyone clambered up into their seats as a couple of early, teaser fireworks were let off. In the rush to get to the grandstand in time, Lexie ended up sitting between Theo and Lucy. Her leg brushed his as they sat and even though he was wearing jeans and she leggings, she still felt the heat of his thigh against hers for a brief moment before he shifted away. She watched the fireworks display get more and more extravagant, purples and reds and blues sparking up the night sky. The cool air bit into her and she shoved her hands into her coat pockets.

She used to go and watch fireworks displays like this as a kid. She remembered a fireworks display in Frome, where she grew up. She, her dad, and her mum had all gone together. She didn't know how old she had been—but it was before he'd left. She'd been clutching a toffee apple, munching her way through the outside, ignoring the healthy apple goodness in the center. She hadn't been paying attention, and one moment her mum and dad had been there, and then she'd looked up and they were gone. She'd panicked, dropped her toffee apple. It had felt like there were strangers everywhere, like she was lost, like her parents might not find her. It had only been a minute or two, her mum had told her afterward. A minute or two before they'd found her, sobbing. Her dad had hoisted her up, carrying her for the rest of the evening. He'd managed to cheer her up, had bought her another toffee apple and made a joke of the whole thing. It was a silly memory—what was another toffee apple in the grand scheme of things?—but it had stuck with her, nonetheless.

As had a different memory, one from a few years later. One where he'd promised to come and take Lexie to a fireworks display, just the two of them, but had never shown up. Her mum had taken her instead, and Lexie kept making her check her phone because she was worried that her dad might try to call, because there had to be a reason he was late, and he wouldn't know where to find them. But he never did.

"I don't like fireworks." She said it quietly, like a secret. She wasn't even sure who she was speaking to—but Lucy was leaning forward and had her phone out to take photos, and apparently hadn't heard. Theo, however, looked her way. She felt his gaze on the side of her face, but she kept looking straight out at the display as she spoke again. "They're pretty and fun and all that, but . . . They make me think of my dad." Stupid, to say it out loud, to admit that vulnerability—especially when Theo clearly thought her dad had been someone to look up to. She felt something bubbling in her stomach, like it was trying to get out. She swallowed, tried to shove the emotion back inside— and forced the memory back too. The noise of the fireworks was a relief. It meant she didn't have to explain—and meant Theo wasn't required to talk, even though he'd heard.

He didn't ask. Didn't question how or why fireworks made her think of her dad, why that made her sad. Instead he said, just as quietly, "I don't like fireworks either." She risked a glance at him, but now it was him staring straight ahead. "I pretend to, for the clients. And they're pretty and fun and all that . . ." She let out a huff of laughter at him using her words. An admission for an admission—was that what this was? "My parents never took me to see them," he continued. "As a kid, I mean. They weren't really big into those kinds of 'overly chaotic and hyperactive celebrations.'"

What had he been like as a kid? she wondered. "Are fireworks inherently chaotic?"

"Well, I suppose they're a bit loud. And some people think that's chaotic, don't they? I think my dad's point was that children go all mental, hopped up on sugar and cider or whatever it is you have when you watch them and then you have to all squish together to watch in that chaos."

"Yes, I've heard kids are all into the cider these days."

Theo snorted quietly. "They said fireworks are bad for the environment," he continued after a beat. "My parents, I mean. I was annoyed for a while, thought they were doing it out of some weird principle or to keep me from doing something I wanted to do. Classic egotistical seven-year-old. But then I realized they're right—they *are* really bad for the environment. The birds get upset and the wildlife panic, and for what? So we can enjoy a pretty show."

Lexie watched the last few fireworks, hearing the laughter, the gasps of delight. "You're right," she said eventually.

"I am?"

"It's as much of a shock to me as it is to you, trust me." She glanced at him, saw his lips twitch.

"Kind of takes the romance out of the moment, doesn't it?"

When the show was over, they all stood up and made their way out of the grandstand. At the bottom, Lucy turned to smile at Theo and Lexie. "I'm guessing that's the main event done with?"

"Yeah, that's pretty much it," Theo said. "We'll hang around for a bit in case anyone wants to grab another drink, though, if you're keen?"

Lucy shook her head. "I'm loving this, but I want to take it easy."

"I can walk you—" Theo began.

"No, don't be silly. I actually want to take a beat, walk on my own. Is that OK? It's on my list of things I want to accomplish this holiday—all part of being braver."

"You got it. But if you need us, you've got our numbers."

"I do." Lucy squeezed Lexie's arm as she passed. "What you and your dad have built is so cool. I know some people might just think it's a silly little holiday, but it's given me the courage to think I can do things on my own again. Maybe on my own for real next time."

With Theo right there in hearing distance, Lexie thought he was going to grumble about the *you and your dad,* but he said nothing. Still, it made Lexie feel funny. It was like a different version of their father-daughter relationship was being posited—one they could have had, if he hadn't left. But obviously she couldn't say that to Lucy, so she just smiled her thanks and said she'd see her in the morning.

Theo and Lexie were quiet for a moment after Lucy left. The crowd was dispersing, but most of their group were lingering.

"Lexie?"

She looked up at Theo.

"I'm sorry about your dad. I should have said that a lot sooner."

She felt the lump in her throat rise back up. She wasn't sure what to do with the apology, wasn't sure what it was supposed to mean. She remembered what he'd said during the solicitor's meeting. *You never bothered to answer your dad's calls—and it's not like you're ever actually around.* Could hear the echo of his voice when she'd overheard him talking to Ange in the office. *She clearly didn't care about her dad, so why would she care about the company?*

But she remembered too what Ange had said. *Let's just say I think he's a little lost, without Richard.* Thought of the way he'd looked, when he'd talked about Richard earlier. *Your dad was good at it too—chatting to people, making them feel welcome right away.* Was that why Theo was so set on continuing what her dad had started? Was it because her dad had made him feel "welcome"?

"I'm sorry too," she found herself saying. "If he meant something to you. I mean, I don't know what the deal was, really, and I'm still totally confused about why he left us both in this mess and why he thought it was appropriate to—"

He coughed, as if pointing out she'd slipped into babble mode, and she flushed. "Well. You know what I mean."

"Rarely, if ever." His voice was dry—but it wasn't mean.

She blew out a breath. "I'm just sorry. I know you lost him too." The words were out before she could think better of them, and she felt the way his gaze lingered on her face, like he was taking in the words. *Too.* You lost him *too,* she'd said. Like they were in the same situation, like there was some sort of grief to be shared.

Theo looked like he might have been about to say something, but then a few other tourists jolted past them, buffeting Lexie out of the way. He grabbed her wrist, pulling her to one side. It was a quick, efficient move. There was no twining of fingers or sensual caress of his thumb over her skin. So why did it make her pulse jump? Why did that point of contact crackle with electricity?

Theo looked up, his gaze snagging on hers. For a second something flickered there, in those firelike eyes of his. Then he let go, looking around to locate the rest of the group. She brought her other hand up to rub the place his fingers had been, trying to soothe away that crackling under her skin—but the feeling lingered, even after he'd moved away.

Chapter Eleven

"Whatever would Mike say?" Lexie shook her head mockingly at Theo as they walked into the hotel lobby, her body welcoming the warmth after so long outside. "Leaving the rest of them like that?"

"Well, I think since Mike has deemed other things more important this evening, he doesn't get a vote. Regardless, they don't want us around. Trust me. Cynthia's husband has finally cottoned on that she's been trying to make him jealous and they are about to have lots of breakup or makeup sex, Mark and Jay are enjoying spending time just the two of them and do not want an audience, Christine—"

"OK, I get it. They want to fly solo." He might not have the immediate warm personality that made you want to chat with him for hours on end, but Theo was pretty good at observing people, she'd give him that. For the business, at least. Lexie glanced around the hotel to check they were alone as they headed to the elevator, then dropped her voice for good measure. "What's his deal, anyway?"

"Given I mentioned at least three 'he's' just now, you might have to elaborate a bit there."

"Mike. I can't work him out. He seems nice—friendly—and he said he knew my dad . . ." What she really wanted to ask was how he'd been friends with her dad, what had brought them together—but she wasn't sure how Theo would take those sorts of questions.

"Mike is . . . Your dad and him had a bit of a complicated relationship."

"Right."

"Mike cares about the company—and wants to make it work." It was a diplomatic answer. A *non*answer, really.

Lexie tried to bring things back onto their newfound neutral territory as they stepped into the elevator together. "So do you think he's listening to see if we're still sniping? Reporting back to Ange?"

Theo laughed a little. "Do you know what? I wouldn't put it past Ange to have arranged exactly that."

"How did *she* meet my dad? Do you know?" She just couldn't imagine it. Ange seemed to have genuinely cared about Richard—and Lexie already knew that Ange was a decent, kind person. So did that mean that Richard had shown himself to be decent and kind, too? She couldn't imagine it, knowing what she did about him. Was Ange just in it for a job? But that didn't make sense to her, either.

"She was there when I joined," Theo said, with a quick glance down at her, like he couldn't quite figure out her line of questioning. "I think she may have been a part of what encouraged Richard to take a chance on me, in all honesty."

"How come?"

Theo shook his head, gave a self-deprecating smile. "Let's just say I don't think I made the best first impression."

"Really? You shock me." His eyebrows shot up, and she felt herself flushing. "So, ah, you don't know? How Ange came to work at the company?"

Theo was quiet as the elevator opened on level two, and they both got out. "I think she'd been let go from her last job, actually. A whole host of redundancies or something." He scowled, like he was annoyed on Ange's behalf, even though it had happened years ago. "And she wanted flexible hours, because she helps with her grandkids, and she was struggling to find somewhere to take her on. Richard hired her because she made the best cup of tea he'd ever had. At least, that's what they both said, if you ever asked either of them." A corner of his mouth pulled into a smile, like he was remembering a specific time he'd done just that. "But really, I don't know how Richard would have done any of it without her. I definitely couldn't do any of it without her—not that she'll ever take enough credit for that."

Lexie went quiet as they approached her room—Theo must be farther down the corridor. She wondered at the side of Richard he was describing—the type of person to take a chance on someone, instead of abandoning them. She wondered, too, whether Ange would mind Theo relaying her story like this.

She wasn't sure how, but Theo seemed to guess at her line of thinking. "She'd tell you herself, if you asked her."

She couldn't work out if that was a dig—at the fact that she hadn't been around long enough to ask, to get to know any of them. It didn't *feel* like a dig, but still. She stopped outside her room, and he stopped too.

"This is me," she said, nodding toward the door.

"Right. Well, sleep well, I guess?"

He half hesitated, like he was waiting for her to say good night too. Instead she took a breath. "Theo?"

He cocked his head. "Lexie?"

"You were kidding, right? When you said we wouldn't sell the company?"

His face shuttered. "How about we talk about this in a few months—it's all academic at the moment, anyway, isn't it?"

She huffed out a frustrated breath. "What's the point? If you're just going to refuse?" He said nothing, so she pressed on. "It's half mine. You can't—"

"It's half mine too," he pointed out, as if she didn't already know that.

"You said after the tax year—"

"I didn't say, I let you infer."

"Oh yes, so clever with your fucking semantics." She closed her eyes for a beat, hating the way he brought out an argumentative streak in her.

When she opened them, he was considering her. "I could buy you out."

"With what money?"

"How do you know I'm not rich?"

"Are you?" He said nothing and she pulled a hand through her curls. "God, I should have just walked away in December."

"You're making way too big a deal about this. It's all completely irrelevant anyway until the year is up and I turn a profit."

"Until *you* turn a profit?"

"Yes. Because you walked away."

Lexie folded her arms, leaning back against the door in an attempt at nonchalance. "OK, let's just get a few things straight. One—"

"Oh great, you're a list girl."

She got the next words out through gritted teeth. "One, just because I didn't stay in England doesn't mean I don't care; two, you were the one who suggested the idea; three—"

"How long is this list going to go on for? Just so I can prepare."

"Would you stop!" She stood up straight, pushing off the door in frustration. But he didn't move, so that only served to bring them closer together. "Fine. I'll just leave. You can't make me do anything, so there's no point—" She was already turning away, reaching into her coat pocket for her key card, but he took her arm and turned her back to face him.

"No, you started this. Might as well get it all out in the open."

She glared down at the hand holding her arm, and he let it go immediately. But he didn't let the subject drop.

"So go on. What's three?" He was staring down at her, waiting, barely six inches between them.

She tilted her chin up. She should turn, go inside her room. Instead her muscles had gone tight, holding her in place. She swallowed and saw the way his gaze dropped to the bob in her throat, before coming back to her face.

"What's three, Lexie?" His voice had changed—it was low, rough velvet coursing over her skin.

The tingle down her spine was a warning. She tried to take a clear breath, but only breathed the smell of him in more deeply. He was still waiting for an answer—but she couldn't actually remember what three was going to be. She settled for scowling at him, feeling like it was *his* fault that she'd forgotten.

He backed away a step. "We can talk about it when you remember." He moved back again, a little farther, and without really thinking about it, she reached out, placing a hand on his forearm to stop him. He glanced down at it, then at her face.

"Three, I don't appreciate you assuming you know what I'm thinking or why."

He stared at her for a long moment. Then, "OK."

"OK?"

He nodded. "OK. That's a fair point. I don't know what

you're thinking, you don't know what I'm thinking. I guess we can both try to work on that."

"Well, then." She realized she was still holding on to his forearm and let go.

Their gazes held for a moment. Then Theo said, "Truce?"

She huffed out a half laugh at the word, the formality of it—the *ridiculousness* of it.

"Or something less binding?" he continued. "A ceasefire?"

Lexie couldn't help it—she laughed properly this time. And saw his features soften in response, too. "That's a pretty strong word. Implies we've been getting out weapons or something."

That scarred eyebrow shot up. "And you *haven't* been getting out weapons?"

She rolled her eyes. "OK, fine. Truce." She held out her hand and he took it. His fingers clasped around hers, his grip warm and firm. At her wrist, her pulse flared, like it was stretching to reach the end of his fingertips. She met his gaze, saw the amber flare. He didn't let go right away, his thumb sliding over hers.

His gaze dropped to her mouth, his pupils seeming to grow blacker. When he looked back up, she felt her breath catch.

You do not like him, Lexie. But apparently, just because she didn't like him, that didn't mean she didn't, right now, want to know what that mouth tasted like.

Had she pulled him closer? She didn't remember doing it, but her free hand was on his arm, as if stopping him from leaving. *Let go of his hand, Lexie.*

But he was frowning at her now—a considering frown. And he was leaning toward her. Waiting. Like a dare. And even though there were a million reasons not to, it was *her* who closed the gap, unable to back down as she caught his mouth with hers.

And then she didn't *want* to back down because her mouth was moving with his, and she could taste the lingering lemon, and something deeper, darker. She gripped his arm more tightly, her nails biting into the fabric of his coat, searching for skin underneath. His teeth caught her bottom lip, and goosebumps spread. And when he pressed her back against the door, she let out a half moan at the pressure of his body against hers. She felt a low, liquid pull in her core—just from a fucking kiss.

This is a terrible idea, Lexie.

But the voice was dim in her head, and there was the feel of his hands to contend with, on either side of her waist now, tugging her closer. At some point she must have moved her hands to his shoulders, because she could feel the muscle underneath there, and it made her want to hold on. His lips broke away from hers and she might have let out a growl of frustration, which turned into a soft groan as his lips skated over her jaw, down her neck, teeth just grazing her. She arched her spine, pressing into him, and his teeth bit harder down her throat as she did. Her hands were in his hair, and she was trying to tug him closer, even as his hands moved, skimming to the bottom of her coat, then up under it as she ran her hands down his back.

Distantly, she heard a nervous giggle down one end of the corridor. It was enough to jolt her back to reality and she pulled away from him in one violent motion, snapping her hands back to her sides. In the same moment he must have realized what they were doing too, remembered that it was *her* he was kissing, because he stumbled back, leaving cool air as a line between them.

There was a beat of silence, like they were both trying to figure out what had just happened. Then she cleared her throat. "Ah, so . . ."

He shook his head like he was trying to clear it. "Bad idea?"

"Yeah. Yeah, *really* bad idea."

His eyebrows shot up. "I'll do my best not to be offended by that."

"You said it first. And besides, you and I don't kiss." She said it as firmly as she could manage.

"Hate to point out the obvious, but apparently we do." His eyes were back on hers, inky black.

"You and I *shouldn't* kiss." It came out as barely a whisper though, and her breathing was still ragged, her skin hot and needy beneath the layers of clothing. Her body was playing catch-up to what her mind already knew—that this was *Theo,* that he was not someone to go around kissing in hotel corridors. Not someone to go around kissing anywhere, in fact. She bit her lip, saw him follow it with his gaze. And God, maybe it didn't matter that they didn't like each other, if he kissed like that.

Shit. Shit! This was a bad move, a very bad move. Kissing him more would be an even worse move. She couldn't work out from the look in his eyes whether he thought the same.

He was looking at her mouth again as he said. "I think you should go into your room, Lexie."

"What?" *Come on, Lexie, keep up.*

"Please." His voice was a half plea, though his gaze was still on her mouth. "Please go into your room. We can talk about this tomorrow." When she didn't immediately react, he reached out, stuck his hand in her coat pocket. Her nerves jumped, skin sparking in anticipation. But he only took out her key card, opened her door, then practically shoved her through it. He backed away, pressing the key card into her hand, then let the door slam between them. She heard his heavy footsteps as he walked away down the corridor.

Numbly, she switched on her lights, shrugged off her coat. She tried to push it away. Tried not to think of how it had felt to have him pressed against her. *You are not allowed to like kissing someone who hates you, Lexie.* But she *had* liked it, hadn't she?

Point fucking Theo.

Chapter Twelve

Lexie told herself not to overthink anything as she picked up her rucksack and headed downstairs to check out. She'd kissed plenty of men before—and she was a master at keeping things casual. She had literally never had a serious relationship in her life—if anyone could play this cool, she could. It had been a random moment of confusion, misreading adrenaline from their argument as chemistry, that was all. He'd said they would talk about it today, so they'd talk, no doubt put it behind them, and she would do her best to be polite and professional moving forward. Especially because she didn't think that the two of them just ignoring each other from now on was going to work. The trip had gotten her thinking—no doubt Ange's intention. She couldn't just run from this. She wasn't actually sure where that left her—and despite her restless night, when she'd been unable to stop her thoughts churning around, all she'd arrived at was that the current plan with Theo was not going to work.

She had an earlier flight than everyone else, so she was heading to the airport on her own—and as a result, it was only Mike and Theo waiting in reception to see her off. Her stomach lurched at the sight of Theo, despite what she'd told herself. She could only see the back of him, but that didn't stop her mind immediately remembering what it had felt like to have his mouth on hers, how his fingers had dug into her waist, the feel of the length of his body against hers. *Not useful, Lexie.* She realized she was scowling and tried to smooth out her expression—scowling didn't really lend itself to polite and professional.

Mike and Theo seemed to be having another hushed conversation as she crossed the sleek wooden floors, her pumps squeaking a little in a way that made her feel unnecessarily self-conscious. Whatever the two of them were talking about, it must have been very serious, given Mike's expression. She couldn't see Theo's, but he had that stillness of intense focus. The stillness she'd felt last night, when his attention had been solely on her. *Stop it, Lexie!*

Mike only noticed her when she was right there, putting down her rucksack and fishing out her key card to hand in to reception, and he jumped in an almost comical way before pasting on a smile. They'd been talking about her, then. Or something they didn't want her overhearing. Come to think about it, talking about her made a lot of sense—she'd have been talking about her too, if the situation were reversed. It didn't matter, she told herself. They could think what they liked. She tried really hard to believe that as Theo spun to look at her. Unlike Mike, who she'd not seen out of a suit all weekend, he was wearing jeans and a long-sleeved dark blue T-shirt.

He gave her a little nod. "Lexie."

"Theo." It was so ridiculously formal that for a second, she wanted to burst out laughing—an entirely inappropriate reaction.

"So you're ready to be off, are you, Lexie?" Mike asked. "Enjoyed your holiday, I hope?"

"Yes, I—"

But Mike's phone rang, and he made a show of fishing it out

of his suit jacket pocket, holding up one finger as he checked the screen. "Have to take this, so sorry." He stepped a few feet away before answering, wandering down into the bar area.

Lexie felt a sudden rush of nerves as she glanced up at Theo. Then she told herself to get a grip. She was an adult; she could handle being alone with him.

Theo cleared his throat. "So about last night," he began, and she nodded, mentally preparing her answer. It shouldn't have happened; she didn't know what they'd been thinking; it couldn't ever happen again. "If the truce still stands, I'd like to propose we hold fire on any discussions about the future of the company until later in the year."

She stared at him, trying to catch up. Truce. He'd suggested that before he'd kissed her. Or before she'd kissed him—she still couldn't quite work that one out.

The company—he was talking about R&L. *We'll talk about this tomorrow.* But apparently he'd meant continuing the argument they'd been having *before* he'd kissed her. So what, they were just going to pretend it hadn't happened? She bit the inside of her lip. OK, fine. She could do that. Maybe it was better, actually. No awkward conversations.

He was still looking at her, his dark gaze assessing her expression as he waited for a response.

"Right," she managed. She couldn't think of much else to say.

"OK. Great. And look, I'm sorry about—"

"Sorry about that," Mike boomed from behind Theo. He came up between Lexie and Theo, as Lexie bent to pick up her rucksack just for something to do. Had Theo been about to talk about the kiss? *I'm sorry.* OK, well, that was good, wasn't it? It meant he knew it was a mistake, meant they could just put it behind them.

Mike was smiling at Lexie. "Well, I suppose this is the last we'll see of you for a while, Lexie? Off back to the Alps, I presume? I'd love a bit of skiing time right now, but far too much to do." It was said in that boasting way that she'd heard so often—people making a point that their lives were busier and more important than hers, people who assumed she was frivolous, assumed that the way they'd decided to live their lives, saddled with responsibility, was somehow inherently better than hers.

Maybe it was because she was annoyed at that. Maybe it was because the weekend had made her realize she couldn't just ignore the fact that she *did* have a responsibility now, like it or not. Or maybe it was because she didn't want Theo to be able to use the fact that she'd been away the whole time at the end of the fiscal year, somehow tricking her out of her share when the company sold. It was probably a mix of all those things but the words were out before she could think better of them.

"Actually, I think you'll be seeing more of me." She directed the words to Mike but felt Theo's gaze on the side of her face. She angled her head toward him, very deliberately. Everything between them felt like a challenge, she was learning, and while she might have lost last night, she met his gaze directly now. "I've decided I want to be more involved after all. Properly fulfill my side of the contract."

"Well," Mike said, clearing his throat and rocking back on his heels, eyebrows sky-high. "Well, I mean, that's—"

"That's fine." Theo was totally calm. He still hadn't broken eye contact, and despite herself, something in the base of her stomach fizzled. *Don't be stupid, Lexie.*

"So I'll just tie some things up, and I'll be back in the UK in a week or so." She matched his calm tone, no big deal, but her palms were already starting to prick with sweat. What was she doing? She'd have to leave the Alps, leave her friends. But really, it would only be two months until she was done anyway; this was just speeding it up a little. She'd broken eye contact with Theo as her thoughts went haywire, and she took a breath to calm herself.

"That's fine," Theo said again, while Mike tugged at his collar.

"It is?" She'd expected more of a protest. More *You don't care about the company so why should you be involved?*

"Yes. I'm away on annual leave for a few weeks then anyway, so you'll have time to settle in. And if you're still there when I get back, we can figure it out then."

Ah. So that was it. He thought she'd have bolted by the time he was back from holiday—thought he wouldn't have to deal with her. "I'll still be there," she insisted, stubbornness setting in.

"OK." He gave her half a smile. "See you then."

"Well," Mike said, stopping Lexie from reacting to the bland *OK*. "What a pronouncement! Looks like we'll be seeing more of you, in this case." He reached out to shake her hand—a clear dismissal. Which was for the best, actually, because she had a plane to catch, and she wanted to be alone to think through what the hell she'd just done.

She didn't know whether to shake Theo's hand. After last night, touching seemed like a bad idea. So instead she nodded politely.

"Yeah. You'll see me then."

It was in the taxi on the way to the airport that she saw she had an email from Ange, sent this morning. She opened it up. It was a ticket back to the UK from Austria. No explanation, only three words in the subject line.

Just in case.

Chapter Thirteen

"So he's back in a week?" Fran asked as she and Lexie took a seat by the window of the independent coffee shop that Fran deemed *the best in Bath*. Mainly, as far as Lexie could gather, because of the fact that they often had little pieces of cake to sample for free alongside your coffee—and today's white chocolate brownie had been good enough to tempt Lexie into buying a whole one.

"Yes. A week." And the thought made Lexie's stomach squirm uncomfortably. She'd moved back to the UK two weeks ago, after wrapping everything up in Austria—but Theo hadn't been back in the office yet.

Lexie stared out the window while Fran stirred her Creme Egg latte—it was Easter in a couple of weeks, and the café had gone mad on the theme. Easter was supposed to signal spring, though, wasn't it? Outside, Bath felt distinctly un-springlike. It was cold and gray, and the sky held that pale glow that sometimes meant snow was on its way. Despite that, it was still beautiful. From here Lexie could see the River Avon running beneath Pulteney Bridge, the majestic buttermilk limestone bridge that was an iconic feature of the city. But Lexie scowled at the city, even in all its Georgian splendor.

"Seen something terrible in the water?" Fran asked.

Lexie tapped her fingers on her knee. "It's annoying," she said, ignoring Fran. "I feel like I've made the decision now—I've come back, I'm going to stay until the company sells, and because Ange is helping me, I actually stand a chance at finding my feet. But I just know he's going to come back and ruin all that."

" 'Ruin' is a strong word," Fran said diplomatically.

Lexie turned to her friend, picked up her oat-milk latte. As a teenager, Fran used to resolutely dye the tips of her hair purple, but the lawyer in her had stopped the habit and now her long, dark, and slightly bushy hair sat around her shoulders. Lexie also remembered her favoring ripped jeans and T-shirts with band slogans—often bands Lexie had never heard of—but now, even though it was a Saturday, she was dressed in what Lexie thought of as "adult work clothes"—black jeans, a smart top, and a blazer. Still, despite the difference in appearance, she was the same Fran. And unlike a lot of their old school friends, who all seemed so *sorted,* with husbands and houses and children and dogs, Fran didn't make Lexie feel completely left behind. Yes, Fran had a career, which Lexie didn't have, and yes, she had bought a flat, but those things didn't seem like such a big barrier. It was probably because, unlike a lot of her other friends, Fran never seemed to judge Lexie for how she chose to spend her life. She didn't make Lexie feel inferior, or like it was a phase she should have outgrown by now. That was just one of the many brilliant things about her.

"He doesn't want me there," Lexie insisted.

"*You* don't want *him* there either."

"Only because he's making things difficult. If he'd just help to, I don't know, find some kind of balance, then we could crack on with work, turn a profit, and—"

"Sell the company."

"Exactly."

"Which he doesn't want to do."

"Well no, but—"

"And you are refusing to see his side of it."

Lexie turned her scowl on her coffee. Around them, the sound of coffee beans grinding swelled over the laughter and chatter. "As my friend, aren't you supposed to be automatically on my side in situations like this? Because you're not doing a great job at it."

"I'm just saying, it must be hard for both of you."

"Well, he doesn't have to be such a dick about it," Lexie grumbled. "It's not my fault Richard left me half his stupid company."

"It's not Theo's fault, either."

"Is this how you are in divorce negotiations—all diplomatic and shit? Because I'd think that would make you a terrible lawyer."

Fran didn't give in. "I'm just pointing out the obvious."

Lexie tapped her fingers on her knee again, unable to stop twitching. "What do I do if he just refuses to sell the company?"

"Would it be that bad to keep it? I know you're doing this so you can sell it—but is there a chance you might actually *enjoy* it? You seemed to have a good time in France, after all."

Lexie's mind immediately went to that hotel corridor, before she shoved the memory aside. "It doesn't fit with my life," she said firmly, choosing not to discuss France or anything that may have happened there. "And it's my dad's company, Fran."

"I know. Which he left to you." Fran had experienced the highs and lows of Lexie's relationship with Richard firsthand. She'd met him when Richard had taken Lexie and Fran on a Saturday adventure, over to a nearby woodland, with cliffs that you could climb up if you were feeling brave. Lexie had been so excited. She'd been desperate to show Richard off—she'd hated him for not being around, yet she'd still been proud to introduce him to her best friend. He'd been brilliant that day, dealing with the two of them when they'd been at that awkward age between children and teenagers, making the whole thing feel like a cool adventure—then taking them to the pub later, chatting with them like they were all equals. But Fran had seen the other side, too. She'd seen Lexie trying to hide her tears when he canceled on her last-minute, had been there to deal with the fallout at her twenty-first birthday. And throughout it all, Fran had been firmly on Lexie's side, changing her opinion of Richard along with Lexie herself—until now, apparently.

"He left it to me without speaking to me about it," Lexie pointed out. "And that's so not the point."

"Did he try to talk to you about it? Before he died?"

"No!" Lexie exclaimed, even though the word "died" sent something hard shooting to her stomach. It was stupid. She'd been at his funeral, for God's sake—and it had been months now. But she still didn't like hearing that word out loud.

"He never called or anything?" Fran pressed.

Lexie shook her head. She didn't want to think about it. Talking about his company was one thing—it felt practical, and she'd managed to start thinking of it as one step removed. The truth was, her dad had tried to get in touch a few times in the last couple of years. And they'd had one disastrous meet-up, just under a year ago. She'd agreed to meet him for a coffee when she was home visiting her mum—had come to see him in Bath. He'd tried to tell her he was sorry for how he'd been, for not being there for her more when she was growing up, but the apology had felt uncomfortable, and like it was too little, too late—and she'd ended up snapping at him and leaving, coffee only half drunk. And now, she understood why he'd been trying to build a bridge. He'd wanted to connect while he still had time, and she hadn't let him get that far.

"He can't actually just refuse to sell it," Fran said. Like she knew where Lexie's brain had gone—and knew not to push it any further. "The contract makes that clear—it's not a unilateral decision. Legally, I suppose he could find a way to buy you out? Or to prove that you haven't fulfilled your side of the contract?"

Would he do that? She'd caught a brief flash of another side of him in France. But she still knew nothing about him, really. For all she knew, he could be that callous, that harsh. Unbidden, a memory of the feel of his lips on hers flashed through her. She'd dismissed it, was actively not thinking about it. But had that been part of a bigger plan, too?

"You're back now," Fran continued, and Lexie nodded.

Where was Theo right now? He hadn't said where he was going on his leave, and she'd made a point of not asking anyone in the office. Where did he go for a holiday, given he got to go so many cool places with the company? She supposed it was different from being somewhere for work—though since being a kid, she'd only been able to afford to go abroad when it was for a job, and for her that never took away the thrill of seeing somewhere new. Who was he with? A friend? She had no idea what his life was like outside the company. Was he with a girlfriend? She shouldn't care. Apart from the fact that he'd kissed her. And cheated on his poor girlfriend. His poor girlfriend she didn't even know he had.

"What are you thinking about?"

"Nothing," Lexie said too quickly.

"Yes, you are: you've got that expression where you're all preemptively annoyed about something. It's the same one I remember from when we were kids and you were scowling at Ellen Bates for stealing a pencil she hadn't got round to stealing yet."

"I'm doing some pointless spiraling. And Ellen Bates would have stolen the pencil if I hadn't thought to prevent it."

"Spiraling about the company?"

Maybe she waited a beat too long before saying, "Yes."

Fran's eyes narrowed. "Or about a certain someone in the company?"

Lexie picked up her nearly empty coffee cup. No wonder she felt jittery—this was her third cup of the day. *Note to self: drink less coffee.* "What do you mean?"

"Oh, we're pretending we don't know who a certain someone is, are we? I'm confused because you keep bringing him up every five minutes. And just so you know, this is my sarcastic voice."

Lexie rolled her eyes. "Thanks for the heads-up." She shook her head. "I keep bringing him up because he annoys me and I have to work with him and he's arrogant and condescending and . . . Can we talk about something else?"

"You're the one still talking about him."

Lexie sighed. "You're impossible."

"I'm delightful."

"How's Noah?"

"Oh. I think that might be over."

"What? But you sounded so keen."

"That was until he told me he's not really into monogamy."

"Where do you *find* these people, Fran?"

"I'm on all the apps. You've got to be, if you want to meet someone." Lexie couldn't help thinking again how weird it was that the divorce lawyer was a serial dater.

"Well, good. Being single is better anyway."

"For you. But I *want* to find someone, Lexie."

"Even though you see how it can . . ." She put her mug down, decided not to finish that thought.

"How it can end? With divorce, you mean? Yes, even then."

Time to change the subject. "And you're still going to stick with it? The . . ."—she waved a hand in the air—"lawyering?"

Fran frowned slightly. She had a great frown, Fran—it was like she frowned with her whole face, her lip sticking out, her cheeks pulling in. It was weird, the things you missed when you didn't see people enough. "I made a list and decided the pros outweigh the cons. It was color coded and everything."

"Of course it was."

Lexie's phone buzzed on top of the table between them, and she reached for it. A WhatsApp—from Rachel. Her heart gave an extra-large thump. She didn't open it—didn't want Rachel to know she had yet—but she could see the message flashing on the top of the screen.

I hear you're back in the UK. Maybe we could talk?

"Everything OK?" Fran asked.

Lexie smoothed out her expression. "Yeah. It's just my mum, checking in, you know." She wasn't totally sure why she was lying. Fran was her oldest friend, the one person who had stuck with her—if she could talk to anyone about it, it would be her. But she didn't know what to do about Rachel. They'd never had a relationship before, when their dad was alive—why should it be any different now that he was gone? It would be the house, and Rachel wanting to clear the air. Maybe she should send her a message, telling her it was all fine. Yes, she'd do that. Then Rachel would stop trying to get in touch.

"How is it going, living with your mum?"

"I love my mum," Lexie said slowly, putting her phone down again.

"But?"

"But living at home is not super-fun. Despite the fact I have a reason to be here, it feels very much like a regression. She is brilliant and kind and cooks me pasta almost every night—but if this continues I'm going to start to look like a piece of penne, and I'm going to say something I regret when she asks me to pick my clothes up off the floor in my bedroom."

"You could move in with me?"

"What, really?"

"Sure, why not? I've got a spare room in the flat since my last housemate moved out. As long as you only leave clothes on the floor in your room and not everywhere, I'm cool with it."

"You had a housemate?"

Fran laughed. "And that shows how much attention you pay."

Lexie winced. "I'm sorry. I should have been around more. I should have—"

"Lexie, relax. It wasn't a dig. I'm sure there are things I don't know about your life, either. That's just what's going to happen, given our lives aren't twined together anymore. I don't blame you for living your life. And the offer's there, if you want it."

"In that case, that would be bloody brilliant, thank you. Shall I get us another coffee to celebrate?"

"Only if you make yours a decaf. I don't think I can stand to watch much more of your jitteriness."

Lexie gave her a wicked grin. "Oh, you are *so* going to regret inviting me to move in."

Chapter Fourteen

"Is it like *In Bruges*—you know, the film?" The man looked up hopefully from the Christmas brochure that Lexie had handed to the little family of three.

"Isaac!" The woman—his wife, judging by the ring on her finger—snatched the brochure out of his hand, while their son, who couldn't have been older than about seven, studied Lexie with a seriousness that was a little unnerving. "Please excuse my husband," she said, adjusting the pair of sunglasses she'd propped on her head when she'd entered the shop.

Lexie smiled at them. "I actually can't say I've ever seen the film. Is it good?"

"Oh, it's great," Isaac gushed. "Very funny. You know Colin Farrell? He's great in it."

"There's a lot of shooting," his wife added. "And various people die."

"Wait, who dies?" piped up the boy.

"No one, sweets. It's a film Daddy likes."

"I want to watch it."

"It's too old for you."

The boy scowled, then went back to observing Lexie like she was about to do something untoward. Out of the corner of her eye, Lexie saw the door at the back of the office open. Her heart gave an unpleasant little stutter as Theo stepped in, glancing around the office. He must have been upstairs this morning the whole time. Ange hadn't told her he was back! Something coiled in her stomach. If she'd known, she could have prepared. His gaze moved toward her, and she looked away before the moment of eye contact, forcing herself to turn her attention back to the family, who were watching her expectantly.

She cleared her throat, trying to pretend she hadn't noticed Theo go out again—toward the back room. "Ah, well, we try to steer away from shooting and death on our holidays."

Isaac smiled a little guiltily, while the woman muttered, "Quite right," under her breath.

"But if you want somewhere to celebrate Christmas, then Bruges is brilliant. It honestly is like something out of a fairy tale—the houses are covered in snow, and you can stroll down cobbled streets and feel like you're in a snow globe. The canals often freeze over, and there are market stalls in the squares of the city if you want to check out the Christmas offerings. Plus the food is amazing—you've never had waffles like theirs—and we work with this brilliant little waffle shop who have a secret family recipe."

"Waffles?" The boy looked at her less suspiciously now.

"And chocolate," Lexie said with a wink. "Belgium is famous for its chocolate, and they go wild at Christmas." He offered her a small smile at that, then glanced up at his mum hopefully.

"That sounds good, doesn't it, Isaac?" Without waiting for an answer, she turned back to Lexie. "What are the next steps, if we want to go for it?"

Lexie took them through the booking process, added a few more details on the trip, then backed away, leaving them to ponder. No one liked to be pushed—and she was pretty sure they'd go for it without any further intervention on her part. After a few weeks in the office, this was the part she felt she could do. She'd done a lot of customer-facing work over the years, and though she'd not sold holidays before, it was a similar skill set—and something she actually enjoyed doing. She liked trying to figure people out, liked the easy conversation— and she was finding she liked trying to work out what they were after in a holiday—which place they might like to get to know through a local celebration—and matching it up as best she could.

Lexie glanced around the office. Harry was talking to an older couple at what Lexie thought of as *his* desk, though they were supposed to be communal, nodding along to a story they were telling him. Apparently Christmas ties were not the only festive-themed items in his wardrobe—he was wearing a blue tie with yellow chicks on it as a nod to Easter today.

Most of R&L's business was actually done online, Lexie had learned, but they kept the shop open for anyone who wanted more personal interaction before deciding which holiday to book. As a result, there was a lot of remote working—she hadn't even seen Mike since moving back, and Ange told her he hardly ever came in to the office. Harry was in most days, manning the floor, and Ange was in a lot, but she wasn't strict about hours. So far, Lexie had been coming in every day. Ange had given her a company laptop, but she had no idea what to do at home, sitting on Fran's sofa and frowning at the screen, trying to figure out whether she was supposed to be coming up with some grand idea to make loads of money. At least in the office she could talk to people and feel useful.

What would Theo do, now he was back? Would he mostly work upstairs from the flat, or would he be down here, in the office?

She watched as the little family headed to the nearest desk—

the one where Lexie often sat—and picked up one of the business cards. The boy made to grab a handful of the chocolate eggs, wrapped in colorful tinfoil, from the bowl there, but the woman stopped him and handed him just one; then Isaac snuck him a second while the woman pretended not to see.

"We'll book online," the woman said with a smile as she headed past Lexie and back out onto the street. "I'd better get Belgian on my Duolingo!"

"You're good at this you know."

Lexie spun to see Ange standing behind her. Her lips were painted her usual bright red, and she was wearing dangly carrot earrings—presumably because of Easter. Lexie put a hand to her heart. "Jesus, you don't half know how to sneak up on people. And good at what, exactly?"

"Putting customers at ease. Figuring out what they want and offering them the chance to take it. Not everyone can do it." She gave Lexie a wry smile "You made it sound like *you* wanted to go there."

Lexie smiled too. "That's the problem—I do want to. Every time I'm talking about somewhere, I want to go there."

"You can't be good in a travel business if you don't want to travel yourself."

"I saw Theo come in," Lexie said, in a would-be casual voice.

"Yes, he got back last night, said he wanted to jump straight back into work. Speaking of which, we've got our company meeting in ten. Can you go and remind Theo to come up to the flat? He's in my office." It wasn't technically *hers,* but no one ever corrected Ange on this.

Lexie hesitated. She wondered if she could tell Ange to go and get Theo herself, or if that was a step too far on the immaturity scale. Ange seemed to read her mind. "You're going to have to face up to him," she said, in a very no-nonsense tone. "And he shouldn't be scaring you off, so don't let him. No matter what he says, you did the right thing coming back—and I know he knows that."

After that, she could hardly refuse, could she? She turned away, then looked over her shoulder when Ange called her back. "Lexie? Just a heads-up—he's never in the best of moods after he comes back from Ireland. Something to bear in mind."

"Fantastic," Lexie muttered as she headed to the back room. Though at least it answered the question of where he'd been. As usual, there were coats hung up in a haphazard sort of way, along with general clutter, including a box of new brochures that hadn't been unpacked yet. There was a small window high up on the wall, showing the bright blue sky outside. And there was Theo, sitting at Ange's computer, frowning at the screen. She had no idea why he had chosen to come down here and work—the flat was much nicer.

She cleared her throat and he looked up. His hair had grown a little longer since she'd last seen him, and he had more stubble too, like he hadn't bothered to shave for a few days. She wished it didn't look attractive. She wished *he* didn't look attractive. "So, you stayed," he said.

"Yes. I stayed." He nodded slowly, and she resisted the urge to push her hair back self-consciously. "Ange says to remind you we've got a company meeting in ten, upstairs in the . . . in your flat."

He turned his attention back to the computer screen. "It's not mine." Well, a change from when he'd posited the opposite, in the solicitor's meeting that started all this. It was true, though—he only rented it from the company. Which meant he risked losing it, if the new owners wanted it for themselves. She didn't want to feel guilty about that, but the thought had crept in despite herself.

"So, the meeting?" she prompted.

He frowned at her, clearly distracted. "What? Oh right. Yeah. I'll come up. Thanks." It wasn't exactly gushing, but it was civil, at least.

"OK. Well, I'll head up now. Make everyone a coffee beforehand or something."

He stood abruptly. "I'll come with you. I could do with a coffee." He strode toward her but didn't seem to be quite looking *at* her. He slipped a hand into the back pocket of his jeans—she'd never seen him wear anything more formal—and pulled out a key, tapping it against his other palm without seeming to notice what he was doing. She was thinking about what Ange had said, wondering what was in Ireland that had made him come back so tense and distracted.

Given she couldn't exactly refuse to walk up with him, she followed him up the stairs. He said nothing as they climbed, though she caught him spinning the key between his fingers.

"So. Ireland." He glanced back questioningly, clearly still not quite in the room, and she shrugged a little. "Ange told me."

"Course she did," he said on a sigh.

"She said you'd be in a terrible mood and likely to bite my head off." Which was hyperbole, but if anyone could handle Theo, it was Ange, so she wasn't too worried. "And I said, 'Surely not, Theo is always only sunshine and rainbows.'"

He shook his head and she *thought* she heard the tiniest snort of laughter. "You did not say that."

"No, OK, I didn't, but I think it was implied by the incredulous look on my face."

He turned as they reached the top of the stairs. "Feeling extra sassy today, are we?"

She wrinkled her nose. "No one has ever described me as *sassy*. I'm easygoing." There was a pause in which he gave her a *look,* and she sighed. "Just not with you, apparently."

"Not sure if I should take that as a compliment or an insult."

"Whatever your evil villain heart desires."

OK, that was *definitely* a laugh. A small one, one he tried to hide—but still a laugh. It made her smile a little in response.

Then he cocked his head, and the way he looked at her made her remember all too clearly the way he'd looked in that hallway in France, just before they'd kissed. *Don't go there, Lexie.*

"Isn't the villain dependent on whose point of view the story is told from?"

Lexie lifted her gaze to meet his. "So I'm the villain, not you?"

"I guess that remains to be seen." He no longer seemed distracted. Instead he was a little *too* focused as he looked at her.

She cleared her throat, looking around for something else to say. "So. What's in Ireland, then?"

He raised his eyebrows. "Well, there are a lot of green fields, some beautiful cliffs by the coast, and some excellent pubs, if you know where to look."

She just about stopped herself from rolling her eyes this time. "You know what I mean. How come Ange thought you'd be in a bad mood?"

He considered her for a moment, and she thought he'd tell her to drop it, that it was too personal. Which might have been fair enough, given how well they knew each other. Instead he said, "How about we make a trade?"

"A trade?"

"I'll tell you what's in Ireland, if you tell me one of your wishes."

Lexie frowned. "What?"

"You know, the ones you put in your jar thing. At Christmas."

Lexie's frown grew deeper. "Why do you want to know?"

"It's an evil villain thing," he said, very seriously. "We have to know what people's wishes are, so that we can stop them coming true."

It got a surprised snort of laughter from her, and she swore his eyes lightened at the sound of it. And because he'd made her laugh, because he seemed *pleased* to have made her laugh, she caved. "When I was thirteen, I wished my hair would grow purple naturally."

It was an easy wish to offer him. She'd wanted so badly to dye it, but her mum had refused. By that time, Lexie had stopped taking the wishes so seriously—both because she was older, and because her belief in the tradition had been marred. But there had been a part of her that still secretly hoped the wish might come true—because her mum wouldn't have been able to do anything if her hair had just grown like that.

"Why are your lips twitching?" she demanded.

"It's called a smile, Lex."

"Maybe you ought to look in a mirror before making that claim," she tossed back. But he only smiled more widely.

Then he blew out a breath, his expression shuttering in that way he had. "My parents are in Ireland." He turned to open the door, gestured into the flat before she could ask any more. "Shall we?"

Chapter Fifteen

"So the only other thing left to discuss is the Madrid trip," Ange said, flicking a page in her notebook, pen in hand as she took minutes. Ange and Theo were sitting on the sofa, with Harry squished between them, and Mike and Lexie were in the two armchairs facing each other over the rug on the wooden floors. *What did they ever do if there were more than five of them in a meeting?* Lexie wondered. Apparently Harry often stayed downstairs to mind the shop, but they'd closed it up for this meeting so that he could join.

The flat was so tidy, it was almost like no one lived here. She thought she was a master at living light, but apparently Theo was too, if the sparse bookshelf was anything to go by. Unless he kept all his clutter somewhere else. In his bedroom, maybe. Not that she was thinking about his bedroom.

"Madrid?" she asked, pulling herself back to the room. Behind Mike, she could see the massive windows, typical of this Georgian style of building, and the glimpse of the city below, with the abbey in the distance.

"We've been talking about setting up a new trip there for next year," Mike said. He'd acknowledged her at the beginning of the meeting with a booming, "Lexie! Wonderful to see you sticking it out, good for you," which Lexie was trying not to hold against him. "There's a big cultural festival there in May," he continued, "the Fiesta de San Isidro." His put-on Spanish accent was just as bad as his French one.

"Yes," said Ange, "and you've just about got time to do a recce this year, if you get organized and decide on a strategy." Lexie noticed Ange tended to do this—refer to "you," rather than "we." It reminded her of what Theo had said, about her not taking enough credit for what she did for the company.

"I have no idea why Richard didn't ever get this one off the ground," Mike said, shaking his head. "Old boy was missing a trick."

Lexie saw Theo clench his jaw at that, though he said nothing. She wondered if he was upset about the slight on her dad. Did he feel he owed Richard something, maybe—for giving him a job, and now, for giving him a chunk of the company?

"We don't have anything else in Madrid, do we?" Ange asked pragmatically. "Nothing this will clash with?"

"Makes no sense that we haven't done Madrid in all this time," Mike said. "Seems obvious, doesn't it? Plenty of people will want to go there and we can sell the Spanish dancing and tapas and the like. Be perfect for anyone who imagines themselves a bit of a romantic and wants to dance the salsa or whatnot."

"I went to Barcelona once," Harry said. "But it was with a bunch of friends when I was eighteen, and I don't remember much about it, if I'm honest."

Lexie chose to look out the window rather than engage in the conversation. Her dad might not have set up an R&L trip to Madrid, but she knew for a fact he'd been there at least once before. She pressed her lips together tightly. Bitterness was not helpful—and she could do nothing to change the past.

"I can make time for a weekend recce," Mike was saying. "Kate loves Spain. I'll take her along."

"I don't know if you'll be able to do a proper recce if you take your wife along," Theo said, and though his voice was mild, Lexie heard annoyance layered under it.

"Nonsense, Kate will love it."

"Mike," Theo said, with the air of someone dredging up patience, "Kate is lovely, but she will not want to have a full-on weekend like that. And you won't want to go to some of the places either—you told me that you hated the dancing on the Mexico trip."

"Well, we won't actually *do* the dancing; it's more about watching it, isn't it?"

"And are you actually going to make time to investigate all the places, or are you just going to take Kate out to the best places for lunch?"

"Now, listen here, old chap, I've been part of the company longer than you have, and I've been on enough of these things without you stepping in to tell me what I can and can't—"

Lexie glanced at Ange, but she seemed to be doodling in her notebook, waiting for the argument to pass. Harry was swiveling his head back and forth between Theo and Mike as they argued.

"I'm not telling you what you can or can't do. I'm *asking* you if you think Kate will make things difficult, which you've mentioned before that she has a tendency to do on work trips."

Mike made a sort of blustering noise before saying, "Well, I'll go on my own, then."

Theo took what Lexie imagined was a calming breath, and Harry used that opportunity to pipe up with, "I would *love* to go to Madrid. Just in case that's useful for anyone to know."

Lexie thought Theo might shut Harry down immediately or point out that a comment like that wasn't helpful just now, but instead he just shook his head, and she saw the smile he tried to stop when Harry grinned at him.

"We'll get you out on a trip soon, mate, I promise, but it can't be a recce. I think for this one it might be better if I—"

"I'll go." Lexie hadn't fully thought it through before she said it, but now that the words were out, she found she meant them. She'd wanted to go to Madrid for a long time—why not now? And she wanted to prove she could do more than answer customer inquiries. She wanted to be able to prove, at the end of the year, that she'd helped the company turn a profit—and helping to set up a new trip was doing that, wasn't it?

Mike gave a tinkling laugh, while Ange looked up from her notebook and gave her an approving smile. "Lexie," Mike began, "I admire your enthusiasm, honestly I do, but you won't have the first idea what you—"

"I've got a good few weeks before I'd have to go," she pointed out. "That's loads of time to do some research, figure out what to check out, come up with a rough itinerary, and then see if it could work. I can talk to you and Theo about previous trips and figure out what I'm looking for. OK, I haven't done a 'recce' for you before, but I *have* traveled a lot. I'm good at talking to new people, and I know how to throw myself into something."

Mike opened his mouth to talk over her, but Lexie cut him off. "Plus, I own half the business. Doesn't that give me the right to at least try?"

Mike blustered to himself, Ange gave her a wink, while Harry said, "Hear hear." Theo was looking at her, frowning slightly, but he didn't immediately shoot her down. She made herself face him.

"I won't mess it up," she said, trying to speak calmly and professionally. Technically, she knew, that wasn't something she could promise. She could *try* not to mess it up, though.

"I, for one, am all for it," Ange piped up. "She *is* good at the people side of it, after all."

"I know she is," Theo said. It surprised Lexie enough that she didn't immediately say anything. She thought of what he'd said in France, when he insisted he was trying to give her a compliment. Apparently he'd meant it.

"Right," she said after a beat. "And I can work with you on the business side of things before I go, can't I? Because I know you have more experience on that front." She spoke directly to Theo, knowing that, really, it was only him she had to convince. And although she wasn't sure about volunteering to spend more time with him, even if it was just for work, she could try to meet him halfway here—if he was admitting she was good with people, she could admit that he was probably better on the business side. Even though she would try to avoid the word *better* if she could.

Theo looked at her for another long moment, then nodded. "OK."

She blinked. "OK?"

"Yeah. You should go."

A smile spread across her face. "What, really?"

"Yes. Ange is right. And you're right. If you're going to stick it out for the year, you need to get involved."

"Yes," she said, nodding. "OK. Well, that's—"

"But I'm coming too."

She tried to stop her mouth from falling open. "I don't think—"

"Mike is right as well. You don't really know enough about

the business yet to fly solo. So we'll both go, work together on it like you said."

"Yes, but I didn't mean . . ." She trailed off, distracted by the way he was watching her, waiting.

"Well, that's settled, then," Ange said, while Mike looked between the two of them, frowning. Harry was grinning, and nudged Theo in the ribs, apparently delighted. And Lexie saw no way out of it—not when it had been her idea in the first place. "So unless anyone has anything else they want to talk about, I think that's it for now?" Ange shut her notebook, then flapped her hand as they all started to stand up. "Oh no, wait! Theo, you wanted to talk about your idea, didn't you?"

For some reason, Theo's eyes flicked toward Lexie, then away again, before he answered. "No, don't worry. Maybe it's best we put that on hold for now."

"Well, we might as well *talk* about it while we're all here," Ange pressed, opening her notebook again.

"What idea's this?" Harry asked. "Oh no, wait, is this your local business thing?"

Theo pulled his hand through his hair. "It's not *my* thing, it's . . ." He looked around at all of them. "It was something Richard and I talked about, before he . . ." He broke off, glancing at Lexie again, like he wasn't sure whether to go on.

Mike frowned. "The investment project?"

Lexie felt like she should put her hand in the air, though she just about resisted. "So . . . What's the project?"

For the first time since she'd met him, Theo looked uncomfortable. "Well, the company already supports local businesses, with everything we do," he said, shifting in his seat, "but I figured—and Richard agreed—that we could go a bit further. Like, what about putting some of our profit back into local businesses—people who want to start something, in one of the places we run trips? So, for example, we have this Christmas trip in Belgium—"

"Lexie was talking that one up to a family just now," Ange said.

Theo glanced at Ange, then back at Lexie, seeming to take a moment to gather his train of thought again. "Right. Cool. Well, you know about it, then. But there's this woman there who makes the most amazing hot chocolate—with, like, actual chocolate, and she can do vegan hot chocolate too, in a way you wouldn't believe, and she has this idea for a chocolate café, but she hasn't been able to get the funds together to start it up. So we could support her, investing in the business—and make her café a part of the itinerary for the trip, so it all links together." He frowned, shaking his head at himself. "I'm not sure if I'm explaining it very well. But Richard got it, I think." The way he said the last part, like he needed to reassure them all that someone else had vouched for the idea, opened a little window into a side of him she'd not seen before.

"No, I think I get it," Lexie said. "And it's really cool. I think it's a great idea." And she meant it. She couldn't work out whether it had been Theo's or Richard's idea in the first place— she couldn't match the idea up to what she knew about either of them—but that didn't stop her from being all for it.

Theo looked at her like she wasn't quite getting something. "Yeah, it's just . . . Well, if we do that, then we risk the margins being quite close to the wire, profit-wise, at the end of the year."

She glanced at Ange for help as she tried to catch up. Then she realized. "Oh."

"Yeah. Oh."

"So you mean, put *all* the profits back into local businesses?"

Was it selfish, that she'd asked that question? But how could the company even function if it didn't turn a profit? She didn't know much about business, admittedly, but wasn't that the main point of them?

"No, not all of it. But we've had a rough couple of years recently, and we're not fully back on track yet, so maybe . . ." He sighed. "Maybe now isn't the right time."

Lexie hesitated. "Maybe we can see where we're at in a few months?"

He nodded, his gaze flickering across her face, like he might have been trying to figure out the truth behind her words. "Yeah. Yeah, OK."

"Excellent!" Ange clapped her hands together. "You'll have plenty of time to talk about it while you're in Madrid together."

Chapter Sixteen

"And have you—?"

"I booked the flights last week. Which I told you at the time, remember?"

Theo drummed his fingers on the other side of Lexie's desk, where he was standing, looming over her. "That wasn't what I was going to ask."

Lexie cocked her head. "Oh no?"

The drumming fingers stopped for a moment. Then, "Fine. I was just checking. Usually Ange books them, so forgive me for wondering—"

"If I'm capable of booking two seats on a flight to Spain on the right day without any hiccups?" She waved a hand in the air when he opened his mouth. "Ange has enough to do, which I told her. So consider looking up flights and clicking the 'Buy Now' button just another of my many talents."

The drumming fingers started again. "You need my full name. And passport details."

"I know that," Lexie said idly, clicking on another link she'd found detailing all that was to offer at the Fiesta de San Isidro. The problem wasn't going to be finding enough to fill a week-long holiday—it was going to be trying to figure out what the best parts were, and how to really make the guests feel like they were getting to know the city through the tradition. "I went up-stairs while you weren't looking, broke into the flat, and rummaged through your bedside table drawers until I found it." She gave him a sly look. "You really ought to consider what you keep in there."

His eyes narrowed, and she let out a half laugh.

"Relax, T-Rex. Ange gave all your details to me."

He gritted his teeth at Ange's nickname for him, then ran a hand through his hair, making it stick up at odd angles. "OK. Well, good. Tea?"

She looked at him, like he might be pulling a trick on her with the friendly gesture, but he only raised his eyebrows in question. "Ah, sure. Can I have—"

"Lots of milk, two sugars. I know."

"How do you know?"

"I observe."

She didn't comment on that, not quite sure if she should be suspicious. He got to his feet, stretched. His T-shirt rose a fraction with the movement, exposing a line of very toned-looking stomach. She snapped her gaze away immediately, looking back at her computer screen and getting up the Word document for the itinerary for Madrid.

"Although you really shouldn't have so much sugar in your tea."

She fluttered her eyelashes at him. "Because I'm sweet enough?"

"Because the man at the shop where I buy most of my groceries is starting to think I have a serious sugar addiction and I'm pretty sure he's going to report me to Sugar Anonymous any day now."

Lexie let out a snort of surprised laughter. His lips twitched in response and something warm lit his gaze, a sign that he was glad at having made her laugh. She felt a little flutter at that, though she tried to shove it back down where it belonged.

Harry saved her from thinking too deeply about it by calling out, "I'll have a tea too, my man, if that's OK. A green one, if you've got it."

Lexie went back to pulling together what they'd already decided on for Madrid, trying not to track Theo's movements out of the office. She looked up automatically when the front door opened. Her hand went dead still on the computer mouse. The woman came inside a little tentatively and brought one hand up to run it through her curls—curls that were so similar to Lexie's.

"Hi!" Harry bounded over in his puppy-like fashion. "Can I help you?" There were no holidays to theme his outfit around at the moment, but that didn't mean he hadn't tried. Given they were talking a lot about the Madrid trip these days, his current tie was bright yellow-and-red stripes in honor of the Spanish flag. Lexie had asked him once where he got his ties from, and why he had so many, and he'd just nodded along and said, "I know, they're cool, aren't they?" proving that his habit of not actually answering questions was not limited to customer inquiries.

Lexie realized she was still frozen at her desk and ducked, nearly smacking her head into her computer monitor.

"Oh, hi. Sorry, I'm not actually looking for a holiday. I mean, we could all do with a holiday, couldn't we?" Rachel gave a nervous laugh. "Sorry, what I mean to say is, I'm looking for Lexie Peterson."

Lexie had asked her mum, once, why she'd never changed her surname back to her maiden name. And her mum had said that it was too much hassle, that it was just a name—and that, besides, taking his name had meant something, at the time, and that even if it hadn't turned out the way she'd wanted, you couldn't just erase years of your life with a piece of paper. Lexie wasn't quite sure about the latter part, but she *did* agree with her mum that a name was just that—so sharing her father's surname didn't tie her to him in any meaningful way. Though did Rachel think differently?

"Oh sure," Harry said, and Lexie wanted to groan.

Obviously she was being stupid. She couldn't hide behind a bloody computer monitor—though it had been worth a try.

"She's right over there."

Lexie straightened, trying to look like she'd been bent over for a perfectly legitimate reason, like tying a nonexistent shoe-lace, or picking up a pen. Then she stood all the way up, because it felt weird to be sitting down as Rachel walked over to her.

Rachel didn't look entirely comfortable either. She was twist-ing a bracelet on one of her wrists, and her eyes kept darting to Lexie and then away again. When had Lexie last seen her, not counting the funeral? She couldn't actually put a finger on it. She was struck again by the confusing sensation that Rachel was so much older than when they'd last met—and yet still so young. Young enough that it should have been Lexie being the bigger person here.

Lexie tried to work up a smile. She could do this. "Hi, Ra-chel."

Rachel stopped playing with her bracelet and dropped her hand to her side.

Lexie noticed her fingernails were bitten all the way down, the skin around them red and raw-looking. Had she always had that habit? Lexie couldn't remember.

"Hi." She took a deep breath, and under her denim jacket,

Lexie saw her chest heave with the motion. "Look, I'm sorry to barge in like this. It's just, you haven't really been answering and I thought we ought to . . . well, talk. And I heard that you were working here now, so . . ."

"Right." Lexie felt uncomfortable heat rush down her spine. "Well, I can't really—"

But she was cut off by the sound of Theo's voice—he had apparently slid in the door without anyone noticing. Lexie was ready to take his appearance as a get-out, explain that she needed to talk to him about something—but he wasn't even looking at her. Instead, balancing three teas in his hands, a grin spread across his face as he looked at her sister. A real grin—one she didn't think she'd seen before.

"Rach!" He strode in, dumped the mugs on the corner of Lexie's desk, then wrapped Rachel in a big bear hug. "How the hell are you?"

Lexie stared at the two of them. He *knew* her? Of course he did. Rachel and Richard weren't estranged, were they? Something hot and ugly bubbled at the base of her throat, even as she tried to swallow it down. She wasn't even sure *why* she was feeling like this. But seeing Theo greet Rachel like this, like an old friend, compared to the way he'd treated her when they'd first met . . .

She swiped her tea—the milkier one—off the desk, spilling liquid over the rim and wincing as it seared her fingers. She cleared her throat and the two of them broke apart, Rachel looking a little flushed, but happy, the edges of Theo's grin still lingering. "I'll leave the two of you to catch up, then," she said, gesturing with her tea to the door, and the back room she was going to hide in. It was childish, to try to escape like this, but right then, she didn't care. Rachel shouldn't have just *sprung* this visit on her. And Theo—he should have told her he knew her sister.

When, Lexie? In all those heart-to-hearts you have?

"Oh no, wait," Rachel said, her voice quick and jittery, the flush in her cheeks deepening but her smile fading. "It's you I wanted to talk to."

"Right," Lexie said. "But I'm a bit busy just now." She gestured around, trying to convey a general workplace busyness. "Sorry you came all this way."

She hesitated, clocking the way Rachel's face was falling. And tried to push away the guilt.

"Sorry," she said again, her voice quieter. "Another time, yeah?" Another time, when she'd had time to prepare. When she didn't have Theo right here, watching the entire conversation.

She walked quickly, doing her best not to spill her tea in the process. When she reached the back room—and thankfully it was empty—she sank into Ange's swivel chair, cupping her mug between her hands for comfort.

Shit. Was she really that pathetic, that immature, that she couldn't handle a quick conversation with her sister? Her *little* sister, no less? She glanced at the door. She should go back out there. Suggest they go somewhere else—away from prying ears.

But just as she was thinking it, the door swung open, and Theo came barging in, a scowl already set in place. "What the hell was that about?" he demanded.

She scowled right back at him. "None of your damn business."

"You were so rude to Rachel. She's your *sister,* and you just completely blew her off."

"I'm well aware of who she is, thanks." But she could feel heat in her cheeks and found herself gripping the mug more tightly.

"I think you should go back out there, apologize."

"*Do* you, now?" She tried to control the anger curdling in her gut. "Well, thanks for your input. But seeing as how, as mentioned, it's none of your business, maybe you ought to keep your opinions to yourself."

He folded his arms. "She's upset. I know her, and she's trying to hide it, but she is."

"Yes, you know her. I got that." Her voice was a snap.

"What, so now you're upset that I've met her before?"

"Don't be so ridiculous." *Was* that what she was upset about? It had shaken her, yes. But right now everything felt tangled and she couldn't work it out. One thing was sure, though—Theo clearly knew Rachel well enough to care whether she was upset or not. Whereas, with Lexie, he hadn't cared one bit.

"She lost your dad too, Lexie."

His voice might have been gentler, but hers grew louder. "I know that! For fuck's sake, what are you after here? Don't you ever consider that I might have my own emotions to deal with?" She set her mug down on Ange's desk and got to her feet, suddenly unable to sit still. She started pacing. "Doesn't it occur to you that the reason I can't talk to her is *because* our dad is gone? And because she had a completely different dad from me, and I don't know what to say to her about that? Because I don't want to make it *worse* for her?"

She glanced over at Theo to see a flicker of a grimace there. "Shit, Lexie, I'm—"

"But no. You don't think, do you? As usual, you are jumping to assumptions about me, and then *blaming* me for those assumptions, like I've done something terrible to you, personally."

"I don't—"

"Maybe *next time,* Theo, you can keep your opinions to your damn self. Maybe you could remember what you said in France—that we *don't* know what each other is thinking." She stopped a yard or so away from him, folding her arms and mimicking his pose. God, she shouldn't have let herself get drawn in, even for a second—should have remembered the many reasons she did not like this man.

"You're right," he said quietly, the fire in his eyes banking a little. "I'm sorry."

She frowned. She didn't know what to do, when he came barreling in one minute, then apologized the next. "Right," she said. "Well, then."

"I shouldn't have jumped to conclusions."

"Why buck a trend?" she muttered under her breath. But he was apologizing here—and she didn't want to keep arguing. So she lifted her chin, looked him in the eye. "OK, fine. You're sorry."

Yes, great, sound more *like a petulant child, why don't you, Lexie?*

He took a step toward her, and it seemed careful. "I really *am* sorry. I just didn't like seeing it."

"Rachel getting upset?" she asked quietly.

"Both of you getting upset."

He kept his gaze on hers as he said that, and she felt her breath hitch, just a little. Found herself remembering what it had been like, to pull him toward her, to feel his mouth on hers.

"But I know it's not that easy," he continued, then shook his head cynically—not at her, she realized, but at himself. "Trust me—despite the incredible lack of judgment I've displayed when it comes to you, I do get the whole complicated family thing. And I have a habit of projecting sometimes."

He took another careful step toward her, and she swallowed. There was only a matter of inches between them now.

"I'm sorry," he said again, his voice no more than a murmur.

His eyes held hers in a way that was both too intense and impossible to look away from. Would it be the same, if she kissed him now? Would it send her blood humming? Already she felt a pull inside her, one that she wanted to deny. What was *with* this? How could she go from being mad at him to wanting him within the space of minutes? The air between them thickened, and she felt sure he knew exactly where her brain had gone. Seemingly of its own accord, her own gaze dropped to his mouth. When she looked back up, the amber in his dark eyes flared.

Then the door swung open, and the two of them jumped apart.

"Well," said Ange, looking between them. "I'm all for a healthy argument, but poor Harry out there has turned up the music so loud that it's impossible to get any work done, even in the flat." Lexie cringed internally. "Now, Theo," Ange said, turning to look at him sternly, "leave Lexie alone. She's right. Her relationship with her family isn't any of your business, unless she wants it to be." He winced a little. "And Lexie." She gave Lexie a once-over, like she was checking for damage. "I'm all for not bottling everything up, but I doubt you want strangers overhearing you, so maybe take a beat and come back out when you're ready?"

Lexie nodded, and Ange gave them both another glance, before turning to leave.

The door clicked shut behind her, and Theo and Lexie looked at each other again. There was a moment of silence between them. Then Lexie made a snap decision. She grabbed her coat off the hook and headed for the door, Theo moving out of her way as she did so. Because as much as she still wanted to put off talking to Rachel, she didn't like the idea of her hurting. And because, in that moment, running after Rachel seemed like a safer option, all things considered, than staying in this room with Theo.

Chapter Seventeen

Lexie saw the back of Rachel's head as she stepped out of the office. "Rachel!" She ran the few steps to catch up with her, as Rachel turned, eyes a little guarded. She had that rare combination of dark hair and blue eyes, and it was really quite striking.

"Wasn't sure I'd catch up with you," Lexie said, pulling her jacket tighter to her. It was bright and sunny outside, but right now the chill in the air was still biting.

"I was moving quite slowly," Rachel admitted. She had a soft Welsh accent—and the contrast between that and Lexie's own accent was another thing that marked them out as different. "I was hoping you'd change your mind."

"Did Theo tell you he was going to go after me or something?"

"No. But I guessed that's what he was going to do after he stormed out after you."

Lexie scowled and shoved her hands into her jacket pockets. "He's an arrogant coal-eyed demon bat."

Rachel let out a quiet snort.

"Actually that's not really fair—bats get a bad rap and are actually quite cute."

"Theo's quite cute, to be fair," Rachel said.

"No, he's not." Cute was definitely not a word she'd use to describe him. "Shall we walk?" Lexie gestured down the street and Rachel nodded.

Together, they started walking, past some of the shops that Lexie had gotten to know since being here. She imagined it would go away after a year of living here, but for now she loved this, just meandering through Bath, especially on a day like today. There were a few places, in all her traveling around, that made her feel like she belonged, like the place was welcoming her in—and Bath was one of them. It was hard to imagine anyone would dislike it here—the gorgeous architecture always gave you something to look at, and there was always another cool little side street to explore, with a café or an independent shop waiting for you.

"He is once you get to know him. Theo, I mean."

Lexie glanced at Rachel. She had to be around ten years younger than Theo, but still . . . "Is there something going on between you two?" She figured it would be better to know now, if so.

Rachel laughed, making Lexie feel instantly ridiculous. "No. He's not my type, trust me. We're just . . . friends I guess."

"You guess?"

"Yeah, well, we'd spend time together with Dad, sometimes, like we'd all have dinner together or whatever, and we sort of . . . got to know each other, through that." She shot Lexie a glance, like she might be worried about bringing Richard up so soon.

And there it was—another reminder that Theo knew Richard, the Richard of more recent years at least, a hell of a lot better than Lexie did. They took a left, and Lexie knew they were heading toward the abbey courtyard. For a moment they walked in awkward silence. Lexie tried to think of an arbitrary question to ask but came up blank.

They stopped as the courtyard opened up, a decent-size crowd sitting at the cafés on either side and milling about the shops, even though it was a weekday. A building with big sandstone pillars stood to their right, majestic in a way only a café in Bath could be, and up ahead was the Abbey itself in all its glory. Gorgeous stained-glass windows, columns of honey-gold stone, and towers that stretched into the blue sky.

"I really want a coffee," Rachel said. "Don't suppose you fancy one?"

Lexie was trying to cut back, but the smell of it was lingering in the air. So they got one to take away, then sat on one of the benches in the middle of the courtyard, facing the abbey.

"This is awkward, I know," Rachel said, when they couldn't pretend to be busy with balancing their coffees anymore. "And I know it's weird to just show up and I know you sent me that message saying it was all fine, but I . . . I wanted to talk in person." She took a big gulp of her cappuccino and then winced, like it was too hot.

"About the house?" Lexie asked after a beat. Might as well get it over and done with.

"Yeah. Partly. Mainly."

"Is that why you're over this way? To check up on the house? Because you don't live here, right? You live in Wales?"

"I live in Cardiff now, yeah. And yes, I mean it's useful to pop into the estate agents—selling a house is, apparently, really complicated. But I came here to see you."

Lexie glanced sideways at her. "You drove all the way here to see if I was around?"

Rachel wrinkled her nose, and Lexie had the flash of a little Rachel, no more than five, who had made an expression just like that behind her mum's back when she'd been asked to finish her broccoli. Did Rachel still hate broccoli? Probably not.

"I've been told I can get a little obsessive at times," Rachel admitted.

Lexie found herself laughing, and Rachel gave her a guilty smile. "Good to know," Lexie said.

Rachel lifted her coffee to her lips again, and Lexie caught the glint of a ring on her finger, a blue sapphire.

"Nice ring," Lexie said casually.

Rachel glanced down, then positioned her hand so that the ring was obscured by the coffee cup. "Thanks." It was a weird reaction to just a ring, but Lexie didn't pry—she knew what it was like when you didn't want to talk about something.

"You're selling the house, then?" she asked instead. "You weren't tempted to live there?" Although, at twenty-two, maybe a house would be a bit too much responsibility to take on? It certainly would have been for her, at that age. Come to think of it, it still sounded like a bit too much commitment, even now.

Rachel bit her lip. "I didn't want . . . I didn't want to move here and, you know, intrude. I knew you were going to be here for a bit."

Lexie wondered how she'd gathered all her information. Theo? Though of course it had been in the will, so Rachel would have known from that that Lexie had inherited half the company. Maybe Rachel didn't know Lexie had run from it at first.

Lexie blew out a breath. "Bath's not *mine,*" she said. "My mum doesn't live here—she's still in Frome. And I'm only here for a year—less, now, actually. You shouldn't not live here because of me." She hadn't even thought that this would be a consideration.

"It's not just that." She twisted the ring on her left hand, not seeming to notice she was doing it. "I already have somewhere to live. And it's . . . It's Dad's house, you know?" Lexie nodded, even though she *didn't* really know. She didn't know what it would be like, to go into his house and see everything he'd left behind—but she didn't think she'd feel the same about it as Rachel did.

"I'm sorry," Rachel said quietly. "About the house."

"Don't be," Lexie said simply.

"But I—"

"Rachel, I didn't think he'd leave me anything at all in his will. The company stuff. I don't know. I have no idea what I'm doing, but I'm working through it. But his house—I wouldn't have wanted it." It was true, she realized. It might have been easier, but it would have felt way too personal. She'd gotten hung up on it because it was easier to focus on, to look for proof as to how Richard had valued his two daughters. But that was unfair to Rachel.

Rachel glanced at her, clearly trying to read her, before looking at the abbey again. "So where are you living now, then? With your mum?" Maybe she was returning the favor—changing the subject.

"I was—but I'm living with a friend of mine from school now."

And she'd been amazed at how easy it had been. She'd been forced to share space with a variety of people over the years, but it had been so much nicer sharing with someone who already knew the bad parts of you as well as the good. She knew Fran could afford to live alone, but for now, it was perfect—and Fran insisted that she liked the company. She'd expected her mum to be disappointed, but instead she'd seemed almost relieved. Maybe living with an adult daughter was just as hard on the parent—and perhaps she hadn't appreciated the fact that her mum might actually enjoy having her own space.

Lexie checked the time on her phone. "I should probably get

back to the office." No one would blame her if she didn't, everyone very much kept to their own schedule, but still. "We're planning this Madrid trip," Lexie explained out loud. "And I want to make sure I've done all my research." Especially as Theo was going to be with her, and she didn't want to risk things going wrong.

"Oh, that's so fun!" Rachel beamed. "I've been to Madrid. I was only about nine, so I don't remember the ins and outs, but it was so cool—we went to see these Spanish dancers, and we ate all this Spanish food—I remember the *patatas bravas,* though I just thought they were posh chips with tomato—and they were amazing. It was so hot, and Dad and Mum seemed really happy—though that might have been the sangria. I got obsessed with this Spanish red dress and Dad actually bought it for me and I wore it to every party for like a year and . . ."

She trailed off, looking at Lexie, and Lexie realized she must have been letting something show on her face. She tried to smooth out her expression, but her gut was twisting, imagining the scenario Rachel was describing.

"Oh my god," Rachel said. "I'm so sorry. I didn't even think."

Lexie shook her head to let her know it was fine, but Rachel plowed on, her voice a touch higher.

"I'm such an idiot. I'm sorry, I—"

"Rachel, it's OK. You're allowed to have memories of him." Rachel looked like she was about to cry, her lip on the verge of wobbling. And Lexie didn't know what to do.

"I shouldn't have . . . You didn't get to have a trip like that."

"No. I didn't." She heaved in a deep breath. "I wanted to come," she said quietly, figuring she owed Rachel some explanation. "Dad told me about Madrid, said you were all going—and he said I could come too. Not my mum, obviously, but she never let on that she was anything other than delighted at the prospect of me going." Despite how much it must have hurt her, to have Richard invite Lexie along to a holiday with his new family, her mum had kept that to herself in a way Lexie had never truly appreciated until now. "Anyway, a few weeks before the trip, he canceled."

Rachel's expression twisted. "I didn't know. I'm so sorry, Lexie. He never said you were going to come. Although . . ." She bit her lip. "It might have been my mum, you know. She was very set on family time, and she's weirdly . . . traditional." She started twisting her ring again. "It might not have fit with her idea of how a family was *supposed* to look or whatever." Lexie might have thought she was just saying it, trying to make excuses for Richard, trying to make Lexie feel better about it—if it wasn't for the way Rachel's eyes darkened, the way her mouth pulled into a tight line.

Then Rachel closed her eyes, and when she opened them, they were shining with tears—and Lexie was struck again by her complete inadequacy. "Oh, god, Rachel—"

Rachel dashed a stray tear away. "I'm sorry. I just . . . Dad's gone. He's really gone, and it keeps hitting me—like I keep waking up, thinking it can't be true, and then it is and I . . ." She swallowed, and Lexie saw how hard she was trying to swallow the tears down, not to break down in front of her. "My mum won't talk to me about it. About him. They separated a few years ago—I don't know if you . . . ?"

"I knew that, yeah," Lexie said quietly. And she'd noticed that Rachel's mum wasn't at the funeral, hadn't she? She wanted to ask why—why Richard had abandoned his second family—but now clearly wasn't the time for that.

She wanted to tell Rachel that she could talk to her. She

wanted to be kind and offer an olive branch and be there for Rachel, in the way everyone needed someone to be when they were going through grief—ideally someone who knew the person who had died. But the problem was, she *didn't* know that person—she didn't know the same dad as Rachel, and it was still hard and confusing to hear the memories Rachel was sharing. Like her dad had dropped one family, picked up another, and not even noticed the first one's absence. Just carried on. Until he'd left that one, too. And of course Rachel would have had a lovely time on those holidays—because when he'd been there, he was the perfect, fun dad. But any memories Lexie had of him being there became few and far between, replaced with memories of him letting her down.

So maybe the best she could offer right now was truth. "I haven't figured out yet how I feel about it all. How I feel about Dad being . . ." She swallowed the final word, unable to say it. "I don't really know how to process it—I don't know if I'm sad, or if I'm just angry, or what to think. So I guess I'm . . . I don't know. Waiting?"

"I get that. I think I do, anyway. For me, he was always my dad. He was a bit flaky at times, but in general he was great, and he was there for me when I needed him."

Though he still left your mum, Lexie thought—but she didn't say it out loud.

"I'm sorry," Rachel said on an outward breath. "You must think I'm awful. I would, if I were you."

Lexie gave Rachel a little smile. "Of course I don't. I don't blame you, if that's what you're worried about. You had as much say in it all as I did. I just . . . I'm not very good at facing up to things, I guess."

Rachel tucked a curl behind her ear. "I know that we don't

know each other very well. And I know that all we have in common is Dad, and that he was a different person to both of us. But, I'm just going to throw it out there—things with my mum aren't easy, and I don't have much in the way of family, and I know being sisters might be a bit much after all this time, but I'd . . ." She shot Lexie a glance. "I'd really like it if we could be friends."

Lexie nodded slowly. You had to admire Rachel, for putting her heart on the line like that. And because she admired it, because she couldn't ignore how vulnerable Rachel was in that moment, she decided the least she could do was meet her partway. "How about we start with something a little easier, and build up to friends?"

To her credit, Rachel didn't look offended by that. Instead she pursed her lips, thinking. "Mortal enemies?"

Lexie snorted out a laugh. "If we're looking for something easier and less intense, mortal enemies isn't the way to go in my experience."

Rachel cocked her head, her curls spilling to one side the same way Lexie's did. "Have many of them, do you?"

Theo's face flashed into her mind. Was that what he was? It wasn't exactly the term she'd use to describe him, though she wasn't sure how, exactly, she *would* describe him. "Oh, I collect them daily. Look at me—I'm just the right build for someone to pick as an enemy."

Rachel gave her a little look up and down. "You're pretty much the same height as me."

"Exactly. We're little but not *too* little, so people don't feel mean about picking on us."

"I'm not sure I have any idea what you mean."

"No. Well, you wouldn't be the first."

"So . . . We'll be something less intense than friends, then?"

"Well, I suppose we can try, at least. I know you like coffee. That's one good thing about you for starters."

"I can't drink too much of it," Rachel said, almost an admission. "I get all jittery."

"Me too!" She was, perhaps, a little too enthusiastic in the exclamation, given people getting jittery on caffeine wasn't exactly a rarity. And surely that wasn't the *only* thing she knew about Rachel? She tried now—really tried—to think if they'd had anything in common, the few weekends they'd been forced together. But all her mind could conjure up was a memory of Rachel when she was a toddler—Lexie couldn't have been older than ten at the time. Lexie had been baffled by this tiny human—by the fact that this little girl had been all it took to tear her own family apart. She'd been cross and feeling resentful—but then Rachel had made her laugh. The thing was, she couldn't remember *what* exactly had made her laugh. Something silly, like dropping a toy in a comical way—nothing that stood out. But she remembered laughing. Remembered Rachel laughing too. And she'd seen her dad, standing in the doorway.

Hey, Little Lex. So what do you think? You up for having a sister? He'd said it like it would be inclusive—like she could be part of the family too.

Lexie had looked at Rachel. *Maybe.* Rachel was picking up a toy now, handing it to Lexie, and Lexie took it almost reverently. Weirdly, she could remember exactly what toy it was—a stuffed tiger. Funny, the things that come back to you.

I don't really know how to be a big sister, Lexie had admitted. After all, she'd gotten used to referring to herself as an only child.

Well, as I see it, there's no right way to be a big sister, her dad had said.

And then Rachel's mum, Jody, had slipped in. And Lexie could still remember her muttering in an undertone. *I told you not to leave her alone with Rachel, Richard.*

Her dad's sigh. *What do you think she's going to do, Jody?*

But Jody was already stepping in, picking up Rachel and chatting to her, telling Lexie she'd make them some lunch. And taking Rachel away from her.

In the present, Rachel was watching her, nerves plastered on her face—and Lexie realized she'd been quiet for too long. "I'm sorry I've been so crap," she said quietly. "I'm sorry you felt like you had to literally force me to talk to you."

"Don't be," Rachel said. "Everyone processes this stuff differently. I know that—and I didn't want to intrude, but I . . ."

"Did it anyway?" Lexie grinned to show she was joking, and Rachel laughed.

"If you'd really sent me on my way, I would have dropped it. For a bit, anyway."

Lexie nodded and stood up. "I really do have to get back."

"OK. I'm going to stay here for a bit."

Lexie wasn't sure if Rachel was just saying that to offer her an out—but then again, maybe Rachel also needed some time to sit, to process. To be in the city her dad had lived in, without anyone watching how she dealt with that. She supposed the fact that her heart broke a little at the thought of that showed she wasn't such a terrible person.

"Rachel?" She waited for her to make eye contact. "Thank you for coming."

Rachel smiled, her eyes shining. "And thank you for coming after me."

Chapter Eighteen

Lexie tapped her foot impatiently, waiting as the queue of locals and tourists edged forward, painfully slowly. It was warm and sunny in Madrid, and even though it was only May, Lexie could feel the heat of the sun on her shoulders, thanks to the strappy dress she'd worn. She craned her neck to see how far they still had to go—it felt like they'd been standing in the queue for literal hours. And for what? The small building—San Isidro's "hermitage"—did not look all that impressive, and she couldn't even *see* the fountain they were all trying to get to.

"I just don't think this should be part of the schedule." She'd already said it, but waiting around was making her cranky enough to repeat herself. "People will get bored waiting."

Theo frowned. "It's part of the tradition."

"The big heads were better." Earlier they'd seen the parade of weird giant-headed figures being marched through the main streets in the center of the city—which had been bizarre, but cool.

"We can't just miss this bit. It is literally the whole point of the festival—the patron saint, his magical healing properties."

"It's the water that has healing properties."

"Right, so where's your water bottle?" Indeed, a fair number of people had their water bottles ready, waiting to fill them up. "Thought you would have been into magical water, what with your wishes and all."

"Thanks, but I'm all good and healed at the moment." It wasn't too hot in the city at this time of year, but it was far too hot in the queue, everyone bunched together like this. "I just think it's a bit of a waste of—"

"Let's see, OK?" His voice was a bit too sharp, almost a snap.

"Jeez, what is up with you? Back to the sniping phase of our on-again, off-again hatred?"

He looked like he might smile, then shook his head. "I'm just a little . . . worried. It's . . . Look, things are looking a bit tight at the moment. Budget-wise. I mean, we're doing OK compared to the last couple of years, but travel is still bouncing back and . . ."

"We're not on track to turn a profit?"

He said nothing, confirming it.

"Why didn't you tell me!" Should she have known? She'd looked at the numbers, but they had confused her. "What happened to our truce? And working together?"

They edged forward, the group in front of them surreptitiously looking back at them at her outburst.

"It'll be fine," he insisted, though the way his fingers tapped nervously against his leg suggested otherwise. "It's just . . . your dad used to do all this stuff and I know you're learning the ropes, but this is something *I'm* still learning too, OK? As Mike was quick to point out." He dragged a hand through his hair. She couldn't quite see his eyes, hidden behind his sunglasses, and didn't like that she couldn't fully read his expression as a result.

"We could have figured it out together." Not that she was necessarily qualified. But still.

"Look, the new Christmas holiday is already looking good— we've had lots of early bookings already. The margins are small, but with another trip on our books, I think we'll be OK."

"Iceland?"

"No, not Iceland. That will have to be next year, if we go for it—with a recce this year."

She felt somewhat relieved by that, though she didn't voice it out loud. "Where, then?"

"Vienna."

"Oh. Yeah." She'd actually been part of that conversation.

"How far behind budget?" she asked.

"Like I said, if this new trip comes off we should be fine." That wasn't an answer, and she opened her mouth to point that out, but he jumped in. "Why don't we sit down when we're back—when we have everything in front of us? And then, if you have any suggestions, we can go through them."

She blew out a breath. "OK. Fine."

He gave her a wry look. "Way to muster enthusiasm."

She returned that same look, then remembered something. "What about your investment idea? For the local businesses?"

He shook his head. "That all becomes irrelevant if we don't have the profit to invest back in."

She conceded with a nod—it was true. So at least they were on the same page about that. Though if they sold the company, would whoever took it on pick up Theo's idea and run with it? Or would they change the company into a more standard travel firm, focus less on the values it worked so hard to support right now? *Not your problem, Lexie.* She tried to believe that voice— but it was getting harder each time she thought about the future of the business.

When they finally reached the fountain, Lexie couldn't help but feel slightly underwhelmed. It seemed small, up against a cream-colored wall, with a plaque behind it, in Spanish. They had to bend down to wet their hands with the water, and the whole thing felt rushed, due to the pressure of the queue behind them.

They left the little building behind and headed toward San Isidro's meadow, or "la Pradera de San Isidro"—which was basically a beautiful green park, as far as she could tell.

"Go and find us a spot, will you?" Theo asked. "I'll catch up."

Lexie headed onto the grass, finding a space under one of the big leafy trees. The atmosphere was brilliant, she'd give it that. The whole park was buzzing, people all around having picnics, the sound of laughter filling the air. Still, her annoyance was getting the better of her, and she sat down with more force than necessary, regretting it when it sent a twang along her coccyx.

She couldn't see any sign of Theo. Maybe he'd gotten fed up with her and decided to leave her here. Well, that was fine, she knew the way back to the apartment. She blew out a breath and pulled her sunglasses down from the top of her head before closing her eyes and tilting her head back to warm her face in the sun. She wasn't even sure why she was so annoyed. Because Theo had seen something about the profit margins that she hadn't? He was better at the business side of things, she knew that. Her dad must have known it, too, she thought. Was that why he'd paired them together? To even out each other's gaps and continue the legacy of the company he'd created? Because he'd cared about the company, she knew that. More than he'd cared about either of his families, perhaps? And maybe *that* was why she was so annoyed.

"Here." She opened her eyes to see Theo standing above her, holding a big plastic cup of something out to her. "It's *limonada*. It's the traditional—"

"—drink made with wine, lemon, sugar, and chopped fruits."

She reached up to take it. "I know—I did the research too, remember?" But now she was just being snippy, taking it out on him for no reason. "I mean, thank you," she said, and the corner of his mouth twitched.

She took a sip—it really was delicious, like a brilliant wine cocktail that shouldn't work but totally did. He sat next to her on the grass and leaned back on his elbows, shifting so that his legs stretched out in front of him. Maybe it was just the taste of citrus that was reminding her of what had happened in that hotel corridor in France, but she was suddenly aware of how little space was separating their thighs.

"Oh, I bought us some of these, too." He reached behind his head for a paper bag full of little doughnuts. *Rosquillas,* Lexie remembered. There were different types, but these ones had powdered sugar. She took one, bit into it. It didn't taste like any doughnut she'd tried before—it wasn't quite as sweet, and it had a hint of anise, with a perfectly fluffy middle. It was great, actually, and she took another, then licked the sugar off her fingers.

She leaned back on her hands, feeling the tickle of grass on her palms. She could imagine bringing a group of people here, talking about the history of the festival, drinking *limonada* and eating a picnic made from local food, and giving everyone a chance to chat and bond. She felt sure this part of the itinerary, unlike the fountain, would be a winner.

"Maybe we could give people the option," she said out loud. "Separate the group into those who want to go to the fountain and those who don't. And we—or whoever—" she added, remembering it wouldn't be her on these trips in the future, "can fill people in on the tradition and the history behind it regardless—and then all meet up here in the park."

Theo grunted in what she thought might be agreement.

Lexie looked around. There were some people—locals, maybe—dressed in the proper traditional garb as they ate lunch. The *chulapos* and *chulapas*—she'd committed it all to memory. Apparently they'd initially been working-class people who were proud of where they came from and wanted to celebrate it with an elaborate style. The men were in trousers, a cap, shirt, and waistcoat—understated, she thought. But the women looked glamorous in their long skirts and shawls, with little bonnet-type things she couldn't remember the name of on their heads. She'd seen some of the traditional outfits for sale as they'd wandered through the streets earlier and had been tempted by a pale blue one—but she knew she'd never wear it.

"This is in my wish jar," she admitted into the quiet between them. "Coming here."

Theo tilted his head to look at her. "To San Isidro?"

"No, not specifically. But to Madrid. My dad took his other family." She frowned at how that sounded. "Rachel and her mum, I mean. He took them to Madrid on holiday. Or they went. Whatever. He said he'd take me too, but he didn't—got cold feet about us all being together, I suppose."

Theo's eyes were still hidden, but she saw the way his brow was furrowed.

"What?" she asked, feeling a little self-conscious.

"Nothing. I just . . . It's weird. The Richard I knew . . . I'm sort of figuring out he wasn't just *that* Richard. He used to talk about you a lot."

Lexie said nothing—though a part of her wanted to know.

"And he would mention memories, of a trip you guys had all taken. He talked about Rachel, too—and I saw him and Rachel together, so that never felt like it was in question. But the way he spoke about you—like he missed you, like he had all these great memories of you . . ."

Lexie pressed her lips together before speaking slowly. "That version of him . . . That's not the version of him I knew. Not for the last fifteen-plus years, anyway. And I know you think it's my fault, for not being around—"

"I'm sorry." He sat up straight. "I never should have implied that. I was still reeling from losing him and I . . ." He gave a shrug that looked a little self-conscious. "I missed him. And I'd only seen Richard's side of it and . . ." He rubbed the back of his neck. "But regardless. I shouldn't have taken it out on you. Richard, he used to talk about you—and I knew he wanted to talk *to* you. I didn't know he was going to leave you half the company."

She raised her eyebrows at that, not really believing him. He'd disliked her from the moment he'd first seen her, after all.

He plowed on, ignoring her reaction. "But it sounded like he thought highly of you, and I guess I just let myself believe that he was a father trying to reach out and you'd always been too busy." He paused for a long moment. "You didn't even know he was sick?" he said quietly.

She risked a quick glance at him, but his face gave nothing away. "No, I didn't."

"Sorry, I don't mean . . . I mean that I assumed you *had* known."

She pursed her lips. "You assumed he'd told me he was dying and I hadn't come home to say goodbye?"

He grimaced. "God, that sounds awful, doesn't it? But yeah. Something like that."

Lexie blew out a breath. "Doesn't paint me in a very good light, does it?"

"I figured it out. After you were around more, I realized I'd been wrong. And I had to . . . recalibrate. Which is totally my fault, not yours." He sighed. "I don't really have an apology that's big enough, but in the aftermath, I was so mad and, I don't know . . ." He waved a hand in the air. "Lost, I guess. He was the first person who seemed to give a shit about me—the me I actually am, I mean—and then he died, and he hadn't told *anyone* how bad it was, not until the last moment. He'd kept it hidden. But despite that, I thought you would have known."

She nodded slowly, trying to process that. An explanation, for how he'd been with her at the beginning.

"And then I saw you leaving the wake early and I . . ."

"You thought I didn't care?" Lexie guessed.

He grimaced. "I jumped to conclusions I shouldn't have. I should have known that families are always more complicated than they seem—that you may have been processing things differently or had your own reasons for leaving."

"Yeah," she murmured quietly. "Maybe you should have." But it helped, to understand why he'd disliked her so much at the beginning. To realize it hadn't really been about *her,* but some perception of her—the idea that she didn't love her father, the way she was starting to realize Theo must have loved him. Maybe she should have allowed for that a little more than she had done. She probably hadn't helped all that much by snapping back all the time.

She hesitated, then said, "I think he tried to tell me. That he was ill. But I wouldn't let him."

"Yeah, maybe. Doesn't put you in the wrong, though."

"Maybe I should have tried harder to be around." She felt like she could say it now, out loud.

Theo opened his mouth, closed it, then shook his head. "Look, I don't know the ins and outs. But I do know what it's like to have a complicated relationship with your parents. And if he wasn't around for you, at the time when you needed him the most, if you didn't think you could rely on him . . . That's a lot. I don't think you can be expected to just turn around and magically move on from that. And looking back, I don't think he expected that, either. He used to hammer home to me that we couldn't change our past—but we could try to do better in the future. I thought he was talking about me, because I'd never stuck with anything before I found the company, but I reckon now he must have been thinking about you. I think in the end, he was just sad, and he knew time was up, and he was full of regret."

To her alarm, Lexie found herself blinking back tears. At the thought of her dad, knowing he was going to die. At the thought of him sitting in the office—the office she now worked in—regretting the past, and feeling sad and alone, because he wouldn't fully confide in anyone. He'd made *her* feel sad and alone a fair amount over the years, even if her mum had always been there to pick up the pieces. But still, it hurt to think about.

"Shit," Theo said, shifting, and raising a hand like he wanted to touch her but wasn't sure where. "Sorry, I shouldn't have said all that. Crap. Please don't cry."

She'd thought she was doing a good job of hiding that, what with her eyes behind her sunglasses, but apparently not good enough.

"It's just . . ." Lexie's voice was thick. "He's gone. He's . . . He's dead." She said the word out loud, and her chest cracked. "And it feels like . . . He hasn't been my dad properly, in so many ways, since he left. I've been so mad about it. But I still remember stuff from before—and stuff from after he left, when he'd show up and he'd be my dad again, you know? And I'm still sad, about losing *that* dad."

She took a shuddering breath. "When I was twenty-one, I had this big party planned. I felt weird about it for some reason—turning twenty-one. Like I should be this adult, but I didn't really feel it, you know?"

Theo just nodded, staying quiet so she could talk.

"Anyway, I'd invited him along. And he'd seemed so happy. I was renting a room at the local pub, and he said he'd bring the cake along—he wanted a job. He was going to pick me and my friend up from my house on the way—my mum had wanted to go early to decorate, and I let her because I thought she might feel weird, being in the same car. It felt like that sometimes, like I had to limit her exposure to him, even if she never said anything. A divorced parents thing, I think. Anyway, he didn't show. I waited thirty minutes after we were supposed to leave and then called Mum. He messaged to apologize the next day but . . . well."

She hugged her knees to her chest. "It's silly," she continued quietly. "We made the party. We didn't have cake, but we made the party. But I was late and flustered, and I ended up crying in the bathroom with Fran that night. And I just decided enough was enough." She looked down at the grass because it was easier than looking at Theo. "But now, I think I'm realizing that I always assumed there would be another chance. Even though that was years ago, I thought maybe there would be a day when I was ready, and then maybe I'd be able to talk to him without feeling angry. So I miss the person he was to me, before he left, before he let me down—but I also . . ." She swallowed, and it was painful. "I also feel guilty, for not letting him tell me he was ill, for not giving him a chance—*us* a chance, to . . ." But she didn't know how to finish that sentence. And her voice, which had been steady the whole time, was now breaking.

"He could have tried harder to tell you," Theo said gently. "If you didn't know, that's not on you. It's because he didn't really want you to know."

The tears were still coming despite her best efforts, silently streaking down her face.

She felt Theo shift, then his arm came around her, a heavy, comforting weight.

"Why are you being nice to me?" she mumbled, her voice hitching on a sob. She felt his arm tighten briefly around her.

"Because there was never a reason not to be. It just took me far too long to realize that."

For some reason, that was enough to break the last hold on herself. She let out another sob and he pulled her toward him, so that she was pressed against his side. She let her head drop onto his shoulder, let his sandalwood scent wrap around her. There were people all around her, enjoying the festivities, and still she could not stop crying.

"I'm sorry," she said between sobs. "I don't know how to . . ."

"You don't have to." His voice was calm, and his hand ran up her side and back down again, soothing.

And there, with Theo's arm around her, Lexie let herself cry for the first time since her dad's funeral. She cried for the man she'd known as a kid, for the loss of that man when he'd left. And she cried for the man who had died in December, for the man she'd now never get the chance to know.

Theo didn't offer any words of comfort—like he knew, somehow, that there would be no right thing to say. Instead he sat there with his arm around her, letting her sob it all out—no judgment, just the offer of silent companionship.

Chapter Nineteen

Slowly, Lexie managed to stem the sobs. And when she did, she became distinctly aware of the fact that she was curled up against Theo, his arm still around her, his T-shirt wet from her tears. She pulled away, and he dropped his arm. She slipped off her sunglasses and brushed away the remaining tears. She didn't want to look right at him, embarrassment at her outburst now curdling in her stomach, along with an awareness of how blotchy and tearstained she must look.

He leaned back onto his palms. "So, one of your wishes was to go to Madrid, huh?"

Lexie laughed, though the sound was a little watery. But it was, in that moment, the best thing he could have done. "Yes," she said. She took a deep breath. Later. She'd figure out her feelings about her dad later. "It was the wish I made the Christmas after he'd taken Rachel here. I think I was more wishing that he hadn't left," she admitted. "Or that he hadn't chosen to take them and not me, or that I wasn't so easy to leave behind." And they, too, were feelings she was still trying to face up to.

"I'm so sorry you had to feel that way," Theo said quietly. "I should have realized there are always two sides to it. I knew your dad felt guilty, but because of what he'd done for me, I just assumed that the guilt was misplaced—or that he was overexaggerating or whatever."

She hugged her knees to her chest. "What did he do for you?"

"Well, he gave me a job, for starters."

She knew that couldn't be the whole story. And actually, she *wanted* to hear the whole story. Not just because she wanted to know Theo better—which she did, she realized—but also because she wanted to know what her dad had been like for them. What he'd done to inspire such loyalty in people like Ange and Theo.

Theo didn't elaborate though. "Can I hear another one of your wishes?" he asked instead.

Lexie tapped her fingers against her knees. "How about we trade again? For every wish I tell you, you answer a question."

"A wish for a truth?" Theo seemed to consider for a moment, then nodded. "OK, that seems fair."

"When I was five, I wished for a hamster. We went to pick him up after Christmas—I called him Fred, and he lived a grand total of two years. But I was heartbroken when he died."

Theo shook his head. "Poor hamsters—they have a bit of a bad lot, don't they?" He looked up at her, waiting for her question.

She thought about it. Decided to start easy. "What's your favorite color?"

He laughed. "Really? You could ask anything and that's what you lead with?"

"You can tell a lot about a person from their favorite color."

"Can you, now?"

"I don't know." She wrinkled her nose. "Probably."

He went quiet, looking out at the park for a moment. "I think it's probably green."

"Green," she mused, like she was reading into it. He laughed again. She liked the sound of his laugh, she realized. This laugh, the one that seemed open and genuine.

"I grew up in Ireland—"

"Hence the Irish accent."

He made a face. "Right. Thought I'd mostly got rid of that."

"Not quite."

"Well. Anyway. I left when I was twenty-two, because I couldn't wait to get away, but living in a city, I still sometimes miss all the green from where I grew up." It was more than she'd expected him to reveal, and she found herself storing the little nugget away. He helped himself to one of the remaining *rosquillas* and gave her an expectant look.

"When I was fifteen, I wished that this boy, Mike Freeman, would decide he fancied me. I was totally in love with him." She took a sip of her *limonada,* and though it had warmed a little in the sun it was still delicious.

"Did it work?"

"Well, he asked me out. But only after he'd been out with and dumped three other girls that year."

"Ah. So not a catch?"

"No. Although he is now happily married with three kids, or so I hear—so maybe his player days are behind him." She put down her *limonada*. "How did you get that scar?" She reached out, nearly brushed her fingertips over it, then thought better of it and pulled her hand away.

He grinned. It wasn't the cocky grin she'd seen on him before, but one that seemed more fun. "People always have theories about the scar. Bar fight. Attack in the street. I once told a girl I got it in a snowboarding accident at the Snowboard World Cup."

"Did she fall for it?"

His grin turned sly in a way that said it all, and she laughed.

"So? If you didn't get it from snowboarding or fighting?"

"It's actually totally ridiculous."

"Now I *really* want to know."

"I was about eleven, I think. Mum was trying to teach me how to cook—she was very insistent that I had a rounded education, and even then she wasn't super-impressed with my grades, so she was on a bit of a mission to help me find my calling, so to speak. Anyway, she left me alone chopping onions for a bit, and they started to sting my eyes and I, like, reached up to rub them or something and sort of . . . forgot I was holding a really fucking sharp knife."

"Oh my god, Theo! You could have taken your eye out."

"So I've been told, many times."

"Your mum must have been so scared."

There was the tiniest beat of hesitation before he said, "Yeah. She was. Your turn."

"When I was six, I wished for a new bike. That one *did* come true, but only because I not-so-subtly told my parents what the wish was."

"Is that why you do it? Because you want to believe the wishes will come true?"

She rolled her eyes. "Maybe when I was like five." She didn't want to go into how much she'd believed in the magic of it once—they might have been opening up a little, but that was a step too far. "I know you think I'm stupid, but there are limits."

"I never said you were stupid. And I definitely don't think that. I guess I'm just trying to work it out—the whole wish jar thing. You seem so . . ." He gestured around into the park.

"Green?"

"*Green?*"

"You're gesturing at the grass. Though if green is your favorite color, maybe I should take that as a compliment?"

"Right. Well, I'm not, I was gesturing into space, for emphasis."

"I seem so . . . spacey?"

He made a sound that was a cross between a choke and a laugh. "So . . . I don't know. Real."

"Yes, I've often been complimented on my realness. Those poor imaginary people out there, never having any validation."

"What I mean is, you don't, like, often reference star charts or horoscopes or anything. I had a girlfriend once who was obsessed with horoscopes—to the extent that she broke up with me because her horoscope told her that she was about to meet the man of her dreams, and she took that to mean she had to get rid of me first so she was ready for him."

Lexie laughed, feeling lighter, then pressed her lips together. "Sorry. That's not funny."

"It's a bit funny now. Felt a bit harsh at the time. But wishes—don't they fit into that category? Sort of, you know, wishing something would come true instead of . . ."

"Working for it?"

"Something like that. Not that *you* . . . I just mean, that's the thing. You seem to go after stuff. You're always off—"

"Waiting on posh people in the Alps and having a frivolous time skiing?"

A wince. "Another thing I shouldn't have said. I don't always think things through before I speak."

And for now, she decided to let him off the hook. "So what you're saying is . . . You're not the wishing type?"

"My mum was big into wishes. Like wishing I would do better in school, wishing I would get a different job, wishing I would propose to my 'aspirational' girlfriend." He sighed. "Just generally wishing I was different. I guess you could say it put me off a bit."

So maybe that partly explained why he always came back from Ireland in a bad mood, then. She couldn't think of what to say in reply—but she knew what it was like, to think you weren't enough. So she kept it light and said the thing she'd want to hear. "I think you turned out OK. When you're not being all argumentative and annoying."

He laughed, which was what she'd been aiming for. And she realized she liked that she was able to make him laugh.

"I mean, you stuck with the company, didn't you? So maybe you were just waiting for the right thing to come along. Not everyone has to immediately find their feet and get all grown up and sorted."

"Yeah. I guess. Though I only really stuck with the company because Richard made me." He pushed up off the grass, took his sunglasses off as he looked at her, and asked her a question before she could push him on that. "What would you wish for now?"

"Honestly?" A beat. "I don't know. I didn't make one this past Christmas. After he died . . ." She took a sharp breath. "I thought of a few wishes, when I found out what he'd left me."

"I'll bet."

"But I couldn't think of the right one. And even though I don't put them in there because I believe they'll come true . . ." She hesitated. "It's sort of like I'm setting them free. Like, by putting a wish in the jar, I won't wish for it anymore. And I didn't know what I wanted that thing to be."

He looked at her for a long moment before saying, "You get one more question. For the last non-wish."

There were lots of questions that were probably way more interesting, important ones. But she couldn't help saying, "You said you had a girlfriend who was into horoscopes." He raised his eyebrows and she was surprised he couldn't see where this was going. "Do you . . . I mean, are you with anyone now?"

The eyebrows shot up farther, but he simply said, "No." He stood up. "Come on, we'd better go."

He held out a hand, pulled her to her feet. But he didn't let go once she was standing and every part of her hummed at the point of contact.

"Lex?" His thumb brushed, ever so gently, over hers. "Just so you know, if I was with anyone, I wouldn't have kissed you in February." It was the first time either of them had explicitly mentioned the kiss, and it made the back of her neck grow hot at the same time as something pulled, low in her stomach.

"OK." Somehow now all she could focus on was the curve of his mouth, but she managed to get out, "Noted."

He gave her a wry smile, acknowledging she was repeating his own word back to him. And as they turned together to walk out of the park, instead of dropping her hand, he kept hold of it, lacing his fingers with hers.

Chapter Twenty

Daytime in Madrid during the Fiesta was one thing—but nighttime was a whole new level, where the party atmosphere hung in the air, so that it felt impossible not to feel the buzzing under your skin. There were a few places to enjoy the evening festivities, but they'd settled on Las Vistillas. It was a big garden with a huge fountain in the center of it. Some people were sitting on the edge of it, sipping their drinks and chatting, others out on the grass, but the majority were congregated around the pop-up stage at the end of a concrete path, where there were various pop-up bars and food stalls. They'd been here in time for sunset, had watched the low pink-and-orange glow filter through the grass, but evening had set in now, and the two of them were sitting at a table near the stage, drinking what was left of their sangria. They'd hunted down tapas for dinner—something that would have to be on the itinerary for guests—and Lexie had decided Rachel had been right about the *patatas bravas*, the Spanish restaurants she'd been to in the UK just couldn't quite match the food she'd had out here.

Earlier, there had been traditional dancing onstage—the *chotis,* a far cry from the salsa Mike had imagined, where it seemed to Lexie that the men mainly stood still while the women moved around them—but now the music had shifted into something more modern and sensual, and the whole place was alive with celebration as people danced all around the garden.

There weren't all that many tables to sit at, and Lexie and Theo were bunched next to another couple, who kept awkwardly leaning over to kiss in a very public display of affection. Given the lack of space, Theo's knee kept bumping hers under the table, sending heat shooting up Lexie's thigh each time it happened, in a way that made it hard to think straight. The band playing up on stage was a useful distraction, and she kept making a show of watching them during the pauses in conversation. She'd had a message from Fran earlier in the evening, asking whether she was coping with Theo and telling her that her latest date had gone terribly wrong because the man in question had kept trying to touch her thigh under the table after about five minutes of knowing each other. Lexie had then proceeded to imagine Theo's hand on *her* thigh under the table, and so when she'd replied saying she was just about coping, it had felt like a lie.

The Spanish couple next to them leaned across the table to kiss each other again, apparently oblivious to how close to them Theo and Lexie were sitting.

"When I was sixteen," Theo said loudly, as if to make it obvious to the couple that they were not alone, "I got a tattoo on my back. I thought about getting it removed but it seemed like too much hassle and money, so it's still there."

"You have a tattoo? What of?"

"Nothing, really. It's basically just a black squiggle."

Lexie grinned. "You make it sound so macho."

"It's really not. It was a decision sixteen-year-old me made and although I don't spend much time looking at my back, so can't be sure, I'm pretty sure the guy made it uneven when it's not supposed to be—which I suppose is what you'd expect from a dodgy tattoo shop that didn't bother to ask how old I was."

Lexie laughed. "Will you show me?" She immediately regretted it. If it was on his back, he'd have to be at least semi-naked for her to see it, and seeing him semi-naked would not be a good idea. *Picturing* him semi-naked was not a good idea either. *Stop it, Lexie.*

He cocked one eyebrow in that way of his. "Maybe one day."

She cleared her throat, tried to brush past the moment. "Did your parents find out?"

"Yeah. My mum went mental, but that was sort of the reason I did it, so mission accomplished. I think my dad just sighed and went back to reading the paper." He gave her a meaningful look. Right—a truth for a wish. She could feel his eyes on her, even as she looked to the band—her safety net. And right now, she was wishing her body didn't react like this to him, wishing the music and the sangria and the evening shadows weren't getting to her so much.

"Ah . . ." She glanced back at him, shifted enough that their knees brushed under the table. An accident. Mostly. His eyes turned heavy on her, enough to make heat gather between her thighs. She cleared her throat and uncrossed then recrossed her legs. He followed the movement, and his glass of sangria paused, resting on his bottom lip for a second before he took a sip. She wished she didn't remember what that lip tasted like. Wished she didn't wonder if it would be the same if she kissed him again.

"Would you like a dance, mi amor?"

Lexie started and looked up into the face of an attractive Spanish man who had approached their table without her noticing. He was clean-shaven and had a mess of dark hair, and his eyes sparkled as he smiled at her, his hand out in a question. She nearly declined. Then she glanced at Theo again, who was watching her a little too carefully, and decided that, actually, a dance with a random Spanish man sounded like a great way to get a little space from Theo so she could get control of herself. So she put her hand in his and let him pull her into the throng of people, all dancing under the stage.

The music thrummed under her skin, and though she wasn't a hugely talented dancer, she could move well enough, and she caught the rhythm easily as the man put his hands to her waist, guiding her through the steps. She closed her eyes for a beat. She'd forgotten how much she loved to dance, just for the hell of it. The man twirled her under his arm, twice in quick succession, and she let out a laugh. The night air was cool, but it was hot enough with all the bodies pressed close together that she could feel sweat dampen her back.

"You are beautiful, mi amor," the man said, in what was clearly supposed to be a low, seductive tone.

She laughed to cover up the slight awkwardness she felt. "Thank you." She hadn't had a chance to change today—the days here had been very full-on, trying to fit in as much as possible, and her strappy dress felt less suited to a nighttime of dancing than it had to a picnic in the park. Her skin felt warm and tight, a warning that she'd been out in the sun for too long, and her hair was messed up in a way that was definitely on the "dragged through a hedge" rather than the "beachy" side of the scale.

His hands traveled up her sides, back down again, in a way that felt a little too intimate. She pulled away slightly and he got the message, kept them on her waist as they moved to the beat. It was definitely a salsa vibe, though the music added a modern spin on the traditional, so that it felt a little wilder. She glanced over to the table where Theo was still sitting, saw him scowling at the man dancing with her. She felt herself flush and looked away before he caught her eye. Was he *jealous*? But she was allowed to dance with someone else, wasn't she? They were just colleagues—colleagues who had barely even tolerated each other until recently. And OK, fine, they'd ended up having a nice afternoon in the park, but all they'd ever done was kiss—once—in a moment where they had mixed up hatred with lust. And he'd held her hand this afternoon as they'd walked—but just in comfort, because she'd cried about her dad, and he felt sorry for her. Right?

But despite the way she tried to reason it out, to convince herself that the heat now licking at her insides was only because she felt embarrassed—or guilty for leaving him at a table alone—she couldn't quite hide behind it. Because she knew that somewhere over the last few days she'd fallen into liking him—even if she wasn't sure she wanted to. And she also knew that if *he* was up here dancing with someone else, she'd feel . . . well, a bit like the way he looked, scowling over at them. She'd probably have stalked off, leaving the party altogether, or else found someone of her own just to show she didn't care and—

"Mind if I cut in?"

Lexie jumped, moving out of the Spanish man's hold as she did so, at the sound of Theo's voice behind her. Her breath whooshed out—partly in surprise, and partly in relief, that he hadn't gone off to find some other girl, like in the scenario her overactive imagination had been playing to her.

He took Lexie's hand and gave the Spanish man a one-eyebrow look that clearly told him to sod off. The man looked for a second like he might say something, but maybe her earlier protest at him getting a touch too grabby had made him decide he wasn't going to get what he wanted from her, so he gave a shrug and headed into the crowd to find someone else.

Lexie felt a rush of indignation at being moved from man to man like she was a *thing* to claim. She pulled back from Theo, shoving at his chest. His hands moved to lightly rest on her waist, not keeping her there, just barely touching.

"What are you doing? What if I wanted to—?"

But his hands slid down her waist to her hips, his fingers curling there, and her skin heated. And really, who was she kidding? Because being this close to him, even surrounded by other people, she knew there was no point in trying to lie about it—to him or to herself. She might not really have understood why, but it was *his* hands she wanted on her right now.

"Wanted to what?" he asked.

She swallowed. "Nothing. Forget it."

"Gladly," he said, his voice low, on the edge of a growl. He started moving, pulling her with him into the beat. Her hands went to rest on his shoulders, and she told herself firmly to keep them there.

She cleared her throat, trying to ease some of the tension between them. "When I was twenty-one, I wished for a 2:1 in my course at university. I was studying biology, which in hindsight was a terrible idea—I'm really not good at it."

His eyes stayed level on hers, and the corner of his mouth crooked up. "And?"

"I got a 2:2."

"Better than me—I didn't even go to university. As my parents like to remind me on a regular basis." He looked at her expectantly—she was supposed to ask a question.

She searched his face briefly before asking. "Why do you care so much about the company? Why . . . What was the deal with you and my dad?"

He didn't falter as they kept in time to the music, but she saw his brow pull together. "Your dad . . ." He glanced down at her, like he was figuring out how much to say—or what would upset her to hear. "So, you know how I called you flighty?"

"I vaguely remember the implication, yes."

"Yeah, well. The thing is, I jumped to that conclusion because *I* was like that. After I left Ireland, I moved around a lot. I couldn't settle and I went through a phase of fucking everything up. What you do, moving around . . . It's something that clearly *works* for you, and that's what I didn't get. But for me . . ."

His eyes weren't focused on her anymore, so she could look at his face freely, watching the expressions play out there.

"I tried so hard, to be what my parents wanted—and then, because it never worked, I suppose I tried to be the opposite. It might be a cliché, but it's true. Bounced around a lot, didn't try too hard because I didn't want to fail."

She wanted to ask more—about why he wasn't what his parents wanted, about what he'd done while he bounced around. But she also didn't want to interrupt, in case he stopped talking.

"I got the job with Richard through coincidence, really—saw an advert for a junior position at a travel company, thought, hey, that sounds like fun for a bit. He took a chance on me—and I think I've already said that Ange may have had something to do with that. But I hit a snag early on, screwed something up. Funny thing is, I don't even remember *what* I screwed up. But it was enough that I tried to quit—you know, get out before you get fired. Before I failed. But Richard wouldn't let me. Just kept refusing to let me leave—and instead he spent time with me, teaching me stuff, not getting worried if I got things wrong. It was the first time anyone had ever done that. And because I stuck at it, I got better at it. So Richard, he made me feel like I was good at something. He listened when I talked, too, and made me feel like my ideas were, you know, valuable." He shrugged like it was no big deal, and she could sense some embarrassment there, at admitting all this. "And now, I think the company is cool, and I want to carry it on for him. He loved what he did, and it was something he poured everything into—and when he died, I didn't like the idea of that being lost."

Lexie went quiet, thinking, as the music changed, slowed. She tried to imagine it. The man who had left her, who had let her down repeatedly—this was also someone who had helped Theo, who had made him feel a little less lost. And that was why he'd hated the idea of sharing the company with her in the first place, wasn't it? Because he'd wanted to keep the legacy alive, and she'd wanted nothing to do with it.

"Why? Why do you think he didn't let you give up?"

He shrugged again rather than answering.

"He didn't tell you?"

"I never asked." He hesitated, and it was like he knew she needed more than that. "I was with him when he found that restaurant in Menton—you know, the one we ate at during the Lemon Festival." Lexie nodded, remembering. "He admired those guys so much, because they just weren't giving up. It was something he talked about a lot—but I think maybe that was the first time it really hit home for me. He used to say that you could never do everything perfectly, but that if you at least tried, you'd have less to regret in the long run."

"I've never really thought of him as a 'trying' or 'sticking with it' kind of guy. What with, you know. Everything."

He nodded slowly. "Maybe that's why, though. Maybe he was so determined to stick with the company—and to help *me* stick with it—because he didn't want to repeat his mistakes of the past."

"Maybe," she said, hedging. And maybe she'd never know for sure. Maybe there were a lot of things that she'd never have answers to, about why her dad had done what he did over the years. She bit her lip as she glanced at Theo, thinking about what he'd said. *I think the company is cool, and I want to carry it on.* Something pulled at her. Because they might have put that conversation on hold, but at some point it was going to come back around to bite them.

Then he slid his hand up her back, fingers grazing the exposed skin above her dress—and she decided not to think of that. Not right now.

"When I was fourteen," she said, "I wished for dance lessons. I was going through a phase of thinking I would be a dancer when I grew up—even though I'd never taken ballet as a kid or anything. I was imagining some kind of dancing like *Step Up* or *Save the Last Dance*. They're films," she added when he looked at her blankly. "I think I thought I'd be cast in a film and play this cool, tormented soul who lived to dance. My school didn't have dance lessons, and I'd found this academy thing. Mum couldn't afford the lessons—seriously, way too expensive. But I thought I might get a scholarship. For the space of about two weeks I was weirdly confident I'd get in, before the auditions."

"I'm guessing you didn't get in?"

"No—I was about as good at dancing as I was at biology."

He spun her around, brought her back to him and drew her a little closer than they had been before. He managed to do it so easily, she couldn't help wondering if *he'd* ever had dance lessons. "You seem like you can dance OK to me," he said, and his mouth was close enough that his breath caressed her ear.

Her insides seemed to shimmer at the sound of his voice, but she forced herself to keep it easy. To keep pretending. "That's because you are weirdly good at this."

He grinned, then skimmed his hands down her sides. "Would you tell *me* a wish?" she asked. "What would you wish for—if you were the type to make wishes?"

He let out a low laugh. "I don't think you want to know what I'd wish for right now, Lexie."

She bit her lip, felt a flare of satisfaction as his attention zeroed in on it. "What if I do?" What if she wanted to give in to it, stop pretending?

His eyes darkened, and something pulled low in her stomach.

He said nothing, but his right hand skimmed down her spine, the other coming to her hip. Her hands moved to his neck, and she saw his pulse jump at the base of his throat as his gaze dropped to her mouth. They were so close, breathing the same air—close enough that his nose skated down hers as he shifted his head. Her heart was hammering hard enough that she was surprised they couldn't hear it over the music. They'd slowed out of time now, moving in their own rhythm as her hands traveled over his shoulders, down his muscled back. His fingers at her hip dug in, and the hand on her spine flattened, pressing her against him. They were both breathing heavily now, their lips separated by less than an inch, the air buzzing in the space between them. She moved her hands to his stomach, spread her fingers there, and he shuddered a little, moving his own hands lower behind her. There were people all around them, dancing, but she didn't care. She couldn't think outside the two of them, couldn't do anything but stare at him as she remembered what he'd tasted like last time. As she wondered what it would be like to have *more*.

Then it started to rain. The heavens literally opened, seemingly without warning, and though it might have been warm in the daytime here, there was a chill in the evening air, and the water was cold, a shock to the system. Like the world was reminding her to cool the hell off and take a goddamn shower.

Chapter Twenty-one

Lexie let out a little scream as the rain hit her head, and most of the people around her did the same. Theo grabbed her hand and pulled her out of the crowd, toward the cover of the nearest tree. Only, other people had had the same idea—leaving nowhere to shelter. They looked at each other through the rain. Theo was grinning, and he looked so bloody cute in that moment that Lexie couldn't help laughing. Onstage, the band was still playing, employing a definite *fuck it* attitude—though that was helped by the fact that the stage was sheltered. Some other people were carrying on dancing, and the music grew more vibrant, feet stomping as people laughed and jumped in the rain.

"Think we're going to have to make a run for it!" Theo shouted, above all the noise around them.

Lexie hesitated. A part of her wanted to get drawn back in, to dance in the rain. But it was getting colder, and she could feel her damp dress clinging to her skin. So she nodded.

When they made it back to the apartment they were both drenched and breathless from the run. Theo got the door open and they stumbled in, Lexie laughing in a way that only made her breathing heavier. Theo looked at her and grinned at her in a way that let her know she looked like a drowned rat. She shrugged out of her jean jacket and hung it up on the coatrack to dry, then reached up to wring out her curls.

They'd rented an Airbnb as it had been cheaper than a hotel:

they had found a good deal in the city center, near the Plaza Mayor—though they'd spent some time checking out local hotels where their future clients would stay. Still, the apartment was gorgeous—proper wooden floors all the way through, a bright and airy open-plan living and dining room, which led onto a balcony so you could crack the doors wide open as you had a coffee first thing in the morning. There were houseplants dotted around, with a beautiful big fern right next to the comfy white sofa. The two bedrooms were both a decent size, with a separate bathroom down the corridor, so there had been no competition as to who got which room. The apartment was plenty big enough for both of them and they'd coexisted well enough for the two days they'd been here, only really using it for breakfast and to sleep. But right then, when Theo shut the door behind him, Lexie was suddenly very aware that it was just the two of them here, completely alone.

"Do you want first shower?" Theo asked, stripping off his jacket and revealing a wet T-shirt clinging to his skin.

"Sure. Thanks."

But neither of them moved, still just inside the doorway.

"I'll, er, let you know when I'm done," she said.

"OK." His eyes were too intense on hers, making her face heat. She made herself take a steadying breath. She might have decided he wasn't as bad as she first thought and she might be attracted to him, but they still had to work together, and they still wanted different things from the company in the long term. They were still, ultimately, on different sides.

Averting her gaze, she made to move past him, but he grabbed her hand. "Lexie . . ."

She looked up at him. They stayed like that for a moment—like he was waiting for something. Her pulse picked up speed and although she knew she should feel cold, heat flared through her. She didn't pull away—but she didn't move toward him either.

He blew out a long breath, dropped her hand. "Never mind."

Bad idea, bad idea, bad idea. Then, "Screw it." She reached up, pulled his head down to hers—and kissed him.

Theo grabbed her waist, pulled her closer and kissed her back in a way that made her breath catch. "Thank fuck for that," he said, his words murmured against the line of her jaw. He kissed his way down her neck, and Lexie closed her eyes, grabbing his shoulders and holding on. Outside, she heard a rumble of thunder—a warning, one she chose to ignore. Their chests were pressed together, their wet clothes sticking together, and a current of electricity pulsed between them. His hands traveled over her waist to her hips and she ran her hands down the muscles of his back, wishing she could reach farther, trying to tug him even closer.

"You actually want this?" Lexie managed to get out, her voice catching as his teeth lightly scraped against her neck.

"Is that a trick question?"

"Last time we kissed you shoved me inside my room afterward to get me away from you."

He laughed, low and dark-sounding, and her stomach flipped. "Lexie, I was about a second away from tearing off your clothes in the goddamn corridor. Getting you away from me seemed like the safest thing to do."

God, she knew that feeling, and a thrill ran through her that it wasn't one-sided. His mouth caught hers again roughly while his fingers ran up her thighs, bunching her dress at her waist. She moved her hands around him, up under his shirt, and felt him shudder slightly at the feeling of her fingers against his stomach.

"And in case you don't remember," he continued, his mouth quirking up at one side, "it was *you* who said we shouldn't."

He started walking her backward, his eyes level on hers the whole time. The backs of her knees brushed the edge of the sofa, just as he turned her and pulled her down so she was sitting on top of him, her thighs straddling his. His hands skimmed up under her dress, his thumbs catching on the curves of her hips, and she saw his breath stutter, felt her own do the same. She ran her hands up under his T-shirt, then helped him tug it off.

"Wouldn't want you to catch a cold," she said, and was answered with a grin.

"Could say the same about you," he said, his hands running up under her dress. She bent toward him to kiss him again, felt his fingers dig into her thighs. Then he flipped her in one smooth motion so she was lying back on the sofa, and half a laugh escaped her before he was there on top of her and the pressure of it made her let out a soft groan. His teeth skated lightly down her neck, and she let out a low hum of pleasure. His hands came up to push the straps of her dress down, and he pressed his lips against her bare shoulder. She could feel his erection digging into her and her hips moved of their own accord, demanding some kind of friction. His breath hissed out between his teeth.

"Theo." His name was half a plea and his mouth came back to hers, teeth catching her bottom lip, making her arc against him. Her nails were in his back, urging him closer, and his hands skimmed between her thighs, where she was desperate for him to touch.

But somewhere inside her, there was some logic breaking through. *It was you who said we shouldn't.* She had. She'd said that. And there was a reason for that, she was sure.

She just about managed to get out the "Wait," even as her

hips rolled against his. He backed away, pushing himself up on his hands on the sofa and looking down at her. Her thighs were still around his waist, holding him there, at odds with her words.

"You don't want this?"

"No, I do." She swallowed. "I really do."

His brow furrowed.

"It's just . . . This is . . ." She had to close her eyes to get it out. "Maybe it's not a good idea."

"Seems like a great idea to me right now." He kissed the nape of her neck again and a shiver ran down her back, her mind getting stuck for a moment.

"Seriously," she managed to say, her voice more of a gasp than anything else. "We work together."

"Yes."

"And we have to . . . We're going to have to figure out what to do, at the end of the year."

He looked at her for a long moment, both of them holding themselves still, their breathing slowing a little. And right then, she hated herself. Why did she have to bring it up? *Now,* of all times?

"I just . . . I don't want it to be awkward. I want to be clear that it's . . . that it's a one-time thing." She felt hot around her collarbone for saying it, was briefly pleased that she was still half covered, less exposed—especially given the way he was looking at her right now. Maybe she hadn't needed to say that—maybe that had already been a given for him.

"A one-time thing?" She could feel his erection, still pressing against her, and felt her confidence grow as she lifted her hips to press against him and was rewarded by a sharp intake of breath.

"Yes. What happens in Madrid stays in Madrid." She ran her hands down his bare back again, reached up to kiss him.

He kissed her back, but it was softer than before. His mouth skimmed over the corner of her mouth, his warm breath moving to her shoulder, then to where her pulse was hammering in her throat.

"Fuck," he hissed, his hands briefly tightening their hold on her thighs. "I'm so going to regret this, but . . ."

It was her turn to frown at him, as she brought her hands to rest on his neck.

"I think you're right. I think we should stop."

"What? Why?"

"Because I can literally see you overthinking it."

"Trust me, the way this is going, soon I won't be thinking at all."

A smile pulled at his mouth. "As much as that does my ego a world of good, I don't want you regretting this in the morning."

She opened her mouth to protest, to say again that they could just have tonight—it would be easier, surely, to get all this tension out of the way so that they could move past it.

But he kissed her briefly to stop her from speaking. "When I'm inside you," he said, his voice low, "I want to be sure you want it, just as much as I do." Her insides went liquid and taut, all at the same time. "And if you're already stressing about what happens after, it's not going to be *nearly* as fun as it could be." Then he straightened so his hips were no longer trapped between her thighs.

Her whole body registered the lack of warmth, but she didn't immediately move, and his gaze traveled over her, all of her cells vibrating under it.

"Fuck," he said, and when he bent toward her, she thought he'd caved, that she'd won the silent standoff. But all he did was kiss her cheek. "Good night, Lex."

He stood, and she sat up, pulling the straps of her dress back into place, feeling self-consciousness return. He grabbed his wet T-shirt off the floor, and she caught sight of the tattoo at the top of his back, between his shoulders. Two thick black lines, curving together like antlers. He'd been right—it *was* slightly uneven. But it was also stupidly sexy.

He glanced over his shoulder as he walked away. "I'm taking first shower." Then he left her there, and she heard the click of the bathroom door. And even though it had been *Lexie* who had started the conversation, who had been the one to say it might not be a good idea, she couldn't help but feel the sting of rejection as she headed for her bedroom—and made sure she heard his own bedroom door shut before she ventured outside again.

Chapter Twenty-two

Lexie spent the next few weeks in the office trying to put what had happened in Spain behind her. Trying to pretend that every time she looked at Theo across the room, she didn't remember what it had been like to have him pressed against her, on top of her. And she'd been busy—they'd all been busy, with a lot of customer inquiries, finalizing the plans for the Christmas trip in Vienna, thinking about new ideas for next year's Lemon Festival in France, as well as getting ready for the summer and autumn trips. She had to focus, make sure she pulled her weight.

She was sitting at the desk in the front office and was in the process of inquiring about room availability and a possible group discount at a boutique hotel in Madrid that they'd short-listed for next year, when her phone buzzed on the desk next to her.

Fran.

How's it going?

She'd told Fran what had happened in Madrid, and how she was sure kissing him had been a stupid thing to do. And the last two weeks had been a test, waiting to see if anything would be mentioned, trying to figure out if it shifted the balance between them at all—and she'd needed someone to talk to about that.

> I'm maintaining my impeccable air
> of professionalism.

She got a line of strong arm emojis back, followed by

> I'm going to be late back AGAIN tonight. But if
> you're still up can we have a wine? My client didn't
> get the custody settlement he wanted, my head
> hurts with the stress of it, and I'm so sick of my
> office, I'm thinking I might need to redecorate.

> That sucks, I'm sorry.

> The head—yes. The office—I'm not sure I'm actually
> allowed to redecorate, so that also sucks. But the
> client, not so much. I'm pretty sure he was a bit of
> a dick.

> Well I'm all up for wine. But thought you
> had a date tonight?

> He canceled. Still in love with his ex-girlfriend.

Lexie shook her head at her phone as she switched the screen off. She didn't really get why Fran couldn't find someone, given how she put herself out there. She was—objectively speaking—pretty damn great. In a perfect world, there would be a nice, handsome, kind man she could set Fran up with from her office. But the only single and age-appropriate man was Theo. Theo, who was currently heading across the office and toward the back door, having just come in from the street with Mike. Their heads were bent together, Theo nodding along to something Mike was saying. He caught her eye, smiled briefly, and she immediately flicked her gaze away, back to the computer screen.

It had been a one-time thing, that was all. Or a no-time thing, depending on how you looked at it. But she still felt rejected. He'd wanted her—she'd felt that. Yet he'd walked away. And she didn't quite know what to do with that.

Mike and Theo were through the back door and Lexie could hear their footsteps as they headed up to Theo's flat. It made the second time in one week she'd seen the two of them having some sort of private meeting.

Ange came out from her back office, carrying a cup of tea for Lexie.

Lexie smiled up at her. "It's not your job to bring me tea."

Ange waved that away, and her dangly earrings—dragonflies today—swayed with the movement. "We all bring each other tea."

Lexie took a sip. Somehow, Ange always got tea to be the perfect temperature, right from the outset. "What are Theo and Mike talking about, do you think?"

Ange leaned again her desk. "Nothing Theo can't handle, I'm sure."

"So you're saying there is something to handle?"

Ange looked at her, those pale green eyes assessing her. "Has Theo told you anything about Mike?"

"Only that he and my dad had a 'complicated' relationship. But they were friends, right? That's what Mike said."

"Yes, they were friends. Mike was actually the one to give your dad the loan to start the company."

Lexie set her tea down. "What, really?"

"Not all of it. But business loans aren't easy—and your dad didn't have a lot of savings."

Lexie didn't even know what he'd done before the company. Something in sales—she remembered that vaguely, and it was the line she'd parroted whenever she was asked what he did.

"From what I gather," Ange continued, "and bear in mind this is all secondhand information, Mike and your dad started spending more time together after Richard moved to Bath."

Just after he'd left Rachel's mum, Lexie thought. After he'd abandoned another family.

"Anyway, Mike wanted a new venture, offered your dad some money, and your dad took the loan."

Lexie tried to get her head around this. "But it was never co-owned?"

"Well. Mike owned ten percent up until about two years ago, but he sold the shares back to your dad then, so Richard owned the whole thing."

"Why? Why did he sell his shares, I mean?"

"Well, the travel industry wasn't doing too well then because of Covid, so I think Mike thought it might go bust—probably seemed like the right time to get out, get the money back."

"But my dad didn't think it would go bust?"

"Or hoped, at least," Ange said, with a little smile.

It explained why there had been the subtle undercurrent with Mike, the sense that he wasn't entirely happy with how things were currently panning out. He'd put down money on the company, helped start it. And now he had nothing—just a job on a very average salary. Though, to be fair, he didn't actually seem to *do* a lot for that salary. "Why didn't Richard leave the company to Mike? In part, at least?"

Ange tapped her fingers on Lexie's desk. "Mike . . . Look, I've got nothing against the guy. But he checked out when it looked like things were going badly. He wants back in now, of course, but if it got tough, he'd be out again without a thought. Theo, on the other hand, worked every hour there was, even when his salary was cut. He and your dad were brilliant, refusing to give up even when it was impossible to carry on business as usual as a travel company. When things were starting to open back up again, they started up trips in England first, before the travel restrictions were lifted—were one of the first travel companies to do so. They worked within the rules, figured out how to make people feel safe. So it made sense to me when I found out that Richard had left Theo half the company—even if I'm not sure it has always made sense to Theo."

Lexie frowned a bit at that. She'd never questioned whether Theo thought he deserved his share of the company—or maybe even more than that. But Ange was carrying on now.

"But there's a reason he didn't leave it wholly to Theo—or even to Mike and Theo." She hesitated, then smiled in that kind way of hers. "I know you're unlikely to believe me when I tell you this, but I think the company was always partly yours, in his head—right from the beginning."

Lexie shook her head. "That doesn't make any sense."

"No? The company was built for people who love to travel. For people who crave adventure, who want to get to know a place through celebrating there. Are you really telling me that doesn't remind you of anyone?"

Lexie said nothing. She thought of how she had inadvertently grown up to keep the tradition of spending Christmas abroad, because it never felt right to spend it at home. She thought of Iceland again, and of how she'd felt like her dad had turned their family tradition of spending Christmas somewhere new each year into something that made money. But now, know-ing the company better, she also knew that he likely could have made a lot more money if he hadn't focused on supporting local businesses. It was just another thing she couldn't quite work out about her dad.

Ange gave her another smile, and there was a tinge of sadness there now. "I'm not saying your dad was perfect. Far from it—if my son ever treated his children the way Richard treated you, I don't know what I would do. But people are rarely black and white, are they?"

THEO CAME BACK downstairs around lunchtime and headed straight over to Lexie's desk. "Hey."

She offered him what she thought was a polite smile. "Hey."

"You eaten yet?"

"No, why, is there a meeting?"

"Sort of. Come on." He jerked his head to get her to follow him, then headed for the front door onto the street.

"What . . . ?"

"We're going for lunch," Theo said, holding the door open for her.

"Um . . ."

"Come on," he insisted, waggling the door a little for empha-sis. "Ange?" Lexie followed the direction of Theo's gaze to see Ange emerging from the back room. "I'm taking Lexie out for lunch to discuss a few things."

"No need to explain, you don't answer to me. I'm off early today to pick Ivy up from nursery, but have a lovely lunch."

And that, apparently, was that. Lexie got to her feet and slid out the front door, careful not to brush against Theo as she did so. It was warm outside, a sunny June day, and Bath's golden buildings shone more brightly as a result. It was early enough in the summer that it was still a luxury to step outside in her long skirt and sleeveless blouse without needing a jacket.

She glanced up at Theo. "Is no one else coming?"

"Nope. Just the two of us." He started walking purposefully, and after the briefest of hesitations, she matched his pace.

"Why?"

"Because you've been awkward and weird since we got back from Madrid."

"No, I haven't!" Lexie exclaimed automatically. He raised his eyebrows and she wrinkled her nose, embarrassment heating her cheeks. "Fine, maybe a little. I don't *usually* get awkward and weird."

"So why did you?"

Lexie pressed her lips together, not sure what to say. She didn't really *know* why. She'd had plenty of flings in the past. She supposed the difference was they'd actually *been* flings and usually she was the one to walk away, before they could decide they were done with her.

His lips twitched, something apparently funny in her non-answer. "Besides, we do actually need to run through some things—why not do it over food?"

He led her to an independent café on Margaret's Buildings, a little street that was known for its local shops and restaurants, situated in a hot spot between the Circus and the Royal Crescent. They grabbed a table outside on the paving stones, Theo slipping his sunglasses on and Lexie wishing she'd remembered hers. The café itself was bright green, with paper chains hanging in the window, and had that kind of intimate feel that could never be replicated in a chain restaurant. The outside tables were buzzing and Lexie could see a table of four women, all with Aperol Spritzes, making the most of the early English sun. Given she had to get through an entire hour with just Theo, she was quite tempted by an Aperol herself, but opted for an iced latte instead.

While the waiter was getting their drinks, Theo leaned forward, clasping his hands on the table. "So. Just to clear the air—do you want to talk about it?"

"Talk about what?" Lexie asked slowly.

"What happened in Madrid."

"Nothing to talk about, right?" She tried to keep her voice light, even though her stomach was squirming.

"If you say so."

"It was a one-time thing," Lexie insisted, the words coming easily, maybe down to the number of times she'd repeated them to herself.

"OK," Theo said, his voice casual. He thanked the waiter who brought out their drinks, and they ordered their food. It was all locally sourced, and breakfast was served all day, so Lexie opted for the Turkish eggs

She waited for Theo to press her on the subject as the waiter took their menus, and when he didn't, she frowned—it seemed too easy. But if he wasn't going to push, she certainly wasn't. "Saw you talking to Mike," she said.

"Yeah." An expression crossed his face that she couldn't quite read.

"He's not happy?"

"I'm actually not sure, despite his blustering, Mike is ever happy."

"Ange told me he used to own ten percent of the company."

"Yep."

"And now he owns zero percent."

Theo just shrugged, taking a sip of his citrus juice—a specialty of the café, apparently.

"Even though he lent my dad the money to start it."

"Which your dad paid back," Theo said pointedly, just as their food came out.

Lexie added salt to her eggs, took a bite, then immediately wished she'd forgone the salt—they'd gotten the seasoning just right without it. It was still delicious, though, the garlicky yogurt somehow *exactly* the right amount of garlic. Theo's mushrooms on toast looked good too, and Lexie decided she'd bring Fran here on the weekend.

"Does Mike want it?" Lexie asked after swallowing. "Does he want his share back or whatever?"

Theo sighed. "What Mike wants varies from day to day. He'll want in again if the profit projections are good, but out if it looks like too much of a gamble. Speaking of which—it's looking tight, but if Vienna and Belgium sell out, I think we'll make our targets—and we might even have enough to revisit the investment idea, if it's something you're still open to."

"Of course," Lexie said, though she felt a twitchiness settle over her skin. If she got her way and they agreed to sell the company, it wouldn't be her business whether the investment idea went ahead, would it? Wouldn't be Theo's business either—unless he was kept on. Maybe he would be, she told herself. Surely whoever bought it would need a manager to run the whole thing. Lexie dipped her bread into the runny part of the poached eggs to distract herself. "So what do you need from me?"

"Well, I wanted to run an idea past you."

"Really?" The word was out before she could think about it.

He laughed a little. "Don't act so surprised—you told me

yourself not all your ideas are inherently terrible, so maybe you can tell me whether *this* one is terrible."

In France—hadn't she said something like that at the Lemon Festival? She was surprised he'd remembered such a passing comment. "OK, so what's the idea?"

"So, it's looking like we'll get thirty people booked in for Vienna—"

"Which is actually pretty awesome for a first year, according to Ange."

"Which is indeed actually pretty awesome for a first year. Anyway, it's not *too* big a group, so I was thinking, to sort of try it out, we could do like a Secret Santa."

"A Secret Santa?"

"It's where—"

"Theo. I know what a Secret Santa is."

He ran a hand across the back of his neck. A nervous tic. "Right. Well, the Christmas markets are one of the main attractions in Vienna so I thought as part of it we set a limit, and pull names out of a hat, the whole lot, and send everyone off one afternoon to get their present."

"What if some people don't want to spend money on a stranger? I think it's a fun idea, but some people—"

"Yeah, so we should actually have some money in the budget for the holiday left over after the discount on the hotel, so we can cover something small with that."

She took a sip of her iced latte. "And then everyone could open them on Christmas Eve? That's the big day in Austria."

"Right, exactly."

"I think it's a great idea," she said decisively.

"Really?"

Lexie smiled a little at the fact it was now him asking that. "I can give credit where it's due." But she realized he'd genuinely been asking her opinion—and she remembered how he'd talked about the investment idea in the first place—how much he'd reassured them all that Richard, too, had thought it was a good idea. Like he needed the validation, to know that his idea was worth something. Was this another reason Richard had put the two of them together, because they could help each other? Or was she just looking for reasons when there were none?

"So that's what you wanted to talk to me about?" she asked as Theo finished the rest of his mushrooms.

"Yeah. That—and . . . We've got the Christmas party in two weeks. Plus ones encouraged, by the way."

"I don't have a plus one," she said without thinking.

"I know that." He grinned in a way that made her flush. "But bring a friend. Or your mum or whatever."

"OK," Lexie said slowly. "But, you know it's July in two weeks, right, not December?"

"Yeah, we're doing Christmas in July. It's a thing. The Christmas period is always a bit hectic for us, so we never have it in December. It was a tradition your dad started," he added, his smile softer now, "and I think it might be cool to carry it on—for this year at least."

"Can we afford it? The company, I mean?"

"Yeah, I mean—it might have to be drinks and 'snacks' rather than a full-on three-course sit-down dinner, but given the year we've had . . . I think it would be good for us all to get together and celebrate."

"OK. Yeah."

"You're so agreeable today."

Lexie rolled her eyes. "Agreeable is my usual resting state; you just have a habit of bringing out my bad side."

He opened his mouth and the glint in his eye made her hold up a finger.

"Don't." But a smile pulled at her lips despite herself—the problem was, she *liked* this side of him.

"OK, so at the Christmas party, I was thinking . . . Maybe we could do your wish jar."

"What?"

"Well not *your* wish jar, but you know, the idea."

Lexie frowned and folded her arms.

"I just thought, it's your company too now, and it would be like a way of bringing in a tradition of yours and . . ." He trailed off. "You hate it."

Lexie tried to smooth out her expression. "No. Sorry, no. It's just . . . Won't people think it's kind of silly?"

"I think, after everything that's happened—losing Richard after only just pulling it all back after the last few years . . ." He shrugged. "I just thought we could do with some hope. But I can see you overthinking this."

"You can *see* me overthinking?"

"You get a crease . . ." He reached out, and despite herself her body tensed in anticipation of him touching her. But he didn't quite trace the line between her eyebrows. And really, she should probably work on making her expressions less easy to read.

She batted his hand away. "You do remember the part about me putting wishes in there to let them go, right?"

"Yeah, well, about that. We'll probably aim to have wishes in there that people think they can make come true."

Lexie sat back against her chair. "Are you criticizing my wish jar?"

Theo sat back too, mimicking her pose. "I'm only saying, maybe by 'setting them free'—your words—you are hiding from what you want, making it so that you don't have to hope for things."

"You *are* criticizing it!"

He gave one of his too-casual shrugs. "Just seems like you might be using it wrong."

"It's my wish jar. How can I be wrong about how I use it?"

He crooked one eyebrow at her in answer and she felt a surge of annoyance.

The waiter came, cleared their plates, and Lexie thanked him, then turned her attention to the people walking past, laughing and chatting in the sunlight.

"So you take it with you? The wish jar?"

She frowned, still not looking at him.

"Everywhere you go, you take it with you?" he prompted.

She spared him a brief glance. "Haven't been able to kick the habit."

She didn't really know why she'd kept it up all these years. It had always been something consistent, she supposed, something that made her feel like it was Christmas—and something that made her think of her childhood home. She could still remember the year she'd first started the tradition, with her mum sitting next to her, cross-legged on the living-room floor. It was one of those memories that was a little hazy, and it was hard to be sure if even the parts that stuck out in stark focus were real, or if they had been layered with other people's stories, making her *think* she remembered.

She could remember finishing the wish jar—sticking gems to it that had then fallen off, over the years, and running into the kitchen, to show her dad.

That is the best wish jar I think I've seen. There's no chance the wishes won't come true if you put them in that.

Lexie had looked at the jar in her hand, wanting to believe but also a little suspicious. *How can they come true? I made it, and I'm not magic.*

He had put one arm around her and winked. She could still remember the faint smell of tobacco and mint. *It's the act of making it, Little Lex. It* becomes *magic. And maybe the wishes won't come true right away, maybe not the same year you put them in the jar, but one day, if you want the wish hard enough, it* will *come true.*

But she'd wished, year after year, for her dad to come back, for him to pick her, for things to go back to when it was the three of them—and it had never come true.

"You have a favorite place you've been to?"

Lexie blinked at Theo. "Ah . . ."

"Or a favorite place you spent Christmas?"

"I don't know. They are kind of all my favorite, while I'm there." But she could tell he was trying to change the subject away from the wish jar—probably picking up on her annoyance at him. So she relented. "I actually spent Christmas in Australia one year. It was right after university, and I had no idea what to do, so I decided to go there. You can get a work visa for a year, as long as you don't stay longer than six months in one job, and that sounded perfect. I got a job as a waitress, made a load of friends." Friends she didn't really speak to anymore, because time and distance had pulled them apart. "Anyway, we all spent Christmas on the beach. I was on the Gold Coast—it's in Queensland—and I used to get up early every day to watch the sunrise. I'm not really a morning person, but it's impossible *not* to be a morning person there. So we got up—a bunch of us who were either traveling or were living away from family—and we all went to the beach and had a barbecue on Christmas Day. It was so cool."

"I always wanted to go to Australia," Theo said. "But my moving around tended to be from city to city in the UK, because I was too useless to save up any money or properly apply for jobs abroad." She noticed how harsh he was on himself, but decided not to comment as he asked her another question. "What's the longest you've stayed in one place?"

"Ah, since university? A year, I think." She felt self-conscious about admitting that, even if he wasn't doing what people usually did—remarking that it must be hard to build a life that way, or making fake gushing, admiring noises. "I like it," she added, on the defensive.

"Yeah, I can see that."

She wasn't sure what to do with that, so she deflected. "What about you? You said you moved around a lot?"

"Yeah. Mainly because I couldn't get a job I thought I was any good at and I made things difficult for the poor people employing me as a result."

"Troublemaker?"

He grinned. "Totally." Then his expression evened out a bit as he looked over her head to the street beyond. "When I moved to Bath, I figured it would be the same thing. But because of Richard, here I am, five years later. It sometimes feels bizarre—but somewhere along the line, this place has ended up feeling like home, you know?"

She nodded—though she wasn't sure she totally did know. Home was wherever she was at the time, and she'd gotten good at that. But sometimes it felt exhausting. "And you've been in the flat all that time?"

"Not at first. I was in a shared house for a bit, before Richard and I worked out a deal where I could rent it. It's temporary," he said, bringing his attention back to her. "I wasn't trying to, like, leech off your dad or anything. I'm saving to buy a house—which really does make me sound boring compared to you."

Lexie smiled slightly. "'Boring' is not a word I'd use to describe you." She studied him for a moment. "What was it that made you stick around?"

"Honestly? I think I'd been looking for a reason to stick somewhere. But I was too, you know . . . scared, to stay put—moving around means you don't let anyone down."

Lexie nodded, and she felt a little relieved—because that wasn't the same for her.

"So Richard, him believing in me and making me see that I *wasn't* letting him down—it gave me what I needed to stay put. And because of that, I figured out I *liked* the job. I get to travel, get *paid* to do it. And I like finding holidays for people, like building the itineraries, discovering new things."

She kept nodding, not wanting to admit that she liked that part of it, too.

"Like Iceland—if we can get out there this year, I reckon it's going to be pretty epic, and it's kind of unbelievable that that's my job, you know?"

She registered the "we" and was unsure if he meant the general "we" or if he was referring to her, specifically. Something tightened in her stomach, though she couldn't quite pinpoint why. Because he might want to spend time with her there? Or because, even if she *did* go to Iceland with him, it was only a matter of time before the "we" was obsolete.

"You've got your overthinking face on again."

"No, it's just . . ." She didn't want to admit what she'd really been thinking. "Iceland. It's . . . We had this tradition." And she explained about their family holidays, about spending Christmas in a different place each year. About how they were supposed to go to Iceland the year Richard left. And how now, she couldn't help the thought that he'd been taking the family tradition she'd loved, and the holiday she'd been so excited to go on, and using it to make money.

I promise I'll take you there one day, Little Lex. She remembered him saying that, when she'd cried at the fact that he was leaving. She wasn't really crying about the *holiday,* of course, but he'd latched on to that—perhaps because it was an easier promise. But it was still a promise he'd broken, in the end.

Theo let her talk, listening. And when she finished, he just said, "I'll go in and pay."

"I'll pay my half," Lexie said immediately, but he waved it away.

"We'll put it on the company. We talked about work, didn't we?"

They walked back to the office, the big Georgian buildings seeming to bask in the sun. "You could look at it a different way," Theo said conversationally, and Lexie glanced at him. "You could say that he was trying to treasure something—to honor you and your family tradition. And to me, there are two things that suggest that he was thinking of you, the whole time."

Lexie frowned, and he elaborated.

"Iceland and Madrid, for one. He never did anything in Madrid, and I was wondering about that, until you told me about the trip he took Rachel on. He let you down. It was a dickish thing to do, and I can't even imagine how it must have felt. But he didn't want to do Madrid with the company—and I can't help wondering if that's the reason why."

"But you were planning Iceland," Lexie pointed out.

"Yeah, but he wouldn't work with me to get it off the ground.

It was like he was waiting for something. Maybe he was waiting for you."

Lexie frowned. "What's the other thing?"

He gave her a look. "I'm waiting for you to cotton on to that one."

She rolled her eyes. Then she sighed. "I think that's looking at things with rose-tinted glasses."

"Our choice how to look at things, though, isn't it?"

They were quiet for a minute or so, and then as they turned onto the street where the office was, Lexie spoke again. "Fine, we can do the wish jar at the party. Even though people will think it's stupid."

"Great. You can decorate it."

It made her laugh, and he smiled.

When they got back to the office, he held the door open, but stopped her just as she was about to step inside. "Oh, and Lex?" His voice was quiet enough that he couldn't be overheard—and with just enough edge that it made her skin tingle. "Just for the record . . . I doubt very much that it was just a one-time thing."

Chapter Twenty-three

It had been Lexie's idea to hold the Christmas in July party in the flat above the office. For one, it saved money, but also, they could make it look properly Christmassy, whereas any bar or pub they went to would be in full summer swing. She and Ange had gotten really into it, and weirdly there was something even more fun about putting the decorations up in July, like they were breaking the rules. They'd hung fairy lights around the big windows and along the mantelpiece above the out-of-use fire, had put a wreath on the front door. Ange had cracked out the Christmas tree that they used every year down in the office—it was plastic, but apparently the fake ones could actually be more environmentally friendly if you used them year after year, so Lexie put her objections aside.

They'd had to open all the windows as wide as they could because it was so warm up in the flat—even in the evening—but they'd gone the whole hog and made mulled wine anyway.

They had the Christmas music on by the time everyone arrived, "Santa Baby" currently playing underneath the swell of chatter, but because they hadn't already been listening to the songs on repeat, the music felt fun rather than slightly grating, the way it usually did when you eventually got to Christmas itself. The whole office was here, and because most people had brought a guest or two, the flat felt buzzing. They were confined to the living room and joint kitchen—Theo's bedroom strictly out-of-bounds. Harry was there with a friend; Ange had brought along her son and his wife; Mike had brought *his* wife, Kate, who carried a faint air of disapproval around with her, like she was firmly against the concept of Christmas in July; and Lexie had brought along both Fran and her mum. Theo, she noticed, was flying solo, despite having encouraged everyone else to bring plus ones.

Everyone was in Christmas gear. Ange was in a reindeer jumper with matching reindeer earrings and Harry and Mike were both wearing Christmas ties. Theo hadn't exactly gone overboard, but had dressed more formally than usual, donning a shirt with the sleeves rolled up rather than his usual T-shirt and jeans. Lexie, however, had gone all out in a sparkly black dress, simple but classic, with high heels that she only braved every now and then. And because it was summer, she could wear this kind of outfit and not be freezing, which was a plus. She'd seen Theo glance her way a few times and knew it had had the desired effect. And OK, yes, she wasn't supposed to be going there with him, but that didn't mean she didn't want him to suffer, just a little, for stopping things in Madrid.

Lexie's mum broke away from a conversation with Ange, came over to stand near one of the windows where you could catch the odd breeze to counteract the steaming mulled wine. Lexie had thought it might be weird for her, to come along to something that had once belonged to her ex-husband, to be around people who had valued him, but her expression showed no sign of discomfort.

Instead she beamed at Lexie. "Thank you so much for inviting me, my love. This is such fun!" Lexie raised her mug, and they clinked. "Ange is just *lovely*. I've only ever seen her in passing before, but we're going to lunch next week—she's going to take me to this café at the garden center near her, apparently they do the best toasted sandwiches you've ever had." Lexie smiled. Her mum's cheeks were a little pink, her eyes shining. "And Mike, you know, I knew him a bit before, but it's lovely to catch up. Though I'm not sure about that wife of his."

"You knew Mike?" It was weird, to think of their lives all being intersected like that.

"Oh, not really. But Richard became friends with him back when we were together."

"Really? They knew each other for that long?"

"Oh yes. It's nice, isn't it, that they kept in touch? I think they met in the sales job your dad used to work at." Her mum frowned. "Astra something or other."

Lexie grinned at her mum. "You don't know what Dad did either."

Her mum gave her a weird look.

"What?"

Her expression immediately softened. "Nothing. You called him Dad, that's all. But no, I never totally learned the ins and outs of his job. He explained it a few times but, well . . ." She broke off, looking at her phone, which she'd kept in her hand the whole evening—something that was uncharacteristic. A smile spread at whatever she saw there.

"Who—?"

But Lexie didn't get to finish, because Fran came over, clutching a glass of Prosecco, having declared earlier that "July is not the time for stewed alcohol, Lexie." She was in a dress too— a knockout red one that Lexie had encouraged her to wear, along with a pair of heels, so that she wasn't the only one.

Fran swept her long dark hair over her shoulder. "For the record, I'm totally loving this."

Lexie smiled, and risked a glance over at Theo, who was standing with his back to her now, chatting to Harry by the sofa.

For the record, I doubt very much that it was just a one-time thing.

"My Christmas party wasn't nearly as fun," Fran was saying as Lexie forced her attention away from Theo's back. "It was a sit-down dinner. My boss got way too drunk and told me how much he regrets the last twenty years of his life." She wrinkled her nose. "That'll be me in twenty years."

"Drunk? Or regretting your life?" Lexie cocked her head. "A boss?"

"Probably all three at this rate."

Lexie's mum said nothing to any of this, still intent on her phone, as Ange bustled over, her reindeer earrings swinging. "Lexie, I *love* the wish jar! What a fun idea! We should take the wishes out next year, see if any of them have come true. Or put wishes in for the company? Or . . ." She flapped a hand. "I don't know. There's an idea on the tip of my tongue, I know it, I'm just a little woolly at the moment after the wine. Anyway, I love it, and Theo said it was your idea?"

Lexie shifted uncomfortably. "Ah, sort of."

Beside them, her mum finally stopped texting and looked up.

"Have you put a wish in yet?" Ange asked.

"I did," Fran announced. "I wished for the love of my life. Although, actually, are we allowed to put two in? Because I might wish to win the lottery, so I don't have to do any more paperwork for the rest of my life."

"You're not supposed to tell us the wishes," Lexie said, nudging Fran in the ribs.

"Why not?" Fran asked, her lips twitching. "Because then they won't come true?"

"Oh, I love that you've brought the wish jar here," Lexie's

mum said, beaming. Her eyes shone a little more brightly, and for a moment Lexie was worried she might start crying. "I can remember the first year you did it. And I know it's silly—I moved on from your father a long time ago—but in some ways I wish he were here, to see the tradition still going strong."

Lexie frowned. "Why?"

Her mum fluffed up her hair a little. "Well, it was him who started you on it, wasn't it?"

"No," Lexie said slowly. "It was your idea—remember? We made the first one together." She had that memory, sitting on the living-room floor, sticking gems onto glass.

"We decorated it together, yes, but it was your dad's idea in the first place. He was the one who encouraged you to get it out the year after, too. I think he might have done it when he was a kid, actually. I'm sure that's where the whole thing came from."

Lexie stared at her mum, trying to process her words. It had been her *dad's* idea? She knew she'd always talked to him about it, knew she'd shown him the very first one she'd made, but she hadn't realized it had been his idea in the first place. That particular detail had gotten lost in her memories, somewhere along the line. So it had been *his* tradition she'd been carrying around with her all this time, without even realizing it. And she couldn't quite work out how she felt about that.

"Are you OK, Lexie love?" Her mum was looking at her with concern now, an expression at odds with the sparkle of her bright red-and-green knitted Christmas jumper—the one and only Christmas jumper she owned, to Lexie's knowledge. "I'm sorry to bring it up if it upsets you."

"No, it's OK." Lexie forced a smile. "I'm fine."

For a moment her mum looked like she might say something else, but then her phone buzzed again and in her distraction Fran pulled Lexie away, saying they needed drink top-ups. Within half an hour her mum made apologies to leave early, and the whole thing was forgotten about.

At around nine P.M., they decided to head to the pub. Fran bit her lip at the suggestion, drawing out her phone to look at the time.

"What's up?" Lexie asked, gathering a bunch of empty glasses and dumping them into the kitchen sink as Theo switched off the music and the others all headed out the front door, talking loudly as they clambered down the stairs.

"It's just . . . Tom said I should meet him this evening, if I'm free . . ." Fran had been on two dates with Tom so far, and apparently he seemed nice, normal. Given Fran's track record, Lexie was a little worried that he sounded too good to be true, but she had decided to keep that concern to herself.

Instead she said, "Go! Meet him. Everyone will be calling it quits soon anyway, I reckon. Have fun."

Fran gave Lexie a quick hug, then bounded off out of the flat and down the stairs. Really, you had to admire the hope.

"Where's she off to?" Theo asked, and Lexie spun around to see him bringing the rest of the glasses into the kitchen.

"She has a date."

"Ah." It was quiet, now that everyone had left.

"My mum left early too."

"Maybe she has a date as well."

Lexie made a face. "Don't be ridiculous."

"Is it that ridiculous?"

Lexie frowned at him. "She would have said."

"OK."

She was learning that Theo often said "OK" when he disagreed completely. She supposed her mum *could* have a date.

She must have had dates since her dad left. And she was pretty sure there had been a time when she'd been close to bringing a guy home to meet Lexie, in her teenage years, but Lexie had never given her mum's dating life a huge amount of thought—she'd always presumed that she was just happy being single, after what Richard had put her through.

She was lost in her own thoughts as she continued clearing up some of the mess they'd made—and belatedly realized that Theo was doing the same. Maybe he didn't want to come back to a dump later. She cleared her throat as she put the mugs into the dishwasher, feeling the need to fill the silence. "So what do you usually do at Christmas?"

He poured the last dregs of the mulled wine out of the pan and down the sink. "Work, mostly. I go on the trips quite often, which is fun."

"You weren't working last year," Lexie pointed out. He'd been there when she'd tried to sneak into the office on Christmas morning—coming down from his flat.

"I wasn't abroad, but I was still working."

"Oh."

He smiled at her. "Feeling sorry for me now, are we? Don't be—Ange invited me round for Christmas dinner in the afternoon, so I had the full Christmas experience."

She could imagine that of Ange. Though if he'd told her that on the day itself, she wouldn't have had to feel momentarily guilty, leaving him in the office.

"You don't ever go home to your parents or anything?" she asked as she finished loading the dishwasher. She knew he didn't get on brilliantly with them, but still. And yes, OK, maybe she was trying to dig a little deeper there.

"My parents were never really big on it. We went to church

when I was a kid, but I think out of a sense of obligation—my parents weren't overly religious. But the rest was just awkward."

"Because it's an 'overly chaotic and hyperactive celebration'?" Lexie asked, remembering.

He shot her a glance. "Yeah, that's about the sum of it. Although Mum wanted to do Christmas as it should be done. But for her that meant it was all calm, and that we were seen to be this, like, I don't know, perfect little family with a well-behaved, grateful child or whatever. So she'd host everyone for Christmas Eve drinks and serve these incredibly posh canapés that I hated—and generally she tried to encourage other parents to leave their kids behind, but those that *were* there were supposed to be dressed up in suits. Like a ten-year-old in a suit munching on a goat cheese canapé for Christmas—the whole thing was a little ridiculous." His voice was wry, like he was making a joke, but Lexie couldn't help but wonder what was beneath that. "Anyway," he continued, "the day itself was always painful. Like sitting there and opening our one present each—mine was always something to do with school— and then having this meal that my mum had slaved over while my dad read quietly in the living room by the fire, drinking sherry."

"My mum likes sherry," Lexie said—because she wasn't really sure what else to say.

"Well, there's something we have in common—parents who like sherry."

She laughed a little, and he gave her another of those glances as he got out a dishwasher tablet from beneath the sink.

"I spent the past few Christmases—before this last one—with your dad, actually."

She wasn't sure what to say other than "Oh." She wondered if he'd leave it there, and realized she didn't want him to. "What did you do?"

"Well, three Christmases ago we were in Edinburgh—for work, on the trip there, which always does pretty well as a lot of people want to hang around for Hogmanay."

OK, for work. That made it a bit easier to hear—given all the times she remembered wanting to spend Christmas with her dad, and him not being there.

"I actually think he could have gone on the trip himself, but we'd had a rough couple of years with the business, and I think he knew I didn't really have anywhere to spend Christmas, so he got me to come along." He smiled a little at the memory. "Then the year before last we were in Vienna—we were there for a recce—for the trip that's going to be running this year. We had to postpone it once we realized how ill Richard was."

"Right," she said, thinking she ought to show she was following.

"And Richard flew Rachel out too—not on the company, but she was having a bit of a hard time, so . . ."

He'd flown Rachel out to Vienna, for Christmas, because she was having a hard time. How had he been *that* good a father to her, and completely absent for Lexie? It was also after he'd left Jody, wasn't it? So apparently he hadn't abandoned Rachel when he left Jody, the way he'd done with Lexie.

Lexie realized Theo was watching her carefully, as if wondering how she was taking all this, and she tried to school her face. "So what did you do, on Christmas Day itself?" she asked him.

"We actually got a bit carried away on Christmas Eve, which is the big celebration over there—Richard had found this amazing family restaurant that was open on the day. No idea how he found it, to be honest, because it was very much geared toward the locals, but it was amazing. The traditional Christmas food in Vienna leaves something to be desired—it's all about breadcrumbs. But these guys managed to merge the traditional and the modern and the food was incredible. And there was so much wine—Rachel ended up almost passing out on the table and we had to practically carry her home." His brow furrowed a little, while Lexie felt a pang at the family scenario he was describing—with her dad and her sister. "Which in hindsight was a little irresponsible of us, given Rachel must have been like, what, nineteen or something?"

"She's twenty-two now," Lexie said, her voice quieter than she'd meant it to be. But at least she knew that.

"Right. Well, anyway. On Christmas Day itself we wandered around the city—Rachel had been hoping for snow but there was none. It was still so beautiful, though, and we were trying to figure out where we could take clients for the day itself, for those people who didn't want to be alone, and it became sort of, I don't know, like a game." He shook his head, clearly thinking about it; then his voice changed a little. "It was just before he found out he was ill, I think. I mean, I can't know that for sure, since he never told me, but I think it must have been before he . . ." He broke off, clearing his throat, and seemed to force lightness back to his voice. "Anyway, it was a lot more fun than Christmas with my parents. What about you? You spend it with your mum usually?"

As a change of subject it left a little to be desired, but Lexie went with it. "Growing up, yeah, it was mainly me and Mum. She always made such an effort, and we played games, and on Boxing Day we'd always go and meet friends. It was nice." The absence of her dad in that sentence seemed to hang in the air around them, after his story. "But, ah, then I moved away and I'm usually doing something to do with work on Christmas now—or spending it with people I've met through work that year. I stopped wanting to come home for it," she admitted, though that made her feel guilty, because of her mum. She sighed. "I know it sounds stupid—it was so long ago—but it never felt the same after my dad left. I was always too aware that he was somewhere else, enjoying it with his new family, and I couldn't shake the feeling of being . . ."

"Second-best?"

"Yeah." She blew out a breath. "Something like that. It's stupid, I know," she said again.

"It's not."

She glanced around. It was tidy enough. "We should go. Ange said they were heading to the Lamb."

They walked to the front door together. "So, we have an Irish trip coming up in August," he said conversationally. "In Warrenpoint. Ever been?"

"No—do you know what? Weirdly, I've never even been to Ireland."

"Well, you should come with me, then."

She glanced up at him, as he opened the front door a crack. "You're going? Thought you didn't like going to Ireland."

"I don't hugely love going back near Dublin, which is where I grew up, but this is Northern Ireland. Besides, Mike hates this one, so he won't go, but we have a tricky customer coming so *one* of us needs to be there."

"One?"

His lip quirked up at the corner. "Or two. Our usual local guide isn't available this year, and to be honest I could use your help, given I know Miranda is going to make life difficult."

"I don't know," Lexie said slowly, still waiting for Theo to open the door wide enough for them to step out.

"Don't trust yourself around me?"

She huffed out half a laugh. Though really—maybe there was something in that. "The others will be wondering where we are," she said by way of deflection.

He opened the door all the way, then very deliberately looked up. Mistletoe was hanging there. Mistletoe she was sure she hadn't hung herself. Where did you even *get* mistletoe this time of year?

Lexie gave him a suspicious look. "You put that there."

His face was the picture of innocence. "Ange did."

"Is that so?"

"Yep. She's big on mistletoe. She met her husband under the mistletoe one year."

"Really?"

"No idea. Wouldn't put it past her, though." He waited, one hand still on the door.

She told herself it was a silly thing, playing at Christmas, a quick kiss under the mistletoe—even if the thought that he'd hung it there just for her made her want to smile.

She thought she was prepared, as she pressed her lips to his. As his hands came up her arms, a soft caress. But he didn't deepen it. She didn't taste the hunger like in Spain, that gut punch she'd been ready for. Instead it was slow, and sweet, and she felt her body go loose and liquid as her eyes fluttered closed. Barely a whisper of a kiss, really. Still enough to bring the heat, still enough that she had to fight not to pull him closer. More than that, though, it was enough to make her heart stutter as he pulled away and took her hand to tug her down the stairs.

She did her best to ignore it. Told herself that it was a physical reaction, that was all. Because kissing Theo was one thing. Falling for him was not an option.

Chapter Twenty-four

Lexie stepped into the Cider House and spotted Rachel at the end of the bar, adopting the default position when you're alone in a pub—scrolling through a phone. Lexie rushed over, hot from having legged it across the city. "I'm so sorry I'm late," she said by way of greeting.

Rachel looked up from her phone, sliding it into the pocket of her black jeans. How was Rachel not *boiling*? But she looked perfectly cool in her jeans and pale lilac blouse, blue eyes bright. Whereas Lexie was sweating in her summer dress. "Don't be," Rachel said with a smile. "I'm chronically early. It's a condition."

The Cider House was packed with the after-work crowd, but even so Lexie could see why Theo had suggested this place. It had a distinctly "quirky" vibe with its multicolored bar, horizontal rainbow stripes adding a fun feel, and industrial pipes on the ceiling. But it wasn't so trendy that you felt out of place, managing to create a welcoming, homey vibe, and the people behind the bar chatted as they pulled pints. Still, despite the positive atmosphere, there was a beat of awkward silence between Lexie and Rachel.

Lexie fixed a smile to her face. "So . . . cider?"

"Got to be, hasn't it?" They each opted for different cider to try, then headed outside to the sprawling alfresco terrace, taking a seat down on the lower part. One side of the terrace had a wooden wall, which had been painted a dark green, with different colored apples and pears against the backdrop. And above the pub stood a line of the Georgian buildings Bath was famous for, looking down at them against the evening sky.

Lexie took a sip of her cider and told herself to be careful—it was delicious and she could definitely get carried away and drink it too quickly. "So," she said, keeping her bright smile in place. "How's the house sale going?"

Rachel took a sip of her own drink. "Well, there's a buyer interested, but it's not gone through yet." She set her pint down on the table. "But we don't have to talk about it if you . . ."

"It's fine," Lexie said firmly. "Honestly." They couldn't just ignore it—and besides, these days she wasn't entirely sure she had actually gotten the short end of the stick. She had to work for the company, yes, had to prove something, and the income wasn't guaranteed—but the longer she worked there, the less black-and-white it had become, and she'd found herself questioning her initial idea that giving Rachel the house had been as simple as declaring her the favorite daughter. Richard had cared about the company, and he'd left it to her—that was saying something, wasn't it? She wondered now if Rachel felt the same way. She'd never shown any sign of it—but had she ever felt bitter that Lexie had gotten half the company? She didn't know how to ask.

"I guess I just feel weird about it," Rachel said now. "Selling the house. It was his home, you know? And I'm just . . ." Rachel waved a hand in the air to finish the sentence.

"Did you ever visit him there?" Lexie asked.

"Yeah, all the time. He moved out nearly four years ago—after I left for uni—but because of, well, stuff with my mum, it sort of ended up feeling more like home than my own house, in the long run. Then Mum moved too, a couple of years ago."

"After they got divorced?"

There was a beat while Rachel glanced at her, then away again. "They didn't actually divorce."

"Oh, I'm sorry. I thought I'd heard . . ." That he'd left her—left another family.

"No, I mean, they did separate, they just didn't get the papers or whatever. I think maybe Dad thought it might not be permanent, but, well . . ." She tapped her fingernails—still bitten down—against her pint glass. "It's been causing a few problems, actually."

"What do you mean?"

Rachel shot her one of those surreptitious glances. Maybe she felt too awkward, talking about this. *Really, Lexie, you could have picked an easier topic to kick things off.*

"Mum thought the house would go to her," Rachel said. "She thought she'd get more than she did, anyway." Rachel closed her eyes. "That's incredibly callous, I know." Was it any less callous than Lexie feeling jealous that Rachel had been given the house, back in December? Her stomach laced with guilt, which sat there uncomfortably as she took another sip of cider.

"How come they *didn't* divorce?" Lexie asked. Then winced. "Sorry, that's intrusive."

"No, it's OK," Rachel said, though her tapping on the glass became a bit more frantic. Lexie caught a glint of the same ring she'd been wearing last time—the beautiful sapphire. "It's just complicated," Rachel said eventually—and Lexie knew to let it drop.

"So how's everything else?" she asked instead. "How's . . . work?" She frowned. "Rachel—what do you actually *do* for work?" They caught each other's eye, and both burst out laughing, easing the tension between them.

"I'm actually training to be a vet. So lots more studying still for me."

"Wow. How did I not know this?" That was a silly question to ask, all things considered, and she decided to plow on. "So you're super-brainy. Good to know."

Rachel wrinkled her nose. "I think I just work hard. And luckily I'm good at exams. But I suppose we'll see if I'm actually good at it later down the line."

"I was terrible at exams," Lexie said. She wondered where Rachel got it from. Had her dad been academic? She didn't really know.

"My mum was very insistent on good grades and all that while I was growing up," Rachel said, like she was reading Lexie's mind. "Dad didn't seem to mind, as long as I was happy, but she went on and on about the fact that I'd be closing doors if I didn't get straight A's or whatever."

"She must be pleased you're becoming a vet, then."

There was a pause, where Rachel seemed to focus intently on one of the hand-painted apples on the wall. "Maybe she is," she said eventually. "My mum and I . . . We're not really talking at the moment." Lexie desperately wanted to ask why, and how Richard factored into it all, but she also didn't want to push. Rachel started to toy with the ring on her hand, twisting it one way then the other.

"You don't have to talk about it if you don't—"

"It's OK," Rachel said. They were both being so careful around each other, Lexie thought. Like one false move might break this tentative step toward something. "Mum had already made compromises, or so she said." She sighed. "Marrying a divorced man was not part of the plan, and she had a lot of guilt about the fact that she was the cause of that divorce, I think.

She's never actually said that to me—we don't have that kind of relationship—but I've come to that conclusion after hours of therapy." She shot Lexie a wry smile, and Lexie's own lips twitched in response.

"I'd always assumed you were the well-adjusted sister."

"Oh, you have *no* idea. Sorry to disappoint."

"Quite the opposite—we'll have much more in common this way."

Rachel laughed a little. "Anyway, Mum dealt badly with all that—it's probably why she stopped wanting you around." Her voice was apologetic now, and Lexie remembered what Rachel had said when they met before, outside the abbey—that it could have been Jody who stopped Lexie going to Madrid. "She didn't want the reminder that she was a home-wrecker."

Lexie's eyebrows shot up at the harsh phrase.

"I know," Rachel said. "Sorry. Apparently I have a few issues with my mum."

"Therapy?"

"Yeah. I'm a work in progress."

"I think we all are."

It was weird, though. She'd never really thought of Rachel's mum as a real person, despite having met her several times. She'd always just been the woman her dad had left for, nothing more. But still . . .

"He could have tried harder to see me." It came out in a small voice, and Lexie took a sip of cider to try to mask that. "Even if your mum didn't want me around, I mean. He could have . . ." She trailed off, not really sure of the right way to finish that sentence. *He could have fought for me?* Was that what she wanted to say?

"Yeah. And he *should* have, Lexie." Rachel leaned toward her across the table, as if to emphasize her point. "I loved him—so much. I still love him. And he was there for me—but he wasn't there for *you,* and that's something I can't understand either."

Lexie swallowed and tried to push down the emotion that rose up at Rachel's words. Tried to keep her voice level as she asked, "So that's why he left? Richard?" She couldn't quite bring herself to say "Dad" in front of Rachel. "Because your mum was difficult or whatever?" And if she was difficult, if she was the type of person to do all this, then why had Richard left them for her?

"No . . ." Rachel twisted the ring on her finger again. "I'm . . . I'm seeing someone. It's pretty serious, I guess." She shot Lexie a look from under her eyelashes. Her eyes were almost exactly the same shade of blue as the sky. "I know I'm only young and whatever, but we've sort of made a promise . . ." She tapped her ring. "We're not getting married now—not until we're more sorted and old enough so that people won't think we're ridiculous, but, well . . . I'm pretty sure this is *it*. You know?"

Lexie didn't know. She wasn't sure she'd ever had the "it" feeling—wasn't sure she'd ever even wanted it. But she could tell from Rachel's voice how serious *she* was. "That's amazing! I mean, yeah, you're young, but maybe if you know, you know?"

"Exactly," Rachel said, nodding. "And I know."

"But, so what are you saying? That Richard left because you're seeing someone? He disapproved or something?" She was trying to follow Rachel's thought process, which had been a bit erratic since she'd started talking about her mum.

"No, he . . ." Rachel blew out a breath. "My *mum* disapproves."

"OK . . ." Lexie said slowly, trying to keep up. "How come?"

Rachel bit her lip, then blurted out, "Her name is Lana."

Lexie frowned. "Right. So is she some sort of, like, drug dealer or something?" She was trying to think of what caused most parents to disapprove of someone on a relationship front—but it all felt very *Pride and Prejudice*.

Rachel was staring at Lexie a little oddly. "No . . . She's a *she*."

"What? Are you serious? She doesn't like that you're going out with a woman?"

Rachel let out a shaking breath. And Lexie saw the tears coming.

"Oh shit," Lexie said. "Rachel, I . . ."

"I'm sorry," Rachel said through a sob. "I promise I'm not usually this emotional." She shook her head, her curls flying everywhere. "That's a lie. I'm sorry for lying. I cry *all* the fucking time, I can't help it."

Lexie laughed, but the sound was panicked. "I'm sorry. I didn't mean . . ." But she couldn't figure out what she'd said wrong.

"No, it's just . . ." Rachel wiped her hands across her eyes, smudging her mascara. "God. It's stupid. I know it's stupid in this day and age, but my mum, she's just not OK with it. My friends are great. Lana is great. And I know it's wrong to be grateful for that, but I just . . . I was worrying about telling you because . . ."

Lexie reached over and took Rachel's hand across the table. And she felt a rush of fury for Rachel's mum, though she managed to stop herself from spewing it out loud—she doubted that was the right thing to do in this situation.

Rachel looked down at Lexie's hand on hers, and the sobbing subsided. She blinked up at Lexie. "I guess I don't fit in her perfect little traditional family unit either."

Lexie snorted. "She's the one who had an affair with a married man."

Rachel's breath was a little shaky. "Yeah. I think that's the thing, though—she felt like she had to make up for that with a perfect family. I think . . . Well, I used to overhear snatches of conversation—you know how you hear things when you're little, because the adults assume that your ears don't work properly?"

Lexie laughed a little. "Yes." She'd seen a bit of that from the other side, nannying in Austria.

"Well, my mum, she always seemed a bit, I don't know, panicked, I guess? That Dad would leave us."

"Like he left my mum and me?" She said the words without really thinking, and Rachel gave her a funny look.

"Yeah, or more like, she was worried he'd go *back* to you."

Lexie frowned, but she wasn't sure how to contradict that without stating the obvious—that if he'd wanted to come back he *could* have. And she didn't want to push that, didn't want to make it into a competition between her and Rachel.

"Anyway," Rachel continued. "That's why Dad left."

Lexie took a moment to catch up, then felt her stomach drop. Lana—Rachel was talking about Lana. "Because—"

"No," Rachel said quickly, clearly noting Lexie's twisted expression. "God, no. I mean that he left because my mum couldn't—or wouldn't—accept the fact that I was in a relationship with a woman. And he was trying to support me. I think he thought—we both thought—she'd come around eventually. But that was several years ago now and, well. He didn't *leave* us, not really. And it never felt like he left *me,* because he was doing it for me—to stand up for me, if that makes sense."

Lexie nodded and pulled her hand back from Rachel's. She didn't know what to say really, or how to process it. This image of her dad, so determined to stand up for his daughter, didn't fit with the image of him she'd carried around with her for years.

Usually, she wouldn't admit to feeling like this. But after what Rachel had admitted to her, she felt like she owed her something in return. So she settled for honesty. "I'm glad he was there for you—honestly, I am. But I . . . I don't know what to do with it, this version of him you knew." She felt her stomach squirm uncomfortably at saying the words and she couldn't quite meet Rachel's eye. But she carried on anyway. "I don't know how to feel about the fact that he was there for you, when he could never be there for me."

"I know," Rachel said quietly. "I would be the same if I were you. I can't really say anything to make up for it."

Lexie finally looked at her. "Not yours to make up for."

"No. But . . ." Rachel heaved in a breath. "Lexie, if you let me, I'll try to be there for you, if I can."

To her alarm, Lexie felt her eyes sting at the total sincerity in Rachel's voice. She nodded, refusing to give in to the lump in her throat, and took a gulp of cider.

Then she bit her lip. "Can I ask you something random?"

Rachel raised her eyebrows. "Sure."

"Have you ever been to Iceland?"

"No. It looks cool, though. I really want to go and sit in one of those hot water things while it's all icy outside. Why?"

"No reason." She didn't think she could find the right words to explain. "And—one more random thing?"

"Go for it."

"Did you ever have a Christmas tradition? Like a family thing or whatever?"

"You mean like Christmas caroling or something?"

"More like something only you and your parents did. Or you and . . . Dad." Because yes, it felt odd to call him Dad—but just as odd to call him Richard.

"I mean, we did presents and stockings and all that. And we had a Christmas meal all together . . ." She looked at Lexie, clearly trying to find the right answer.

"So you haven't ever heard of a wish jar?"

"No." Rachel shook her head apologetically. "Sorry. What's that?"

Lexie let out a long exhale, and felt something in her loosen, just a little. "It's . . . It's just something we did at the office Christmas party a couple of weeks ago." Maybe she'd find a way to explain it to Rachel one day, but not today. She was feeling a rush of relief, at the fact that it was a tradition her dad hadn't just gone on to start again with his new daughter—and she knew how selfish it would be to admit that out loud.

"Right," said Rachel. "Your office does know it was July, right?"

Lexie laughed. "So I told them. It was fun, though. My mum and my friend Fran came along and we all drank mulled wine in Theo's flat and it was just, I don't know, nice and relaxed."

And it was so different, being here in Bath, hanging out with people at the company, from where she'd thought she would be—and how she'd thought she'd feel—back when she got the news in December.

Then a thought occurred to her and she grimaced a little. "I should have invited you." She should have thought of Rachel—maybe she'd have liked to be there.

"Don't be silly," Rachel said with a wave of her hand. "How are you finding it anyway, working with Theo?"

"It's . . . interesting." She thought of him kissing her under the mistletoe and tried to shove the memory away. Yeah, *interesting* just about covered it.

Rachel laughed. "I'll bet."

Lexie gave Rachel a considering look. She didn't think Rachel would hate her for asking. "Did you know that he was going to leave me the company? Half of it, at least?"

Rachel hesitated, then shook her head. "No. I don't think anyone knew what he was planning. I only found out he was sick a month or so before he . . ." She swallowed and looked down at her near-empty cider. "I was so mad at him, for not telling me sooner," she said quietly. "He explained why, that he didn't want the grief to be dragged out more than necessary, that there was nothing anyone could do so he was trying to protect me, but still . . ."

Lexie closed her eyes briefly against the guilt and the grief that wanted to rise up in her. Yet there was something comforting about being here with Rachel, about knowing that, although they were processing it differently, there were still some feelings they shared.

"But no. I didn't know—though it makes sense. You love to travel, right?"

"Yeah. Yeah, I do." She sighed quietly. "I guess no one knew what he was planning. Apart from Theo, obviously."

Rachel gave her a funny look.

"What?" Lexie asked.

"Theo didn't know," she said.

"Of course he did," Lexie said, frowning. "He was so cross at having to share it with me. Dad must have told him before he . . ."

But Rachel was shaking her head. "He definitely didn't know.

I remember talking to him, after he'd found out. He wanted to find out if *I'd* known, and if I could explain the decision. So he called me—I think there was a meeting with a solicitor about it?"

Lexie nodded.

"Yeah, so he called me after that."

Lexie said nothing, her mind playing catch-up. Had Theo really found out at the same time as her? Or just before, she was guessing—maybe that's why he'd seemed so pissed off in that meeting. He'd literally just found out, and was trying to come to terms with it, like she had been.

"I just assumed . . ."

"Nope. Guess Dad wanted to surprise you both with it," Rachel said, with a touch of dryness. "Theo was panicking a bit, actually. He knew what the company meant to Dad and he didn't want to mess things up. He can be a bit like that, sometimes. He doesn't always let on, but I know he worries about letting people down. Certain people, anyway," she clarified, with a small smile.

Lexie thought of the way he talked about her dad. She thought of the way he'd bounced around in his early twenties, moving on before he could fail at anything—and how he seemed to need validation for certain ideas. "Yeah," she said quietly. "I think I can see that."

Rachel glanced down at their now-empty glasses. "So. Another cider, do you reckon?"

"Yes, let's. Though maybe we should talk about something nice and easy like the weather over the next round."

Rachel grinned. "Well, we *are* in need of some rain right now."

"And it *is* hot even for August in the UK."

Rachel collected the empty glasses to take inside. "Quite so."

And Lexie had a flash of a younger Rachel—maybe around five years old—picking up plastic glasses from the picnic blanket she'd made Lexie sit on. At twelve, Lexie was far too old for playing tea parties, of course, but Rachel had been surprisingly bossy about the whole thing. It made her smile a little. It wasn't a detailed memory, and there was nothing to make it stand out—but it was there. It proved she *did* have memories of her sister, even if they were mostly buried. And maybe, if she could find a way to let Rachel in, they'd be able to make new ones.

Chapter Twenty-five

Lexie sat between her two new friends—George, aged five, and Cece, aged seven—her tongue poking out as she concentrated on coloring in Fionn the giant. Around them, the pub was buzzing after the weekend Wake the Giant festival. It was a brilliantly traditional pub, the kind that screamed comfort—and that would certainly be the place to be in winter, when she was sure the now-empty fireplace would be roaring. A light smell of beer and chips hung in the air, and waves of chatter rose above the sound of the live band. The outside of the pub was Lexie's favorite part—bright pink, with flowers hanging in the windows.

"The giant parade was the best bit," George said, answering Lexie's earlier question. He sifted through the coloring pencils laid out on the wooden table, before carefully choosing a yellow.

"That *was* cool," Lexie agreed, coloring in Fionn's hair in a dark brown, to match the "real life" Fionn who had kept them company over the last couple of days. Lexie had never heard of the Wake the Giant festival before Theo had told her about it, but she'd decided it was definitely worth the trip to Northern Ireland. It had been a weekend of storytelling, from when Fionn mac Cumhaill had arrived by ferry, sitting astride his giant motorbike and accompanied by a procession of forty boats. Fionn had watched over the music and shows, a lot of which were grounded in the folklore and legends from Warrenpoint itself. The procession of giants at the end had indeed been very cool—

Fionn leading the way with a line of other walking, talking giants behind—but Lexie suspected the real reason George was calling that his favorite bit was because it was the most recent.

"I liked the disco," Cece said. There had been music all weekend, celebrating the traditional Celtic music and local artists, and a special children's disco, which had resulted in Lexie teaching a bunch of kids how to do "Big Fish, Little Fish, Cardboard Box."

"What about the giant cookies?" Lexie asked and got an enthusiastic "Yes!" from both of them. There had been a giant food trail, which celebrated flavors from the area, as well as, of course, a few "giant" foods thrown in there.

There were fifteen of them on the trip in total, but Lexie and Theo were spending this evening with just four of them, as the others had decided to spend time on their own.

Helen, George and Cece's mum, caught Lexie's eye from across the table, and mouthed, "Are you OK?"

Lexie nodded, and Helen held up her half pint of Guinness in a little thank-you. Both she and Helen were trying Guinness— though Lexie's glass was mostly untouched, because she was struggling with the strong flavor.

Next to Helen, Theo was nodding along to Miranda—the "tricky" client he had mentioned when he first broached the trip to Lexie. She was currently giving a rundown on things she thought weren't up to scratch, including the fact that it was a bit wetter than she would have liked, given it was August (with a gesture outside to where misty rain was setting in), and that the giants hadn't been quite as big as she'd expected. Theo shot Lexie a wink, and Lexie looked away quickly, back to the coloring book.

She still wasn't sure quite how she'd ended up on this trip. It seemed like Theo had mentioned it offhand, and then he'd sort of assumed that she'd be going. And she'd let herself go along with that, for reasons she didn't want to dig into too much.

Helen sighed. "I'd better get them to bed soon."

Lexie glanced up at Helen, who smiled.

"I'm just having such a lovely time—trying to put off the end of things tomorrow."

It had been her first time away as a single parent, Helen had told Lexie earlier this weekend, and she'd gone from being worried about being a nuisance to seeming relaxed and happy in just a few days. Lexie supposed this was where the magic happened. Supporting people on holiday, helping them find a trip that suited their means and lifestyle, whether that was an exotic two-week holiday or a short weekend away. Giving people a break from reality might not be much in the grand scheme of things, but Lexie couldn't deny that it gave her a little glow—it was like the happiness was catching.

"And really," Miranda was saying, in a rather posh English accent, "if so much of it is going to be outside, they ought to set up more gazebos and the like, don't you think? I know it's not *your* fault, but do you think you could put in a complaint about that?" Her eyebrows—plucked so thin you could barely see them—pulled together. "And maybe make it clear on your brochures, you know?"

Lexie couldn't help it—she glanced up at Theo again, who caught her eye, and grinned. She needed to stop *looking* at him, for God's sake. She'd been waiting, all weekend, for him to make some kind of move, but he hadn't, and instead of that making her feel calmer, she felt all jittery as a result. He hadn't so much as held her hand. Because it was a work trip, and it would be unprofessional? Or because he'd changed his mind about it not being just a one-time thing? Maybe, between the Christmas in

July party and now, he'd come to his senses and realized what a terrible idea it would be to take things further. Even if taking things further was pretty much all she seemed to be able to think about right now.

The violins struck up for the next song—a fun, fast piece of music, the type that makes you bounce your knee when you're sitting still. Then the singer started—a woman with a beautiful, soft voice—and Lexie found herself wishing she knew the tune so that she could hum along.

"I want to dance!" Cece announced, getting to her feet to prove the point.

"Oh, I don't know if . . ." Helen began, at the same time as Lexie said, "I'll dance with you." She looked at Helen. "If that's OK with you, I mean?" She could do with dancing off some of the frustrated energy that was pulsing through her.

"I don't mind, but are you sure?"

"Absolutely." There was a small space in front of the band— Lexie wasn't sure if it was *meant* for dancing, but everyone in here seemed friendly enough to at least give it a go. She got to her feet and held her hand out to Cece, who took it, following Lexie out to the middle of the floor, between tables where people were finishing their Sunday evening pints.

Lexie looked over her shoulder. "Coming, George?"

He shook his head, moving around to the other side of the table to half hide behind Helen, like Lexie might be about to force him.

Lexie looked down at Cece. "Just you and me, then." And she spun Cece around, making her giggle.

There had been a time when her dad had danced with her like this, turning the music up loud in their little cottage and spinning her around in the living room. She remembered being a teenager, too, on a day when she'd been forced to go out with her dad and Jody and Rachel. She'd told her mum she didn't want to go, because Jody never made her feel welcome, and because it didn't seem fair that her dad could cancel on her but she couldn't cancel on him. But she'd been overruled. They'd gone shopping—it must have been around Christmastime, because Lexie could remember the lights in all the shops and had a distinct impression of sparkle. Lexie had trailed behind the family of three, feeling like she didn't belong—and feeling resentful because of it. There had been a band, playing in the street—and Jody had danced with Rachel, who was only little at the time. Her dad had tried to get her to dance too, taking her hand and encouraging her into a spin.

Come on, Little Lex, dance with me!

She'd pulled her hand away, scowled. *I'm not that little anymore.*

She still remembered the look he'd given her, before he'd smiled—sad, and something deeper there. A realization, of time passing by? *I know,* he'd said, giving her shoulder a little squeeze.

Lexie pushed away the memory and threw herself into the music with Cece—who danced much more exuberantly than Lexie, oblivious to the potential embarrassment. The singer of the band smiled at them both, a few staff members came over to clear a bit more space, and more people came up to join them. They started linking arms and swinging each other around, going so fast that it made Lexie breathless. She saw, out of the corner of her eye, Helen and George coming to join in, then Theo and Miranda. It seemed like the whole pub was getting involved, and whether or not the band had been expecting this—whether or not it was *supposed* to be the type of place where everyone got up and danced—they were relishing it, barely pausing between songs, the music fast and infectious. Someone had propped the front door open and outside, the rain grew heavier, sheets of it cascading down, but the sound of it only seemed to spur everyone on.

As she danced, spinning in the summer dress she was wearing despite the rain, all the while she was aware of where Theo was. How they were gradually moving closer as everyone linked arms again. She briefly lost sight of Cece, then saw her again with Helen and George, the three of them holding hands and jumping. Then, finally, she was next to him, and when their arms linked it was such a relief to be able to touch him, to feel his bare arm against hers, even if only for a brief moment before they changed partners again. The next time they met, he caught her gaze, held it. She felt her pulse leap at the base of her throat at the way his eyes glowed. Then his lips slowly tugged upward into that cocky smile she hated. Only she realized that she didn't hate it at all. His grin spread, like he *knew* that, and while it should have annoyed her, in that moment it hit her that, despite how she'd gotten here, despite what these past months had entailed, *this* was where she wanted to be right now. In a pub in Ireland, dancing to music that made your soul come alive—with Theo by her side.

Chapter Twenty-six

Later, after Helen had taken the kids back to where they were all staying at the Coach Inn next door and Miranda had retired too, claiming she needed a good night's sleep because the temperature hadn't been quite right in her room last night, Theo and Lexie sat opposite each other at the table in the corner, their knees nearly touching. The candlelight in the pub was flickering and the crowd was thinning out. They both had half a glass of red left, and Lexie knew she was nursing it, in the hope of dragging out the evening.

"So," Lexie said, tapping her fingernails against the glass. "I'd say Ireland isn't that bad, after all."

Theo laughed as he leaned back against his chair. "The last time I was in Ireland, it was to watch my old girlfriend get married." He said it casually, no hint of hurt, but Lexie's heart spasmed. The last time he was in Ireland—earlier this year, when he'd come back all tense?

"Were you . . . Was she . . . ?" But she didn't know what exactly she was trying to ask.

"No, it wasn't like that," Theo said, apparently figuring out her nonquestion. "We were dating before I left Ireland— obviously. She was from just outside Dublin too; her mum and my mum ran in the same social circles. My mum was desperate to impress their family, because they had the right sort of background or whatever." He wrinkled his nose. "It's a side of my mum I don't really get, but she is always trying to impress. Anyway. My mum was desperate for it to work between us—but it didn't, which is part of the reason I left."

Twenty-two. He'd left when he was twenty-two, she remembered. It could still be a childhood sweetheart—the one person Theo never got over—but she didn't think so, from the way he was telling the story.

"Anyway, I hadn't seen her in a while, but when I got the invite from Cally—that's her name—I thought I should try to be there."

"You're still friends?"

"Not really. It was nice to see her again in that way it's nice to see an old acquaintance and feel kind of nostalgic, but she only invited me because of the family connection. That's why I went back—not really for her, but to see my parents. And, well, it didn't go well." He sighed. "Sorry. It's just weird. It's a different country, but we're not far away from them now—they're just down the coast." He took a sip of her wine, then looked at her pointedly. "Your turn."

"What?" He just waited, and realization hit her. A truth for a wish. And maybe the red wine could be blamed for this, but she decided to offer him something a bit different. "If I could make a wish right now," she said, keeping her voice low, "it would be that we could come back here again next year. That we could come back to this same pub, dance to music, have a few days away from everything." She felt herself blush as she said it, and she couldn't meet Theo's eye. Because when she said *we,* she meant him.

"That's a wish you could make come true, you know."

The way he said it coaxed her into looking at him. The corner of his mouth pulled up into half a smile and she became a little too aware of the inches that separated them under the table. She could imagine it, though—her and Theo sitting here again next year. Could they do that? Could they make a pact to drop everything and meet up, once a year, like people did in movies? Her automatic response was *no,* because it was a silly dream— a silly wish that she would be stupid to hold on to. But she remembered what Theo had said about her wish jar before. *Maybe by "setting them free" you are hiding from what you want, making it so that you don't have to hope for things.*

Then a memory of her dad's voice, too. *One day, if you wish hard enough, it* will *come true.*

But a frown pulled at her forehead. Because wishing for something did *not* make it come true, did it? And despite the fact that she was having trouble shaking whatever *this* was between Theo and her, they still wanted different things.

"I don't want to stay in Bath forever," she said quietly. "I don't want to run the company forever." She glanced at him, wondering whether she'd make him snap at her, for bringing this up. He'd been thrown into this too, after all. He hadn't always known he'd take over the company, hadn't been prepared for it. This had changed his life, as well as hers. But the difference was, he had already been *in* this life, whereas she . . . "I like my life. I like traveling."

Theo nodded, his expression mock-serious. "Oh yes, it sucks all this desk-based work we're doing right now."

Lexie rolled her eyes. "I just . . . I worry about the commitment of it all."

"Really? I hadn't noticed that about you at *all*."

She kicked his shin lightly under the table. "I'm trying to explain, OK? I'm trying to make it so you won't hate me, when we're done with all this. Because I'm still figuring out what I want to do, and this was my dad's dream and . . . and I'm not sure it's mine." She broke off, trying to figure out exactly what she was trying to say.

"There's nothing to say you can't figure out what you want to do while also seeing if you like doing this for a bit. It's not a trap, Lex. And I don't think your dad meant it as one."

"No. Maybe he didn't." She took a sip of her wine—the glass nearly empty now. "What will you do if the company sells?" It felt like she could ask now that they were actually talking about it.

"I don't really know. But I was OK before; I'll be OK after. There are other jobs."

There was no blame in his voice, like there had been in the past—but it still felt tentative, like something could shatter if she said the wrong thing. And she realized she was sad, too. She was sad at the idea that she wouldn't have a reason to talk to Theo every day, wouldn't get to see him over the top of her computer or explore new places with him. She'd gotten used to him being there, without even realizing it—gotten used to being annoyed by him, and sparring with him, and them making each other laugh. She realized with a jolt of panic how much she was going to miss him.

She cleared her throat to cover it up. "Were you? OK before?"

He shrugged. "I was getting there. But I've learned how to be OK—and I won't lose that if the company sells." He said it firmly, like he was convincing himself. And she wondered— could she keep it after all? Could she let *him* keep it?

When they finished the wine, Theo stood, wooden chair legs scraping across the floor, and she got to her feet too, following him outside, where it had finally stopped raining, and into the Coach Inn next door. They walked side by side, neither of them saying anything. Their forearms were so close—she only had to move an inch, then they'd be touching.

They reached his room first—both of them were on the ground floor. He cleared his throat. "Well, this is me."

She nodded, though disappointment was coursing through her.

"I'll see you tomorrow?" he asked, shoving his hands into his pockets and rocking back slightly on his heels.

She nodded again, her heart picking up speed in a way that felt a little like panic.

He turned, fumbled with his key to open the door. And she took a breath.

"Theo?"

He looked back at her, and she made herself hold his gaze as she spoke again.

"I wouldn't regret anything in the morning this time. Just in case you were wondering." Her heart was in her throat now, her body held tense. It was a risk, to put the suggestion out there, in case she got shot down. He might not even remember his words from the last time they almost went there.

He didn't drop eye contact, and the space between them seemed to pulse. "Are you sure?"

She gave a firm nod. "Yes."

That was all it took. Theo closed the distance between them, and his mouth came down to hers, catching it firmly, no hint of hesitation. And God, the *relief,* at feeling his lips, hot and firm on hers. Her lips parted for his tongue and she felt his hands grip her waist as she angled her mouth up to meet his. She ran her hands up his back, fingernails digging in, and he let out a soft oath against her mouth. Why had she ever tried to convince herself not to do this? As if this could ever be a terrible idea.

His mouth moved down her throat, slow and hungry. "God," he muttered. "You have no idea how much I've wanted to touch you this weekend."

"Then why didn't you?" Her voice was a little breathless, and when he moved his hand down her thigh, back up under her dress, she felt the burn of his palm on her flesh.

"Because," he murmured. "It would have led to me doing this." He kissed her again, deeper, rougher, and heat flared though her as he backed her again the wall.

"We need to . . ." But her breath caught as his teeth scraped her bottom lip, then down over her jaw. *"Move,"* she managed to get out, though she was still pulling at him, urging him closer.

"Shit." His voice was hot against her skin before he eased back, glancing behind them. "Right."

She let out a shaky laugh at his expression. "Although apparently hotel corridors are our thing."

He moved his hands up and down her arms, leaving goosebumps behind. "Which . . . ?"

"Yours," Lexie said immediately, jerking her head over his shoulder to where his hotel room was waiting. "Closer."

"Good call." He grabbed her hand and pulled her inside, and she laughed again as he pushed the door shut, then pushed her against it. His hands moved down her thigh and she dragged her fingers through his hair. His fingers glided higher and she shuddered as their mouths slipped together again. He tugged at her dress and she lifted her arms over her head, helping him get it off her.

Their movements slowed, became more deliberate. This wasn't an accident on either of their parts—not this time. They stared at each other as their hands roamed, and her breath caught at the intensity between them. One of his hands moved to push one bra strap down, and he kissed her bare shoulder.

"I've been dreaming about the feel of you," he murmured against her skin. "Been remembering the taste of you."

"Can't shake the memory, huh?" Her attempt at lightness was slightly betrayed by the quiver in her voice.

"I don't *want* to shake the memory," he said, then bit down in that space between her shoulder and neck. She groaned and closed her eyes as she arched against him. His hands skimmed down her sides, dug into her outer thighs. Then rose. Her eyes opened, and she grabbed his shoulders as she hooked her legs around his waist, a little wide-eyed as he moved her away from the door and toward the bed.

"You're carrying me!"

He grinned that cocky grin. "I know."

"How are you strong enough to carry me!"

His grin only spread as he dropped her on the bed, and she laughed as she landed. Her laugh changed to a gasp as he grabbed her calves, pulled her toward the end of the mattress. His hands rode up her inner thighs, then his mouth followed, tasting where he touched. She breathed his name, wasn't even sure what she meant by it, then whimpered as he kissed the top of her inner thigh and over her, her hips lifting automatically. She reached behind her, grabbing hold of the top of the head-board to ground herself, as he pressed a hand to her stomach to keep her still, the heat of his mouth pushing her closer to the end.

"*Theo,*" she said again, and now reached down to pull him to her. He rose and she heard the hiss of his belt buckle, before she sat up, helping him out of his jeans. He pushed her gently onto her back and she pulled him with her, groaning at the relief of finally feeling the weight of him on her. He reached behind her and she shifted so he could undo her bra. His gaze went both dark and burning as it scraped up the lines of her body.

"Fuck, Lexie."

She ran a hand through his hair, unable to keep from touching him. "I'll take that as a compliment."

His laugh was a little shaky. "You should. You totally should." His thumb swept the outside curve of her breast and her nerve endings lit up. She moved her thighs so he could settle against her hips, and his mouth dragged down her breasts, catching her nipples. Everything in her went tight. She reached between them to feel him in her hand, and he let his breath out on a hiss as he moved into it.

"Did you bring a . . . ?"

"Yeah." He grinned. "Just in case." He reached for his bedside table, and she knew that he, too, must have guessed where this weekend was going to end. He kissed her hungrily as he worked on the condom, then took hold of her hips, guiding her onto him, his eyes heavy and dark. Everything in her went taut as he held himself there. Then she moved her hips against him, and he groaned as he rocked into her.

"Fuck," he said again, his teeth scraping down her jaw.

She let out another gasp as she pushed against him, her fingernails digging into his back. "And to think, all the time we've wasted not doing this."

"We've done this plenty of times in my head."

"How does it compare?"

"Not even close."

He sat up, pulled her into his lap, and pushed back into her. She braced her hands behind her, working herself onto him, as one of his hands wound into her hair, the other flattened on her back, holding her there. She ran her hands down his back, his muscles rigid with tension, and felt her outline dissolving, the edges of everything becoming blurred. She bit the side of his neck, and his fingers dug into her spine as a rush of pleasure flared through her.

Afterward, he pulled her down on the bed next to him, so that her head was on his chest. She lay there, waiting for her breathing to return to normal, as he traced lazy patterns across her stomach. "Are you . . . ?" he asked.

"Still here," she said. Though in truth she felt a little dazed, like her brain was still catching up to it. Really, if this was what sex with Theo was like, maybe she ought to be doing a lot more of it.

But not tonight. Because if she wasn't careful, she'd end up falling asleep here, and she couldn't be having that. So, a little reluctantly, she moved away, starting to sit up.

He reached out, grabbed her hand. "Stay," he murmured. And despite what she was trying to tell herself, despite the fact that she was trying to keep it safe, her stupid heart flipped. But it was for that very reason that she couldn't.

Instead, she bent over him, kissed his forehead. "I'll see you in the morning."

Because whatever he might want now, she didn't want to come to expect him to always be there.

Chapter Twenty-seven

When there was a knock at Lexie's door in the morning, she answered it without thinking, toothbrush in hand, still in her pajama vest top and shorts, bare legs on show. Of course, it was Theo who stood there, his hair messy, a hint of stubble just starting to grow out. And no matter that he'd seen all of her last night, no matter that he'd tasted practically every naked inch of her, she still had a rush of self-consciousness. It was one thing in the moment, in the middle of the night—another thing entirely with the curtains open, bright light streaming in—and him all dressed and her . . . not. Especially as she hadn't had time to sort her face out and she currently looked like she'd just crawled out of bed—and definitely not in the sexy way. She tried to resist the urge to cover herself as Theo's gaze dropped to her legs, traveling up the length of them. She cleared her throat and his gaze snapped to hers.

"Right. Sorry."

It made her laugh, and the self-consciousness faded a little. He shoved his hands into his pockets. He did that, she realized. When he was working up to something.

"So I wanted to take a trip today. And I wondered if you'd come with me."

She frowned, now not really sure what to do with the toothbrush in her hand. "Aren't we booked onto the flight home with the others?"

"Yeah, but we can get them on the bus and say our goodbyes from here. We couldn't ask the company to pay for new flights for us, but flights home from Dublin are super-cheap."

"From Dublin?"

"Yeah. I've got a friend who lives near Dublin still—he owns a B&B down there. We could drive down. It's only about an hour from here."

His hands were still in his pockets, and he rocked back on his heels. He was nervous about asking her. And that thought made her heart catch, in a way she couldn't help. She thought about it for a second. But the truth was, she didn't want to go home. She didn't want last night to be the end.

His voice, heavy with near-sleep. *Stay.*

So she nodded. "OK."

"OK? Really?"

"If you didn't think I would say yes, why did you ask?"

He grinned at her in that way she loved. "Always worth a shot, Lex."

THE B&B TURNED out to be an old farmhouse and even though she knew Dublin was a stone's throw away, it very much had Irish country vibes. They'd driven down a long drive, fields with horses in them on one side, and a view of a nearby lake on the other. Theo parked the car on the gravel driveway in front of a place that managed to be impressively big while also holding an undeniable "cottage charm." The building was stone gray, with climbing green plants over one side, and flowers in mismatched pots leading up the white steps to the front door. Lexie heard barking, and a collie shot out from around the back of the house somewhere.

"Simon!" shouted a man's voice as Lexie took half a step backward from the bounding dog. It was wagging its tail, though, tongue hanging out and head low, so Lexie held out a hand for it to sniff, then laughed as the dog pressed against her legs for strokes.

Theo and Lexie carried their bags inside, and were greeted in the reception area by a man with scraggly hair and an equally scraggly beard who looked about the same age as Theo. He was dressed very casually for someone in hospitality, his jeans ripped at the knees, a streak of mud down one side of his T-shirt, and he smiled at Lexie when he saw the dog following at her heels.

"Sorry about Simon," he said, then glanced at Theo, leaving Lexie wondering who the hell named a dog *Simon*. "And hello there," the man said, his Irish accent thick. "Can I help you both on this fine day?"

His smile was full of charm, but Theo managed to look suspicious, his scarred eyebrow shooting up. "I called earlier."

"Ah yes. Theo, is it?" The "Th" changed to "T," so that it sounded more like "Teo." "Got a lovely room for yiz both, overlooking the lake."

"I asked for two rooms," Theo said pointedly, before Lexie could jump in. At her shins, Simon nudged her for attention.

"Ah no, we've only got the one room, I'm afraid. But she's a beauty."

Lexie opened her mouth to protest, but Theo pulled her to his side and wrapped an arm around her side. He gave her a very un-Theo-like smile. "What do you think, honeybee?"

She narrowed her eyes up at him as the scraggly-haired man laughed, then came over to envelop Theo in a hug. "Mate! It's been too long."

Lexie couldn't help noticing that his Irish accent was less thick now. So, this was the friend Theo had mentioned. She wondered if Theo had put him up to the joke.

Theo clapped him on the back. "Good to see you. Lexie, this is Kieran. Kieran, Lexie."

"Um . . . hi." She gave a sort of awkward half wave, and then used Simon as a way to distract from that, bending to scratch him.

"Nice to meet you, Lexie," Kieran said. He tipped an imaginary hat to her.

"So—*do* you have two rooms?" Lexie asked, looking up at him.

Kieran laughed. "Yeah. I've had them on standby since Theo told me you were coming a few weeks ago."

A few *weeks*? Lexie straightened and shot him a look, but he studiously ignored her gaze. So, he'd been planning this then. Her stomach flipped with a weird combination of anxiety and pleasure.

"Or one room, if you prefer," Kieran said, with a sly grin for Theo.

Theo glanced at Lexie and shrugged. "We'll figure it out later." And oh God, the awkwardness. "But first, I figured we'd go into Dublin—you've never been, right, Lex?"

"No, I . . ."

Kieran raised his hand in the air, grimacing as he did so. "I may have something that interferes with your plans." He lowered his hand and tugged a little nervously at his beard as Theo waited for him to elaborate. "Your mam *may* have found out you're here."

"Kieran! Did you *call* her?"

"Nah, of course not. But, like, you know how it is. I stuck something on Facebook, her friend saw, she found out, she called me. And you know how I am—can't lie, can I?"

"Do not tell me she's coming here, Kieran." Theo's tone was full of warning.

"I don't *think* so. But she asked me what time you were expected and, well . . ."

Seemingly on cue, Theo's phone rang. He got it out, glaring at Kieran, while Lexie returned to stroking Simon, unsure of what to do. Simon licked her ear as Theo answered.

"Hello, Mam." It was the most Irish she'd ever heard Theo sounding. "I'm sorry, but it was a bit of a last-minute thing." There was a pause. "Only one day—we're flying tomorrow." Another pause. "Lexie." He shot Kieran an evil look. "No, I can't come today. Because I'm with Lexie. Right." He pulled a hand through his hair as his mum continued to talk at the other end of the line. "Right. Look, I'll let you know." He hung up, tugged a hand through his hair. "She wants us to go for lunch. For fuck's sake, Kieran."

Kieran winced.

"We can go for lunch with her," Lexie said, trying to be diplomatic.

Theo shot her a look, but she couldn't quite read it.

"And do Dublin later? I'd like to meet her."

"I'm not sure you would," Theo said dryly. But she was thinking of her own dad now, and of the fact that she'd brushed him off the last time he tried to reach out. Thinking of how these chances were limited—and how you have to take them while you can.

"I think we should go," said firmly.

Kieran clapped Theo on the back. "The room will be ready by the time you get back."

"Rooms," Lexie said, keeping her firm voice in play.

"Ah, sure. Rooms. That's what I meant. And I'll have a pint waiting for you."

Theo sighed. "Fine, we'll go." He looked at Lexie. "But please remember that I warned you." He turned his attention to Kieran. "And that pint better be on you, mate—you owe me."

LEXIE COULDN'T STOP her mouth from quite literally falling open as Theo parked the car in front of his parents' place. It had to be the most gorgeous redbrick house she'd ever seen—and was about five times the size of her mum's cottage. The front lawn was perfectly manicured, complete with pruned bushes. Four turreted chimneys stretched up above the roof, and from the windows she could see, Lexie was sure it must be three floors.

"You're rich!" she hissed at Theo as they got out of the car. She hung back until he started making his way toward the porch, feeling uncertain all of a sudden.

"My parents are rich," Theo said. And like he could sense her nerves, he took her hand, laced his fingers with hers. Even out here, in front of his parents' house, her pulse flared with the contact, and she had to try very hard to stop her mind flashing to how it had felt to have him inside of her last night.

"Isn't that the same thing?" she asked, as they crunched across the gravel. There were another two cars in the enormous driveway—a BMW and a Mercedes.

"Well, definitely not in my case."

But Lexie was still staring at the house, craning her neck back as they approached, feeling a combination of awe and trepidation.

"Damn, I never should have brought you here," Theo said wryly. "Now if I ever ask you to marry me, you'll only be in it for the money I might one day inherit."

She could tell he was joking, but her heart immediately gave a panicked thump at the word *marry,* and she stumbled a little as they came to a stop.

He squeezed her hand. "Lex?"

She looked up at him.

"I'm kidding."

She licked her now-dry lips. "Right. I know that." She gave a weak, very unconvincing laugh.

Theo pressed the doorbell, and Lexie heard it echo inside the house. A woman came out almost immediately, and Lexie knew this had to be Theo's mother. She had the same eyes—dark with amber highlights, though on first glance they seemed more static than Theo's, which were constantly changing. Her tan skin was flawless, her lips painted peach, and her hair was a little lighter than Theo's, with honey highlights neatly streaked through. She smiled, showing impressively white teeth, and leaned in to kiss Theo's cheek. Theo, Lexie couldn't help but notice, held himself a little stiff as he returned the gesture.

"This is my mum, Lexie," Theo said. "Shauna."

"Hi, Shauna." Lexie's smile faltered a little under Shauna's assessing gaze. Shauna then looked away, back to Theo, like she was reserving judgment.

"Your father's in the living room," she said to Theo. "He'll be pleased to see you."

"Doubtful," Theo muttered, so quietly that Lexie was sure his mum hadn't heard.

She squeezed his hand as Shauna led them into the hallway, her heels clacking on the wooden floor. Lexie felt underdressed—not just in comparison to Shauna, who was wearing a flowery dress that looked like it must be designer, but in the face of the interior. The whole place was flawless. The off-white walls were spotless, the beige carpet leading up the impressive spiral staircase pristine. There was a fireplace in the hallway, of all places, with a rug in front of it and two reading chairs, and above them a chandelier hung from the high ceiling. There was artwork dotted throughout, in that way most people could only dream of. She wondered what it must be like to keep a place of this size as clean and tidy as it was—though surely somewhere like this would have a cleaner. It was so at odds with what she'd seen of the flat above the shop where Theo lived that she couldn't get her head around the fact that he'd grown up here.

The walk through the house felt oddly hushed—if it had been her mum, they'd have been talking from the word go. Theo's dad was reading *The Irish Times* when the three of them entered the living room and he only looked up when Shauna spoke his name.

"Patrick? Theo's here. And his friend Lexie," she added, after the briefest of pauses. There was a *piano* in the corner of the living room, for God's sake. She glanced up at Theo, wanting to ask if he played, but he was looking at his dad, his posture stiffening by the second. She pulled her hand from his, tugged at her curls self-consciously.

Patrick peered over the paper. His hair was steel gray, to match his eyebrows, and his eyes were bright blue. He was wearing a suit, despite the fact that it was just the four of them. Lexie decided that Theo's parents must take the concept of "Sunday best" literally. She and Theo *definitely* looked underdressed.

"So you're visiting for the weekend, then?" Patrick asked, not bothering to say hello to Lexie.

"Lexie and I are here for work," Theo said, and he said her name a little pointedly, like he was reminding his dad she was here. It worked, and Patrick glanced at her.

"You work with Theo, do you?"

Jesus, Patrick's eyes were intense. But not in the way Theo's were—his gaze was cold and calculating. "Ah, yes. I'm Richard's daughter."

Patrick's gray eyebrows pulled together.

"My old boss," Theo explained, and Patrick grunted, before folding his newspaper.

"Lunch ready, then, is it?" he asked Shauna.

"Yes, nearly," Shauna said, her tone a little *too* bright. Lexie had a momentary flare of sympathy for her. "You head on through to the dining room and I'll bring everything in. Can I get anyone a drink?"

"I'll have a beer, if you're offering," Theo said.

Shauna pursed her lips. "It's lunchtime, Theo. I've made some lovely elderflower cordial, though."

"That sounds great," Lexie said quickly, because she saw Theo go to open his mouth again—and she *knew* that argumentative look. He cocked one eyebrow down at her, like he knew what she was doing.

Shauna served drinks and an entire Sunday roast on the world's biggest dining table, so that even though they were all sat down at one end of it, it still felt like they were very far apart from one another. Shauna and Patrick sat on one side, Theo and Lexie on the other, and Lexie was put in mind of a formal board meeting—or a job interview. The roast was incredible—a joint of beef, complete with impeccable roast potatoes, cauliflower cheese, creamed leeks, and Yorkshire puddings. How had Shauna been able to get all this ready in time—and still look as immaculate as she did?

"So, Theo," Shauna said brightly, stretching to place more potatoes onto Lexie's plate across the table, "how are things? You're here for work? Is it still that travel agency you're working for, then?"

Theo tore off a chunk of his Yorkshire pudding, dunked it in gravy.

Lexie saw the look Shauna gave him at that, but she didn't say anything.

"Yeah. Still there."

Lexie started eating with gusto, partly to try to cover up the awkwardness.

"So, you're sticking with it, are you?" Patrick said, folding a napkin neatly on his lap.

Theo shrugged, but Lexie saw the brittleness in that action. "I enjoy it."

"Haven't you thought about what we talked about last time, darling?" Shauna asked. "I have a friend who has a contact at that firm in London if you—"

"I'm good. Thanks."

"You haven't grown out of it yet, then?" Patrick asked, surveying Theo over the fork of beef he lifted to his mouth. "Don't want to settle down and do something serious?"

"He owns half the business," Lexie said, unable to stop herself. She felt herself redden as both of his parents looked at her, a little baffled. But seriously—*grow out of it*? It was like what people said to her when they asked why she was still traveling around, why she hadn't gotten a *proper* job yet. Only the judgment from Theo's parents was worse, because he *had* settled down—he was good at running the business, and he had worked hard to keep it going.

"You own it?" Shauna repeated, looking back at Theo for confirmation.

"Lexie and I own it, yeah." Theo shifted uncomfortably in his seat, and Lexie wondered if she should have just kept quiet— maybe there was a reason he hadn't told his parents.

Shauna looked between them, frowning slightly, like she was trying to figure out the exact nature of their relationship.

You and me both, Shauna.

"How much is it worth?" Patrick asked, spearing a roast potato in a way that managed to make Lexie feel *sorry* for the potato.

"I don't know yet, Dad."

"Have you spoken to Cally since the wedding?"

"No, Mam."

"Well, she's doing very well. They went on a *lovely* honeymoon to the Maldives, and I think it won't be long before we'll have more news to celebrate. They're looking to move house, and I heard on the grapevine they were looking around Rathfarnham, and you just know that's because of the schools in the area." She sighed. "I always wonder, if we'd sent you to school there . . ."

She trailed off, but the end of the sentence was implicit, and Lexie thought of how Theo had said before that his mum was big into wishes. Was this one of those—I wish we'd sent you to a different school, so that you'd have turned out differently? Was it about success? But he *owned* his own business now—surely you didn't get much more successful than that? And he had a cool idea, to invest back into local businesses, even if that might not come off in time, but still . . .

She opened her mouth, but Theo caught her eye, shook his head ever so slightly. And really, she didn't want to risk rocking the boat, did she?

"That's nice for Cally," Theo said, ignoring the second part of his mum's sentence.

It went quiet for a moment, and the scrape of knives and forks on china made Lexie wish there was background music. She cleared her throat, trying to dispel some of the tension in the room. "This is delicious, Shauna."

Shauna gave her a smile. "Thank you. I love cooking a roast—it's so soothing. Do you cook, too?"

"Oh, um . . . sort of." She thought of her and her mum's attempts at blinis the previous Christmas—most of which had ended up in the bin. "I make a good spaghetti Bolognese," she settled on.

There was more warmth in Shauna's smile now. "Such comfort food." Then she sighed. "I do wish you'd stuck with the cooking lessons yourself, Theo."

Lexie had never heard the word "wish" sound so cutting. She wanted to reach out, lay a comforting hand on his arm—but she wasn't sure she should, with his parents watching them.

"You know, Reuben from your school is a chef now—and he owns his own restaurant."

Lexie waited for him to snap back, *wanting* him to snap—or to at least stand up for himself. But instead he just nodded—so unlike the Theo she'd come to know. "Good for Reuben."

Shauna turned her attention to Lexie. "So, what else do you do, Lexie?" Lexie wondered if by saying she could make spaghetti Bolognese she had led Shauna to assume cooking was something she "did," and decided, all things considered, to roll with that.

"Um . . ." She glanced at Theo for support, but obviously he couldn't help her here. "I guess I travel a lot."

There was a sigh from across the table from Patrick, barely hidden.

Shauna frowned. "Don't be rude, Patrick." She smiled at Lexie. "I'm so sorry, Lexie. Do tell us more."

"Well, I mean there's not a lot to tell, really." If they thought *Theo* was unsuccessful, she hardly wanted to admit to moving around every six months—and was sure they wouldn't take too favorably to the fact that her last job had been as a nanny. But as the meal passed in uncomfortable silence, she wished she *had* gone into the details. It felt like time was moving incredibly slowly—though it could only have been forty minutes, tops, by the time the plates were cleared and Patrick went back into the living room.

Theo made an excuse, telling his mum they had to get back to the farmhouse for a meeting, and Shauna didn't question it, for which Lexie was immensely relieved. She was starting to feel a little guilty for having forced Theo to accept the invitation.

"Thank you for coming to see us, Theo," Shauna said at the front door, kissing his cheek again. "I do wish you'd visit us a bit more, you know."

"I'll try," Theo said noncommittally, and Shauna pursed her lips at the evasive answer.

Then she turned to Lexie. "It was lovely to meet you. I hope you have the most perfect time in Dublin this evening."

It was said kindly, Lexie was sure of it. But she couldn't help the words from slipping out, over a smile of her own. "Perfection is overrated."

It got a small laugh of delight from Theo.

"But I'm sure we'll have a great time, thank you."

Theo said nothing as they got back into the car, and still nothing as he started the engine, turned around in the driveway.

Lexie let out a long breath. "Well."

Theo ran a hand across the back of his neck. "Yeah. Not what you expected?"

"I don't know *what* I expected, really."

And it wasn't like his parents were horrible. They just weren't *warm*. She could tell that Shauna had been trying, and perhaps she really did have Theo's best interests at heart—she wouldn't be the first mother to want something better for her son. But it was like she hadn't noticed that Theo had been getting more and more tense throughout. So perhaps they were both products of their upbringing, in the end. And even though his parents were still together, Lexie couldn't help wondering if they *should* be—did they even like each other? Or speak to each other? Or was that just where all relationships were destined to end up eventually?

"She cares about me," Theo said, like he was reading her mind. "But I can't help feeling that I'm a disappointment every time I see her. Like she wishes for something better."

"I don't think you're a disappointment." She wasn't sure how much it was worth, but she said it anyway.

Theo glanced at her, something she couldn't read in his expression. "I feel stupid sometimes, for caring about it. There's nothing nasty and they weren't ever abusive or anything—so it feels like I shouldn't be hurt by it, you know? Like what do I really have to complain about?"

Lexie tapped her fingers against her thigh. "I'm not sure things need to be overtly nasty to be hurtful." Over time, constantly feeling like you weren't good enough could do its own damage, couldn't it? Leave its own scars.

"I guess not."

"My dad was never mean," Lexie said. "He just wasn't there."
And that, too, had left scars. She shook her head. "I'm sorry
I made you go today—if you didn't want to. It's just . . . He
tried to build a bridge with me, before he died. Richard. And
the thing is, I might have allowed it, if we'd taken things a bit
slower, so to speak. But he went right in for this big apology and
it was too much. And now, a part of me is wishing I'd taken the
time to listen to him, but another part is wondering if he even
would have done it, if it hadn't been for the cancer. And then I
get really confused, because I don't know how I feel about any of
it—or even who I'm really grieving for."

"I guess you can grieve the father you lost when you were
seven, as well as the one who died last December. It's OK that
he wasn't perfect—and it's OK to feel sad about the fact that he's
not here anymore, even though he left you. I think it's OK to feel
however you feel—I don't think grief is ever simple or straight-
forward, no matter the circumstances."

Lexie looked out of the window. "Yeah. Maybe. I guess I'm
working toward that—and trying to forgive him, too."

"I think it's OK if you can't forgive him. Forgiveness and
acceptance are different things, aren't they? And it might take
some time to work toward either."

Lexie glanced back at him. "Is that how you feel, with your
parents? Because that's where I was going with this, believe it or
not—because I know I'll never get another chance. So that's why
I was so keen for us to visit *your* parents today."

He flicked the indicator on and said nothing for a moment.
Then, "Do you know? This is why I was a bit . . . resentful of you
at first. Because your dad was trying to reach out, and your dad
was just so great with *me*. And my parents—they're annoyed if

I don't visit when I'm here, but really, they wouldn't ever come to visit me or anything, and they disapprove of everything I do. Whereas your dad, to my mind, was just so proud of you, of the way you explored new places. And it looked to me like you just kept throwing it back in his face."

Lexie frowned. "It's more complicated than that."

"I know that now. And I hope you know how sorry I am, for judging you. For making you think I hated you."

"You *did* hate me."

The corner of his mouth crooked up. "Only a little. Only as much as you hated me."

She hesitated, not sure of what to say. Then, "I don't hate you now." It was the best she could offer.

His mouth spread into a fuller smile. "I know."

Something inside her lurched at his expression—something she didn't quite understand. Or maybe something she didn't *want* to understand.

When they got back to the farmhouse, Simon came out to greet them again, following them at Lexie's heels as they headed inside, and they found Kieran slouched in an armchair in the guest living room—which was much more haphazard than Theo's parents' living room, and much nicer, to Lexie's mind, because of it.

"I'll have that pint now, Kieran," Theo said loudly.

Kieran got to his feet, clapping Theo on the back. "Right-oh." He turned to head out, then stopped, fished in his pocket, and held out a key with a bird key chain on it.

Lexie took it. "Thanks," she said. "We'll just have the one room."

"Oh good," Kieran said, tugging at his beard. "Because I've only actually got the one."

Lexie shook her head, then laughed. She glanced up at Theo as Kieran headed out—presumably to get them all a drink. "I suppose you knew I'd cave." Though *she* hadn't been sure she would—because sharing a room felt bigger, more deliberate. No longer just a casual hookup—and something that would be harder to walk away from.

He put his arms around her and kissed the corner of her mouth. "I didn't know," he murmured. "I hoped."

Chapter Twenty-eight

"So what do you think?" Lexie asked her mum as the estate agent walked back to the kitchen to give them some space, leaving them in the bedroom.

Her mum beamed. "I think it's *wonderful*."

But Lexie bit her lip as she took in the bedroom again. It was small, but not cramped, had a built-in wardrobe with mirrors to give it a bigger, brighter feel, and a chest of drawers opposite the double bed. It was furnished, of course, because Lexie had no furniture whatsoever. And it *was* nice. A steal for the location, according to Fran—not as central as her flat, but still.

Even so . . . "It's a twelve-month contract."

"Yes, well, I think that's pretty standard these days, isn't it? Oh, Lex, it'll be lovely to have you so close for another year."

Her mum didn't seem to get it. Twelve months might not sound like a long time to some people, but for Lexie it felt like an enormous commitment, one that made her palms go a bit sticky. And the thing was, she wasn't doing it to stay nearby, was she? Even if it *would* be nice to stay close to her—and to Fran—it was Theo she'd been thinking of when she'd booked a viewing. Of the fact that she didn't want to say goodbye to him. Of him telling her, in Ireland, that she had control over whether they went back there together next year—and all that that had implied.

Her mum seemed to read something on her face. "You can

always move when the contract's up, if you find that living here really isn't for you," she said softly. "A year will go by in no time."

But now that she was here, looking at the flat, she was starting to feel as though she'd be giving up her freedom, the nomadic life that had always suited her perfectly. And for what—for a chance to make things work at the company, and with Theo? To try for a proper relationship? She didn't even know if she'd be any good at a relationship. Look at Theo's parents, look at her own parents—and her dad's second marriage, come to think of it. Relationships didn't always work out the way you wanted them to.

Lexie plopped herself down on the edge of the bed, rubbed her hands over her face. Felt the bed sink slightly as her mum sat down next to her.

"What's going on in that head of yours?" her mum asked.

She knew, Lexie thought, that this was about more than just a flat. She had her suspicions about Theo, Lexie was sure of it. And she must have known that this was all tied up in the company—because if Lexie committed to renting a flat, then she was committing to running the company, wasn't she? At least for now.

Lexie hesitated, before asking the question she wanted to ask. "When did you know that it wasn't going to work out with Dad?"

She'd worried the question might be hurtful, but her mum only seemed thoughtful. "Do you know what? I've asked myself this plenty of times. I've tried to remember if there was a moment when I thought, OK, this is it. But I don't think there was—not until after he left. Richard was . . ." She pursed her lips, thinking. "He was always looking for something better. Not just in a relationship. I mean that he was often convinced there would be something better out there, in terms of a job, or a place to live, or whatever. When I first met him, I loved that about him. It had seemed optimistic, and I loved that he always wanted to go new places, experience new things—that he thought you didn't just have to stick with what you had. But when we had you, I wanted to give you some stability—I guess I'd outgrown always searching for the "better"—I thought I'd already found it. But I don't think he had outgrown it yet."

Lexie couldn't help comparing herself to Richard. Was that what she was doing, by always moving from place to place? Was she always looking for the "better" out there? She remembered too what Theo had told her, about how her dad was so determined to help him stick with something. That didn't sound like the type of man who was always searching for the next thing. Maybe her dad had realized that "better" was something you worked at, not something you found.

"When he met Jody ..." her mum continued, and Lexie scanned her face, to check for any sign that this was a hard conversation for her. It was why she'd never asked before—the fear of upsetting her mum. "I think he genuinely loved her. I was bitter enough, back then, to think he only wanted her because she was new, and young, and exciting. But I think he loved her, in a different way than he'd ever loved me—and that was hard to accept, for a very long time. It made me feel not good enough, and I think that's why it took me so long to, well ..."

She blew out a breath and Lexie put her arm around her shoulders, squeezed. She wanted to tell her mum that she *was* good enough, but she knew firsthand that it wasn't always that simple—and that this was something that had taken years to fix, years when Lexie had been only a child.

"Our relationship was on the rocks before that, in all honesty. It's something I didn't want to admit. It was easier, at the time, to be angry, and to cast Jody as the villain of the piece. Richard too. It was easier to believe that they had stolen all of my happiness, when really, things hadn't been very happy for some time."

"From what I've heard about Jody, I don't think she's exactly a hero," Lexie couldn't help muttering.

Her mum gave her a searching look, then said, "No. Well, people are complicated, aren't they? But what I mean is, we'd stopped working, as a couple. It wasn't anything major, but we were sort of existing around each other, rather than *with* each other. Relationships take work—and eventually I realized it wasn't just him who'd stopped putting in that work. And then Jody came along and I suppose all those little cracks exploded into chasms. I think maybe then I wanted to try—but it was already too late."

It wasn't easy to hear. It felt to Lexie like her mum was putting herself down—because Richard had still been the one to leave for someone else, hadn't he?

Her mum seemed to be reading her mind, because she took Lexie's hand in hers and said, "I don't blame him, Lexie. Not anymore. I don't think, in hindsight, we were right together. I'm not sure we would have been the happy family I'd imagined. And I don't think you can always help who you fall in love with—or when."

"But Jody's so . . ." She wanted to say *awful,* but she caught herself in time. She wasn't sure how Rachel would feel about her relaying her issues with her mum. Instead she said, "I met with Rachel recently."

She said it carefully—she'd never really talked about her sister with her mum before. But her mum only smiled.

"She said something that made me . . . Well, she said that she thought Jody had been worried that Dad might leave them. That he might come back—to us."

It wasn't a question, because she didn't really know what she wanted to ask. But her mum nodded slowly. "He spoke to me at one point, when Rachel was, I don't know, around one or two I think. Jody was . . . Well, I don't really know the ins and outs of it—I never wanted to. I think maybe—not unlike your father at times—she was a little caught up in the idea of what something should be, and perhaps less willing to adjust when things didn't quite match up to what she'd expected. And it sounded to me like she'd had a hard time, when Rachel was first born, and I'm not sure if that's why, or whether she just wasn't the person he'd thought she was when he married her, but he was having doubts."

"He wanted to leave her," Lexie said flatly, and her stomach contracted painfully—because somewhere over the last few months, she'd stopped wanting to see her dad this way.

"I think it was more that he wanted to come back to us, actually. He said he thought he'd made a mistake by leaving us. But he didn't know what to do, because leaving Jody would be making the same mistake again, and she was also saying that if he left her, she'd stop him from seeing Rachel. But by that point, I didn't *want* him to come back, not to me. It was too late by that point. I think he was searching for greener pastures in a difficult moment, and was scared he'd left the greenest one behind. It may just have been a moment of panic, because he felt like he was losing you, but I told him no. I wish he'd been around for you more, but us staying together wouldn't have been for the best for anyone. I also told him that leaving Jody didn't sound like it would solve anything—that you have to really put the effort in to make things work. And apparently, he agreed—because he stayed, and he tried to make it work. And do you know what? Weirdly, I was kind of proud of him for that."

Lexie heard the estate agent's phone ring down the corridor.

She stood up off the bed, knowing they had to leave. If anything, what her mum told her just made it even more incomprehensible that Richard had stayed with Jody, given she had held Rachel over his head like a threat. But maybe her mum was right—maybe her dad had finally grown up a bit, and decided to make the best he could of it for Rachel.

Her mum stood too, linking her arm through Lexie's as they headed to find the estate agent. "I know this must be weird to hear. But all I've got is that people are complicated—and what they do or don't do doesn't always make sense. I suppose all we can do is try to learn from our mistakes and do the best we can. And if it's any consolation . . . I think that's what Richard was trying to do, when he stayed with Jody and Rachel. I think he was trying to learn from his mistakes. And I think his company may have been a little about that, too."

Lexie nodded, not quite trusting herself to speak. None of this really made up for anything—but it did offer her a glimmer of understanding, and that was something.

You can't help who you fall in love with. That's what her mum had said. Unbidden, Theo's face flashed into her mind, even as she fought not to let it. No point in pretending, though, was there? He was the reason she'd be staying, if she took this flat. That, and maybe, just a little, the company, too. Maybe she should give them both a chance—and stop wondering if the grass was always greener elsewhere.

So when she shook the estate agent's hand as they were let out, she said that yes, she would like an application form, please. And felt her mum squeezing her hand, like she was telling her it was the right decision.

Chapter Twenty-nine

Lexie raised her knuckles to knock on the flat door but then lowered her hand again. She paced away in the little space at the top of the stairs, then turned around. She'd filled in the application form for the flat last night and had just found out this morning that she'd gotten it. She had to put the holding deposit down by the end of the day, but she wanted to talk to Theo about it first. She just wasn't sure exactly *how* to talk about it. Was she asking if he wanted to go all in—actually try to make this a relationship? Was she telling him that she wanted to keep the company? Her thoughts were panicked and muddled, and she took a breath to try to calm herself.

She knocked on the door, and Theo was smiling when he opened it. It was the type of smile to make the amber in his eyes light up. She felt her breath loosen a bit.

"Hey, Lex. What's up?"

"Hey. So, I wondered if we could talk for . . ." She trailed off as she caught sight of Mike over Theo's shoulder. She bit her lip. "Sorry. Is this a bad time?" She hadn't realized there was a meeting. Then again—surely it *wasn't* a proper meeting, otherwise she'd have been invited?

"Never a bad time for you." He opened the door wider, gestured her inside.

Mike gave Lexie a look she couldn't quite interpret, before turning back to Theo. "I should go, then."

"I'll walk you down," Theo offered. "Make yourself at home, Lexie."

Mike gave her a polite nod as he and Theo left—leaving Lexie alone in Theo's flat. It was weird—she'd been up here plenty of times for work, but now, since Ireland, there was something strangely intimate about it. Her phone buzzed, and she laughed as she saw a WhatsApp from Theo.

If you wanted to wait for me naked I wouldn't object.

She moved into the living room. There was a bunch of paperwork sitting on the coffee table, all with the R&L Travel logo stamped in the header, along with the slogan. *See the world through celebration.* She'd once thought it was a silly slogan— now, she thought it was apt. The first lot of paperwork was the latest P&L sheet. She made herself look at it properly. They were still on track to turn a profit. Her stomach gave a funny flip as she thought about what that meant—and the conversation she was about to have with Theo. Maybe they could just postpone the decision about whether to sell?

She kept flicking through. After the P&L document was a contract. She frowned, not understanding it at first. Then she saw her name, and her heart did a funny little lurch. She picked the paper up, rereading the top of it. There was Mike's name too. And Theo's.

It didn't make sense at first. The document looked so like the contract the solicitor had given her when she'd first found out about her dad's will. Only parts were changed—and Mike's name was in places it shouldn't be. Her heart was hammering, her fingers gripping the edges of the paper tightly. Because even as she tried to deny what her brain was telling her, she was already cottoning on.

They were planning on cutting her out. It was a draft contract, she could see that—there were no signatures yet. But the wording was clear. She would be out, and Mike would be in—with a twenty percent share of the company, the rest going to Theo. It cited her lack of involvement earlier in the year as a reason. There was no mention of selling the company off. Theo would get what he wanted—to keep the company, run it long-term; Mike would be in, like *he* clearly wanted, after having given her dad the start-up loan; and Lexie would be out completely.

She stared at the document, a lot of it in language that she didn't immediately understand. Bewilderment came first. How could they do this? Could it even be legal? But beneath that, and far more overpowering, was the thought that really mattered. He'd been planning this. The whole time, Theo had been planning it. When they were in Madrid together. When they slept together in Ireland. He'd opened up, got *her* to open up, and talked about future plans, and all the while, he'd been working on a plan to cut her out.

The front door opened, and Theo came back in. She stared up at him.

"Hey, so . . ." He trailed off, and she knew her expression must have been giving her away. He looked at the contract in her hand, and his face paled. And that was all the confirmation she needed. "Lexie—"

She stood up, letting the contract fall to the floor. "Don't."

He stepped toward her, but she moved back. "Lexie, please, it's not what you—"

"Not what I think?" She scoffed, clinging to the anger that was now rising—easier to feel that than the other emotions that wanted to boil over. "I don't think there are any other ways to interpret this, Theo, though granted I've only glanced it over."

And God, beneath the anger she was *hurt*. More hurt than she'd like to be. More hurt than she should have *let* herself be. This was why you shouldn't trust anyone—not completely. She'd been ready to go all in—was about to make herself vulnerable and tell him as much—and all the while he'd been doing *this*. She'd been ready to give up her way of life, to sacrifice that for *him*, but to Theo, she was just collateral damage.

"If you just give me the chance to—"

"No, do you know what? I don't think I will." She walked toward the door, skirting past him. Because she knew he'd try, she was prepared, and dodged out of reach when he tried to take her hand to stop her.

"Lexie," he said again, but she would not stop. She wanted to get away from him, as far away as possible—and she certainly didn't want to listen to excuses. So she ran down the stairs, moving faster as she heard him swear, then follow behind her.

"Harry," she said as she entered the office on the ground floor, her voice hitching on a near sob.

Harry looked up at her, hiding his phone swiftly in his pocket.

"Theo's coming down now. He asked if you could run him through the customer inquiries this morning."

Harry gave her a little salute, and she bolted from the shop.

Behind her, she heard Harry's voice as he lurched into action the moment Theo came down the stairs—and that gave her the chance she needed to get away. Sooner or later, she knew, she'd have to have a conversation with him. Would have to feel the full hurt of what he'd been planning and find out exactly how manipulative he'd been.

But not today.

LEXIE WAS SITTING on her bedroom floor, suitcase open and half filled by the time Fran came in. She heard the jangle of keys from the living room as Fran placed them in the designated key bowl on the kitchen counter, then heard Fran calling out.

"Lexie?"

"In here!"

Lexie stared at the clothes in her suitcase. Usually she was excellent at packing, after all the practice, but right now, she couldn't think of what she needed. Obviously the simplest thing to do would be to chuck everything in her room here into the suitcase and be done with it, but she knew she still had some things at her mum's, too.

"So, I've brought wine because I have some pretty big . . ." Fran trailed off as she came into Lexie's room and stared at the suitcase. "What's going on?"

Lexie bit her lip. "I'm trying to remember where I put my passport."

Why—why had she been so disorganized this time? It must be at her mum's. She glanced at her mobile, which was on her bed. She'd called a few agencies already, looking for seasonal work—after telling the estate agent that she was going to withdraw her application for the flat, of course. She was a bit late, but there was always last-minute availability—and a couple of the agencies had worked with her before, so knew and liked her.

"Your . . . What the hell, Lex? Where are you going? I thought you'd put down a deposit on that flat!"

"No, I changed my mind. And I don't know where I'm going yet." She pulled a hand through her hair.

"You don't know where you're going? What am I missing here?"

Lexie closed her eyes, then sank backward onto her bed. "I'm done. I'm quitting the company."

"But . . . *why?*"

Lexie shook her head. She couldn't bring herself to explain. And to think, this morning she and Fran had been talking about her flat, and when Fran could come round, and planning a moving-in party with Theo's name up at number one on the guest list. Stupid. She was so, so stupid. Then her eyes flew open, and she frowned.

"Wait—you said you had some pretty big . . . what? News?"

Fran's eyes darted from the suitcase on the floor to Lexie, and back again. "Ah, well."

"Tell me!"

Fran jumped, and Lexie grimaced.

"Sorry, I mean, let's press pause on my crisis for a moment. Please tell me."

"Well, I, um, sort of quit my job."

Lexie stared at her. "Are you serious?" Fran nodded, and Lexie sprang to her feet. "Oh my god. Oh my god. Congratulations! Shall we have wine? You're right, this calls for wine." She left the bedroom and hurried to the kitchen, her movements a bit frantic.

"Lexie, don't you think we should—"

"No. I want to hear about you. Tell me what happened." She opened one of the cupboards in Fran's small kitchen and got down two wineglasses. "This is way bigger than my thing," she insisted, aware that she was potentially talking a little too quickly but unable to stop herself. "You've been in your job for *years,* I know how hard you've found it lately." She felt a weird pull at the base of her stomach, realizing she'd also quit her job today, but she brushed that aside, along with all her other feelings.

Lexie saw the bottle of wine Fran had left on the counter and opened it, looking at Fran expectantly as she did so.

Fran seemed to waver in indecision for a moment, before speaking. "Well, I quit. That's the story. End of."

"That is so not end of. What are you going to *do?* Do you mean—are you, like, becoming a different sort of lawyer?" She handed Fran one of the glasses.

"No. I'm going to do something else entirely. I hated my job." She blew out a slow breath, then took a sip of wine. "Do you know what? I've wanted to say that for ages. I hate it. So I'm going to do something else entirely. God knows what, but I have savings and I'll figure it out." She put the wine down on the counter, then stepped up to Lexie and took one of her hands in hers. "And do you know what, Lex? It's because of you. You've been taking the time to work out what you really want to do—"

"Yeah, but that's really just because I'm a complete commitment-phobe and can't figure out what the hell to do with myself." The words slipped out, heightened by the state she was in right now. She didn't mean them, she told herself firmly. She loved traveling—and maybe it was a good thing that she'd seen the contract of Theo's, because it had reminded her that she didn't *want* to put down roots. That she'd have been sacrificing a part of herself—for someone who didn't deserve it.

"Well, I don't see it like that," Fran said firmly. "I see it as you figuring it out. And I think you might have figured it out these past few months—though I don't know what's happened to make you freak out like this. And I thought you'd like to hear that I was inspired by you, Lexie. That you're not the fuckup you seem to think you are. You've done what you needed to do for yourself, and you've made me want to do the same."

Lexie felt a lump swelling in her throat. "I haven't figured it out," she whispered.

"Maybe you—"

"No. I mean, it's not . . ." She swallowed, and then, on a deep breath, told Fran what she'd found in Theo's flat.

Fran looked at her for a long moment, then said, "Did you give him the chance to explain?" Lexie said nothing. "Maybe you ought to talk to him, Lexie." Her voice was calm, and full of sympathy, but Lexie still said nothing—because she wasn't sure she could face talking to Theo. Wasn't sure she wanted to be confronted with the truth of it. And perhaps worst of all, she didn't want to risk him coming up with an excuse, didn't want to risk *believing* him, only for this to happen again, later down the line. It was wrong of her, to be thinking about settling down—because relationships didn't ever work out to happy endings, did they? Not for her, not for Fran, not for her parents, not for Richard and Jody, not for Theo's parents . . . And this had been the wake-up call she'd needed.

Lexie knew her thoughts must have been playing out on her face when Fran gave her arm a little squeeze. "I know that if you keep moving around, there's less of a chance people will let you down. But Lex, it also means less connection with people. And that's OK," she added quickly. "It's a choice—and maybe it's been the right one for you until now. But you can also try something different—you don't have to run before you give people a chance. And I know it's scary, but if you never open up enough to give someone the chance to let you down, it also means you aren't opening up enough to give them the chance to be there for you."

By *people* she meant *Theo,* obviously. But had she not heard what Lexie had said? About what Theo had been planning to do—without even talking to her? All those conversations with Mike, behind her back . . .

"I'm not running," Lexie said firmly. "I shouldn't even have stayed as long as I did. I never meant to in the first place."

"It's just . . . this decision seems a little rushed. Are you sure this is the right thing to do? To leave without even talking to him about it?"

"Yes," she said. And when Fran gave her another look she said, "It *is.*"

Fran's eyebrows raised. "Are you trying to convince me—or yourself?"

When Lexie opened her mouth to insist again, Fran held up her hand.

"I'm just going to say one more thing about it, OK? Then I'll even help you pack, if you want."

Lexie gestured for her to go ahead.

"For me, being brave was quitting my job and throwing myself into the ether. It was forcing myself to take a risk—and who knows, it might play out badly. But I can still go back to the job if I want to. So my question is, what's being brave for you? A lot of people think traveling around, moving from place to place is a brave way of living. And it is. It's amazing. And I know you've loved doing it. But is it the thing you want *now,* even if it scares you?"

Lexie said nothing—silence seemed like a safer bet.

Fran gave her a small smile. "Do what you need to do. I'll always be here, OK? And just know that there's a place for you here if you ever change your mind."

Chapter Thirty

Lexie had her suitcase packed, her flight booked, and a job back in the Austrian Alps lined up by the time she'd worked up the courage to go back into the office. She'd lost track of the number of missed calls from Theo and had deleted several voicemails without listening to them. But much as she didn't want to admit it, Fran was right—she couldn't just leave without having a face-to-face conversation.

Autumn was setting in now, with that definite "back to school" feel in the air as people rushed around the city in the morning. It was slightly cooler than it had been in recent weeks, and there were the very first signs of the leaves beginning to turn. Bath would look beautiful in the autumn, Lexie thought—the light would suit the golden hues, and the russet colors would no doubt compliment the sandy buildings. As she pushed the door to the shop open, she felt a pang of sadness that she wouldn't be here to see it.

Theo was hovering over the computer Harry was working at when Lexie walked in. His expression of relief when he saw her made her insides tighten, and she straightened her spine against it. She would not let herself get drawn in.

They both walked toward each other, meeting in the middle of the shop. She tilted her chin up. "I just came to tell you that I'm leaving," she said, before he could lurch into anything.

"You're *what*?"

Out of the corner of her eye she could see Harry watching them. Theo clearly noticed too, because he grabbed her hand.

"Come with me," he snapped, and pulled her through the office and into the back room, past Ange, who had appeared balancing three cups of tea in her hands. She gave them a quizzical look but said nothing.

Theo shut the door behind them, and Lexie pressed herself against it as he moved away from her, tugging both hands through his hair.

"Look," he began, and she steeled herself.

She'd been expecting this—an excuse, some kind of pleading explanation. So let him get it out, then she could go.

"Yes, the contract you saw was about trying to cut you out."

Her heart jolted. She hadn't been expecting him to come out with it like that. "You—"

"But that was from the beginning of the year, Lexie." His hands dropped to his sides as he looked at her out of those coal eyes. "Mike had the idea before you'd even agreed to come back—before France. And at the time I thought, well, why not—because I'd spent five years working for this company, and you were acting like you didn't give a shit and I wanted to keep it going, because I thought that was what Richard would have wanted, because I thought I *owed* it to him to protect his legacy no matter what." He took a careful step toward where she was still pressed against the door, and she eyed him warily.

"I did give a shit," she said, her voice quieter than she would have liked. But already, she was speaking in past tense. Already, she was cutting herself out of it.

"I know that now. Of course I know that now. And things changed."

She folded her arms, gave him a narrow-eyed look. "What changed, exactly?"

"I got to know you," he said simply.

"But the paperwork I saw—"

"Was old. Lexie, you saw it hadn't been signed, right? It was an old contract, I promise you—I can show you the dates to prove it. Mike was here bringing up the idea again, trying to push because he wants a cut, but I'd already said no when you walked in. It was a stupid thing to think about in the first place. But I wasn't—I'm *not*—thinking anything like it anymore."

She said nothing, and he strode toward Ange's desk, tapped away at the keyboard, then turned the computer monitor to face her. "Here."

She glanced at it, though she was a little too far away to see what he was showing her—some sort of email, apparently. "This is an email chain between me and the solicitor, asking about cementing you as director in the future. If you want it. I wasn't going to say anything, not until the end of the year, because I knew you might *not* want it. But I wanted to check the option was there."

She said nothing, though her insides twisted again. The future. He'd been thinking about the future—the future of the company, sure. But with her. She'd been ready to sign an apartment lease—and he'd been ready to commit to running the company together.

She took a steadying breath. Because that was the problem, wasn't it? She'd been ready to do that, for him, but what did that mean for the part of her that loved her life of living all over the map? It was a part she didn't want to lose. And if she put him first—if she gave up everything just for a relationship with him, if she stayed in Bath and stayed with the company—what would happen if the relationship were to break down in the end? What would be left of her, who she was, if she did that?

"Theo," she began. "I—"

"Don't." His voice was a mixture between a snap and a plea. "Please don't do this. Please don't do what I did—don't keep running away."

She tilted her chin in the air defensively. "You said it yourself. It's different for me."

"I don't think it is, this time," he said quietly—and the truth of his words hung in the air between them. "And Lexie, Mike will back me up, if you want to—"

"It's not about that," she interrupted, and he frowned. "I mean, it is. It was a dickish thing to do, no matter when you did it."

He grimaced. "I know. But I also know I wouldn't have gone through with it. I was just angry and grieving."

"Even so."

He nodded slowly, accepting that.

She heaved in a breath, and her hands dropped to her sides. "But it's not *just* that." She hesitated, trying to find the words to explain why this had made her see that she couldn't stay. In the end, she settled for, "The company was his. My dad's. Not mine."

"Doesn't mean you can't make it yours," he said softly. And when she said nothing, the corner of his mouth drooped down. "Please. Don't do this. Stay." She remembered his voice, his hand on hers in that room in Ireland. *Stay.* She felt a rush of emotion, and closed her eyes against it.

"I can't," she whispered. And when she opened her eyes,

Theo's expression had hardened. Like he knew that it was about him as much—more, maybe—than the company. That this wasn't just her leaving the company, it was her leaving him.

With that thought, she found she couldn't look at him anymore. She turned, fumbling for the door handle. She could hear Fran's voice in her mind. *You're not the fuckup you seem to think you are.* But Fran was wrong, wasn't she?

Even as she got the door open and stepped one foot outside, there was a small part of her that was hoping Theo would grab her, stop her. That he would be able to find the right words to *make* her stay—even if she didn't know what those words would be. But he didn't—he said nothing. So she kept walking.

The fact that Ange came up to her the moment she stepped into the main office made Lexie think she'd been waiting for her. Her pale green eyes scanned Lexie's face searchingly, before her bright red lips twisted and she shook her head, the big gold hoop earrings she was wearing moving as she did so.

"I wish you wouldn't do this, Lexie," Ange said softly.

Lexie didn't ask how Ange knew. She found she couldn't even meet her gaze, looking down at the carpet instead.

"Your dad asked me to look after you for this year," Ange continued, in that same quiet voice. "And I hope I'll be able to look out for you long after that, too. But you're making that rather difficult if you run away."

The carpet was blurring in front of Lexie's eyes, and she blinked to try to clear her vision. She didn't bother to contradict the running away part, like she had with Theo—she knew Ange wouldn't buy it.

Ange sighed. "If you walk away, if you don't fulfill your end—the company will all go to Theo, Lexie."

"It doesn't matter," Lexie said thickly. "He deserves it more than me anyway—this was never mine. And I can help, from afar. I can . . ." She swallowed. "If you need me, I can still help."

When Lexie glanced up, Ange was watching her, her expression thoughtful. "Your dad guessed it might come to this, you know."

Lexie frowned, but before she could ask Ange to elaborate, Ange held up two envelopes—envelopes she must have been holding the whole time, without Lexie noticing. Her name was written on both. Her name—in her dad's handwriting.

"I don't know what's in them," Ange said, and now she weighed an envelope in each hand. "But I was under strict instructions to give you a letter, if it looked like you might quit."

Lexie glanced between Ange's hands, and Ange gave her another small, slightly sad, smile.

"But there's a choice. One letter is for if you really do decide to quit, the other is for if you choose to stay." She held out the letter in her left hand, and Lexie knew—this was the letter Ange wanted her to take.

She felt a lump clogging her throat and it wouldn't go away when she swallowed. Her dad had known she might want to quit. And, if these letters were anything to go by, he'd hoped that she might change her mind, and stay anyway.

"I suppose it's up to you, which letter you take." Ange said, and now she held both out to Lexie. The staying letter in her left hand, the quitting letter in her right. Lexie took a shuddering breath. She didn't want to take *either* letter. She didn't want to read her dad's writing, didn't want to open up the floodgates. But she couldn't leave without taking one. She couldn't turn her back on this final thing her dad had wanted to say to her.

The *I'm sorry* she wanted to utter didn't get as far as her lips, and instead echoed inside her head as she took the letter in Ange's right hand. So maybe she was more like her dad than she'd thought. Because she was leaving his company, just like he'd left her all those years ago. The thought made her eyes blur again, and she turned on her heel, away from the disappointment in Ange's eyes, gripping the letter in her hand.

She didn't know if she'd work up the courage to read the letter. Not right now, that was for sure. Maybe in a while from now, when she'd managed to move on, put the past nine months behind her. Because that's what she had to do—put it behind her, remember her own identity. No matter how much it hurt, no matter how much she was shaking as she stepped onto the street outside, she had to leave it, in order to keep herself safe.

So when the door shut, Lexie didn't look back.

Chapter Thirty-one

In the first few weeks after Lexie left, Theo had been sure she'd come back. Even a month later, he'd still felt convinced that he'd come downstairs to the office one day and she'd be there, ready to dig into him, maybe ignore him for a bit—but he figured, once she was back, he'd be able to talk to her, win her over again. But by the time December rolled around, he'd given up hoping. He'd taken to working upstairs in the flat more—he'd always done it a bit, but he used to like being downstairs for variety. Now it seemed a bit too quiet in the main office without Lexie. Not the actual volume—Harry was good for keeping that up— but the lack of her presence pressed in on all sides, like a constant awareness.

There was a sharp rap at the flat door, then Ange opened it, poked her head in. "I don't suppose you know if Mike's joining us for the team meeting, do you?" she asked by way of greeting. "He spoke to me this morning but is now ignoring my calls."

Theo straightened up from where he was hunched over his laptop on the sofa. "I don't think so." Mike had sort of checked out recently and Theo wasn't totally sure how long he was going to stick around, now that it was clear he wouldn't be able to re-work the contract. He thought Mike had wanted to get back a share out of pride, more than anything else—it had stung, that Richard had left it to Lexie and Theo, when Mike had given him the start-up loan. But it wasn't like Richard had done it to hurt Mike—it was just that Mike's interest in the company blew hot and cold.

Ange gave him a look. "So it's just you, me, and Harry?"

Theo rolled his tight shoulders. Really, he should stop working on the sofa. "Looks like."

Ange seemed to be about to say something, then stopped herself, nodded, and left Theo alone.

Theo glanced out the mullion windows to the city outside. There was a pale winter glow, and even though it wasn't yet four P.M. darkness was already beginning to settle in.

He moved his laptop onto the coffee table and stood, heading for the adjoining kitchen. He suspected Lexie was unlikely to be sitting quietly on her own right now, trying not to feel sorry for herself. Because yes, maybe it made him a loser, but he'd done the classic social media stalking—and hadn't felt any better as a result when he'd seen a photo of Lexie on Instagram, snow-covered mountains as her backdrop, with some blond guy's arm around her. He'd felt bitterness at the sight—enough to stop him texting her again. So the last message exchange with her in his phone was still from the day after she'd left.

Come back. Please.

And her words back, several hours later. A message that had made him leap for his phone when he saw her name, only to feel crushing disappointment.

I can't. I'm sorry.

He understood why she'd left. He knew what it must have looked like, and he knew, didn't he, that she didn't trust all that easily and God, why hadn't he thought to pick up the damn contract and take it with him, shove it back into Mike's hands on his way out? He could have avoided all of this. Then again, maybe she'd still have left—maybe something else would have triggered it.

He clicked the kettle on to boil with more force than was strictly necessary. He'd fucked up. He should never have even entertained the idea of cutting her out—it was wrong on so many levels. But he *hadn't* considered it, not really. It had been a conversation when he was angry and lost after losing Richard, right at the beginning of all this—one that Mike had taken too far.

He felt a surge of anger at Lexie then. She shouldn't have left. She should have understood that he'd never have done that to her—not now. But a part of him knew—she *did* believe him. He'd seen it. He'd had the proof in front of him, and she'd barely blinked. And yet, she'd still left. The anger turned inward, so that it felt like his insides were too hot.

He tried to take a calming breath as he poured hot water into a mug and was distracted by his phone lighting up with a message from his mum. He'd taken a leap, asked if she wanted to come out for a few days this December, told her he could show her around Bath.

We'd love to, Theo—but your dad can't get away
from work. You're very welcome here, of course.
We're having a bit of a soiree on Christmas Eve—
Cally and her husband will be here!

It made him huff out a breath of laughter—at the predictability of it. He tapped out a reply, saying he would likely still be abroad at that point, but he'd try to come over in January. It might be his last Christmas with the company, after all, so he *wanted* to be working—and he'd suggested he take Harry along on the Belgium trip, to show him the ropes. If Harry did well, Theo could even leave him there to handle the last few days by himself—it was the type of thing Richard had done for Theo in the early years, and now Theo felt like he wanted to pass that on. Harry had stuck with the company, after all, and even if it did sell, there was a chance he'd be kept on.

He put his phone away. He was trying. After seeing Lexie grapple with her relationship with Richard, and what they hadn't had the chance to put right, he was trying to work toward acceptance with his parents. His dad would always be a bit detached; his mum might always be wishing for something better. She'd spent a fair amount of time trying to change him and hadn't been able to—but he couldn't change her, either. No one was perfect, as Ange was fond of reminding everyone on a regular basis.

He wondered if Lexie was still trying to come to terms with losing her dad, while she was living it up in the Alps. He still thought of Richard on a regular basis. It was impossible not to—the number of times they'd sat up in the flat together, having a coffee in the morning or a drink in the evening. He wasn't really sure how they'd gone from colleagues to friends. He still felt he owed Richard so much—he was the first person to believe in him, to mentor him, to make him feel like he could stick at something.

He blew on his tea, scowling at himself. Richard hadn't told anyone how bad the cancer was. Theo should have pushed; he should have been there—shouldn't have taken Richard's brushoffs at face value when it was clear he was getting sicker. He'd never really understood why Richard kept it so quiet—though he'd wondered, after getting to know Lexie, if it was all tied up in guilt. Guilt making him think he didn't deserve to be taken care of, at the end? Or maybe being unable to face up to what was happening, not wanting to admit the end was so near before he'd had a chance to fix things? It was all guesswork, though—there were no neat answers.

He remembered Richard taking him along on his first company trip, even though he'd made a big thing about not wanting to go. It had been the Christmas trip, in Bruges—the same place he was going back to in a few days, when he'd be taking Harry on his first company trip, like a weird sort of circle. It was that trip that had been the turning point for Theo. It had been something silly—Richard had said he'd forgotten something, back at the hotel, when they'd been on the way to the evening light show. In hindsight, it was obviously a lie, but at the time Theo had panicked at being left in charge, at the expectant looks on the clients' faces. But *because* he'd been left in charge, he'd had to get on with it. Most people wouldn't think much of that, maybe—all he'd had to do was get everyone from A to B, be polite, make small talk—but for him, it had felt like a really big deal.

That small moment, being trusted like that, had caused something to shift. He'd stopped hiding behind a feigned lack of interest, had decided to actually try. And by trying, he'd found something he was actually good at.

He'd asked Richard, on the plane home, why he'd pushed Theo into taking the shot.

Richard had looked at him out of eyes that were a little lighter than Lexie's. *All this moving around you do . . . It reminds me of someone else I know, that's all.*

Theo had thought, for a while, that Richard had meant himself—and only this year had he begun to figure out that maybe he'd meant Lexie.

Richard had given him a look out of the corner of his eye as they'd fastened their seatbelts. *And I hope this doesn't sound too condescending, but I've made a lot of mistakes in my life.* He'd sighed, and Theo had glanced at him, this conversation moving onto different ground than he was used to. *I can't change the past—but maybe I can help you change your future, a bit.*

And he had, hadn't he? Richard had changed Theo's future, and he'd never gotten a chance to thank him for it.

He'd gotten a note from Richard, after he'd died. The solicitor had given it to him, right before the meeting about Richard's will. He'd had time to read it just before Lexie had walked in—while he was still grappling with the information that Richard had left half the company to him. It would have been nice if Richard had given him a heads-up, but for reasons best known to himself, he'd decided to keep his plans secret. The note had been short, to the point. Sorry for not telling you, but I had my reasons, that kind of thing. He'd explained that he'd been thinking of Lexie when he set the company up, that it seemed only right to find a way to share it with her. And that Theo deserved the company too, for sticking with it, for putting so much work into it over the years and not walking away. Like Richard knew that's what Theo was most proud of in his life.

Richard had asked Theo to look out for Lexie, in his final note. Had said there was a chance they might clash, but that disagreement is sometimes good—and that he hoped he was right in thinking they might find common ground, too. And Theo thought Richard must have known—or at least guessed— that Theo and Lexie would complement each other once they stopped arguing. That Lexie was naturally good at the people side of things, and Theo had figured out the business side.

He should have told Lexie that, Theo thought, with a rush of frustration. He should have told her that, and so much more.

He wasn't sure what Richard would think about Theo falling for his daughter. And he had fallen for her, hadn't he? He hadn't meant to, but somewhere along the line it had become impossible not to. He'd expected more of a fight, before she walked out. Given how much she'd protested about being kept out of the loop earlier in the year, he'd expected her to push back. But no. Instead she'd cut herself off completely.

Maybe it was for the best. Maybe it was better that she'd left before he could make an even bigger mess of things. Before he let her down, sooner or later, like he'd let his parents down. And she'd been let down enough already.

There was a cursory knock before Ange came in, Harry following behind, Christmas tie swinging. Ange gestured for Harry to sit down around the coffee table, waited for Theo to join them, then leveled a look at Theo. "I'm going to jump right to it," she said. "Mike called me earlier this morning to say he's not going to go to Vienna."

Theo was in the middle of taking a sip of tea and choked. Harry jumped up, went to sit next to Theo so that he could thump him on the back.

"What?" Theo demanded.

Mike had made a huge bloody drama about the whole thing—insisting he go to Vienna, saying that Theo had cut him out of Madrid, that he wasn't letting the same thing happen again. It had been right after Theo had made it clear he had no interest in trying to find a legal argument to get Lexie out of the shares and Mike in—and he'd felt sure Mike was putting up a fight just to spite him. But Lexie had just left, and he hadn't had it in him to argue. Mike was supposed to be going out for the first couple of days, get everyone settled, organize the Secret Santa, and meet the local woman on the ground in Vienna that they'd hired to see people through the traditions and Christmas Day itself. Theo had been out to meet her a few weeks ago, and felt confident she would be brilliant, but it was their first time doing this trip, so they needed someone there for appearances' sake and to check that things went off without a hitch. Mike knew that. Which again, lent credence to the idea that this was all out of spite.

Harry put his hand up, bouncing on the edge of his seat. "I could go."

"No, you can't," Theo and Ange said together.

"Besides, you're going to Belgium with Theo, aren't you?" Ange said, with an encouraging smile.

Theo shook his head at Ange. "You need me to go to Vienna." He frowned. "*We* need me to go, I mean." He sighed. "Sorry, Harry, but I reckon we can deal with Belgium by using the people we have on the ground there instead, and—"

"There's no need for that," Ange said briskly.

She sat back against the armchair as Theo looked at her.

"I think we ought to ask Lexie to go along."

Theo swallowed his tea too quickly, and just about managed to stop choking again.

"She's already in Austria," Ange continued, with that way she had sometimes, no-nonsense, no room for argument, "and she'd only need to go for a couple of days—you said yourself our woman there is brilliant. And Lexie is still, technically, a partner in this company, isn't she?"

Theo hesitated before saying, "Yeah. I guess."

They'd had no conversation about it. He hadn't tried, in all honestly. He knew he was avoiding bringing it up, in case it came to a conclusion he didn't want.

Ange was looking at him expectantly.

"I don't know . . ." he said slowly. And when she continued to look at him, he sighed. "OK. Fine. She'll probably say no, but fine, we can ask."

And it would give him an excuse, wouldn't it, to get in touch?

She beamed. "Brilliant. Harry and I will wait."

"You want me to do it *now*?"

"Of course now. When else?"

Sometimes, Theo thought, it was easier not to argue with Ange. So he got up, took out his phone, and headed for the kitchen, trying to get space from Ange and Harry. He tried not to think too hard about it as he dialed her number. Better this way. He couldn't obsess about what to say. He listened while the phone rang. And rang.

When he hung up, he couldn't resist swearing under his breath, before turning and looking at Ange over the countertop. "No answer," he grunted.

Ange sighed. "You made a bit of a mess of things there, didn't you?" And without waiting for Theo to comment on that, she got out her own phone. "Never mind, I'll talk to her."

And when Lexie answered this time, Theo had to fight hard to control his scowl. What had she *thought* he was ringing her about, for Christ's sake? What conversation was she so desperate to avoid?

He could only hear Ange's side of the conversation and felt a stab of jealousy, because Ange got to hear the sound of Lexie's voice, and he didn't. Stupid, he told himself. He needed to get a bloody grip—she clearly wanted nothing to do with him if she was actively avoiding his calls, didn't she? It made him glad he hadn't tried texting her again.

Harry caught Theo's eye and gave him a sympathetic smile—

and Theo realized that Harry had probably cottoned on to a bit more than he'd given him credit for.

"Lexie says she'll help," Ange said, as she hung up.

And that, apparently, was that. They proceeded to talk about the logistics, Ange saying she'd work out the flight and hotel and change things into Lexie's name, and Theo letting her steer the conversation, while all the time wondering—why? *Why* had she agreed to help?

He could go out to Vienna, he thought, his stomach lurching a bit at the idea. Leave Harry in Belgium after a day or two, assuming it all went smoothly. Like with France, all those months ago, he could just show up, and she'd have to deal with it. Though unlike in France, this time he'd know she'd be there—so he could prepare. Could force her to talk to him.

But Ange was giving him a look. "She needs to do this alone," she said, changing topic midflow.

He frowned and she sighed.

"Have a little faith, T-Rex."

And when he said nothing, Ange smiled kindly.

"She still cares, Theo. She wouldn't have said yes if she didn't."

"And yet, she left us."

She left me.

Ange gave him a long look, then stood. "Come on, Harry. I'm sure there are customers waiting who need your attention."

Harry sprang to his feet and headed toward the door.

Ange hung back for a moment, placed a hand on Theo's arm. "You bet against her once."

He remembered how callous he'd been then and winced.

"Maybe, this time, you ought to bet *on* her."

Chapter Thirty-two

Lexie shrugged off her winter coat as she walked into the lounge. Christmas music was on in the background, the sound of Wizzard rising above the chatter and laughter of the packed bar. The lights on the Christmas tree flashed in the corner and the smell of glühwein wafted over to greet her. Almost a year ago to the day, she'd been in this exact bar when her mum had called her with the news about her dad. And here she was again, with it looking just the same, down to the same tinsel decorating the bar.

She headed over to her group of friends—a few of the same people as last year, including Mikkel, who had his arm around a new girl this year. Mikkel smiled at Lexie, and she smiled back, before sliding into a seat next to Amelie. Lexie had been welcomed back this season with open arms when she'd gotten her job on the ski lifts. The way everyone just made room for her in their lives was something Lexie had always loved about traveling—people formed quick friendships, bound together by being somewhere new. She'd expected to fall easily back into that when she'd left Bath behind, but she didn't feel as connected as she usually did, like she couldn't quite embrace it in the same way as she'd once done.

"How was Vienna?" Amelie asked.

"Amazing," Lexie said truthfully. She'd loved going there, hadn't questioned it when Ange had called her about it. She should have guessed that Theo would have been calling about work, rather than anything else, when she'd seen his name flash up on her phone. She'd shut down all possibility there, hadn't she? But she'd panicked and stared at her phone as it'd rung out. She'd been on the verge of calling him back when Ange had rung, and it had been easier to talk to Ange anyway. She'd set up the Secret Santa between the guests, remembering that this had been Theo's idea in the first place, and a big part of her had wished she could stay, be there on Christmas Eve to see everyone opening their presents, after accompanying them to the Christmas market. But Ange had booked the flights, and she'd done her job—she'd gotten everything set up, made everyone feel welcome, and then left them all in the local guide's very capable hands.

Lexie's boss here hadn't been all too happy about her taking leave—but really, it wasn't like she was doing anything vitally important, was it? They'd found someone else to cover her shifts. She thought perhaps that was what she was struggling with. She'd been a part of something, in the company—and now, she was back to doing temporary work, without any sense of direction or future.

A part of her had been wondering if Theo might show up unannounced, after the trick Ange had pulled at the Lemon Festival. And that, she realized, was what had been missing. She'd wanted him to be there with her, to share it—to go ice-skating with him and have him tease her for being so bad at it. She'd wanted to drink hot chocolate with him and exchange stories and laugh together. Failing that, she'd wanted to call him afterward, to tell him about it.

She'd fallen in love with him, she realized. Somewhere along the line, she'd fallen in love with him—and she hadn't been able to fall *out* of it, not even by running to a ski lodge several countries away.

Amelie had moved on to talk to someone else, and Lexie got out her phone.

She opened up the chat with Theo, read the last message exchange.

Come back. Please.

I can't. I'm sorry.

That had been *months* ago. She'd thought, a few times, about texting him—but what would she say? She'd closed that door, had decided it was for the best, and had been trying to move on. Only she hadn't been able to.

She left the bar early, saying goodbye to her friends and leaving them to their drinking. She was staying in shared accommodation a little way away from the main action, so she had to get a bus to and from work. It was a standard single room with a shared bathroom and kitchen. It was fine, and she'd stayed in worse, but she hadn't been able to shake the feeling that it was a little depressing for someone her age to be staying somewhere like this—which had never bothered her before. She'd barely unpacked, so her room was bare—which was just as well, because it was too small to house much. But as with every year, there was one thing she'd gotten out. Her wish jar stood on her chest of drawers, the sequins stuck on it losing their sparkle but somehow still there.

Next to it was the letter from her dad, the envelope propped against the jar, two pieces of him side by side. She hadn't been able to bring herself to open it. Hadn't wanted to read his words of disappointment that she'd quit—or, maybe worse, hadn't wanted to see that maybe he'd *understand* that she'd quit, because he'd quit things in his life too. And maybe she hadn't wanted to open it because she couldn't face reading his final words to her. It was the last connection—to the dad she'd hated, and to the dad she'd loved.

She sat on the end of her single bed, heard it creak under her weight. She hadn't even taken off her coat yet. Instead she just stared at the pieces of paper, folded up inside the wish jar. Yet unlike last year, she knew what she wanted to wish for.

She thought about Theo saying that maybe wishing for things was about hiding behind them, instead of working to bring about something you wanted. And she thought of what her dad had said, too, all those years ago, as she'd shown him her wish jar. That maybe the wishes wouldn't come true right away, maybe not in the same year you put them in the jar—but one day, if you wanted the wish hard enough, it would come true. He'd meant if you worked for it, if you tried hard enough, she thought now. And maybe that wasn't true for everything. No matter how hard she'd tried, how much she'd wanted it, she hadn't been able to make him come back—just as she couldn't bring him back now. But some things you could work for. Some things only came true by trying.

She'd been kidding herself, hadn't she? She'd thought she'd had to leave to keep her identity—because she'd thought she'd have been sacrificing a part of herself to stay in Bath for Theo. But really, it wasn't that at all. Somewhere along the line, that part of her had grown, had changed—maybe even still *was* changing—that had become clear almost the moment she got back to the mountains. She'd wanted the flat and her role in the company, not just for him, but for *herself* too. And that was OK. Maybe that didn't have to be as scary as she thought. Maybe change was good. And maybe not all relationships had to end up broken. She thought of what her mum had said, sitting on the bed in the flat. *Relationships take work.* Simple, but it had stuck with her. Yes, sometimes things still didn't work out, but you had to put the effort in, didn't you? You had to at least *try*.

She took a shaky breath as she brought out her phone again. But before she could scroll through the numbers, she saw a message from Ange.

> Lexie, you are a superstar. Anna from Vienna LOVES you and everyone is very happy. Thanks for saving our bacon—I knew you were still an R&L girl. And look, I know why you left. But if you find yourself in Bath this Friday, we're having a sort of anniversary celebration for your dad. To say goodbye, one year on. No pressure, but we'd love to have you there. Xxx

Lexie sat with it for a moment. She thought about sitting around a table, saying goodbye to her dad with a group of people who had loved him. She'd started to understand something, this year, about saying goodbye to someone—that it isn't always a one-off, that it can be continuous. You could say goodbye over the course of many months, in different ways. And maybe there were parts of a person you never said goodbye to, for better or worse.

She took a deep breath, tapped out a response.

Can I bring a plus one?

Darling, if it means you're coming, you can bring a
plus five. Xxx

LEXIE WAITED UNTIL the plane was in the air and the fasten seat-
belt sign was turned off before she got out her dad's letter. She
felt she'd had to wait, to know that she was truly on her way
home, before she could read it. Her fingertips trembled a little
as she opened the envelope. She still wasn't sure she wanted to
know what he'd thought of her quitting the company. But she
also *needed* to know.

> *Dear Little Lex,*
>
> *I know—you're not so little anymore. And I know I lost
> the right to call you that, but I still remember you as the
> little girl who was so proud to show me her wish jar, all
> those years ago. My biggest regret in life is that I let that
> little girl down—that I let you down.*
>
> *If you're reading this letter, then it means you've quit
> the company.*

Lexie's heart skipped at this, but she kept reading.

> *And believe me, I understand why. I know I was a ter-
> rible dad to you. I know I wasn't there when I should have
> been. I don't think I have an explanation or an apology
> big enough, or one that would make sense of what I did.
> I made a mistake. I made several mistakes—it's as simple*

as that—and they are mistakes I haven't been able to rectify. I fell in love with Jody without meaning to, and I chased my happiness at the expense of your happiness. I was stupid, and naive, and I thought I'd be able to keep you and have her too—but I was wrong. Rachel was a result of that marriage, so I can't be sorry for it—but I am sorry that you got caught in the crossfire. I'm sorry that I didn't keep you in my life as much as I should have done, and sorry that I wasn't strong enough to fight for that, as you deserved. Most of all I'm sorry that I made you feel that I didn't love you, because I promise you, Lexie, the opposite is true.

So I understand, honestly, why you've quit. Ange told me I should have talked to you first, before deciding to leave you half the company. But I suppose I could never find the words—and if you're reading this letter, we both know it's too late for me to find them now. I know I've thrown you into this and I know I've made things difficult, by splitting it between you and Theo. And I know you won't want to be stuck in a city that was my city, a place you didn't choose for yourself.

But I also think you're stronger than all that. I might be wrong about this, but I'm pretty sure, as I write this, that you'll go back. I know why you've run—but I think you're a tougher person than I ever was. So I have faith, Little Lex, that you won't really quit. That you'll see this year through. And I hope the company brings you a tiny part of the joy it's brought me. Even if you sell it in the end—and let's hope Theo has done enough to ensure the profit on that front, so that there's a good chunk of money coming in—I hope that you'll have found something there.

Because it's your company—whether or not you realize that. It was always you I had in mind.

When I left Jody, I felt like a failure. I left for reasons that I won't go into—because it's not wholly my story to tell. But despite those reasons, I still felt I'd failed yet again, unable to see a second marriage through. I left because I wanted to support Rachel—but it highlighted how little I'd supported you. Your mum is brilliant. She is one of the kindest people I know—and despite what I did to her, she never tried to drive me out of your life. She made sure I knew I was welcome, and she filled me in on your life when you weren't ready to. But still, I knew I'd failed.

Do you remember the first time you ever went abroad? You were only three, and we wanted to take you away for Christmas. We chose Germany because we knew it was big on Christmas markets. I had never seen you so excited. There were other kids crying on the plane—but not you. You were looking out the window all wide-eyed. Your mum and I couldn't believe how easy traveling with a toddler was.

What I'm trying to say here, very ineloquently, is that when I started the company it was because I wanted to re-create that joy I'd seen in you. We had a tradition, I don't know if you remember that. Every year, at Christmas, we'd go somewhere new. It was the highlight of my year, being able to explore a new place with you. And I wanted to pass a little of that joy on to other people. And as I pulled it together, I realized so many of the holidays were holidays I wished I'd had the chance to take you on.

I also know how much you still love to travel—your mum has told me some of the adventures you've been on. I wondered, did we start that love of traveling when you were little, from that very first holiday? Or was it always going to be who you were? Either way—this is a company that will build on that love of travel, I hope.

So it's your company, if you want it. R&L—it's a stupid name, isn't it? Mike—you'll have met Mike by now, I'm sure—tried to make me change it, in the beginning. But what better legacy than my two daughters? It wouldn't have been the right fit for Rachel, but I thought it might be right for you, Lexie.

I don't know what time of year it is, as you read this. Maybe you tried to quit the moment the solicitor told you about it. In which case, I hope this will help you to understand why I left it to you—if you decide to go back. If it's partway through the year, maybe it's Theo who's driving you away. He can take a bit of time to get to know, I realize that. But I'd hoped you might become friends, support each other. I'll never get the chance to know if I'm right about that—but I'll hope.

Whatever time of year it is, I have one more thing to leave you with. I know I usually send you a Christmas card with money. I have to get your address from your mum each year—thank her for that, won't you? I'm not sure if money feels a bit impersonal. I suppose I've always been worried that I'll get the wrong thing—or that you'd return whatever I sent you. Plus, money doesn't take up space in a suitcase. But for your last Christmas present, there's one thing I want to give you.

The year I left, we were supposed to go to Iceland. We hadn't bought plane tickets yet, but your mum had been about to buy them when I told her about Jody. I assumed, stupidly, that there would be another chance—that one day, I'd take you to Iceland myself. I want you to know I never forgot that trip, or the promise I made you. So enclosed within are two plane tickets—in case you want to take someone there to enjoy it with you—and a booking for one of the best places to stay in Iceland, or so my research tells me. I wish I could have gone with you, but I hope it will bring you the same joy I saw on your face as a little girl.

And please know that even if I haven't been in your life as much as I should have, you have been in my thoughts the whole time. I can't change the past, much as I wish I could—but maybe, through this, I can be a part of your future.

I'm sorry—and I love you.

Dad

"ARE YOU OK?" the woman next to her on the plane asked, voice low. Only then did Lexie realize she was crying. She dashed the tears away, nodded her reassurance. She looked back at the letter. He'd known she'd go back. Somehow, her dad had known she wouldn't quit—at least not permanently. She closed her eyes, tried to take a steadying breath. He'd remembered Iceland, remembered his promise to her. Theo had been right, she was sure of it—that was the reason the Iceland trip had never gotten off the ground. He'd been saving it—for her.

She folded the letter up, put it back inside the envelope. There was so much there. Things she needed time to process. Things, maybe, that she should have properly realized before now. Like the company being for her. Ange and Theo had both hinted at it, but she'd refused to accept it. But he'd been thinking of her when he started the company. He might not have known how to close the gap between them, but she thought she understood now how he was trying to make up for the past by creating a legacy for her for the future. He was right—none of this changed what had come before. But it was up to her how she moved forward, wasn't it?

Chapter Thirty-three

Heat flooded into Lexie as she stepped inside, allowing her freezing muscles to relax. It was a pub in the center of Bath, one she'd walked past a few times. It had been, according to Ange, a favorite hangout of Richard's, a place he used to take the staff to for after-work drinks on a Friday. There was a jovial, festive atmosphere, with many of the people wearing paper hats, having pulled crackers over an early Christmas lunch. The lighting was low, with fairy lights around the inside of the windows, where winter darkness had truly taken hold. It wasn't yet six P.M., but people were already queuing at the bar, leaning against the wooden top.

Ange was in the corner, wearing a dress that was all sparkle. Lexie's heart gave a kind of anticipatory lurch as she spotted her, then sank into her stomach when she saw Theo wasn't there. Rachel was, though—a tall girl with sleek black hair sitting next to her. As was Harry, his tie sporting Christmas puddings, and her mum, in that one Christmas jumper she owned. As Lexie drew near, her mum got up to give her a hug, her honey-blond hair shorter than when Lexie had last seen her. Lexie breathed in the floral smell of her mum. She hadn't thanked her enough— hadn't *been* here enough to do it properly. But she could change that. She could make sure that she wouldn't have any regrets where that was concerned.

Lexie slid into the booth next to Rachel as Ange beamed at

her across the table, miming to show that she was going to the bar for more drinks. True to form, Ange was wearing big earrings, which swung as she got to her feet. Sailboats? Were they the same earrings she'd worn at the funeral? Funny, the things you remember.

"Thank you for being my plus one," Lexie murmured to Rachel.

Rachel smiled at her. "Of course. Though I invited a plus one, too, so I'm not sure how that counts?" Rachel took the hand of the woman next to her, took a breath like she was gearing up. "Lexie, meet Lana, my future fiancée. Lana, meet my . . ." She broke off, cleared her throat—and Lexie felt a small pinch of guilt. "Meet Lexie."

Lana beamed, a dimple winking out. She had the kind of infectious smile that made you want to smile with her, and slightly crooked teeth, to go with a fringe that looked like she might have cut it herself. Lexie instantly liked her.

"Hi. I'm Rachel's sister."

Rachel's gaze flashed to Lexie's face, and Lexie met it.

"I mean," Lexie said warningly, "I'm not promising to be a great one. But I'm up for trying, if you are."

There were tears sparking in Rachel's eyes. "I'm so up for that," she said, her voice a little thick.

Lexie cocked her head. "Do sisters hug? I think they hug."

Rachel practically threw her arms around Lexie, who laughed and patted her back. When Rachel drew back, she was properly crying.

Next to her, Lana rolled her eyes, though she patted Rachel's knee affectionately. "She does this."

Lexie grinned. "I know."

And that just made Rachel cry harder.

She had a sister, Lexie realized. A sister she wouldn't have, if it weren't for her dad. A sister she'd almost let pass her by because she'd been too afraid to reach out.

From where Lexie was sitting, she could see the door to the pub—and once again, she felt a rush of disappointment when it opened and it wasn't Theo. It *was* someone else she knew, though, and she got to her feet to give Fran a hug. Gone were the smart business clothes she'd gotten so accustomed to seeing Fran in—instead she was in a bright multicolored jumper that reminded Lexie of the teenage Fran.

Lexie pulled back. "Fran, I'm—"

But Fran held up her hand. "We've been through this. You don't have anything to be sorry about."

Lexie blew out her cheeks but nodded. Then she cocked her head, looking for a lighter subject. "No date tonight?"

Fran tossed back her dark hair. "I haven't been on a date since you left," she said airily. And when Lexie's eyebrows shot up, Fran waved a hand in the air. "It's part of this whole figuring out what I want thing."

Lexie grinned, but Fran was looking over Lexie's shoulder now, and from the way her eyes slid back to her, Lexie knew who she'd seen. Fran gave Lexie's arm a little squeeze, then moved away to join the group around the table.

Lexie's heart hammered as she shifted. Theo was standing a few feet away, dead still, staring at her. Across the crowd, their gazes met, and held. Her breath was caught in her throat. Had he always been this fucking gorgeous? Had he always *looked* at her like this, like there could be any number of people in the room, and still he'd choose to look at her?

But then his lips pulled into a small smile, and he nodded. A hello—but not the hello she was looking for. And he turned—away from her, and toward the bar.

She closed her eyes briefly, trying to stop the churn in her stomach. She'd known this might happen. She'd known he might not forgive her. *Don't run,* he'd told her. But that's just what she'd done, wasn't it? She'd come back, yes—but what if she'd come back too late?

When Lexie turned back to the table, she saw Ange studying her. Her face softened into a smile, and she beckoned Lexie over, pouring out a glass of red wine from the bottle she'd brought to the table. Ange pulled out the chair next to her, moving someone's coat off it, and Lexie sat down.

"Welcome home," Ange said, raising her glass to Lexie's to clink. *Home.* Maybe that was right. Maybe it had become home, without her realizing. And maybe it wouldn't be home forever—maybe she'd never stem the desire to keep moving—but for now, it was enough. Just as she'd come to accept that Richard had changed over the course of his life, she realized it was OK if she changed, too.

Lexie took a deep breath. "Ange? I'm sorry for leaving."

Ange shook her head. "We all make mistakes. Nobody's perfect, remember? It's whether we learn from the mistakes that's the important thing. And whatever happens to the company, Lexie—I'm glad to have had you in my life. You might not have realized it, but you brought light this year, when I think we would have floundered without it. I think Richard knew that," she added quietly, while Lexie fought the lump that was rising up her throat.

Theo returned with a beer but didn't look down at Lexie as he sat between her and Harry—and Lexie couldn't work out if that was deliberate or not. An itchy feeling started up under her skin. If he wouldn't even *look* at her, what were the chances a conversation with him was going to go well?

"Now that we're all here," Ange said, projecting her voice, and everyone turned toward her. Apparently Mike wasn't coming, Lexie noted. Had he left the company for good, then?

Ange smiled, her pale green eyes holding just a tinge of sadness. "To Richard," she said. Everyone raised their glasses and drank. For a moment, there was quiet around the table, and the chatter and music in the pub came in to fill the space. Lexie suspected that they were all thinking of Richard in that moment—of whatever he meant to each of them. She thought of the letter, which she was still carrying around with her in her bag. She thought of him teaching her to ski, and of being on his shoulders at the fireworks. She thought of the last time she'd seen him, when he'd tried to apologize. She remembered him leaving, too, of course she did. Remembered him bending to give her a hug. *I'm sorry, Little Lex. But I'll see you really soon, OK? This doesn't mean I love you any less, I promise. And I promise that I'll still take you to Iceland, one day.*

Lexie took a steadying breath. She was who she was because of her dad, wasn't she? For better or worse. Him leaving had made her into the person she was today—and she had to be OK with that. And do you know what? She *was* OK with that. Like her dad said, you couldn't do anything to change the past. But she *liked* who she was today. OK, she wasn't perfect. But she'd had a life full of adventure, and she was sitting in a pub full of people she cared about—people she wouldn't have known, if it wasn't for him.

"I remember when I first met Richard," Lexie's mum said softly, and everyone's attention went to her. "It was in a queue, believe it or not, to the concession stand at the cinema. I was in front of him, and I could sense him behind me the whole time. It made me nervous, and it meant that I dropped the popcorn after I paid, and it went everywhere." Her mouth quirked into a small smile. "He helped me pick up every piece of popcorn, chatting away, then bought me a new bag. And when I went back into the film, I just knew—that man was going to change my life."

Lexie looked at her mum. She hadn't heard that story before. Maybe she'd asked how they'd met, when she was little, but if she had she didn't remember it—and after Richard had left it had felt too cruel to ask.

"I remember when he took us to Wales camping," Fran said. "Do you remember, Lex? We were, what? Fourteen?"

"Fifteen," Lexie murmured.

"Right. And we were so excited because we'd decided it was like going abroad—because Wales is technically a different country—and then it rained the whole time. But your dad found this indoor arcade place, and left us there with a ton of change, and we thought we were so grown-up, because it was practically like being on holiday *abroad* on our own."

Lexie smiled, remembering too. Fran had thought Richard was the *height* of cool after that, especially when he'd taken them to the pub afterward and let them both try his beer. And that was back when Lexie had still been desperate to show him off, to make her friends see the parts of her dad that she loved.

Rachel gave a watery little chuckle, and Lexie saw Lana squeeze her hand. "I love that. I remember when I broke my arm," she continued, her voice hitching. "I was fourteen, and Dad was going out and wanted to take me with him, and Mum wouldn't let him and there was this whole big argument going on. And I was so annoyed that they wouldn't just let me decide for myself. So I took my bike from the shed. Some idiot came around the corner too fast. It was a red car, I still remember that. Anyway, they didn't hit me or anything, but I had to swerve out the way and I hit the curb and fell. And I guess I fell a bit wrong—because it was *so* painful." Rachel lifted her right hand to run across her left arm, as if remembering. "Dad was the one to find me," she carried on. "They realized I wasn't there, I guess, and came looking. Mum was *so* angry." Rachel twirled her glass on the pub table, leaving watery marks behind. "But Dad, he was super calm. And he distracted me from how much it hurt during the car journey on the way to hospital."

Rachel glanced up at Lexie from under her eyelashes. "It was your birthday," she said, her voice barely more than a whisper, so that Lexie had to strain to hear her. "He was supposed to be going to your twenty-first, I think—he and Mum had been arguing about it. But he stayed with me instead."

An apology, Lexie realized—Rachel was offering Lexie an apology, for getting more of Richard than Lexie ever had. So, that was the reason her dad had missed her party. A reason he'd probably tried to explain, only she'd kept refusing to talk to him. It didn't make it OK, all the times he'd not been there before then. But it helped.

Lexie worked up a smile for her sister. "I'm glad he was there for you. Sounds like you needed him more right then." And Rachel had, hadn't she? Lexie couldn't claim to know Jody very well, but she had enough of an impression to guess that Jody hadn't been the mother that Lexie's own mother had been—so maybe Rachel had needed a dad more than Lexie had.

When Theo finally spoke, Lexie felt relief course through her, at the fact that she finally had an excuse to look at him.

"I remember my interview with him, before he offered me the job. I thought I was fuck—ahh—" Theo glanced at Ange, then at Lexie's mum, and cleared his throat. "Messing up so badly. He'd asked where I wanted to be in five years, and I'd just shrugged or something. And he'd given me this look, like he could see through me." Theo shook his head. "It's weird. That was just over five years ago."

And look where I am now, was the unfinished sentiment there. For the briefest moment, Theo caught Lexie's gaze. Something shimmered in the air between them, before he looked away again.

They continued like that for a while—telling stories about Richard. There was something cathartic for Lexie in the remembering—in realizing that he'd been a whole person, good *and* bad. It didn't make things hurt less. But it did smooth some of the ragged edges.

Lexie couldn't help but notice that her mum was texting someone throughout the evening. Every now and then she'd get her phone out and smile. When Lexie moved to sit next to her, she called her out on it. "Who *is* that you keep talking to?"

To Lexie's slight surprise, her mum blushed. "It's my, er . . ." She gave Lexie a somewhat shifty look—one that was a little funny, coming from mother to daughter. "It's the man I've been seeing, actually."

Across the table Theo's gaze snapped to Lexie's, and his mouth twitched into a smile.

She let out a breath of laughter. OK, fine, he'd been right.

"Good for you," Lexie said, as her mum blushed still further. "I hope I get to meet him someday soon."

"Oh," her mum said, looking a bit flustered and patting her hair down. "Well, yes. He'd like that, I'm sure."

So maybe Lexie didn't have to feel quite *so* guilty that she wasn't around all that much. But still. "Mum? There's somewhere I've got to go, this Christmas. But next year, I want to spend it with you again, if you'll have me."

Her mum beamed. "I'd *love* to have you. We'll do the whole lot—I can get stuff in for a proper roast dinner and I'm sure we can do the blinis better than last year . . ."

"Maybe you can invite your mystery man." She waggled her eyebrows for comic effect, and her mum waved her away.

Lexie glanced down to the end of the table, to where Rachel was bent toward Lana, her curls falling around her face. She bit her lip as she looked back at her mum. "And I thought . . . I thought maybe we could invite Rachel. If you're OK with it. Obviously it's completely fine if not. I just thought—"

"Lexie." Her mum squeezed her hand. Across the table, Lexie could sense Theo looking at her again, but she didn't glance over this time. "I would be absolutely delighted to have Rachel—and you—for Christmas. I will spend the whole year looking forward to it." Her eyes were shining. "Do you know, I never had any siblings growing up, and I wanted a second child so that you wouldn't grow up on your own like I did . . . It's lovely to know that you might have ended up with that, despite everything."

It wasn't until the end of the evening that Lexie managed to get Theo on his own. She followed him to the bar, where he was standing before a Christmas-themed beer on tap. Over the smell of spilled ale, mulled-wine spices, and chips, Lexie breathed in the sandalwood scent of him. It was amazing, how her body seemed both to relax into the relief of being near him and also go tense, nerves jangling under her skin.

"I don't think we should sell the company," she said by way of greeting.

He glanced at her, his eyes scanning her face, as if looking for clues.

"At least for now," she continued, words coming a bit too quickly. "But . . ." She swallowed. "But I want to be involved. I want to run it with you, and I want to do your idea, of investing profit back into local business and . . . and everything," she finished, somewhat lamely.

He looked at her for another long moment, before saying, "I want you to be involved too."

"You do?"

"Yes. You're smart, and good with the customers, and you have good ideas." Right. He meant on a professional level, not a personal one.

"OK." She was bobbing her head, like one of those silly nodding dogs. "OK, good. Well. That's, um, settled, then."

Theo paid for the drinks the barman was handing him, scooped them up to take them back to the table. "Great," Theo said, his voice cool and professional. Distant, in a way he'd never really been with her—one way or another. "We can chat about it after Christmas, maybe?"

"Right," Lexie said again. "OK."

He turned to walk away. And she nearly let him. Because it would be easier than risking being hurt. But she'd vowed to try, hadn't she? So she took a breath. "Theo?"

He looked back at her.

"I'm sorry for leaving. I'm sorry for not listening. And I'm sorry for not coming back sooner."

His body had gone very still, so that the only movement was the liquid in the glasses, sloshing gently from side to side.

"I thought it was a sign, that I shouldn't be here. I thought . . ." Her throat was constricting. God, why was this so difficult? "I thought I might be losing myself, and I didn't want to risk things going wrong."

I didn't want to risk getting hurt. But I'll risk it now, if you will. She was on the verge of saying those words, as stupid as they might sound said out loud, when Theo sighed.

"Maybe it was for the best."

Lexie felt a crushing weight coming in to sit on her chest.

"I'm not sure . . ." He broke off, shifted position. "I want us to run this company together, Lex." His voice was a little less cool now. Kinder. But it still wasn't the tone she wanted to hear. "It's yours as much as it is mine. More, maybe. But . . . maybe I'm not right for you. Maybe you were right and we'd make a mess of things, down the line. So maybe we should keep things professional?"

Even just a few months ago, this would have been enough to shut down hope for her. But she thought she could hear it, the vulnerability under what he was saying. The worry that *he'd* make a mess of things—that he'd be a disappointment to her, like with his parents. She hadn't thought enough of that, when she'd bolted, but she was thinking about it now. And she was thinking about her dad's letter, and how he was right—you couldn't change the past. But you could take chances in the present.

He was walking away from her when she called out. "I'm going to Iceland." She moved away from the bar, took the few steps she needed to close the gap between them. Over at the corner table, she thought she saw a few of their group looking their way, but she didn't care. "I leave tomorrow, and I'll be there over Christmas." She reached into her back jeans pocket, drew out the ticket that she'd been carrying around with her all day—and slipped it in the crook of Theo's arm.

"My dad got me tickets to go," she explained. "He got me *two* tickets, in case I wanted to take someone with me." She met his gaze unflinchingly. "And it's you I want with me, Theo. Not just for this, but always. But only if you want that too." She hesitated, then gave his arm a brief squeeze, before turning away. She didn't need an answer right away. She knew he wouldn't be ready to give her one now, just after she'd dropped it on him like that. But at least, when tomorrow came, she'd know she'd tried.

Chapter Thirty-four

Theo hadn't come to the airport. She'd looked for him as she'd arrived at Heathrow, scanning the terminal as she'd headed to check-in. Through the security queue, her heart had leaped each time she'd seen someone that *could* have been him from the back, then sunk every time each man had turned around. She'd kept hoping, right until the plane took off. Maybe he'd be let onto the plane late, maybe he was one of those passengers they were doing the final call for. But when they were in the air and the seat next to her was still empty, she'd had to accept it—he wasn't coming.

She'd allowed herself to mourn that, on the plane. To think about what might have been, if she'd not scared Theo by running away in the first place. And then she'd let that go. Because even if the ache around her heart felt like it was settling in to stay, even if she had no idea how she was supposed to go back to Bath after Christmas and find a way to be colleagues—and nothing more—with Theo, she could look back on this moment and know that she'd taken a chance and put herself out there. And that, maybe, she was strong enough to deal with the fallout from that.

Besides, she wasn't just here for Theo. She was here for her dad, too. She was finally in Iceland, at Christmas. She wished she could reach back in time and tell seven-year-old Lexie all about it. About how dark it was here, with only four hours of daylight, so that time was already distorting, even after only a couple of days. About going into Reykjavík today, on Christmas Eve, and seeing the holograms of the Yule Lads projected onto buildings around the city, and about meeting the Christmas Cat—the illuminated giant cat sculpture in Lækjartorg Square. She'd imagined her dad's voice, when she'd gone up to the cat. His voice as it would have been, had they come here together all those years ago. *Look, Little Lex! What do you think his name is? He'll come alive on Christmas Day, you know.* An imagined conversation, of course. But one that had made her smile.

There was so much she wanted to do while she was here. She wanted to go to one of the thermal pools, of course—the thing she'd been most excited about when she was little. Tomorrow, for Christmas Day, she planned to go to a concert at one of the churches in the city and she wanted to go to one of the ice caves on Boxing Day. For now, though, she was spending Christmas Eve evening curled up in her pajamas in the log cabin her dad had booked for her. It was out in the countryside, where the darkness was more complete, with trees around the outside, frosted with white. Snow was sitting on the wooden roof when she'd arrived, making it look like something out of a fairy tale, and she'd already made use of the hot tub out back—there was something so decadent about sitting in steaming water while snow lay practically untouched around you. There were a few cottages nearby—all part of the same group—but it was blissfully peaceful.

Her wish jar was set on a bookcase, right next to the woodburning stove. She'd been through the wishes this evening, reading them for the first time since she'd put them in. Some of them had made her laugh, remembering how much she'd wanted something so silly—she definitely no longer felt the desire for her hair to grow purple naturally, for instance. But some of them were things she'd hoped for and had been too scared to go after, and that had given her a pang. So this Christmas, she vowed it was going to be different from now on.

On the little table next to the sofa she was curled up on, there was a pen and paper, ready when she was ready. She really wanted to write, *I wish Theo was here.* But that wouldn't be a wish for *her,* not really—it would be about *him,* and she couldn't control what he did. Just like she hadn't been able to control her dad. Instead, she thought, from now on she would write things she'd like to do in the future—wishes she might be able to make come true.

She was staring at the flames licking the inside of the wood burner when there was a knock at the door. It would be Freyja, who ran the cabins. She'd come by around the same time yesterday on her snowmobile, checking in to see if Lexie needed anything. Lexie got to her feet, pulled on her thick slipper socks, and crossed to the door. It wasn't Freyja, though, who stood on the other side of the door.

Theo was standing in the snow, hands buried in the pockets of his blue winter coat, his expression uncertain, almost guarded. How had he found her? That was her first thought. Her second was that she really wished she wasn't in her flannel pajamas, about the least sexy thing she could imagine, her face bare of makeup after the shower she'd had earlier.

And then, it was like it caught up with her—the fact that he was here, standing right in front of her. "*Theo?*" It was like she had to check, by saying his name out loud.

He managed a small smile, though his eyes were still guarded, the amber in their depths banked. "Thank God it's you. I've knocked on three of the other cabins already, been invited in by a friendly-seeming old man, and been asked by a child if I'm one of the Yule Lads. I was on the verge of giving up, thought I must have the wrong place."

He was babbling. *Theo* was babbling. And she could think of nothing—*nothing* to say.

"You're here," she stated dumbly. *Great, Lexie.* But her heart was hammering, the fingers of her left hand still curled around the wooden door. Like she couldn't really believe it. Like she might break the spell if she moved or said something to scare him off.

Theo ran a hand through his hair, down the back of his neck. "I . . . Yeah. Yeah, I'm here."

"You weren't on the flight."

"No. I missed it. Ange gave me an earful about it."

Despite her shock, Lexie laughed, the sound slightly too high, and bouncing around the snow-covered trees. "I can imagine."

"But then she helped me find a new flight. So, well . . ." He opened his arms to finish the sentence.

"Jesus." She pushed the door open fully. Then, not knowing what to do with her arms, she folded them. "You could have texted, given me a heads-up."

The corner of his mouth quirked up. "I was going for the grand gesture." But he still wasn't making a move toward her. He wasn't sweeping her into his arms or bending to kiss her. They were both just standing there, either side of the threshold, staring at each other.

"Why are you here, Theo?" Lexie asked quietly. She needed to know, for sure. Needed him to say it.

"I . . ." He swallowed—and she saw how nervous he was. Maybe it should make *her* feel nervous too, but oddly, it calmed her down a little. "I wanted to tell you something."

Her body went tight in anticipation, like every part of her was holding its breath. She was getting cold now, the heat of the log cabin fighting with the icy cold of outside—but neither of them had crossed the threshold. Like they were both waiting for something.

"We don't have to keep the company," Theo blurted out.

Lexie's heart plummeted. "Oh. Right."

"No, I don't mean . . . Not like that. I just, I wanted to make it clear that you don't need to keep it because of me."

Lexie frowned. "But you love it."

"Yeah. But I'd rather have you." He met her gaze, his tone dead serious, without the playful edge she knew so well.

"Oh." But it was a different "oh" this time, and she couldn't help but smile, as a lightness settled over her.

Seeing her smile, Theo's expression softened too, and he took a careful step toward her, so that she had to tilt her head to look up at him. "I can find other jobs I love," he continued. "But I won't find another you." Her heart actually *skipped* at this. "And I don't want you to keep it, just because you think that's what *I* want. We can sell it. Use the money to go to the Caribbean or whatever."

Lexie laughed, and took her own step forward, meeting him just outside the threshold. His arms came around her, *finally,* and every part of her body hummed, while a deeper part of her, the part that really counted, seemed to settle.

"Let's keep it," she said, wrapping her arms around him too. "For now. And when we're ready, when it's the right time, we'll sell it. If we want to." It was a little terrifying, committing to that—to a version of the future that meant committing to something, and more, committing to *him.* And yet, there was a spark of excitement inside her, too. Of *hope.*

His fingers flexed on her back, digging in through her flannel pajama top. And the way he was looking at her right now, the way his gaze dropped to her mouth, back to her eyes again, made her sure that it didn't matter in the slightest what she was wearing.

Lexie cocked her head. "You came all the way to tell me that, did you?"

"Well, I've heard the signal can be pretty bad in Iceland, and I didn't want to risk a patchy conversation, so-o . . ."

Lexie laughed. She loved that about him—about *them*. She loved that they could make each other laugh.

Theo lifted one hand to her hair, tucked a stray curl behind her ear. "I came to tell you—"

But Lexie had just seen something in the sky, over Theo's head. "Oh my god!" She pulled away from him and ran a few steps, out in front of the cabin. Under her slipper socks, the fresh snow crunched. Soon, the icy water would seep in, freezing her feet, but she didn't care. Because there, up in the clear night sky, was the aurora borealis. Swirling rivers of green-blue light danced against the darkness, vivid and bright and *beautiful*. Lexie knew there was a scientific explanation for seeing them, but right then, it felt magical—like something otherworldly, just out of reach.

"How did I not notice this?" Lexie exclaimed, twisting her neck up, still unable to believe what she was seeing. "How did *you* not notice?" she demanded of Theo—but she didn't look at him, unwilling to take her eyes off the lights that looked so *alive,* in case they disappeared.

She felt Theo come up next to her. "That was not there a minute ago, I swear."

"Does it come on that quickly?"

"I have no idea."

"Me neither—but it seems like we *should* have an idea."

There was a moment of quiet between them, and in the quiet of the countryside, Lexie could hear someone from one of the other cottages exclaiming too.

Then, "Lex?"

Lexie looked at Theo, and hit one hand to her head. "Right! God, I'm so sorry." She stepped to him, took his hands in hers. His fingers were cool to the touch, proof of how long he'd been outside. "You were saying . . . ?"

He huffed out a small laugh. Then pressed his forehead against hers. "I was saying, I'm pretty sure I'm in love with you."

Lexie breathed in the smell of him and closed her eyes as her heart swelled. As, irrationally, her throat tightened, warning of tears on the way. "Well, that works out well," she whispered, "because I'm *definitely* sure I'm in love with you."

"Thank fuck for that," he breathed. He drew back just an inch, and for a moment they ran their gazes over each other's faces, like they were committing this moment to memory. Then he bent his head and kissed her—and it felt like coming home.

When they broke apart, he came up behind her, wrapped his arms around her, like he couldn't stand to not be touching. She let her head fall back on his chest as she looked up at the northern lights. "Do you know how lucky we are, to see this?" She kept her voice quiet, out of respect for what they were seeing.

"Yeah. I'm feeling pretty lucky right now," Theo murmured.

Lucky—that was right, wasn't it? She was lucky, to have found him. They were two people who would probably never have met if it hadn't been for her dad, bringing them together.

Theo kissed her neck, sending a shiver down her spine—one that was only partly because of the cold. "Happy Christmas, Lex," he said, his breath caressing her ear, in a way that made her think of the hot tub, and the cozy cabin waiting for them, and a Christmas Day spent just with Theo tomorrow.

She thought of the wish jar, sitting inside—of the wish she'd wanted to write, but hadn't. The thing she'd wished for most as a child hadn't come true, but knowingly or not, her dad had made her last wish—a wish that felt like it might be the most important one ever—come true.

Maybe, through this, I can be a part of your future.

She thought of her dad's last words in that letter—the last words she'd ever have from him.

I'm sorry—and I love you.

She looked up at the green lights dancing in the sky once more. She felt Theo's hand on hers, gently pulling her inside—noticing, no doubt, the way that she was starting to shiver. She stayed put for a moment longer, squeezed Theo's hand to let him know she was coming.

Goodbye, Dad—and I love you too.

And she wondered if, wherever her dad was now, he too could see the lights. It might sound fanciful—but here she was, staring up at something that seemed impossibly magical. So although she didn't say the words out loud, who was to say, in that moment, that he couldn't hear her?

Chapter Thirty-five

"Oh crap, I forgot to take the arancini out the oven."

Theo smiled over at Lexie from the other side of the kitchen as she came in, having disappeared briefly to sort her hair out. "I got them out."

"OK." Lexie smoothed down the dress she was wearing—pure sparkle, in honor of New Year's Eve. "And do you think we have enough Prosecco in the fridge? I couldn't find any more space, but I think we have ice so—"

"Lex." He closed the gap between them, took her hands in his. "We're ready, don't stress. Besides, it's not like any of them will care if the arancini are a bit burnt or we run out of cold Prosecco at some point."

Lexie nodded, thinking of the burnt Yorkshire puddings they'd had at Christmas at her mum's house just a week ago, and smiled a little. It had been Theo's idea to have a small New Year's Eve party at their new flat. They'd moved in a few weeks ago, just in time to put a Christmas tree up—signing *both* of their names on the lease. Surprisingly, it hadn't made Lexie break out in hives—she kept waiting for the panic to hit, but so far she'd felt nothing but the buzz of excitement. Harry was now renting out the apartment over the office—at a discounted rate, of course. It had made sense for Lexie and Theo to go for somewhere a bit bigger, and Lexie had wanted something that felt like theirs from the get-go, something shared—and Theo had been all for that.

Her mum and Jacob—her mum's boyfriend, though her mum routinely blushed and waved it away whenever Lexie called him that, claiming she was too old to have a boyfriend—were the first to arrive. It was the first time they'd been to the flat, and Lexie's mum had brought a houseplant as a moving-in present. *And look at that,* Lexie thought. *An apartment lease and a houseplant to take care of, it doesn't get more settled than that.* Jacob kissed Lexie on the cheek, shook hands with Theo. He had silver-gray hair that suited him and blue eyes to rival even Rachel's, and he had an easy way around him, which made him instantly likable. He and Lexie's mum had met at a book club, of all places, both of them having been invited by a mutual friend—like something out of an actual fairy tale. Lexie and Theo had gotten them a trip on the company as their Christmas present—the Madrid trip, which to Lexie felt like as much a gift to herself as to her mum, given she was able to share something she was proud of creating. They'd still do their regular tradition of spending a day with each other later in the year—Lexie was pretty sure she'd convinced her mum to try skydiving with her.

Ange and Harry arrived within minutes of each other—Harry in a black tie with gold champagne glasses on it and Ange wearing her signature red lipstick and cocktail-glass-shaped earrings. Because of the successful year they'd had, Lexie and Theo were planning to promote Harry in January—give him more responsibility and let him start leading some trips on his own. Lexie had wanted to tell him this before Christmas, but Theo had insisted they had to get the paperwork sorted so it was all official. Still, it was something to look forward to. Theo took them both on a tour of the flat at Ange's insistence, while Lexie resisted the urge to squeal when she opened the door and saw Fran there—her boyfriend, Chris, in tow. Fran had been strict about a year's no dating policy, figuring out what she wanted to do—and she'd met Chris completely by accident, a few months ago, at a party. They'd taken things slow, and it was still very new, but Fran just seemed *different* this time—and Lexie was holding out hope. It may also have had to do with the fact that Fran was less stressed. She was in the middle of a teacher training course, changing careers completely, and while Lexie thought this sounded rather stressful in and of itself, Fran seemed to be genuinely enjoying it.

"Chris, Lexie, Lexie, Chris," Fran said, gesturing between the two of them as she came in, hanging up her coat on the coat stand Lexie had put together earlier for this exact purpose. Fran looked a little nervous, tugging at her black dress, so Lexie worked up her best warm smile for Chris.

"It's so lovely to meet you."

His eyes creased at the corners as he smiled. "Likewise. I've heard you may be able to give us tips on the best place to spend Easter this year." Lexie did not miss the *us* there, but did not react.

"Oh, I *so* can." She led them to the kitchen to get them a drink each, and swore she heard Fran let out a quiet exhale behind her.

Rachel and Lana were the last to arrive, apologizing profusely—Lana blaming Rachel for not being able to find a shoe. Lana's black hair had been cut short recently in a way that suited her perfectly, and Rachel was in a knockout red jumpsuit that, Lexie thought, only a few people would be able to pull off.

"Are we all here?" Ange asked, breaking off from her conversation with Lexie's mum in the living room. The Christmas tree was still up, lights glowing in the corner, and Lexie had put fairy lights around the window too. The flat was on the second floor, high enough that you could still make out Bath's sandstone buildings sprawling below, streetlamps lighting up the winter darkness.

"Well, I think we should all toast to a brilliantly successful year, don't you?" Ange asked, raising her glass. "We may be a smaller team even than before, but we have proven we are mighty. To R&L, and to Lexie and Theo." Everyone echoed the sentiment with a "Cheers," clinking glasses with those nearest them, while Lexie felt the smile tighten her cheeks, even with the faint flush of embarrassment at hearing her name like this. But it really *had* been the most successful year—they'd put another two new trips into rotation and had managed to put Theo's idea of investing into local businesses into action. For the first time, perhaps ever, Lexie felt like she had purpose—and like she was doing something she could be proud of.

Theo came up alongside her, clinking his glass against hers, his sandalwood scent wrapping around her. "And to another year, just like this one," he said, quietly enough that the others couldn't hear.

She met his gaze, marveling at how even after a year, the way he looked at her like that could still make her skin tingle. "Well, I don't know if it'll be *just* like this one," she said, her tone playful. "There might be a few more conversations about the washing up, now that we're living together."

He laughed just as Rachel came up, tugging Lana along beside her. Theo excused himself, heading to get a Prosecco bottle and top everyone up.

Rachel took a deep breath. "So, before I drink too much and

mess up the invite, I wanted to ask you what you're doing on September the twenty-seventh?"

Lexie raised her eyebrows. "How incredibly specific of you. Why, what are you . . . ?" She looked between Rachel and Lana, who were both beaming at her. "Oh my god! You've set the date?"

Rachel grinned, her blue eyes shining. "We've set the date."

"Well, I don't know, I might have plans that day . . ."

Rachel hit her lightly, and Lexie laughed, then hugged her tightly.

Theo came over with the Prosecco, topped Rachel and Lana up, then swung his arm over Lexie's shoulders. "What's going on over here? I feel like I'm missing out on something exciting."

"They're getting married!" Lexie exclaimed, gesturing to Rachel and Lana.

"Amazing! Congratulations. I mean, I sort of thought you guys were already engaged, but . . ."

Lexie elbowed him in the ribs. "They've set the date. September the twenty-seventh. Keep it free, you can be my plus one."

He raised one eyebrow. "You say that like I wouldn't have been invited anyway." He turned to hug Rachel, then Lana. "Can't wait. So happy for you guys."

"We're happy too," Rachel said, smiling as Lana put her arm around her. "And actually, Lexie, I wanted to ask you . . ." She bit her lip, glancing at Lana before saying, "Would you want to be a bridesmaid? I mean, my friend from school has already claimed maid of honor since the moment I met Lana, but I would love it if you . . . I mean, you absolutely don't have to, it's just—"

"Rachel. I would be totally and completely *honored* to be your bridesmaid." And actually, she felt her throat closing, her eyes stinging a bit even as she blinked to try to cover it up. Theo clearly noticed, because he gave her shoulder a gentle squeeze. "Just swear you won't do some awful color for the dresses, OK?" The attempt at a joke was marred a bit by the hitch in her voice, but Rachel nodded in a fake somber way.

"I swear."

Rachel hesitated, then added, "My mum is going to be there."

Lexie couldn't think of a single thing to say other than "Oh." Then she cleared her throat. "I mean, that's great!" Her voice was a bit too high.

"It's just, we've met for coffee a couple of times recently and things are . . . Well, she's apologized, tried to explain some stuff to me."

Lana's lips were tight, like she was not so willing to forgive and forget—but she didn't say anything. Lexie worked up a smile for her sister—because if anyone could understand the desire to move beyond the mistakes of the past it was her.

She reached out to squeeze Rachel's arm. "That's great, Rach."

The rest of the evening passed in a whirlwind of chatter, laughter, and dancing—they did, in fact, run out of cold Prosecco, but Theo had been right and no one seemed to care. And as Lexie watched them all, having to pinch herself that they were all really *here,* in her flat—in a flat that she was renting with a man she loved, in a relationship that she was no longer scared of—she had that sense of pure contentment, something that only settles on you every now and then. Because she felt sure, as they began the countdown to midnight, that even if she and Theo ever did sell the company, even if they left Bath, she'd never lose what she had here. Because these people were, thanks to her dad, her home. And really, it didn't get much better than that, did it?

Acknowledgments

I'm learning that finishing a new book each time feels like such a milestone—and I'm so grateful for the people that bring that book to life. In the UK, thanks go to my talented editor, Sherise Hobbs, who has nurtured me and helped me to grow with each novel, and whose enthusiasm, energy, and support never wane. Thanks also go to Isabel Martin for some excellent editorial ideas. I'm so lucky to have two brilliant editors on the U.S. side—enormous thanks to Hilary Teeman and Caroline Weishuhn for their creative ideas, excitement, and attention to detail. Thanks so much to Katie Green for brilliant attention to detail and finding things we missed at the copyedit stage! I feel very lucky to have you all on my side!

Bringing a book into the world is such a team effort. At Headline, thank you to Oliver Martin for securing some brilliant review coverage and championing my books in an incredibly competitive space, as well as Hannah Sawyer in marketing and Amy Cox in the creative team. At Dell, thank you so much to Megan Whalen for your boundless—and very catching—enthusiasm, which always makes me feel a real part of the team, and to both Taylor Noel and Melissa Folds for helping spread the word and find new readers.

Four books in and I'm still getting news about rights deals, for which I'm incredibly grateful! Thank you so much to Rebecca Folland, Ruth Case-Green, Grace McCrum, and all in the

Headline rights team for continuing to look for opportunities in different territories.

As always, thank you to my agent, Sarah Hornsley, for always being there and having my back, and to Cara Lee Simpson for your support.

I always feel so incredibly lucky when readers share reviews or get in touch to tell me that they enjoyed one of my books—it can help combat the nerves and self-doubt, and make being an author feel really "real"! So huge thanks to anyone who has taken the time to read and recommend one of my books in any way, shape, or form—the only reason authors can write is if people read, and I never underestimate that!

A
Winter Wish

EMILY STONE

Random
House
Book Club

Because
Stories Are
Better Shared

A BOOK CLUB GUIDE

Questions and Topics for Discussion

1. Lexie has a complicated relationship with her father, and it takes her a while to process her grief when he dies. Could you understand the way she went through her grief? Is there any one "right" way to grieve for someone?

2. Lexie was at times very angry with her father. Can you relate to her anger and feeling of abandonment? Is there anyone in your life who you have felt abandoned by in a similar way?

3. Lexie's father tries to apologize to her in a letter he leaves her. What do you think of his actions? Do you think he did enough to reach out and apologize to Lexie?

4. Lexie is very reluctant to enter into a "serious" relationship with Theo and to commit to him. Could you understand why she felt this way?

5. Lexie travels around a lot and claims she loves to do so. Why do you think she moved around so much? Do you think she will keep up this lifestyle?

6. Lexie is, at first, angry about her father leaving the company to her. Did you come to understand why he did so?

7. Theo treats Lexie a little unkindly at the beginning of the novel—at least in Lexie's mind. What did you think of his behavior? Do you think he could have handled things differently?

8. Lexie initially feels a little jealous of her sister's relationship with their father. Can you relate to this feeling? Would you have felt differently if you were in her shoes?

9. Lexie worries that she is not qualified to be a "big sister" to Rachel and thinks she doesn't know how to be a sister at all. Why do you think she feels that way? Do you think there is a certain type of sibling relationship to adhere to? How do you think Lexie and Rachel's relationship changes over the course of the novel?

10. At the end of the novel, Lexie wants to commit to both Theo and the company. What do you think she has to go through in order to be ready for that? Have you ever been in a situation where you've struggled to commit to something?

© EMILY STONE

EMILY STONE is the author of *Always, in December, One Last Gift,* and *Love, Holly.* She lives and works in the UK and wrote her first novel in an old Victorian manor house with an impressive literary heritage.

X: @EmStoneWrites

Instagram: @EmStoneWrites

A B O U T   T H E   T Y P E

This book was set in Granjon, a modern re-
cutting of a typeface produced under the direction of George W. Jones (1860–1942), who
based Granjon's design upon the letterforms
of Claude Garamond (1480–1561). The name
was given to the typeface as a tribute to the ty-
pographic designer Robert Granjon (1513–89).

Don't miss these other novels from
EMILY STONE

Follow Emily Stone on Instagram
@emstonewrites

DELL

Learn more at **PenguinRandomHouse.com**

RANDOM HOUSE BOOK CLUB

Because Stories Are Better Shared

Discover

Exciting new books that spark conversation every week.

Connect

With authors on tour—or in your living room. (Request an Author Chat for your book club!)

Discuss

Stories that move you with fellow book lovers on Facebook, on Goodreads, or at in-person meet-ups.

Enhance

Your reading experience with discussion prompts, digital book club kits, and more, available on our website.

Join our online book club community!
f g randomhousebookclub.com

Random
House
Book Club™

Because
Stories Are
Better Shared

 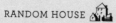